MURDER ON THE PINEAPPLE EXPRESS

FAR OUT CHRONICLES #5

TOM SADIRA

Copyright © 2024 by HIFI Press LLC, Tom Sadira

All rights reserved.

Print ISBN: 978-1-948588-15-7

No part of this book may be reproduced in any form or by any electronic or mechanical means, including information storage and retrieval systems, without written permission from the author, except for the use of brief quotations in a book review.

To Agatha Christie, Seth Rogen, and Isaac Asimov.

We probably wouldn't have hung out in real life, but in my head the four of us had a blast writing this book.

1

Captain's Log. Stardate 9602.4.

The crew of the Galactic Federation vessel *Undertaking* has spent the last thirty-seven ghatikas in pernicious peril.

That is, until we were saved, most unexpectedly, by a colossal golden pineapple.

Yes, I'm afraid it's going to be another one of *those* log entries.

Before I get into the pineapple, it's important, at least for insurance purposes, that I explain where we were, how we got there, and what we were doing when the inexplicable encounter occurred.

But before I do that, please allow me to set the table, if you will, about the unusual circumstances leading up to our predicament. The fact that these circumstances were unusual did not surprise me in the least; having served aboard this vessel for more than half my life, the unusual has become rather usual.

The *Undertaking's* missions, unlike those of our sister ships flying under Gal-Fed Command, often lead us into uncharted sectors along the outskirts of the quadrant: high-churn planets no one in their right mind would dare step foot on, unexplored nebulae so dense with unclassified starstuff that even the most sophisticated scanners would only shrug, making first contact with lifeforms so hideous and unapproachable they would make your skeleton slide out of your skin and do a swan dive into the nearest black hole.

These unusual missions stemmed from the equally unusual Gal-Fed charter bestowed upon the *Undertaking*, all those years ago when I took the helm:

"To exploit strange new worlds, and to seek out new life and new civilizations to forcibly trade with...or else."

It was never made clear for whom that thinly veiled threat at the end of the charter was aimed—the new civilizations or me.

Anyway, those are not the most inspirational marching orders, are they? Perhaps it goes without saying that as a former colonist and ex-slave, I, Captain Dikhard, do not align with their aggressively capitalistic undertones. Would you have me resign in protest? The thought has crossed my mind on more than one occasion, but I shudder to think who they might replace me with. Besides, I signed up for the relentless exploration of new worlds *and* unlimited refills on my jasmine green tea. Both have proven quite sufficient for an old adventurer like me.

Can't believe I'd admit such things on an official log entry? I've never received a single reply to any of these entries. I doubt if anyone from Gal-Fed even listens to these recordings.

Let's put that theory to the test, shall we?

Gal-Fed Supreme Emperor Oozo's mother is so fat you can see what's behind her due to gravitational lensing. She's so ugly that a mere glance in her direction can kill a tardigrade. She's so stupid she can't pass a Turing test with cheat codes.

See? No one's listening. As long as this ship's ROI is in the black, they don't care about the details.

So why do I bother logging any of these recordings?

For one thing, I like the sound of my own voice.

Also, I hope that one day someone might listen to them and behold the vast, beautiful chaos we have confronted during our exploration of the galaxy.

What vast, beautiful chaos was I talking about just now?

Ah, yes. The incident leading up to the gargantuan pineapple. The encounter at Gamma Velorum.

The *Undertaking* and her crew had returned from the Rift only a few kiloghatikas ago. Once the ship was finished receiving necessary repairs and upgrades, we set course to a quaternary system named Velorum to investigate claims of an asteroid threatening to destroy the only inhabited planet orbiting the system's blue giant star, Gamma Velorum. The planet has no official name as they've yet to be contacted by extraterrestrial visitors such as us. The plan was to deflect the asteroid, save the fledgling civilization, and, as per Gal-Fed regulations, get them to sign on the dotted line. Then we'd leave them with a receipt and a pamphlet explaining that a follow-up emissary would be sent from Gal-Fed to begin assessing how they might share their vast natural resources.

Seems we weren't the only party interested in the fledgling planet. The Kroliks arrived a few ghatikas ahead of us and deployed a magnetic mine array to keep us away from Gamma Velorum. No matter which course we took, the mine array remained between us and the planet. As we puzzled over the mines, a Krolik warship uncloaked and locked every weapon they had onto the *Undertaking*. They said they'd let us live to watch the destruction of the planet, but whether they let us go afterwards would be determined by how much technological booty we could provide: matter compilers, biogenetic harmonizers, even our only method of propulsion, our warp core.

You should feel rather fortunate if you've never encountered a Krolik. There's absolutely nothing to be gained by meeting one and much to lose, including your skull, which they collect and display in glass curio cabinets throughout their ships. That is, unless you know how to play their infantile mind games. Which I do, and I have, more times than I care to remember. I've beaten those scoundrels every time. And I have the log entries to prove it. Not that anyone's ever going to hear them. Oh, dear. Why do I bother?

What was I saying?

Oh, yes. Back to the Kroliks. They're a disgusting, verminous species of violent swindlers and thieves. They admire and emulate the Reptilians, which says it all, really. The worse part is that the Reptilians encourage these demented fanboys to run amok along the outskirts of the sector, knowing that the trouble they stir up is good for business. Nothing makes a planet roll over for a new overlord quite like the threat of being pummeled back into primordial ooze.

Which is basically the same racket the Galactic Federation runs; we're just more outwardly civilized about it.

So the Krolik warship kept the *Undertaking* pinned behind a heavily armed blockade as the asteroid hurtled through space toward the unsuspecting planet. It was a good thing for everyone involved that I, Captain Don Duke Dikhard, had a plan.

Our scans indicated that the doomed planet orbiting Gamma Velorum had a magmatic core consisting mostly of a rare mineral called azidozium. Azidozium, in its liquid form, is highly unstable and must undergo a lengthy cooling process in order to be transported safely. The resulting scoria can be carved into many useful shapes, most notably heat shields to contain the highly unstable warp cores required for interstellar travel—like the one we have stashed away twelve decks below me in the *Undertaking's* engine room. Without its azidozium casing, the heat emitted from our warp core would vaporize the ship in about two point five millighatikas.

Right away, I saw the twisted logic in the Kroliks' plan. Why expend resources subduing an entire civilization and then mining their planet's core just so you could wait a hundred kiloghatikas cooling down each metric ton of the stuff? Especially when another method for cooling azidozium is to expose it to the vacuum of outer space.

This method was well known but generally avoided because, as many interstellar corporations found out, any attempt at transporting the stuff from a planet's core into space would only end up costing you a ship. Eventually, they all caught on and just started building surface-side cooling facilities to process the liquid slowly over time. It was better to wait for your profit than have none at all.

The Kroliks had found another way. If, by chance, an asteroid rips a azidozius planet apart, then the process of solidification becomes instantaneous. If there happen to be indigenous lifeforms on said planet when this happens, so be it. They'd be long gone with their invaluable cache of scoria by the time anyone raised a fuss.

And no one ever does raise a fuss over such things. Especially not when the stakes are a no-name, unclaimed planet like the one orbiting Gamma Velorum. Most other planets have their own problems to deal with. In fact, some might prefer a catastrophic asteroid impact over what they'd suffered at the hands of the Reptilians.

Even I had to admit that from a purely economic point of view, it made perfect sense. If anyone besides the Kroliks, say the Escari Triads or the Cyborg Continuum, had stumbled onto the opportunity, they'd likely have done the same.

That is, anyone but the *Starseed*. From what I've gathered over the course of my galactic journeys, they might be the only ship in the sector besides the *Undertaking* who'd help out. There was simply too much to gain by doing nothing.

Sadly, if I had reported the situation to Gal-Fed Command, Admiral Marin would likely have ordered me to stand down while simultaneously sending out a clean-up crew.

Which is why I rarely report anything to Gal-Fed Command until I've taken action.

I ordered my Chief Technology Officer, N-FO, to whip up some covert chicanery on the Outernet while I handled negotiations with the vile Krolik Commander. The asteroid was growing closer, so there was no time for chit-chat. I got right to the point.

I explained that we'd kidnapped their Krolik King and were holding him hostage on the planet. If they wished to save his life, they would direct their magnetic mines to knock the asteroid off course and spare the planet. We'd then return their stolen monarch, who would be most appreciative and probably reward his rescuers. To sweeten the ruse, I even hinted at the possibility of us going halfsies on the azidozium if they immediately de-escalated.

As expected, the commander was skeptical. Which is why we included a link to a video that had been allegedly circulating the Outernet. N-FO's deep-faked video made it look like we'd roughed up the malevolent monarch quite a bit—our digital puppet looking out from the holographic video and ordering all Kroliks to come trade for his life.

By that time our recording was ranking on all sixteen thousand public feeds. I watched the commander's eyes—or whatever those bulbous things atop their ugly heads are—as he watched the video and took our bait hook, line, and sinker.

The Krolik Commander believed the story, alright, but rather than obey his king he laughed and shared a video stream of the doomed planet in his own public feed.

This is hard to say about a Krolik, but I'd underestimated his feculance. He must have reasoned that by doing nothing, not only would he score the largest azidozium payload in galactic history, but he'd simultaneously execute a coup and inherit the entire Krolik dynasty.

I was done playing nice. I ordered my second-in-command, Lieutenant Spiker, to ready all weapons. I commanded Enson Thrusher to prepare the ship for a Qu'trox Maneuver. We were going to get past their embargo and nudge that asteroid off course if it was the last thing we did.

The Krolik ship reinforced their forward shields and readied their arsenal as well.

Just as I opened my mouth to give the command to fire, our bridge was alerted to an unknown vessel approaching at a great speed. Its trajectory put it on course to fly between the *Undertaking* and the Krolik warship, straight through the Gamma

Velorum system. It was approaching faster than anything listed in the Gal-Fed ship repository, and its size exceeded the distance between the *Undertaking* and the Krolik ship.

I ordered the crew to set the engines to full reverse. We moved just in time to avoid the passing vessel. The Krolik warship did not. When the golden blur had passed, all that was left of their ship was a cloud of space debris. No one on my bridge shed a tear.

To the naked eye it looked like nothing more than a huge golden and green smear across the stars. As soon as it appeared, it vanished.

N-FO was able to take a quick snapshot of the object as it passed. He threw it up on the bridge's main screen and I could not believe my eyes. It was not a ship at all.

It was a giant golden pineapple.

Curiosity tempted me to follow the strange interstellar fruit, but decency demanded I first complete the mission at Gamma Velorum. I ordered my crew to target our incineration ray on the approaching asteroid. We fired and vaporized all 3 million kilotons back to stardust.

We turned our attention back to Gamma Velorum and its fledgling planet, ready to do the same thing the Kroliks were trying to do, but with more finesse, when we noticed both Gamma Velorum and its planet were no longer there.

We verified our own bearings—the *Undertaking* hadn't moved in inch. The impossible scene before us was true. The entire star system was gone.

As I stared out into the empty blackness, I summoned my crew and ordered N-FO to play the short distress call we recorded from the passing pineapple:

"I repeat, this is Captain Chuck Stonerly of the Pineapple Express. *If you can hear me... please help, man! We can't stop and we're headed straight for a—"*

2

ONE WEEK AGO

Rush hour in Los Angeles.

A bazillion cars spewed exhaust in a gridlocked labyrinth. A bazillion commuters, trapped inside their Priuses and Teslas and BMWs, honked and cursed at one another in a cacophony of mass frustration. A bazillion patiences worn thin, just a fender bender away from explosive road rage.

Except for one.

Charlie Hong had all the patience in the world.

He slouched at the rear of the bus as it inched its way through the Beverly Crest hills, ignoring the palatial estates that wealthy Angelenos owned for the sole purpose of having a view of the Pacific, his bloodshot eyes instead fixed eastward toward the valley.

Somewhere down in that sprawling urban grid his father was probably working on something new for Whizcom. Charlie thought about calling him to say goodbye, but knew it would be pointless. When his father was heads-down on one of his high tech projects, the world, including Charlie, was practically non-existent.

Which is why his mother had left all those years ago. Was she still down there somewhere, or had she gotten as far away from California as possible? Had she eventually started a new life, a new family? Did she ever think of Charlie?

Charlie stared out at the city and tried to ignore the sickly brown smudge smeared across an otherwise immaculate California sky. Ignoring the smog, like the growing cluster of problems in his life, was about all he could muster these days.

Besides, why should he care about the smog? Smog was one of the few things wrong with the world that wasn't his fault. The only vehicle he'd ever owned he bought for the sole purpose of driving to Phoenix to trade for a few weed clones.

As depressing as it was, and despite an offer from his best bro Nate for a lift, he'd chosen L.A. County Public Transportation as his final commute. His personal contribution to the city's air quality had nothing to do with it.

He knew getting into Jorge's compound would be easy, but getting out alive was pretty much impossible. The last thing he wanted to do was add Nate's murder to his recent streak of epic fuck-ups. Plus, the bus only went as far as San Vincente and 26th St, which meant he'd have to walk the remaining two miles.

The only other time Charlie had been invited up to the Santa Monica Mountains was when he arranged the deal with Jorge. He distinctly remembered feeling very lucky to have left with a pulse.

This time he didn't feel so lucky.

The bus made a u-turn at the west end of its route and stopped. On his way down the aisle Charlie slipped his pre-paid bus pass into the hand of a homeless lady sleeping across a row of seats. He wouldn't need it again, and it seemed a shame to waste.

As he strolled along the winding road that led up to Jorge's compound, Charlie wondered if it wasn't too late to run. He could grab his latest batch of seedlings—his *magnum dopus*—and get as far away from California as possible. Never speak the name Jorge again and never look back. Start a new life in Portland or

Phoenix or even somewhere far away and forgettable like Albuquerque.

Then he remembered he didn't have enough cash to make it to the Cali border, let alone to start a new life. And besides, the Feds had a longer reach than Jorge, and they wanted him just as badly.

Sure, he could've asked his dad for help. His chances of escaping both Jorge's wrath and prison would've been much better with a small loan and access to good lawyers. His dad's lawyers were the kind that specialized in keeping rich, white people out of prison. Problem was, Charlie was neither rich nor white. He knew the law would come down hard on a half-black, half-asian pot grower. Weed might be legal in Cali, but only with a medical license, which Charlie had never bothered getting because... who has time for all that paperwork? If the Feds made good with their warrant, he'd end up spending the rest of his life locked up with a whole community of Jorges in a federal penitentiary.

And the worst part was, last time Charlie checked, they didn't let you grow weed in prison. His seven young seedlings—the culmination of a decade's worth of selective breeding—would wither and die before they had a chance to make it into anyone's rolling papers.

Fuck that, Charlie concluded. *They can take my girls from my cold, dead hands.*

He found himself standing before the gates of Jorge's palatial estate with nothing but the hope that some good ole Charlie Hong bullshitting could save his ass once again.

A few heavily armed guards led him into an office with a wall of glass that commanded a view the Pacific. Jorge stood with his back to the room, gazing out at the burning red orb slowly sizzling into the ocean. His long stringy hair hung wetly over the bathrobe he wore, and he sipped milky brown liquor from a glass tumbler.

"Just in time," he said, not bothering to turn around.

"Actually, it's Charlie Hong. But I'd be happy to go find this Justin guy for you. I'll just head out and—"

"Sit down, Charlie."

Charlie sat.

Jorge turned around and stared at the stoner. Charlie was wearing his usual getup: black Converse All-Star sneakers, baggy blue jeans, and a faded brown hoodie. His skinny frame, brown skin, and short, dark afro gave him the appearance of a chocolate cotton swab, but Charlie always thought it made him look like Jim Kelly from Bruce Lee's *Enter the Dragon*—minus eight inches and thirty pounds.

Jorge sipped his drink and smirked.

"You supposed to be Black Belt Jones or something?"

"You know Black Belt Jones?" stammered Charlie, a smile creeping onto his otherwise terrified face. "I loved that movie as a kid, man. Still do. If you got an old VHS laying around, I got the time. Or we could check Netflix. It's gotta be on the Outernet somewhere."

"Outernet?"

A touch of pink appeared on Charlie's brown cheeks. "I mean *internet*. The internet. You know, memes and online porn and all that other stuff. I have no idea why I said Outernet. Weird. Hey, speaking of the internet, have you ever visited—"

"Shut up."

Jorge swirled the brown drink lazily and sighed. "I'm impressed you showed up. Those stories about what I do to my enemies who try to run away must be getting around."

"Enemy?" Charlie's voice cracked as every muscle in his body tensed. "Naw, man. But I've heard about how merciful and forgiving you are, especially to your *employees*, who, like me, make tiny little mistakes every now and again."

"Little mistake. Is that why you think you're here?"

"Well, uh… yeah, man. As a loyal and dedicated *employee*. Not an enemy. That's just crazy to think that I'd ever cross you. No way! Never."

"Good point, Charlie," said Jorge, pausing to sit at his desk and steeple his hands together. "Employees are people I trust to do a job and produce something. Is that how you'd describe our situation?"

Charlie got a good look at Jorge for the first time in months. Long hair, short goatee, glasses. Always lounging around in a bathrobe and Crocs with a smug, condescendingly laissez-faire attitude. First impressions would tell you he was just your average over-the-hill Democrat boomer living on welfare. First impressions would be wrong.

Jorge was a cold-blooded killer. As were the two guards standing beside him and the small army of goons he commanded in the streets of L.A.

Charlie knew that if he was going to find a way out of this office with his pulse intact, it wasn't going to be through backflips and kung fu punches. This wasn't a Jackie Chan movie. No, once again, he'd have to rely on the only strengths he possessed: growing marijuana and spewing bullshit.

"But you *did* trust me, right?" Charlie offered the coolest grin he could muster. "Until last week you trusted me with your biggest grow operation in the county. Three farms, producing over six hundred pounds of the highest quality ganja in SoCal."

"Funny you mention that." Jorge returned the grin and hit a button on his computer. Behind him, a display screen descended from a slot in the ceiling and buzzed to life. The screen showed a spreadsheet with graphs and columns of data.

"Wait, you use Excel?"

Jorge raised both eyebrows. "You seem surprised?"

"Well, yeah. You never struck me as a spreadsheet kind of guy."

"You try running a worldwide drug cartel without spreadsheets and tell me how it goes. Anyway, as you can see, the operations you managed produced over seven hundred pounds of weed this year, which sold for just under two million."

Charlie squinted at the screen and said, "But we lost that second crop due to powdery mildew. That dipshit amateur we brought in from San Jose contaminated the whole room, man. Didn't you torch all those plants in the incinerator?"

"C'mon, Charlie, do you really think I'd just toss out a *hundred pounds* of weed? We treated it with a topical fungicide and shipped it out to less legal markets, where we made more than twice as much."

"Fungicide, man? But isn't that way more toxic than the mildew?"

Jorge shrugged.

"Turns out the gringos in Indiana don't care what's in their weed as long as it gets them high."

"But I saw your men fire up the incinerator..."

"Something went into the incinerator that night, Charlie, but it wasn't the weed."

Charlie's heart pounded in his chest and he fought the urge to run. He knew the goons standing at either side of the desk were packing heat and wouldn't let him get halfway to the door.

"On the topic of torching weed, this next slide shows how much you lost in that structure fire at our grow room on the south side last week."

Charlie opened is mouth to defend himself but quickly closed it when Jorge raised a hand.

"The fire from your warehouse spread to four other buildings on my lot. What the fire didn't consume, the cops took as evidence. Total loss to the business—plants plus buildings plus bribes—comes to ten million dollars. That's the price for restoring my trust in you as a loyal and competent employee. Do you have ten million dollars, Charlie?"

Charlie squirmed in his seat. Before he could speak, Jorge answered for him.

"No. No, you do not. Not even that pencil neck father of yours has that much. Don't look so surprised, Charlie. When someone owes me money, I check to see if they have any family or friends who might be able to help them out. In your case, you have no one besides your father, and you don't even talk to him much, do you? You have no one. No one to notice you're suddenly not around."

"Hey, man, that's not true! Axo and Zee and Swarm will know! They'll come looking for me, and when—"

"Who the fuck are they? *Axo?* That Ukrainian or something?" He glanced at the goon to his left, who shrugged. "You working with some other gang in town, Charlie?"

Charlie opened his mouth to speak, but his mind went blank and he shook his head.

"I don't know why I said those names. Anyway, I have friends, man. Lots of friends."

"No, you don't. We checked. Which will make this go much easier."

He sighed, leaned back in his chair, and looked Charlie over.

"The business I'm in dictates that I must kill your stupid, lonely ass. Otherwise my customers, my competitors, and your former co-workers will think I've gone soft. Weak. They'll start fucking with me. They'll start stealing from me. I can't have that.

"Charlie, I'm not a particularly bloodthirsty guy these days. Sure, I may have slaughtered people—*lots* of people—to advance my business interests. But here, inside," he tapped his chest, "I'm not some cliché drug lord from the movies. I started off much like you, just a grower who loved my plants all the way from seed to roach. Which is why I'm gonna make it look like I threw you in the incinerator, but I'm actually gonna let you get the fuck outta town and never, ever come back."

Charlie couldn't believe his ears. All those terrifying stories about Jorge had been bullshit, just to keep his business in line. Or maybe this was just an exception. Either way, he wasn't going to stick around to find out. He leapt from the chair and started backing up toward the door.

"Mr. Cervantes, sir, I thank you for your mercy," stammered

Charlie. "I promise I'll never show my face in L.A. again. Thank you, sir. If one of your bodyguard dudes would just unlock this door, I'll be out of your hair forever. You know what, nevermind. This window over here is probably fine, too. I'll just—"

"Sit. We're not finished."

Charlie sat.

Jorge refilled his tumbler with straight Kahlúa, drank it all in one gulp, and set it down with a thunk.

"Stupid pendejo."

"You're right, man. I'm the stupidest pendejo of all time. Which is why I'll just get the hell out of your office and your town," he said, slowly rising from his chair, his hands held up in surrender. Before he knew what was happening, Jorge's empty tumbler thunked against his forehead and fell to the floor, unbroken.

Jorge was on his feet, glaring at Charlie from behind the desk.

"Did you not think I'd see *how* the fire started? Did you not think I would review the security footage to find out how a dumb fuck like you could fuck up so bad that you burned one of my grow operations to the ground?"

"I, uh, fell asleep, man," Charlie said, nursing the bruise above his left eye.

"You fell asleep, huh? Tell me, Charlie, what were you doing that made you so tired that you fell asleep in the curing room with a goddamn blunt burning in your hand?"

"Well, see, I'd been up half the night—"

Jorge interrupted him by throwing his laptop at Charlie's head. One of its corners struck him above his right eye, spurting blood all over his brown hoodie.

"Fucking my daughter in the storage room!"

"What?" Charlie asked in earnest as he wiped a streak of blood from his brow. "No! I mean... wait, she wasn't *your daughter*, man! She was just some new bud trimmer who showed up after-hours to get a tour of the place!"

Jorge flipped a photo frame around on his desk so it faced

Charlie. It showed Jorge on the beach with his arm around the bud trimmer chick Charlie had slept with the night of the fire.

"Oh, fuck me."

"You took advantage of my sweet, innocent Carla!" Jorge roared. "She was back from college for one day—ONE DAY! The ink on her degree was still drying, and you fucked her on top of a hundred pounds of my weed!"

Charlie slunk in his chair.

"So that whole letting me go thing is no longer on the table?"

"Oh, don't worry about the incinerator, Charlie. That won't come till much later. *Much* later." A smile crept across his reddened face. "By the time I'm done with you, you'll be begging for the incinerator."

The guards moved toward Charlie. Without thinking, he reached into his hoodie pocket.

"Golden Ticket!" he yelled, holding up a rolled joint.

The goons stopped and looked at Jorge.

"What the fuck is that?" Jorge squinted at the joint. "What, you wanna smoke one last joint before my guys get started on you? Is that it?"

Charlie loosened up and repeated himself.

"Golden Ticket. It's my latest strain. My *magnum dopus*. Highest THC in the galaxy, man. I've been developing it for years. Here. Take it. I want you to smoke it and if you like it…" he paused, reluctant to finish the sentence. "If you like it, which you will, I have seven seedlings ready to be transplanted. Saved them from the fire on my way out."

"You're telling me that instead of grabbing the computers or other evidence that linked the illegal grow operation to my business, you saved a tray of seven seedlings?" Jorge snorted. "Man, you really are the stupidest pendejo I've ever met."

"Just take a hit, man. One hit. It might just change your mind."

"You think one little joint's gonna make me spare your life after what you've done?"

"Like I said, highest THC in the *galaxy*." Charlie leaned back in his chair and risked a cocky smirk, although inside he was a dense ball of anxiety.

"This isn't like other weed strains, man. This shit is the *apex* of the *vortex* of cannabis engineering. This is what our grandkids are gonna be smoking. Listen, I could grow my girls out a bit, cut clones, fill your warehouses with them by spring. You'll make way more than your ten million back. You'll rule the world with this weed, man."

Jorge reached across the desk, snatched the joint from Charlie, and sniffed it long and hard, from one end to the other. He handed it to the goon on his left who quickly popped it between his lips and fired it up. The goon held onto a chestful of smoke as long as he could before his face turned purple and he exploded into a coughing fit. His newly bloodshot eyes met Jorge's and he gave a thumbs up. Jorge took a long, slow hit of his own and handed it to the goon on his right.

"Where'd you get this? From those gringos up in Humboldt?"

"No, man, *I* bred Golden Ticket. I've been cross-breeding for years, man."

"*You* grew thisss?" Jorge said, letting the last of the smoke billow from his mouth as the 's' in his voice hung around for longer than it should have. "In *my* warehoussse? Without my permission?"

"Uh, well, I used my own nutes and the lights were on anyway so I figured—"

"Where'sss the ressst?"

Charlie took a second to stare at the enraged cartel boss, wondering if his weed had given the guy brain damage or something. Besides the white in Jorge's eyes turning a deep pink, his pupils had narrowed into slits and his irises had become a sickly yellowish color.

"Like I said, there are seven more seedlings ready for transplant. I can bring them here so you can…" Charlie trailed off. The goons' eyes were doing the same yellow-tinged narrowed slit thing and all three men were sweating profusely.

"You guys okay? Want me to get you a glass of water or call 911 or something?"

Charlie popped out of his chair to help, but the goons closed in on both sides.

"Sssit down, ape!"

For the third time, Charlie plopped back into the chair. Jorge leaned over his huge desk and scowled, his fingernails easily two inches longer than they'd been a minute ago.

"Here'sss what'sss going to happen, ape. I'm going to take your stash and your plantsss." He crawled across the desk toward Charlie, a long black tongue flicking from his lips and tasting the air. A scaly green tail whipped the air behind him. "I'm going to grow them myssself, take all the credit, and then take over the world."

What crawled toward him on four legs was no longer an aging cartel boss in a bathrobe. It was barely human.

Charlie sunk deeper into his chair and tried his best not to piss himself.

"O-okay, man. Sounds like you have a plan to make back the money I owe you. I'll just get out of your way and you'll never see or hear from me again. Sound good?"

Jorge's saurian lips cracked and split as they opened to reveal a row of razor-sharp fangs.

"You'll be out of the way, yesss. Because when I'm done with you, there won't be anything left but a pile of ash and the echoesss of your screamsss."

Before anyone could react, the wall of windows shattered inward and the roar of an engine filled the room.

"Get in, Charlie!" someone yelled from behind a single working headlight.

Both lizard goons reached inside their jackets for their guns, but before they could pull them free there was a deafening belch and both men were splattered with a sticky blue goo. They struggled, but the goo glued their arms to their bodies.

"Come on, yo! What are you waiting for?!"

Charlie flipped backwards out of his chair, rolled awkwardly across the floor, and knelt to get a better view of the vehicle that had just crashed into Jorge's office. Right away he recognized the mismatched door panel and the rust patches. His heart burst with joy.

It was Nate's old beat-up truck. Nate, his *numero uno* friend since college, who'd offered him the ride to see Jorge that very morning.

But the person leaning out of the driver's side window wasn't exactly Nathan Hale.

The facial features were Nate's, but that's where the similarities ended. His skin was the bright turquoise of Native American jewelry. His trailer trash mullet had been replaced by long, purple, soggy dreadlocks. Instead of mirrored aviators, he wore tarnished copper goggles that clung to his face with leather straps. When Nate leaned halfway out of the driver-side window and motioned for Charlie to get in, he noticed his friend's blue hands had thick sails of webbing stretching between each finger.

"C'mon, yo! They're almost done reverting back to—"

He was interrupted by a violent hiss and the smashing of Jorge's desk into splinters. What had been a dumpy drug lord only minutes earlier was now a human-sized lizard pounding its claws on the rubble while snapping its jaws at Charlie. Both of the goons had also finished transitioning into giant reptiles, and were biting at the blue goo that bound their arms.

"Hurry, yo!" Nate said, his voice sounding less *Texas shit-kicker* and more *California surfer* than Charlie remembered it.

Something wasn't right, and it wasn't just that everyone had morphed into some kind of human-animal hybrid.

Beyond all the roaring and angry tongue flicking and his best friend yelling, Charlie couldn't help but notice the song blaring from Nate's truck. "Gonna Fly Now," the theme from the movie *Rocky*, was growing louder with each passing second.

Nate always hated that song, Charlie thought. *But lately I've been using it for my—*

Just as the chorus hit the crescendo of the last "Flyyyyyyyy!," the room shattered into a supernova of photons. The office, the truck, turquoise Nate, and the three human-sized lizards were all gone.

3

Charlie opened his eyes to find himself twisted up in sweat-soaked blankets, staring up at the ceiling of his captain's quarters aboard the *Starseed*.

Beside him on the nightstand his alarm clock trumpeted the energetic crescendo from "Gonna Fly Now." He slapped the snooze button, pulled the comforter over his head, and groaned.

Of the strange and horrific cast that had visited him in his dream, one image remained burned into his brain—turquoise skin, soggy purple dreadlocks, copper goggles, webbed fingers.

Another dream about Axolotl, he thought. *Goddamnit, man! When will they stop?*

Charlie knew that somewhere else on the *Starseed*, the massive, living ship that he commanded as captain, sloshed a vast ocean of water called the Pond. The Pond existed for the comfort of the billions of aquatic lifeforms taking refuge aboard the ship at any given time. Like all other areas of the ship—the bridge, the Ring, the Transit Bay, the other passengers' quarters—its exact location was always changing, always adjusting, for the sake of accommodating biological harmony.

Despite being captain for the past few months, Charlie had yet to step foot in the Pond. It wasn't that he couldn't swim or that he was worried about drowning. He knew the *Starseed* would somehow make it possible for him, an air breather, to walk along the bottom of the Pond without suffocating. The ship accommodated everyone regardless of their required atmosphere, gravity, or diet, which allowed the 500 billion organisms onboard to remain safe and happy for the duration of their stay.

Somewhere in the Pond was a home he'd been invited to many times but had never visited. Charlie assumed it was a structure of some kind, although he wouldn't be surprised if it ended up being a cave or a giant shell, or even a huge, hollowed-out pineapple. As absurd as it seemed, after being exposed to a never-ending parade of bizarre alien lifeforms from every corner of the galactic quadrant, the possibility of a humanoid yellow sponge in square-shaped pants didn't seem that unlikely.

Somewhere in that home was Axolotl, his first mate, his *numero uno*, suspended in a healing chamber that was being monitored and maintained by Mother, the ship's computer. To call Mother "artificial intelligence" would be a gross understatement. She was the mind of the *Starseed* itself, a sentient neural network that connected each inhabitant to the ship and to each other. And, as usual, Mother was cleaning up after another one of Charlie's catastrophic failures. The healing chamber kept Axo in a comatose state while she slowly, carefully adjusted each of Axo's epigenetic switches with the hope of returning him to the fun-loving Nommosian he was before Charlie had gone and screwed everything up.

Somewhere very near that healing chamber was Axolotl's mate, Sally. He hadn't officially met her yet. Sure, before Axo's accident she'd invited Charlie to dinner at their place countless times, but every time he'd found some excuse to bail. It wasn't that he didn't want to meet Axo's mate and their thirty-seven wogs. He'd always meant to take her up on the offer... eventually, once everything settled down. But life on the *Starseed* had a tendency to never settle down. As if it wasn't awkward enough to get plucked from Earth and thrown into the maelstrom of interstellar life, Charlie had always found it uncomfortable to meet new people. Especially those whose opinions carried so much weight. If Sally hadn't liked him—and why would she?—what would happen to his and Axolotl's friendship?

After what had happened on their last adventure and despite the safety that the *Starseed* afforded its inhabitants, he wasn't sure he should risk meeting Sally any time soon. If he couldn't face her before Págos 9, he definitely couldn't face her now.

At least Del came back from that adventure with his mind intact, even if it was trapped inside a cactus.

But that was his own fault, thought Charlie. *Who the hell gets their body repossessed?*

Until Axo and Del were all healed up and back to their old selves again, Charlie needed to focus on two things: protecting the rest of his crew and keeping the *Starseed* out of Reptilian hands. Which meant his days of being a lazy, fearful pothead were over.

Well, at least the lazy and fearful part.

The brief snooze expired and "Gonna Fly Now" started again from the top. The room was pitch black except for the neon green "4:20 a.m." buzzing on the face of his small digital alarm clock. When he'd woken up a few minutes ago it had also read 4:20. The time it showed when he'd fallen asleep the night before was 4:20.

The concept of hours and days had no meaning when you weren't rooted to a revolving planet. So instead of trying to keep track of Earth time while zipping through outer space, he permanently set his bedside alarm clock to the time that put him in the right mindset—to tackle another *wake cycle* on the most amazing ship in the galaxy.

Summoning his best impression of Sylvester Stallone in *Rocky*, Charlie slapped the snooze button again and threw off his blankets. His bleary eyes found the familiar purple cylinder sitting on the coffee table across the dim room. He scraped the boogers from the corners of his eyes and smiled faintly. Big Willie, the latest incarnation of the bong he'd accidentally smashed and re-morpho-printed multiple times on the *Starseed*, smiled back.

Yawning, he scuffled across the room toward his old companion. He took the bong with one hand and blindly dragged the other across the table until it found a jar and a lighter. He unscrewed the jar, yawned again, and proceeded to stuff nugs of gold-speckled cannabis into the bowl protruding from Big Willie's stem. Once it was full, he sparked the lighter and covered the bong tube with his mouth.

Slosh. Sizzle. Gurgle.

Thick white smoke was pulled down the stem, through the water, and up into the bong chamber. Charlie inhaled deeply until the bong tube was completely opaque with smoke. Then, in one smooth motion, he pulled the bowl from the stem and sucked the condensed cylindrical cloud into his lungs. He clenched his throat shut to keep the smoke from escaping and began counting to ten.

Charlie only made it to seven by the time the snooze on his alarm clock expired again and "Gonna Fly Now" started from the top.

His tired eyes flew wide open, then narrowed with intensity. He puckered his lips and expelled a geyser of smoke into the dim room. Light from the alarm clock's glowing digits reflected in the cloud that settled around him, wrapping Charlie in a neon green aura.

The luminous smoke reminded him of that first week after becoming captain of the *Starseed*. His battle in the heart of the ship, the THC Chamber, against a rhino-sized spider mite queen and her army of doobie snatchers. Charlie, riding on the back of a giant chicken, rushing headlong into battle to save the *Starseed*.

Where had that Charlie been when the repo-men came to collect Del's body on Zosavuta? Where had that Charlie been when Axolotl got contaminated on Págos 9 and evolved into something terrifying?

He'd inherited the job almost by accident, being the only person the former captain could trust to carry on with his plan to take down the Reptilian scourge before it consumed all life in the quadrant. As he lay dying, Major Tom—a human-skinsuit-wearing Reptilian double agent—named Charlie his successor as captain of the largest and most advanced space vessel in the known universe.

Charlie, the community college dropout.

Charlie, who'd never held onto a real job for more than one paycheck.

Charlie, the fugitive pot grower who'd spent the past year living alone in Northern California growing seven special plants to pay off his debt to a violent drug lord.

Major Tom's proclamation was enough for Mother and the *Starseed* to make it official. Despite initial resistance from the alien crew, Charlie'd been able to win them over, one far out adventure at a time.

Then he went and lost half of them.

Charlie tossed his beloved glass bong over his shoulder where it shattered against the green marble floor. Glass shards and ashy bong water spread out in all directions, but like all trash on the *Starseed*, every last molecule was absorbed within seconds of hitting the ground.

With Rocky's training anthem still blaring from his alarm clock and the warm buzz of his Golden Ticket strain flowing through his veins, Charlie decided it was time for him to hit the ground, too. He quickly stifled a yawn and let himself fall forward without any effort to catch himself. Instead of smacking against the cold, marble floor, his body was caught by the cushiony softness of a thousand marshmallows.

Mmmmm marshmallows, he thought, resisting the urge to take a bite out of the floor.

He'd seen Martha, a plump red hen, and technically the only other Earther on the ship, peck at the floor as if eating bits of marble, but he hadn't been hungry enough—or high enough—to try it himself. Not yet, anyway.

The floor, just like everything else on the *Starseed*, was

designed to adapt to whatever the lifeforms aboard her needed. That included automatic failsafes like the nerfing of absolutely anything that could harm you, including gravity. In Charlie's case, turning the marble floor into a marshmallowy cushion in the blink of an eye was just what he needed.

Charlie fought the urge to fall back asleep. Instead, he slipped his hands underneath himself and pushed. The floor hardened to accommodate. His arms spasmed as he struggled to straighten them below his skinny frame.

The *Starseed* refused to offer him gravitational assistance when doing a simple push-up, but he didn't want help anyway. No more confronting the galaxy with velvet gloves. No more waiting for Mother or the *Starseed* or its crew to rescue him. After months of shirking his duty as captain, Charlie was finally ready to take on the quadrant all by himself if he had to.

Which he really, really hoped he didn't—at least not until after his breakfast blunt.

Charlie managed another half pushup before his elbows gave out. Happy with his new personal record, he scrambled to his feet and caught a glimpse of himself in the full-length mirror hanging nearby. His short afro had grown a couple inches since arriving. His brown skin somehow looked pale and the neon green glow from his alarm clock turned his blue boxer shorts grey.

The naked, scrawny silhouette looking out from the mirror wasn't a heroic starship captain.

But it was a man who'd tear himself apart trying to become one, or die trying.

Charlie flashed a quick flex in the mirror before bolting for the room's only door. His hand stopped an inch away from the knob.

The door led to the rest of the *Starseed*. To another wake cycle of mingling with bizarre alien lifeforms in a nonstop parade of weirdness. To another shift on the bridge... without Del or Axolotl. To his last wake cycle before heading to the Trapezia system for the big peace summit.

The peace summit was to be his first official test as captain.

The whole quadrant would be watching via Outernet feeds. Besides just his galactic reputation, billions of lives spread across three planets were on the line.

No matter what happened, no matter how it all turned out, Charlie knew one thing for sure: he'd be high as fuck from start to finish.

He closed his eyes and imagined a pre-rolled joint growing out of the wall. When he opened them a moment later, a small vine had sprouted beside the door topped with a plump flower bud bulging to open. He touched it gently and the petals unfurled, revealing a perfectly rolled joint.

Charlie plucked the joint, popped it between his lips, and swung the door open to begin his morning jog to the bridge.

4

Charlie caught the door frame just in time to avoid tripping over the mob of alien children crowded outside his door.

"Good morning, Captain!" a tiny chorus of voices called out in unison.

He recognized the mob of grubby, disheveled, soggy children as the wogs—Axolotl's kids.

A *mob* was how Charlie had come to think of them, even after he'd learned the official name for a group of Nommosians was a *maelstrom*. Considering they were one of the most destructive forces of nature in the galaxy, *maelstrom* definitely suited them, as would have *cyclone, tsunami,* or *hurricane*. Charlie figured it was actually pretty generous to refer to them as a plain old *mob*.

Each wog was a two-foot-tall clone of their parents: smooth pastel skin that glistened wetly, webbed fingers and toes, a plump belly situated on a slight and slightly-slouching frame, a mop of soggy dreadlocks dangling over a face consisting of two large eyes, a wide dopish grin, and tiny holes for ears and nostrils.

Their clothes, usually t-shirts, shorts, and flip-flops, were severely faded and well-worn and generally looked like they'd been plucked from the trash bin behind a secondhand store.

Despite their shabby veneer, the wogs always looked happy and healthy enough to cause mountains of mischief.

The only way Charlie'd been able to tell them apart was to match the color of their skin and hair with a particular outfit. The chatty reddish one with the stained khaki carpenter shorts was Lara. The shy purplish one with the green shorts was Anora.

Or was it Enola? Maybe Ebola?

Anyway, the other's names would usually come to him eventually, once he'd hollered at them to turn the music down or to stop throwing cereal or to leave the stuffing inside the couch cushions.

Despite the minor differences in color, size, and clothing, every one of the thirty-seven amphibious humanoids was a spitting image of their father. Every one was a little reminder of what happened to him on Págos 9. Every one was a two-foot-tall guilt trip.

Which is probably how Charlie became their de facto babysitter.

With their father in a healing tube and their mother by his side, the wogs had the run of the ship, which allowed them the freedom to spend as much time as they wanted loitering on the short stretch of beach outside Charlie's quarters. After a series of visits his guilt had prompted him to invited the mob inside for pizza and video games. It seemed like the least he could do.

Since then, the mob of soggy little demons had returned every few days to eat all of his Earth junk food, watch movies, play video games, and raise hell. They'd broken everything in his quarters at least a dozen times, which would've upset him a hell of a lot more if all the stuff hadn't been instantly re-morphoprinted out of the ship's substrate.

Charlie lowered a stern glare at the mob.

"Not today, guys. I'm busy."

A collective groan—and more than a few belches—rose up from the crowd of small amphibious humanoids.

"But Mama screamed that we were being too rowdy," croaked

an anonymous wog somewhere on the left side of the mob.

"She sent us out to play, yo," another added.

Charlie shook his head.

"Nope. No way, man. That's not gonna work today. Now let me pass so I can go on my morning jog."

"Since when do *you* jog?" a tiny voice asked.

He scanned the mob looking for a clue as to who had spoken, but was met with thirty-seven innocent pairs of eyes blinking up at him.

"Of course I jog!" Charlie hesitated, then added quickly, "Well, you know, starting today I do."

"In your underwear?" asked another. A wave of giggles rippled across the tiny crowd.

The blood rushed to Charlie's face, turning his brown cheeks pink. In his hurry to kick off his new morning routine, he'd forgotten to get dressed.

He quickly ducked back into his quarters, which the mob took as an invitation to flood through the open doorway.

Charlie sighed and waited for the last of them to enter before slamming the door closed.

"Look, you can come in while I finish getting ready, but then you kids gotta scram..." His voice trailed off as he watched the mob disperse across his quarters.

A half dozen wogs were already having a jumping contest on his bed. Ten more were plundering his fridge. Where his sofa had been just moments ago now teetered a mass of multi-colored, soggy dreadlocks fighting over two measly game controllers.

His quarters were, once again, officially *wog-inate*d.

Charlie grumbled and pulled on a pair of baggy jeans.

"Whatever, man. You guys can hang here while I go to work."

"I thought you said you were going jogging?"

Before Charlie could answer, another wog belched loudly and added, "We read in a book about Earth that it was dangerous for brown-skinned humans to go running."

"That's true, but I'm only *half* brown. My dad's Chinese."

"Our dad's in a healing tube right now, fighting for his life," a wog called out from somewhere in the kitchen.

Charlie's heart sank.

He shook off the guilt and slipped a clean t-shirt over his afro.

"Look, man, I don't care what you little demons get into around here, but keep your slimy little flippers off my stash."

"Awww, smeggin' smeg! When are ya gonna let us try some of your Golden Ticket, yo?"

"When you're old enough, that's when," he said before his head disappeared into his brown pullover hoodie.

"When'll that be, Captain Chuck?" another wog called out over the ruckus.

A basketball-sized black cotton ball appeared in the neck hole of the hoodie and pushed through until Charlie's face reappeared. He patted his short afro back into shape and sighed again.

"When your mom says so, that's when."

"Which mom, yo?" croaked another little voice. "Mom or Mother?"

"Take your pick. Hey, man, get off that—"

He was cut off by one of his tall upright speakers tipping over and crashing onto the marble floor.

"Smeg yeah!" a few wogs cheered, pumping their tiny fists into the air.

Charlie forced back a smile and shook his head. "Easy on the smeg, guys. Your mom might not be able to hear you, but Mother is always listening."

"Mm-hmm. That's right, Captain," said a warm, southernly voice that seemed to come from everywhere all at once. "I'm always here to keep an eye on my babies."

Charlie raised an eyebrow at the ceiling. Despite the sound of her voice being a perfect replica of his elderly grandmother, which immediately put him at ease, he knew it was just another one of the many tricks she used to accommodate him—and get her way when she needed to. Mother's strategy was to scan each Seeder's brain to find a voice from their past, one they absolutely associate with trust and love, and then use that voice when 'interfacing' with them to make communication smoother for everyone. Charlie's *consolatio persona* was his long-dead grandmother from back on Earth, which he had to admit, worked like a charm.

Yet, based on the dangerous situations he kept getting into aboard the *Starseed* over the past few months, he'd grown suspicious of Mother's so-called omnipresence. She always seemed to be around when he was doing something perfectly mundane and harmless, like taking a dump. But somehow, when the stakes were high—like when the ship was being invaded by giant mutant spider mites—she seemed to be unreachable for one obscure reason or another.

Whether or not he ever got any actual privacy aboard the *Starseed*, or whether there was a method to her madness, was still yet to be seen. At the end of the day, he knew he could trust her. Or at least he slept a lot better believing so.

"Glad you're here, Mother," said Charlie, relaxing. "Think you could, you know…?"

A bottle of something whizzed right in front of his face and shattered his mirror into a million wet shards.

"No problem, honey. I'll keep an eye on this mob while you run off to save the galaxy."

"Geez, talk about pressure!" he said. "I mean, we're just talking about the Trapezia system, not the whole galaxy."

"Billions of lives across three planets ain't nothing! And let me remind you of something, darlin'. Every life carries within it the sweet spark of creation. Every spark has the potential to grow and spread and thrive. To change the course of this galaxy. You downplay the importance of one life, honey, you downplay the importance of all life."

"Yeah, yeah. I remember," Charlie said. "Speaking of the sweet spark of life… is it ready yet?"

Mother gave a little chuckle.

"It will be, honey. Real soon. Don't you worry. By the time you need it, it'll be plenty ripe and ready for plucking."

5

Swarm's thorax rattled like a tin can full of gravel each time he rounded a corner and didn't see the bridge doors.

His crewmates were often late, each offering their own pathetic excuse, but not him. He was never late. Especially not on a day like today.

At first, he tried to lighten up and enjoy the stroll through the Circuit. Mother, with her eerie insight into his subtle biological needs, would sometimes extend his morning commute to get his blood pumping a little more than usual. But once he realized the dim white aura guiding him wasn't getting any brighter, he began clacking his mandibles and growling to himself. Today wasn't the day for a brisk walk.

He picked up his pace and ignored the myriad of distractions along the way: the wonderful fragrances that gently caressed his antennae; the tempting fruit dangling from the vines that grew along the walls; the many chance encounters with Seeders he hadn't spoken to in a while.

Chance encounters, he scoffed to himself. *Yeah smeggin' right. Like anything in the Starseed is a chance encounter.*

Swarm had left his quarters with plenty of time to make it to the bridge, but he also knew the *Starseed* didn't always comply with an individual organism's plans. The vast network of corridors known as the Circuit was as alive as he, moving and adjusting to accommodate the collective needs of every last Seeder. Usually that accounted for slight variations in distance between two points on the ship. This morning's commute was already taking twice as long as usual, which, based on his experience as Chief of Security, could only mean one thing: something was up.

He tapped the chatter pinned to his chest and repeated his urgent request.

"Captain Hong! Zylvya! *Anyone!*" he growled into the metallic green badge embossed with a silver pot leaf. "Come in, you two! Smegging hell! This isn't funny!"

After waiting a minute without a response, Swarm's compound eyes flicked up to the ceiling where he imagined Mother hovered over him.

"I know you're listening," he rattled under his breath. "And I know you know what's going on. I demand you stop this nonsense at once!"

As with every other attempt he'd made that morning to call on Mother, there was no response.

He sighed and kept stomping toward the guiding aura that stayed just out of reach.

Swarm didn't freak out—not yet. He knew the radio silence and the extra distance added to his morning commute were not necessarily cause for panic. What he found much more concerning was that, although he was Chief of Security, no one ever listened to him. Not Mother, not the crew, and especially not his so-called Reserve Security Crew.

He tried to shake off a particularly useless thought that haunted him at times like this. If he hadn't flown his ship into that temporal rift, if it hadn't hurled him backward through time, he'd still be part of the Hive that will emerge in the galaxy a million years from now. He'd still be a respected Squad

Commander with thirty ships under his command. He'd still be with her.

Like so many other Seeders, the *Starseed* had rescued him as he floated through the vastness of space in his busted escape pod. He owed his life to the ship, which only made it marginally easier to accept the disorganized chaos that came with his new environment.

Axolotl was the only crew member who occasionally followed orders, but ever since he'd returned from Págos 9, he'd been stubbornly floating in healing fluid with his eyes and earholes closed. No matter how many sleep cycles Swarm sat beside the healing tube and ordered his Nommosian brother from another mother to wake up, the little smegger wouldn't comply.

I should have been there, Swarm thought. *It was my job to protect him and that greasy-haired dweeb, Del. But I was too busy planning this smegging peace accord. The peace accord I'll never get to if I'm stuck wandering these smegging corridors for the rest of my life!*

He distracted himself from his frustration by running through a checklist of the *Starseed's* life support systems.

The temperature seemed fine. The personalized local gravity and atmospheric fields seemed to be working without a hitch. He hadn't lost a single meetle yet, which meant the ship's morphic fields were intact and operational. No sign of invaders or space pirates. No laser blasts. No explosions.

As usual, something was up with Mother. And when something was up with Mother, it usually meant Mother was up to something.

Just as he was about to grumble into the air again for her to answer, he saw the light of the ship's augmented guidance system settle onto one of the generic, round purple doors at the end of the corridor.

Finally!

Swarm raised his claw to open the door, but stopped when he noticed a painful groaning come from the other side.

He placed his triangular head against the door to listen more closely. The groaning had stopped, but he distinctly heard a heavy thud followed by muffled cries. There was no mistaking it —someone on the bridge was calling out for help.

Swarm's antennae went rigid behind him as he lowered himself into a fighting position. He slapped a claw against the door and dove through without waiting for it to spiral all the way open.

He rolled into a crouch, extending all four arms to grapple with whatever foe had dared invade the *Starseed's* bridge. The ten thousand receptors that made up his large compound eyes quickly scanned the room in all directions at once.

Besides the circular control console sitting in the center of the round room, the only other occupant was Captain Hong. The skinny brown ape was pinned to a low, padded bench by a metal bar that had thick discs attached to either end. His face was purple and his eyes bulged from their sockets. Panicked, unintelligible syllables sputtered from his lips. His scrawny arms struggled ineffectively against the bar that pinned his throat to the bench.

Swarm started forward to free his captain from the strange, cruel torture device, but stopped to steady himself on the control console as his legs became suddenly weak. A strange racket— certainly some kind of sonic weapon—filled the room and nearly brought him to his knees.

Some kind of electronic gadget was sitting on the floor behind Captain Hong. It was rectangular in shape, had knobs and switches along the top, and had two round speakers vibrating at either end. The sound it emitted was worse than the skull-melting cry made by a Venusian Banshee in heat. Swarm had to consciously clench his morphic field just to stop his meetles from skittering away in panic.

He decided to deal with the sonic weapon first. If it was having such a devastating effect on him, who'd only just arrived, there was no telling the damage it may have already caused to Captain Hong.

Swarm pushed off from the console, did a forward flip through the air, and brought a fisted claw down on top of the gadget with all his weight behind it. The sonic weapon was instantly smashed down the center, each half spilling its wires and coughing up sparks. Most importantly, the terrible ruckus that had been blaring from its speakers was gone.

"Swa—! Hel—!" cried Charlie, still pinned to the bench by the weighted bar. "Plee—! Hurr—!"

Swarm skittered to his captain's side. He knocked the bar away and lifted Captain Hong off the bench with two of his claws. His other two swayed menacingly in the air, ready to ward off any invisible attackers.

"Captain! Speak to me! Are you okay?"

Captain Hong sputtered and coughed, trying to catch his breath.

"Who did this to you, Captain?" rattled Swarm.

He smacked Charlie once on the back.

"Where are they now?"

When Charlie didn't answer right away, he smacked him lightly across the face.

"Can you hear and understand me?"

When Charlie's arms flew up to block the next swipe, Swarm knew he'd be okay.

"Knock that shit off, man!" he cried. "Let me go!"

Swarm did. Captain Hong fell a meter to the *Starseed's* green marble floor, which, as expected, caught him gently by going all cushion-y. Charlie settled in, rubbed his throat, and took a deep breath.

"Thanks, Swarm. Turns out that Wikipedia page on bench-pressing was right. You really should use a spotter when lifting." Charlie swallowed hard and winced. "Weight training can be dangerous, man! Know what I mean?"

Swarm answered by driving his elbow into the middle of the padded bench, turning it into a capital 'M'.

"No, Captain. As usual, I have no smegging idea what you're talking about."

He lifted the thick metal bar with ease and twisted it into a crude knot, weights and all.

"How about you start by telling me who they were and how they got onto my bridge."

"Huh? You wanna know who *they* were?"

"For starters."

"Who?"

"That's what I'm asking you! Who was behind the sonic weapon I just destroyed?"

"Sonic weapon?" Captain Hong asked, propping himself up on his elbows to look around. When he noticed the broken device and the electronic guts all over the floor, he lay back again and sighed.

"Dude, that wasn't a weapon. That was just the B-Boys droppin' beats from my ghetto blaster."

"Bees? Blaster?" Swarm swiveled his triangular head to scan the bridge's high dome. Nothing but stars and distant nebulae filled the space above them, but the distant memory of a thousand heavily-armored, laser-tipped stingers pointed right at him sent a shockwave of chills through his morphic field.

"Holy smegging hell, they must've cloaked. Or phased to another part of the ship. But how? A squadron of those bastards must've followed me through the temporal rift. Or maybe…"

Or maybe the temporal rift has opened again, he thought. *Which means maybe…if I could locate it…*

The thought of returning home sent more than a shockwave of chills through his morphic field. What he felt was something completely foreign to both his personality and his insectoid species: emotions. A whole flurry of them. And pleasant ones, at that.

He quickly cast his feelings aside and focused on the immediate threat.

"Captain, we need to lock down the Transit Bay at once and prepare for battle. If the Bees are here, then we must prepare!"

"Bees? No, man, I said the B-Boys. As in, *The Beastie Boys*. Rappers from Earth."

Swarm's antennae drooped slightly, then went rigid once again.

"Ah! I see! Beasts who wrap their prey in metal bars after stunning them with sonic blasters have followed you from Earth. Let's warn the others and—"

"No, man, they *rap*, not *wrap*. And they're not literal beasts. That's just their band name. They're humans, like me."

"Humans did this? Last time I checked, Earthers hadn't even discovered gravity distortion fields yet. How the smeg could they follow us way out here?"

Charlie chuckled and shook his head.

"You got it all wrong, Swarm. The Beastie Boys are just normal humans who make music. Rap music. Hella good rap music."

"Music?"

Swarm recalled learning about the concept from Axo. Apparently some lifeforms produced sounds not strictly intended for hunting, mating, or conversation. They made sounds for pleasure, whatever that meant. In fact, Axo's entire Nommosian civilization had been based on sound—until the Reptilians destroyed it, along with their planet.

Swarm relaxed and dropped his guard.

"Captain, if no one attacked you then why were you paralyzed on that primitive stretcher? Looked to me like you were seconds away from having your respiratory airway crushed!"

Captain Hong's face flushed pink.

Smegging hell, he thought, *I'll never get used to how these fluid-based lifeforms are always changing skin color.*

"Uh, well...that was just me working out."

Swarm looked him up and down.

"Working out what? Your personal problems?"

"My guns, man!" Captain Hong said, hopping to this feet and flexing his scrawny arms.

"What? Mother doesn't tolerate weapons on the *Starseed*! Was Nylf behind this?" Swarm grabbed Charlie's arm and pinched it roughly. "There's no projectile weapon installed inside there!"

Captain Hong yanked his arm away.

"Not literal guns, man! *Muscles*! I'm done being a weak-ass human. I'm not losing any more of my crew."

With those last few words, everything suddenly made sense. Swarm sighed and placed a claw on the captain's shoulder.

"I don't plan on going anywhere, Captain. And we both know Zylvya's too damn stubborn to let anyone tear her away from her post here on the *Starseed*."

"Thanks, man. And hey, call me Charlie. That 'Captain Hong' shit is just for when others are around."

"Sorry, *Captain Hong*, but you'd better get used to that kind of formality. With the Trapezian peace summit right around the corner, we need to get our heads in the right place."

The captain's face lit up.

"I totally agree, man! We need to get our heads in the right place. Which is why I brought plenty of *this*."

Captain Hong reached a hand inside the tangled furball on his head he called his "'fro" and produced a pair of joints.

"Should we spark up now, or wait for Zee?" Before Swarm could answer, Captain Hong tossed him one of the joints. "Good call. Her loss for being tardy."

Captain Hong held his own joint up to his forehead, closed his eyes, and then popped it between his lips. He thought of the ignition word he'd just imprinted on the joint, and the brainwaves triggered a reaction between the sodium and water molecules embedded in the joint's tip. A small flame flared up and vanished, leaving behind a glowing orange ember.

The captain took a few quick puffs to get the ember going, then took a long, hard drag. By the time he stopped, the joint was a half inch shorter.

Swarm had to give it to him, the captain could handle his ganja. On the other hand, that seemed to be the only thing he was good at.

Still, he wasn't about to be outdone by some Earther ape in baggy clothes and a "'fro." He mentally impressed an ignition word on his own joint, popped it between his mandibles, fired it up with a single thought, then took a mighty drag.

Captain Hong waited for him to exhale before spewing his own lungful of smoke into the air. After sharing a few more puffs in silence, a dense, sweet-smelling cloud had formed around them.

"See, it's helping already!" Captain Hong cheered. He let what was left of the joint dangle haphazardly from his tilted grin.

"Helping what, exactly?" bellowed Swarm, who suddenly remembered the argument they'd had during the previous wake cycle. "We're still at a critical impasse and we have no time left to argue about it."

Captain Hong sighed contentedly and gazed into the star-filled dome above them.

"I didn't really like that ghetto blaster anyway. Too tinny, if you ask me. The bridge needs something with a little more range, ya know?"

Just then, two pillars of marble surged upward from the floor and morpho-printed into a pair of standing speakers. Between them a smaller column morpho-printed into a sound system, complete with cassette deck, rotating 100-disc CD player, and an old-fashioned record player.

His control over the substrate is getting stronger every day, Swarm noted to himself. *He's already far surpassed Captain Major Tom's proficiency with morpho-printing.*

"Seeing as how you interpreted the B-Boys' jams as a sonic weapon, I'm thinkin' you're not ready for rap just yet."

He paused to take a small puff while he considered the problem.

"Maybe we should start off with something a little more digestible. Something to help set the tone of the meeting."

"How about you stop smegging around and decide how to handle the problem we're faced with? If we don't leave for Trapezia soon, we'll miss the planetary conjunction, which means an opportunity for peace won't arise for another eighty solar cycles."

"Don't worry, man. We won't miss the whatever you just said. But in the meantime...oh, I got it! The *Beatles*! You know, since you're made up of them and all, you oughta love them!"

"Then you've decided we won't miss the conjunction? I'm glad you've come around to see things my way, Captain," said Swarm. "When Zylvya gets here, we'll break the news to her gently. Or not so gently. Either way is fine."

"Break what news to me?" a voice said from behind them.

Swarm spun around to find Zylvya standing just a meter away, an emerald eyebrow arched on her forehead. She looked the same as always: smooth, wood-grained skin; a long green braid slung over one shoulder; hands fisted on her mammalian curved; a resting bitch face aimed directly at him.

Smeg! I hate when she sneaks up like that, he thought. *More than that, I hate that she was able to sneak up like that. My antennae must still be recovering from that ruckus the captain was playing earlier.*

"So glad you finally decided to join us, Twiggy," jabbed Swarm.

"Stuff it, Bugbrain," she said, walking past him. "Mother had me meandering from one end of the ship to the other. And worse, she's not responding. You guys had any luck, or is she dodging all of us?"

"She's busy right now," said Charlie, failing to hide a mischievous smile. "I've got her working on something secret. Something beyond awesome."

"There's no smegging time for secrets today, Captain," growled Swarm. "We're behind schedule as it is! Now break the news to Zee and let's set course for the Trapezia system at once."

Zylvya stepped forward and raised a fist.

"There are over *three billion* lives that need our help on Lusus! Their star is about to go supernova! Not sure if either of you heard, but no one else in the galaxy cares. If we don't save them, they're dead. Every lifeform on Lusus, wiped out."

Swarm raised his own fisted claw at the star field above them.

"Tau Ceti Prime is on the other side of the smegging quadrant and it's not supposed to blow for at least another million solar cycles!" roared Swarm. "Obviously the Reptilians have tampered with it to distract us from the peace summit!"

Zylvya, who stood a foot shorter than Swarm, stood on her tiptoes and put her face directly in front of his.

"That's exactly why we *must* save them! If the Reptoids are doing this because of us, their stardust will be on our hands!"

"We've already committed to saving the stardust on the *three* inhabited planets of Trapezia! This summit has been scheduled since Captain Major Tom was in charge! If we turn our backs on them now, *countless* Trapezians are dead!"

"Trapezia is full of brutal, warmongering, zilch-heads who are just reaping what they sow!" Zee cried, although the green fire in her eyes was abating. "Lusus, on the other hand, is a young, peaceful planet. For their light to be extinguished like that, especially because we stood by and did nothing..." She trailed off, turning away to hide her anguished expression.

"I agree this choice sucks, Zee," Swarm said, softening his tone to match hers. "But unless the *Starseed* can be in two places at once, we have to choose. Yesterday we agreed to leave it to Captain Hong. Today he has an answer."

"I sure do," said Charlie, a smile still plastered on his face.

Zylvya looked him over.

"How can you stand there and smile when so many lives are at stake? And what's with all the broken junk everywhere?"

Charlie got to his feet, his half-joint dangling from his lips, and started digging around in his 'fro. A moment later he offered a fresh joint to Zylvya.

"You know the rules," he said. "When the going gets tough, the tough get stoned. Go on, don't be shy, Zee. You know you can't resist my *magnum dopus*."

She rolled her eyes. "Fine, have it your way."

There was a blur between them, but before Charlie knew what was happening Zee had already turned away. The unlit joint remained in his outstretched hand, yet smoke was already billowing around her.

"Hey, man!" complained Charlie when he realized his own half-joint was no longer between his lips. "I brought you your own joint this time so you'd stop stealing mine!"

Zylvya smirked and exhaled a long stream of smoke.

"Let's have it. What's your decision?"

"Yes, Captain, tell us," rattled Swarm. "Are we setting course for Trapezia to fulfill our obligation of facilitating peace in a system that's only ever known war?"

"Or are are setting course to evacuate Lusus before their star explodes and consumes all life on the planet?" Zee added.

Captain Hong's big, dumb grin returned to his lips between puffs on his newly lit doob.

"Yes," he answered.

Both Swarm and Zylvya squirmed and grew tense.

"There's no time for nonsense, Captain!" roared Swarm. "You *must* choose! The *Starseed* can't be in two places at once!"

"You sure about that, man?"

"Yes, Charlie!" raged Zee. "Swarm and I may disagree on everything else, but we both understand the basic limitations of physical reality!"

"Well then, get ready to have that understanding shattered," Charlie said, barely able to contain himself.

6

An invisible hand swept delicately across the surface of a vast green ocean. The endless expanse of dense fan leaves and swollen flower buds had just enough time to settle before another breeze stirred them to life once again. Above, a moonless starfield stretched in all directions but not a single star twinkled.

Charlie stood with his crew in a small clearing at the center of seven massive cannabis plants. These seven plants were not only much larger than the rest, but they were also slightly yellowed and wilted. Their golden, resinous luster was still visible but had been diminishing steadily over the past few weeks.

When Charlie wasn't rehashing traumatic memories in his dreams or babysitting a mob of wogs, he was up here, in the Garden, trying everything he could to nurture them back to health. So far, nothing had worked. Their sickness or deficiency or *curse*, as he'd come to think of their condition, had only worsened. He knew he had little time left before they'd start dropping their leaves and then...he didn't want to imagine what would happen next. The bottom line was that if he didn't figure out how to save them, and soon, he'd lose them forever.

Back in the remote mountains of Northern California where Charlie had spent the better half of a year hiding from Jorge—*and* the Feds, *and* his father, *and* any semblance of responsibility—he'd planted the seven seedlings and raised them as best he knew how. His girls soaked up the bright, warm sun. Their roots expanded freely through the fertile soil. They thrived like no cannabis plants he'd ever grown before. No pest could phase them. No dry spell could wound them. Hell, even after being ripped from the earth, sucked up into the sky by a grav beam, then replanted here on the surface of the *Starseed*, they hadn't shown the slightest hint of transplant shock.

Then, shortly after returning from Págos 9, Charlie noticed the first signs of stress in the tips of their leaves. A touch of yellow here, a speck of brown there. Having grown cannabis for years, he thought he'd seen it all, but whatever was plaguing his girls was something that didn't fit any known illness—at least not any Earth illness he'd even encountered. He didn't think they'd caught a space bug from the Garden since none of their neighbors seemed affected. Despite every attempt to heal them, each of his seven plants continued to get sicker and sicker.

Charlie didn't know what he'd do without his *magnum dopus*. They were the culmination of decades of cannabis engineering and cross-breeding. They'd been his only companions during his forced retreat in the mountains. Some people had college degrees or gold medals or multi-volume autobiographies to show for their life's work. Charlie had his plants.

Swarm and Zee had spent the last week arguing over which billion lifeforms to save, but all Charlie could think about were his girls. No matter the outcome of the peace summit in Trapezia nor the fate of planet Lusus, he knew one thing: he'd spend every spare second tending to his seven sick plants.

"Ground control to Charlie."

Zylvya's voice broke through his thoughts.

"Hello? You still with us?"

"Oh, right," he said, pulling his eyes away from his plants. He took a few quick puffs from his joint, buying himself a moment to remember why he'd dragged them up to the Garden. "Nice up here, isn't it? So quiet on the surface, you'd never think this ship was crammed full of aliens."

"Yes, Captain. It *is* nice up here," she said slowly, as if she were talking to a mentally-challenged child. "The Garden is very tranquil compared to the interior of the ship. Did you bring us here just to gawk at your plants? They're not looking so hot, by the way."

Charlie quickly took another toke, and, as intended, a warm stoniness surged through him and dulled the desire to lash out at her for insulting his life's work.

While he ransacked his tattered memory for the reason why he took them on a field trip to the Garden, the ground began to tremble. The trembling grew stronger and closer, until finally a tapered, pitch-black column sprouted from the spongy soil. The column rose above the canopy, above their heads, then relaxed into a writhing black worm-creature the size of a tree trunk. The worm pointed its tapered end at them and spewed gusts of smoke as it spoke.

"Caaaaptaaaain Hoooong! Coooome agaaain tooooo heeeeaaaal yooour plaaaants?"

"Hey, Mu!" said Charlie, spewing a stream of smoke directly at the thing.

It leaned its tapered end into the cloud and seemed to bask in it. Wherever Charlie's smoke touched the worm's impossibly black skin, a faint neon-green pattern emerged.

"Not today, homie. Today I've come to... well, see... the crew and I were here because..." He trailed off, too embarrassed to keep stammering.

"Smegging hell, Captain!" rattled Swarm. "Can't your porous Earther brain hold onto a thought for more than one millighati-ka!? If we don't leave for Trapezia soon, we'll miss the—"

"That's it! The peace summit!" Charlie interrupted, dangling the joint from the side of his mouth while he checked his watch. "Alright everyone, should be any minute now."

"*What* should be any minute now?" cried Zee.

"Shhh! It's a surprise, man. Just look in that direction and, I dunno, take another puff while you wait. You're gonna need it."

Before Zee could continue the banter, something large and white blurred overhead. There was a flutter of wings, a half-squawk, and then a tall, slender bird-like creature joined them in the clearing. It was Vargoni, the *Starseed's* Chief of Transit, who was responsible for all the incoming and outgoing vessels and passengers.

"Hello there, fellow crewmates!" he said, adding his signature squawk at the end of the sentence. "Big day, it is! Big day, indeed!"

"Hey, Vargoni," said Zee. "I guess the captain's already filled you in on his little surprise."

"Damn straight I did! I needed some expert advice."

Charlie pulled another joint from his afro and tossed it high into the air. Vargoni caught it delicately in his beak, closed his eyes, and the joint was lit.

Charlie checked his watch and grinned. "Alright, it's time. I know this'll look crazy, guys, but you'll just have to trust me."

"Do we?" Zylvya asked, rolling her eyes. "Mother, why are you never around when we really need you?"

"Don't worry, baby. I'm here." Mother's sweet southern drawl filled the air. "Sorry for keepin' y'all worried again. I was... well, I was *indisposed* helping Captain Hong with his glorious project." She tried to stifle a giggle and failed.

Charlie whispered into the sky, "Mother, queue up the music!"

All around them the low stirring of a bassoon signaled the start of Strauss's "Also Sprach Zarathustra" from *2001: A Space Odyssey*. Along the ship's horizon, a glowing gold-orange disc of light peaked over the swaying foliage and began climbing the dense starfield. Two bassoon notes followed the first, their pitches climbing in unison with the young star. Just as the full shape of the glowing orb broke the horizon, a blast of horns and drums exploded with the song's signature melody that's been blissing out sci-fi nerds for ages.

But the star wasn't the point, nor was the uplifting classical music. Both of those were just props in service to Charlie's surprise, which was the silhouette positioned at the center of the glowing disc.

"Well?" Charlie paused to take another toke, giving them time to gather their thoughts.

"What do you think, man? Pretty much the coolest thing you've ever seen, right?"

Zylvya opened her mouth to speak, let it hang open for a moment, then, torn between disbelief and rage, promptly closed it. She had to admit that for the first time since meeting Charlie, he'd finally left her speechless. Whatever she was witnessing, whatever the hell Charlie was up to, she was going to let Swarm break the awkward silence.

"If I'm not mistaken, that's a..." Swarm trailed off, his antennae twitching. "Guessing by the size of its silhouette in relation to our position to the local star...Smegging hell! Where's Del when you need him?"

"Last I checked," Vargoni said helpfully, "he's still in his terracotta pot located either in Nylf's workshop or—"

"We all know where Del is, Featherhead!" growled Swarm. He clacked his mandibles silently and threw all four arms into the air. "Whatever the smeg it is, it's really big."

"Yeah, but what *is* it, Captain?" Zylvya asked. "Is it... some kind of Earther fruit?"

"Bingo!"

Charlie held his hand up to give her a high five. When she showed no sign of returning the gesture, he popped his joint between his lips and gave himself a high five with his free hand.

"You grew a gigantic Earther fruit called a 'bingo' and put it in orbit around the *Starseed*?" asked Swarm.

"No, 'bingo' means—nevermind. It's a *pineapple*, man!"

"Let me repeat the question. You grew a gigantic Earther fruit called a pineapple and put it in orbit around the *Starseed*?"

"Well, I can't take all the credit, man. Vargoni here helped with most of the ship-science stuff and Mother did all the heavy morpho-printing. I was the idea guy, you know? It was my vision, man."

Swarm and Zee exchanged a look. She raised her eyebrows and flicked her eyes toward Charlie. Swarm got the hint and cleared the gravel from his throat.

"Exactly what vision would that be, Captain?" he asked, although his tone made it seem like he might not want to know the answer.

"The *Pineapple Express!*"

"Wait a second," said Zylvya, realization dawning on her. "That's not just a fruit, is it? It's a—"

"Starship!" cheered Charlie. "Yeah, man! A pineapple-shaped starship!"

"*That's* a starship?" asked Swarm.

"Hell yeah, it is! Fill them in on all the deets, V-man!"

"Sure thing, Captain," squawked Vargoni. "Not quite as fast as the *Starseed*, but faster than most ships in the quadrant these days. Has all the bells and whistles, just on a smaller scale! A mini-Transit Bay, a mini-Ring, a mini-THC Core Chamber, a mini-bridge—"

"With a mini-fridge!" added Charlie.

"Yes, yes, Captain was most insistent on the mini-fridge full of Earther beverages and snacks."

Zylvya turned her face up to the pineapple silhouette.

"Mother, you helped make this… ship?"

"Mmm-hmm, little sprig, I sure did. Grew it from my very own bosom. Allocated 1% of my substrate toward the captain's vision. That's why I was out of reach this morning. Maintaining simultaneous conversations with over 500 billion lifeforms isn't that hard when you've been doing it for as long as I have, but doing it while giving birth… well, baby, that's not so easy."

"Ha!" Swarm bellowed. "Captain, when I look past the sheer stupidity of what you've created, I can see the genius of your vision!"

Zylvya placed a wood-grained hand between Swarm's large compound eyes and gave him a concerned look.

"Mother, we need to get Swarm some medical help immediately."

"Pull the twigs out of your head, Zee!" Swarm said, pushing her hand away. "Don't you see? Captain Hong found a solution! This is how the *Starseed* can be in two places at once! You can take the captain's novelty starship to evacuate Lusus while the rest of us on the *'Seed* set course for Trapezia, as planned."

"Wait a second! No way! I'm not taking that *thing* to Lusus!"

"Ouch," said Charlie. "The way you said *thing* right then made it seem like you don't like it. I designed it with you in mind, you know. You, and well, the movie."

"Movie?" she asked. "You mean one of those two-dimensional videos you're always staring at in your quarters?"

"Duh, man. *Pineapple Express*. Wait, you've never heard of *Pineapple Express*? The stoner comedy flick with Seth Rogan and James Franco and that other hilarious dude... shit, what's his name? He was in that other movie they did about the end of the world. Whatever, forget the movie. Surely you've heard of the incredible weed strain?"

"Anyway, the Pineapple Express strain won a bunch of Cannabis Cup awards a few years back. Everyone started growing it. All the shops carried it. Are you kidding me? Why are you looking at me like you're never heard the words *Pineapple Express* before?"

"Because we haven't," rattled Swarm. "Nor do we care. All I want to know is when Zee and that giant fruit ship will be setting off to Lusus."

"Wrong, Bugbrain," Zylvya said, snatching the last of Charlie's joint from his lips and putting it between her own. "I'm not flying *that* thing anywhere."

"Okay, fine," Charlie said coolly. "It wasn't for you anyway."

"What?" grumbled Swarm. "Wait, if you think *I'm* going to

pilot that giant fruit to host a peace summit, you're sorely mistaken. Not gonna happen, Captain. No way."

"Cool. That's your call, man. Stay here with Zee. You two can save Lusus together while I take my awesome new ship to the Trapezia system and save three times the people—and have ten times the fun."

"Smegging hell." Swarm buried his face in his claws. "If I let you go alone, you'll just get them high and spend the whole time eating junk food while watching old Earth cartoons."

"It doesn't have to be just cartoons, man. We can take turns watching whatever everyone wants to watch. Geez. Just because I'm the captain doesn't mean I have to be a dick. We'll take a vote or something."

"I can't believe I'm saying this," grumbled Swarm, "but if you're taking that thing to Trapezia, then I'm going with you."

"Alright! Great meeting, everyone," Zylyva said, smiling. "See you when you get back. Safe travels!"

She turned to go but Charlie grabbed her arm.

"Wait!" he cried. "You can't leave yet! You haven't seen the best part!"

"I don't care if you're my captain or not," Zee said. "If you don't get your hand off me in three seconds, I'm going to return it to you in pieces. Three… two…"

Before she could finish, the ground began to tremble and Charlie let go to catch his balance.

"Hey, Mu, you have family dropping by?" Swarm asked as he ducked to scan the rows running between the endless cannabis plants.

"Noooooot tooooodaaaay," Mu said, then shrank back into its hole.

As soon as he vanished, the ground lurched and shifted beneath their feet.

"Vargoni, the four of us will call you from the mini-bridge of the *Pineapple Express* in an hour."

"You got it, Captain! I'll start toking the passengers aboard at once!"

The tall bird creature flapped its mighty wings and disappeared over the *Starseed's* horizon.

"Four of us?" asked Swarm. "I know you're high as smeg right now, Captain, but without Featherhead and Mu, there are only three of us."

"Habu's right over there, sleeping under one of my girls. Hey, Habu, say hi!"

A scrawny human arm poked out from one of Charlie's plants and waved.

"What? We're bringing that weird ape we picked up in the Reptilian moon base orbiting Págos 9?" roared Swarm. He added quietly, "He's bad news, Captain. There's something about him. He's hiding something."

"Well, for now, he's helping me take care of my girls. Oh, and if you haven't figured it out by now, I'm bringing the girls, too. Gonna see if I can try to fix them in my downtime."

"*Fix* them?" Zylvya put her fists on her hips. "With that attitude, no wonder they're wilting like this."

The quaking beneath their feet intensified. A crack appeared in the spongy soil and formed a circle around the seven sick plants, including the small clearing between them that contained Charlie and the others. They nearly lost their balance as the massive clump of soil tore free from the hull of the *Starseed* and began floating upward toward the *Pineapple Express*.

"We're on our way, guys! Better hold on to your butts!" cheered Charlie. "And Zee, as usual, let me know if you need a hand."

7

Swarm studied the *Pineapple Express* with both sets of arms crossed. His compound eyes fixated on the bottom of the fruit, where a hole was widening to receive their floating platform.

Wisps of greenish smoke began zipping past them going from the *Starseed* to the *Pineapple Express*, causing Swarm to clear his gravelly throat and ask, "We're bringing regular Seeders with us, Captain?"

"Before you get your wings all bent out of shape," Charlie said, pausing to expel a lungful of smoke, "I did some research on the Outernet about the route we're taking along the galactic fringe, and it looks pretty sweet, man. Big psychedelic stardust clouds all throughout the sector. Not much traffic out there, so lots of peace and quiet."

"Captain, it's quiet outside of every ship no matter where it is. Sound doesn't travel through a vacuum," said Zylvya.

"Whatever. I knew that. Anyway, the *Pineapple Express* is so big it felt like a waste to leave it empty."

"Couldn't you have just made it smaller?"

"Hey, it's not the size of the pineapple that matters, it's how you use it."

"Exactly!" Zylvya sighed. "Why do I bother trying to argue

with someone who can't see their own absurd cyclical contradictions?"

"Sounds like you could use a little *space cruise*, Zee! Sure you don't wanna join us?"

"Space cruise?" Swarm seethed, barely able to contain his rage. "You introduced a massive security risk to a delicate peace accord in order to fill an unnecessarily large vessel, and now you're calling it a *space cruise*?"

"No! Well, yes. Kinda. Man, you got it all wrong. All I did was invite a few Seeders along for the trip."

"I'm counting more than just a few tokes coming from the *Starseed*!"

"Okay, so it was more like a few hundred Seeders. Maybe a few thousand? I wasn't counting, man. I let Vargoni and Mother handle the vetting process. You probably know this already, but there are a lot of nice aliens—I mean, er, people—who could use a little getaway after all the traumatic shit the galaxy's thrown at them. Also, the peace summit will be held on a secure deck without any possible interaction between the Trapezians and our vacationers."

"Captain, I can see the *vacationers'* toke streams entering the mini-Transit Bay right now. Do you have a separate, secure transit bay just for the Trapezians?"

"Hold up, Swarm. Weren't you planning on hosting the peace summit on the *Starseed*? If you think about it, by only allowing a few thousand Seeders on the *Pineapple Express*, I'm actually making it waaaay more secure."

Swarm opened his mandibles to speak, but not even a gravelly rattle came out.

Zylvya didn't bother trying to stifle her chuckle.

"You guys will have to argue later," she said. "We're here."

As they approached, the soil platform rotated so they were suddenly rising upward into the gaping orifice at the bottom of the *Pineapple Express*. Inside was a huge receiving bay with tunnels and corridors leading in all directions—an exact replica of the Transit Bay on the *Starseed*, only much smaller. The floor was made from the same swirled green marble, but one key difference was that the walls and the domed ceiling were golden and shimmered with a juicy sheen. The effect made Zylvya's stomach simultaneously queasy and hungry.

Every few seconds a puff of greenish smoke would zip through the open port, swirl frantically into a person-sized tornado, then condense into a Seeder clutching their luggage.

The parade of Seeders was less dense than the one Charlie routinely encountered in the corridors of the *Starseed*, but just as bizarre. A pair of five-foot-tall pink crustaceans appeared and skittered off carrying small handbags in their tiny claws. A family of shin-high, cloaked furry things appeared and bounced in unison down another corridor. A creature that looked to Charlie like a starfish teetering on three flexible stilts appeared beside them and stepped over the crew before it climbed the domed wall and crawled into one of the higher tunnels.

"Smegging hell," groaned Swarm. "This whole Transit Bay will have to be quantum-sanitized before we set course for Trapezia."

"The whole *mini*-Transit Bay," corrected Charlie.

"Whatever. I can't believe Mother went along with this!"

"I think it might've been her idea, man."

"Of course it was." Swarm shook his head.

"Look, I'm sure MOM will handle all the scrubbing and security stuff. Come on, this is our stop," Charlie said, ushering them off the soil platform. As soon as they disembarked, the platform and the seven wilted plants recommenced their upward journey through the air.

"Meet up with you later on, Habu!" Charlie called out, waving.

The scrawny arm that waved to them earlier reappeared in the foliage and flashed a thumbs-up. Once the platform reached the apex of the dome, another orifice opened to receive it.

As Charlie led them toward a particular corridor, Zee asked, "Did you just call Mother '*MOM*'? That's a new one."

"Close, but no spliff for you," said Charlie. "I designed the *Pineapple Express* to be grown from the *Starseed's* substrate, which means it contains all the same features: the personal gravity and atmospheric fields around every organism; a hyperspace drive and THC tube for fuel; and its own copy of Mother that I've named MOM, which stands for *My Other Mother*."

His droopy eyelids lifted to reveal wide, bloodshot eyes." Pretty awesome, eh?"

"You made a copy of Mother?" Zylvya said, making a face that showed she thought it was the opposite of awesome.

"Yeah, I guess. Well, actually, I have no friggin' idea how it works, but Mother said it was a perk of using one percent of the *Starseed's* mass to form the *Pineapple Express*. She said when you do that, you get another Mother in the deal. You know, someone to watch over all the passengers and make sure we're all fed and taken care of, just like Mother does on the *Starseed*. Shit, I almost forgot! Wanna see the best part?"

Zylvya and Swarm exchanged a look and shrugged.

"Watch this!"

Charlie pulled them close to one of the glistening golden walls, reached out with his forefinger and thumb, and pinched the surface of the wall. A small, irregular cube of squishy material broke away and dripped juices down the back of his hand. After making sure they got a good look, he smiled and popped the cube into his mouth.

"It's pineapple!" he cheered, through a mouthful of juicy flesh.

Zylvya's emerald eyes widened. "You didn't."

"I did! Perfectly ripe, every time! Go on, try some!"

She shook her head. "I'll pass."

"Come on, Zee! You gotta try some! It's made from *real* pineapple. Well, technically, it's just the same substrate we use on the *Starseed*, but I tweaked it to be eatable."

"Edible," she corrected. "But… why?"

"Why?" Charlie looked offended. "Why ask why? Why not ask 'why not'?"

He plucked another small cube from the wall and popped it between his lips. Juice ran down the sides of his mouth as he continued, "Besides, it's not just pineapple. On the molecular level, it'll provide all the nutrients and shit each individual lifeform needs. It's the perfect healthy snack, man!"

Zylvya groaned and offered a weak smile.

"I guess that's one way to keep everyone fed."

"Exactly!" Charlie cried, snatching a whole handful of the wall and shoving it into his mouth. The fist-sized crater he left behind rippled and bulged until the wall was perfectly smooth again.

"I've never heard of another *Starseed* captain attempting anything like this before," Swarm said, scratching the underside of his mandible. "How do we know this ship, the life support systems, and MOM are stable?"

"No idea, man. We had to move super fast to get the *Pineapple Express* created in time. But think about it, if Mother did the growing, how could her copy be anything less than perfect?"

Zylvya sighed.

"Obviously you haven't been on the *Starseed* long enough to know the answer to that question."

Charlie finished swallowing and turned his face up to the ceiling.

"Hey, MOM! You there?"

A voice filled their heads, just like when talking to Mother aboard the *Starseed*.

"Affirmative, Captain Hong. I cannot be anywhere else but here," the voice said. Unlike Mother's natural flow and sweetly southern accent, MOM's voice sounded stilted and synthetic, like a computer-generated voice from an automated spam call.

"Do you have orders for me, Captain Hong?"

"Uh, no. I'm all good at the moment," Charlie said, then changed his mind. "Actually, I'm trying to find my way to the mini-bridge but the augmented navigation aura thingy I'm following seems really dim. Could you brighten it so it's easier to see?"

"Affirmative, Captain. I'll increase the visual intensity of the automated guidance system for you and the crew."

"HOLY SHIT! TOO BRIGHT! TURN IT DOWN, MAN!" he cried as he shielded his eyes.

Swarm and Zylvya did the same, clenching their eyes shut as tightly as possible.

"Affirmative, Captain. Please specify the level of brightness you'd like to see when using the augmented guidance system."

"Back to where it was before is fine!"

The aura dimmed and the crew relaxed.

"Charlie," Zee said, rubbing her eyes. "At first I thought the *Pineapple Express* was a decent idea—idiotic, obviously, but decent—but now I'm not sure it's safe to rely on a version of Mother that's comprised of only one percent of her faculties."

"Naw, Zee, it's fine. She might take a little getting used to, but think about it—Mother's the one who morpho-printed the *Pineapple Express* and MOM. Would Mother send us out into the vacuum of space on a ship that's not totally, completely, one hundred percent safe?"

"Like I said before, you haven't known her long enough. Anyway, you're the captain, you can do whatever you want. I have to go prepare the *Starseed* to save Lusus. You boys have fun. And try not to die before reaching Trapezia."

"Lieutenant Zylvya, would you like me to toke you back to the *Starseed?*" MOM asked.

"Uhm, no. That's okay. I've already got a ride."

She tapped the chatter badge on her chest and spoke into it.

"Vargoni, you there?"

"Yes, yes! I'm on the bridge, patiently awaiting word from Captain Hong. Is he okay? Did something happen? Oh, dear..."

"Everything's fine, Featherhead. I just need you to toke me back to the *Starseed*. Direct to THC Core Chamber, please."

"You got it! Toking in three, two, one."

Zylvya had just enough time to shoot Charlie a worried look before she evaporated into green smoke and swirled down the corridor the way they'd come.

"Now what?" grumbled Swarm. "Are we ready to depart?"

Charlie checked his watch.

"Let's give the Seeders a few more minutes to board while we check out our new base of operations."

They stepped into the mini-bridge and a round door spiraled shut behind them. Like the mini-Transit Bay, the mini-bridge was a smaller version of the *Starseed's* bridge—circular in shape with round purple doors along the perimeter and a high domed ceiling that appeared to look out at a vast starfield, but which was actually an illusion created by light-emitting bacteria.

Charlie headed straight for the small metallic cube sitting at the center of the room.

"You gotta see this mini-fridge, man. Stocked full of Snickers bars, Red Bull, kombucha, and *this*."

He reached inside and pulled out a bottle filled with some kind of dark, fizzy liquid.

"THC-infused, pineapple-flavored mocktail! Here, try one."

"Maybe later, Captain. Now, about the summit, I think—"

"One of these costs like *ten bucks* back on Earth!" interrupted Charlie. "No alcohol, but they have like 25mg of THC in each bottle, so if you drink too many they'll really fuck you up. You gotta sip 'em to make sure you don't get *overstoned*, know what I mean?"

"Barely, and less so with each word that leaves your mouth," rattled Swarm. "Drink whatever you want, Captain. As for the trip to Trapezia, we should—"

"Dude, the mini-fridge has whatever *you* want. Just think of any beverage or snack and it instantly morpho-prints inside. Cool, huh? Come on, give it a shot. Come on! We've been working all morning without a break. I know you've gotta be thirsty."

"We've been working all morning?"

"What'll it be?"

Swarm sighed, which sounded like a rainstick had been flipped over and a million tiny seeds were working their way down its hollow interior.

"Fine, I'll think of something." His long antennae twitched behind him. "I'll take the purple bottle."

Charlie smiled, reached inside the mini-fridge, and handed Swarm the bottle of murky purple fluid.

He watched Swarm take a long swig and asked, "What is that stuff?"

Swarm wiped his mandibles with his claw.

"The fermented spinal fluid of the Hive's arch rivals, the Bombus. Or *Bees*, as you referred to them earlier. After defeating them in battle, we'd collect their frozen corpses from all the space debris, drain their central nerve into crystal barrels, then let the stuff age for a few kiloghatikas. There's nothing like it in the galaxy—or at least there won't be for another million years or so."

Swarm held out the bottle of purple stuff. "Try a sip, Captain."

Charlie clinked his bottle to Swarm's and smiled.

"Nope, I'm good with this for now. Hey, wanna hit the mini-Ring next? You gotta see some of the vendors we were able to pull over from the *'Seed*, man. That noodle cart dude brought along a—"

"Enough!" Swarm bellowed, a small burp escaping from his mandibles. "What I want to see is a schematic of this ship. Every floor, from top to bottom. Then I'll have to establish security checkpoints in high-traffic areas. If I can't dissuade you from turning this mission into a pleasure cruise, the least I can do is make sure we don't have Seeders strolling through secure areas."

"Come on, man! You really think I'd design this ship so that random Seeders could just walk in on official business?"

Before Swarm could answer, a small voice called out behind them.

"Charlie!"

They turned to find three Seeders standing just inside the

mini-bridge. They were bipedal insectoids, vaguely similar to Swarm, yet covered in soft, medium-length brown fur instead of iridescent red scales. Their compound eyes were smaller and positioned closer to the fronts of their heads, and instead of mandibles, long proboscises curled into spirals beneath their faces. The two adults stood slightly shorter than Charlie while the third came up to his waist. All three were wearing colorful Hawaiian shirts and flower leis around their necks.

"You were saying, Captain?" grumbled Swarm.

Charlie ignored him and straightened up, slipping his bottle behind his back like a guilty teenager caught drinking a beer.

"Hey, look! It's the Glimwickets! Welcome aboard the *Pineapple Express*! Let me introduce you to Lieutenant Swarm, my Chief of Security."

Swarm glared down at the family and crossed his upper set of arms.

"Greetings. How exactly did you access the door to the bridge?"

"A-hem," interrupted Charlie. "The *mini*-bridge."

"The doors to this room should be among the most secure on the ship. If any random Seeder can get in here, then—"

"The Glimwickets aren't just some random Seeders! We picked them up shortly after I became Captain, and they, uh, sometimes invite me over for dinner. I can vouch for them, man."

"How nice. I still want to know how they opened that smegging door."

"Multi-pass!" answered the smallest Glimwicket, holding up a laminated card that hung from a lanyard around his neck. "Captain Charlie had one sent to our quarters before we toked over. Said we were VIPs, which is an Earther term for *very important persons*. Didn't he tell you, Lieutenant Swarm?"

Swarm produced a low, guttural growl from his chest, prompting the larger Glimwicket to step between them.

"So nice to meet you, Lieutenant Swarm. The name's Bobomo

Glimwicket, Sr., but everyone just calls me Bob," he said, extending his four-fingered hand.

When Swarm's arms didn't budge, Bob squirmed uncomfortably and placed his hand on the smallest Glimwicket's shoulder.

"This here is my son, Bobomo Jr.—also known as Bob. And last but not least, this beautiful bundle of brown fur is my wife, Bauble Glimwicket. And, if you haven't already guessed, everyone calls her Baub."

"It's very nice to meet you, Lieutenant Swarm," she said. "With all due respect, if you don't stop glaring at my son like that, I'll shove that bottle straight up your carapace and into your—"

"Hey!" interrupted Charlie, slipping between them. "This is all my mistake, man. I'm sure we can clear this up and get the Glimwickets safely to their room. Right Swarm?"

Swarm glared for a moment longer before relenting.

"Fine, I'll reset the bridge's door access after you leave, and I'll be taking that." He snipped the lanyard from Bob Jr.'s neck and snatched the multi-pass before it hit the ground.

Mrs. Glimwicket narrowed her eyes.

"Lay one claw on my son and I'll—"

"You'll have to excuse my wife," interrupted Bob Sr., his proboscis nervously uncoiling and recoiling as he spoke. "We're expecting another little one soon. Only a few weeks left before the little bugger arrives. That's why we took Captain Hong up on his offer for one last vacation before the big day. It's a girl. Probably. We'll have to see which egg hatches first—you know how it is—but we're hopeful."

Bob Sr. placed his arm around his wife and they became the perfect portrait of wholesomeness in the form of humanoid moth creatures.

"Anyway, Charlie's told us so much about you and your adventures together. It's an honor to finally meet you, Lieutenant."

"The honor is all mine," replied Swarm, keeping one eye on

Bauble. "Now if you'll excuse us, we have important business to attend to."

"Sure, sure! We need to find our quarters, but the augmented guidance system here on the *Pineapple Express* seems a bit dimmer compared to the one back on the *Starseed*—unless my middle-aged peepers are finally starting to deteriorate. Ha!"

Bob Sr. laughed, but no one else did.

Charlie smiled and pointed to the ceiling. "Have you tried out MOM yet? I'm sure she can help you find your way. Hey MOM, you there?"

"Affirmative, Captain Hong. I am always here."

"Would you mind escorting the Glimwickets to their room? Maybe try turning up the aura brightness on the augmented guidance system so they can—HOLY SHIT! TOO BRIGHT!"

8

After reviewing an excruciatingly boring security checklist, Charlie finally gave Swarm the slip by pretending to be overstoned on pineapple-flavored mocktails.

Yeah right. As if a few hundred milligrams of THC could slow me down, he thought, as the mini-bridge's door spun closed behind him.

Ten minutes later, another door spun open in front of him revealing a portal to plant paradise. A paradise for Charlie's seven humungous pot plants, that is.

Like most rooms on the *Pineapple Express,* this room was circular in shape with a domed ceiling, but instead of shimmering golden walls and an illusory starfield above, every surface was smooth and white. Squadrons of spherical drones, each about the size of a golfball and covered in powerful LED lights, buzzed around the room frantically pumping each individual leaf full of photons. Before zipping off to their next target, the grobots would squirt a gentle puff of mist from their backsides to keep the air perfectly humid and hospitable for plant respiration.

The result was a work of art—a technological symphony of the best agricultural equipment Charlie could find on the Outernet.

The best part of setting up this cannabis paradise (or *infirmary*, if he was being honest with himself) had been ignoring the price tags. Even hi-tech gear he found on Earth's internet, which was a minuscule subset of the galactic Outernet, could be morpho-printed in mere seconds. All Charlie had to do was click the print icon displayed at the top of any webpage he browsed from his *Starseed Operating System* and a lump would appear nearby and morph into the desired object. No credit card required. No delivery fee. No taxes or surcharges.

Watching the tiny grobots zip around the dense foliage and swollen, resinous buds, offering every square inch the perfect balance of light, warmth, and moisture, he knew there wasn't a more advanced cannabis grow room in all the galaxy.

Then why the hell do my girls still look so awful? he thought.

Which was why, after weeks of trial and error on the *Starseed*, pulling out every gardening trick he could think of, he finally had to suck up his pride and hire some outside help.

Charlie took a pair of dark sunglasses from his hoodie pocket and put them on before walking into the clearing at the center of the seven plants. Even though the purplish light emitted from the LEDs didn't seem as glaringly bright as the high-pressure sodium lights of yore, they still had a way of overwhelming your vision.

"Hey there, Happy," he said, lifting one of the baseball-bat-sized clusters of densely packed nugs. He drew the terminal bud to his face and sniffed. "You smell wonderful, as always. And damn, girl! Sticky as ever, too."

Charlie released the bud, wiped his hand on his jacket, then turned to address the adjacent plants. "Hello, Doc! Lookin' very pretty. Hi, Sleepy, Grumpy. You both look especially vibrant tonight. Bashful, is that new growth? Damn, Sneezy! Your fragrance is incredible, as usual. Dopey, you look as stunning as ever, man."

When he was done lying to his plants, he searched the spongy soil under them for his new consultant.

"The guy bailed already? Thanks a lot for the recommendation, Mother."

"Sorry, Captain Hong, but Mother is not accessible here on the *Pineapple Express*," MOM answered in her flat, stilted tone. "Yet the *Starseed* should remain within extended communication range for another thirteen Earth minutes. During that time I can convey your message of gratitude to Mother, or any other messages you would like to send. Would you like me to do so now, Captain?"

"Thanks, MOM. But I'm good for now."

"Sorry, Captain Hong, but I do not understand how your generic qualitative status answers my query. If you are interested in measuring your skill level at something, I am programmed to perform a detailed assessment of over twenty thousand tasks and proficiencies, including—"

"Nope, I'm good. I mean, *er*...I won't be needing any assistance at this time," he said, peeking underneath Sleepy's lower canopy. "Actually, you can tell me where the hell this Habu guy went to?"

Before MOM could respond, a toilet flushed nearby. There was the brief sound of running water and someone humming quietly to themselves. The tune sounded familiar, although it was too faint for Charlie to figure out. When the running water stopped, a door panel slid open along the perimeter of the room and an elderly Chinese man wearing a long purple robe emerged. He was bald but for a tuft of white hair and had two thin strands of mustache dangling almost all the way to the floor.

The old man looked shocked at the way Charlie was looking at him.

"What, you've never had to drop a log?" Habu said. He shrugged and stepped through the plants into the clearing.

"I don't remember putting a bathroom there. It wasn't in my schematics."

"Schematics? Ha!" laughed Habu. "You mean those scribbles you gave Mother? You should feel lucky she took some creative liberties or else you'd be standing in a pile of steaming shit right about now!"

Dammit, he's right, Charlie thought to himself. *I planned on spending whole days in here, but I completely forgot about adding a bathroom. What else did I forget?*

"Don't worry, Captain! Mother provides! She always knows what we need even when we don't."

"Sorry, but Mother is not accessible here on the *Pineapple Express,* nor will she be tending to your needs. I, MOM, am here to assist you with anything you need."

Habu rolled his eyes and gave Charlie a look.

"Let's hope we don't need any assistance, am I right?"

"Assistance is exactly what I need right now. That's why I hired you, man. To help me get my girls back on their feet."

"Ha! Shows what you know! Plants don't even have feet—well, they do on Saptek Prime, but that's besides the point." The old man shook his head. *"Get them back on their feet?* No wonder they're having such a hard time right now."

"Hey, listen up, man! This isn't my first grow room, okay? I've grown hundreds—no, *thousands*—of cannabis plants. I've never lost any before, either."

"Really?" Habu said, looking around. "Then where are they, huh? I only see seven plants and they don't look like they'll be around much longer. Oh, I know! Why not print each of them a nice pair of shoes for their feet? Maybe some matching jewelry, too!"

Charlie could feel heat rising in his cheeks.

"If you're just gonna insult me and my girls, then maybe I don't need your help after all."

Habu shrugged.

"Sounds like you have everything under control. I'll just spend the rest of the trip sampling whatever grub found its way into the mini-Ring."

Charlie sighed and held out a hand to stop the old man from walking past.

"I'm sorry," he said. "I admit I don't know what's wrong with my girls and I need help before it's too late. If Mother said you can help, I believe her."

"Well, if Mother says so, it must be true," Habu said, then buckled over with laughter.

When he recovered, he clapped his hands together and scanned the nearest plant.

"Before we begin, I must collect an advance on my pay. Let's see, which one of these nugs looks good… Ah-ha! This one will do just fine."

With one hand he plucked a medium-sized nug from Doc and with the other he produced a long, curved jade pipe from inside his robe.

"Uh… you can't smoke a wet nug, man. You gotta dry it out before it'll combust properly."

"Nonsense!" the old man said, holding the nug up between them. "The *Starseed* always provides."

"Sorry, but that assertion is partially incorrect," announced MOM. "You are not aboard the *Starseed*. You are currently traveling on the *Pineapple Express*. If you would like to return to the *Starseed*, I can produce a single-passenger transit vehicle that can take you there. The trip may take several years, as the *Starseed* and the *Pineapple Express* are currently traveling in opposite directions at very high speeds."

Habu shot Charlie another amused look.

"With a computer like *that* running the ship, you should've named this vessel the *Nonsense Express!* Ha!"

"Sorry, but I do not understand the context of the advice that was just offered. Captain Hong, would you like to rename the vessel?"

Charlie rolled his eyes.

"Naw, I'm good, man."

"Sorry, Captain Hong, I do not understand how your generic qualitative status answers my—"

"MOM!" Charlie interrupted. "Listen, we don't need anything

right now except a little privacy. We don't have much time till we reach Trapezia, and Habu and I have a lot to discuss."

"Affirmative, Captain. I will disable all sensory communication to this room until you state my name. In the case of an emergency, I will proceed to—"

"Thanks! We'll let you know if we need anything."

Charlie waited to ward off another reply, and when none came he turned back to Habu. The old man was puffing vigorously on his jade pipe, tendrils of smoke wafting up around his face.

"Man, that nug was super fresh. It was full of moisture and hadn't been cured yet. How'd you even get it to light?"

"Ha! You think the *Starseed*, a living ship that can simultaneously control the atmosphere, gravity, and language translations for all us Seeders, a ship that can give birth to another vessel like this one, can't remove moisture from a tiny little nug?"

"Good point, man. I've only been here for a few months—Earth months—so I'm still getting used to everything."

Habu nodded and sipped from his pipe.

"You should've seen how much trouble your predecessor had! It was like giving a quantum dual-optimizer to a Xarnaxian!"

"You knew Captain Major Tom?" Charlie said, rummaging around in his afro for a joint. He found one, popped it between his lips, and started puffing as soon as it autonomously sparked itself up.

"Knew him? He was my pupil before he became Major Tom, and then again, briefly, after he became captain of the *Starseed*."

"Wait... you knew him *before* he became Major Tom? That means you knew, uh, he wasn't exactly what he seemed to be."

"Ha! Anyone with half a cortex could figure out what he really was in five millighatikas! He made it so obvious with all his lumbering around and shouting orders all the time. Hardly ever took time for contemplative moments such as these."

Habu closed his eyes and took a long, slow hit from his pipe.

"Holy shit, man," Charlie said, then took a long hit off his joint while Habu's words sank in.

"I can't believe you knew Captain Major Tom! The *real* dude underneath his, uh, disguise. He confided in me just before he died, man. He and the *Starseed* had accidentally picked me up when they swung by Earth to steal my girls."

"Accident? Ha! There are no such things in the universe."

"No really, I was just a stowaway. When I saw my girls getting sucked up into the sky, I clung to Happy over there and I wouldn't let go. The next thing I knew I woke up in the Garden on the outside of the '*Seed*. I'm lucky to have survived the trip through Earth's atmosphere."

"That so?" asked Habu, clenching his smile shut to hold back laughter. "Let me guess what came next. You and Major Tom took a little trip back to Earth to help free the *Starseed* from some nasty Reptilian trap? But something went terribly wrong with his plan, and when he figured he was done for, he handed you the job, right? Ha! See, weed makes me psychic! You can't hide anything from Habu!"

With that, he lost control and burst out laughing, spewing mouthfuls of smoke into the purplish light.

"Whatever, man. Mother must've filled you in on how I became captain. Look, I didn't ask for any of this. Before I got picked up by the *Starseed*, I was just a regular guy... on Earth... trying to take care of his plants."

Charlie's words seemed to ignite something in the old man. He stopped laughing, sat up straight, and looked Charlie in the eyes.

"What are you now, Captain?" he asked in a very serious tone. "And what are you becoming? We all change once we bond with the *Starseed*. It happened to Major Tom after he was rescued, adrift in his little tin can. It happened to every crew member and every Seeder who has had the privilege to step foot on that great living vessel. Even *me*! Believe it or not, I wasn't always so congenial!"

The carefree and somewhat unhinged smirk had returned to his lips as he sucked smoke from his pipe.

Charlie shrugged off the questions and started pacing, the smoldering joint dangling from the corner of his mouth.

"I'm not worried about me right now. I'm worried about my girls. Look at them, man. I've been growing cannabis for over a decade and I've never seen plants take such a bad turn so quickly."

"A whole decade, you say?" taunted Habu, again on the verge of laughter.

"Dude, can't you be serious for *one minute*? My girls are dying! You're supposed to be some kind of cannabis guru, but all you've done so far is get high and laugh at your own jokes!"

"From what I hear, sounds like you and I have a lot in common."

"C'mon, man! My girls are more than just plants to me! They're all I have left of my old life, of who I used to be back on Earth. Look at them, they're *dying*! I don't know how to help them. I don't even know what's wrong. I'll admit it, if that's what you're waiting to hear. *I need your help!*"

Charlie was surprised to notice his hands were balled into fists and his whole body was trembling.

Habu noticed as well and let his smile fall away.

"I'm sorry to have upset you, Captain Hong," said Habu softly. He took a tiny puff from his pipe, held it for a few silent seconds, then blew it toward the apex of the dome.

Charlie waited for him to say more, and in that short time regained a little composure. He ran a hand through his short afro and sighed.

"I didn't mean to get so intense, man. My girls are special. I'm afraid of losing them. And right now, not only are you the only other human I've seen in months, but apparently you're the only one who can help me. Who can help *them*."

Habu raised an eyebrow. "I am?"

"Of course! Why else would you be here?"

"Believe me, Captain, I've been asking myself that same question."

"I know Mother well enough by now to know how she works. She somehow manipulated things to get you aboard the *Starseed* so you'd be able to help me. If you're really some incredible cannabis-growing guru, then please—pretty please with *kief* sprinkled on top—help me!"

Habu closed his eyes and took a deep breath. When he opened them, all levity was gone and Charlie sensed a deep sadness.

"You and I may be more alike than you think, Captain. But never forget that there is much about us that is different. Although I've spent some time on Earth, I was not born there. I, too, was plucked from my home world and sent on a mission that I never asked for. I, too, have been without my kind for many, many years. I, too, have suffered the loss of those I care about. All of that has affected me in ways that are hard to explain. And this," he lifted his jade pipe, "has kept me sane. It's been my only companion on this journey through the vast emptiness of the quadrant. My only true ally. And, as you seem to be able to understand, my dearest friend. It's clear this is a close friend of yours, too. Therefore, I swear upon our mutual friend that I will help you solve your problem."

"You will? Great!" cheered Charlie. "Alright then, man, let's get started! I've already checked the soil, and its acidity is perfect for maximizing nutrient uptake, so I was thinking we could—"

"No!" interrupted Habu sharply. "None of that is necessary. The problem has nothing to do with soil or light or nutrients."

"Then it's a disease of some kind? Some kind of space virus or something?"

"No."

"Okay, fine. Since you're the expert, I'll just shut up so you give me your professional opinion. What's wrong with my girls, man?"

"There is nothing wrong with these plants, Captain."

"What? Don't you see them? Their leaves are yellow and wilting. Their branches seem weak and brittle!"

"The problem resides in *you*, Captain. It's clouding your mind and poisoning your relationship with them."

Charlie took a step backward and stared at the old man. As much as the answer made him want to start yelling again, a sudden wave of nausea swept over him and his legs became weak.

"What does that mean?" he managed to say, although part of him didn't want to know the answer.

"I've diagnosed the problem for you, Captain." Habu motioned to the plants with his pipe. "But only they can give you the solution. If they're such good friends, have you tried simply talking to them?"

"Why not ask *them* what they think is wrong. And then," he paused, his face turning grim. "Be prepared for the answer to be quite different than what you might have expected."

Charlie looked at his plants, then back at Habu.

"Talk to them? I talk to them all the time!"

"Ahh, but how often do you listen?"

9

"I guess that old kook isn't completely useless after all."

"Don't take his side, man!"

Swarm shrugged his upper pair of shoulders.

"I don't know, Captain. Sounds like he gave you the answer you were looking for."

"Wrong, dude! If he'd given me the answer, my girls wouldn't still be sagging halfway to the goddamn floor!" fumed Charlie. He clenched his fists as he walked alongside the insectoid. "That geezer doesn't know the first thing about growing weed! The only thing he knows how to do is mooch off my plants. Man, I don't know why I listen to Mother anyway. She's always got some hidden agenda."

"Sorry, Captain Hong, but Mother is not available here on the *Pineapple Express*." MOM's artificial voice filled the air around them. "I am MOM, a replica of Mother, and I am fully capable of assisting you with your elevated stress levels."

"I'm not stressed!"

"Although you may not consciously feel any adverse effects, your vital signs indicate you are, in fact, experiencing extremely high levels of stress. Your heart rate is elevated, your blood chemistry contains an abnormally high level of cortisol, and your vocal patterns indicate a frustrated and/or aggravated mental state. May I offer you a mild sedative to help calm your nervous system?"

"Fine," seethed Charlie. "How about a fat blunt filled with my *Golden Ticket?*"

Up ahead, a vine sprouted from the glimmering pineapple wall and unfurled into the corridor directly in front of Charlie. By the time he and Swarm arrived—just a few seconds later—an oblong flower bud had already swelled and opened to reveal a thick brown blunt. The moment Charlie plucked it the vine retreated and the tip of the blunt sparked to life.

Without missing a beat, Charlie popped the other end of the blunt between his lips and puffed its ember to life.

"Thanks, MOM. This really hits the spot. We'll let you know if we need another one."

He turned to Swarm.

"So what do you think I should do, man? Should I trust that Mother sent him to help me, or should I fire his ass and figure this thing out by myself?"

Swarm snatched the blunt from Charlie, took a long drag, then handed it back. He was silent for a moment, as if lost in thought, then spewed smoke from between his mandibles and asked, "Permission to speak freely, Captain?"

"Definitely, dude! Unless you're gonna take his side again."

Swarm stopped, faced Charlie, and put a claw on his shoulder.

"The truth is that I lost interest in this conversation a long time ago. Do whatever the smeg you want with your plants. Space the old kook for all I care."

Charlie chewed the end of his blunt and sighed heavily. "Gee, thanks for the advice, man."

Swarm produced a coarse grumble from his thorax and pulled Charlie along at a faster pace.

"Don't take it personally, Captain. We just have bigger mummichogs to fry right now."

"Mummi-what?"

"Is there anything besides smoke inside that head of yours? The peace summit is upon us and we're not ready!"

"Whoa, hold up. What do you mean *'we're not ready?'* Look around, man. We have the *Pineapple Express!* It's all taken care of. Piece of cake."

"It's a piece of something, alright, but not cake."

"Ouch, dude," said Charlie, nursing his ego with another puff from his blunt.

Swarm yanked Charlie aside just in time to keep him from walking into a huge, oily blob that was rolling in the opposite direction. The blob opened its four eyes and its dripping mouth to say something, but Swarm had already dragged Charlie around another corner.

"Smegging hell! The augmented guidance system on this ship is awful! We should already be in the Transit Bay!"

"You mean the *mini*-Transit Bay," corrected Charlie. "And it's fine, man. I designed it to be large enough to park their vessels alongside our transit nugs. Plenty of room for everyone. No problemo."

"If you think parking their transport vessels is the most important challenge we'll face this week, this summit is doomed."

"Even if they arrive without us there to welcome them, it's all good," Charlie said through a mouthful of smoke. "I've instructed MOM to receive them with maximum hospitality and then show them to their super-secure quarters until all the peace stuff happens tomorrow."

"All the peace stuff?" grumbled Swarm. "Captain, did it occur to you there won't be any peace stuff if all three parties arrive at the same time and kill each other?"

"Shit. That would suck. Wait, *three* parties? Aren't wars usually between *two* factions?"

"While you were conducting your 'research' for this peace summit, did you actually learn anything about the millennia-long, interplanetary, three-way civil war happening in the Trapezia system?"

"Three-way? The Trapezians are having a three-way?"

"This is not the time for innuendoes, Captain!"

"Listen, I handled the problem with the *Starseed* not being able to be in two places at once, remember? I figured you knew all the peacemaking stuff already, seeing as how you haven't shut up about this summit since I became captain. Hey look, man! We're here!"

Charlie slapped his palm against the round purple door and it spiraled open to reveal the Bay with its gaping hole in the center and small, seed-shaped nug transports lined up along the perimeter.

"See! We're early, man! Now, I'll finish this blunt while you quickly get me up to speed on all the war and peace stuff. Keep it simple though, I'm getting hella faded over here."

"No time for a history lesson, Captain. I need to contact their vessels to arrange a properly staggered boarding sequence. But, in the meantime…"

Swarm snatched the blunt away from Charlie, then reached another claw into his carapace. He hesitated.

"I didn't want to have to resort to such crude methods, but we have no choice. We'll have to risk shoving a whole lot of information into your brain all at once."

He peered into Charlie's bloodshot eyes and sighed.

"What am I saying? You're no stranger to permanent brain damage."

Swarm opened his claw to reveal a tiny colorless crystalline pill.

"Swallow it. Quickly."

"No thanks, man. I stopped popping strange pills back in college."

"It's just a data pill, you smeghead. Information distilled in quantum entangled bits of silicon chlorine. Eating it will instantly upload into your brain the entire Trapezian history, the war details, and everything else that's at stake."

"I don't know, man. It's not labeled or anything. What if someone cut it with fentanyl or something?"

"Smegging hell! I imprinted it myself, thinking we might need it for this exact purpose. It's not going to melt your brain," he said, then added quickly, "*probably* not."

"Well… just data, huh?" Charlie said, eyeing the pill. "I guess this beats studying."

"That's the spirit! Now swallow it fast!"

Charlie pinched a large chunk of pineapple from the closest wall, snatched the pill from Swarm's claw, then shoved them both in his mouth.

10

WITHIN A NANOGHATIKA OF THE DATA PILL MAKING CONTACT WITH Charlie's tongue, his entire universe went black.

Not only was there a complete lack of light or sound, he couldn't feel the vague tug of gravity or any other physical sensation. He wasn't breathing because there was no air and he had no lungs to breathe with. The *whoosh-whoosh* of his heartbeat was gone.

The only thing his awareness could latch onto was an impossibly distant electrical hum that he somehow recognized as his nervous system. The oscillation was familiar, comforting, and much too far away. Sensing that he was on the brink of a great abyss, he desperately focused on the hum with his untethered awareness. Some primordial instinct told him that if he were to drift just a little farther away, if he were to lose the hum, he'd lose something vitally important—he'd lose himself.

His consciousness suddenly buzzed to life with something resembling coherent thoughts.

Hadn't he swallowed something?

Was it medicine? Was he sick?

Was he actually a pot-growing-stoner-turned-rogue-starship-captain?

Was he actually Charlie Hong from Los Angeles, California, United States, Earth, Gal-Fed Quadrant, Milky Way, Local Group, Virgo Supercluster, Laniakea, Pisces–Cetus Supercluster, Multiverse Simulation #42, Blah-Blah, Dada, Shamba-Lamba-Ding-Dong?

Was any of that real? Or was it just a dream?

A gravelly voice broke through the infinitely expanded emptiness.

"Is this thing on? Hello? Testing... Testing..."

After a few seconds of silence, the fabric of spacetime surrounding Charlie's untethered consciousness rustled and crunched like a piece of cellophane being crumpled into a ball and then flattened out again.

"If Del were here this would've taken two millighatikas! How the smeg am I supposed to know if it's recording or not?" asked Swarm. "I really hope this doesn't melt the ape's brain."

Charlie didn't feel his mind melting. Instead, he felt his mind shatter into coarse gravel churning inside a metal garbage can full of broken glass. He recognized it as Swarm clearing his throat.

A blurry spotlight blinked to life somewhere in front of Charlie's mind's eye. Standing inside it was an eight-foot-tall, four-armed, bipedal insectoid covered in countless iridescent red scales.

"Uh, hello, Captain Hong," he rattled nervously, twitching his antennae. "If you're seeing me and hearing this, that means you were stupid enough to swallow the strange pill I offered you. As your Chief of Security, and as a rational sentient lifeform, I must advise you to never, ever do that sort of thing again. Even from someone you think you know. Even me. For all you knew, I could've been replaced by a clone or a cyborg! Smegging hell, it doesn't matter now. I'm wasting quantum bits. Just use your brain next time—if you still have one after this."

"In the case that you refused the pill and I either forced it down your throat or tricked you into eating it, I don't apologize.

You'll thank me when you don't look like a complete fool during the Trapezian peace accord."

"The good news is, if you can still see and hear me this far into the data transmission, congrats! That means your brain hasn't melted and your consciousness *should* be able to reharmonize with your synapses without causing permanent damage. I guess we'll both find out when the data pill wears off."

"Let's get on with it. Based on the instructions I found on the Outernet, I'm supposed to infuse this thing with terabytes of structured data files on whatever topic you need crammed into your memory. In this case the history and current events of the Trapezia system. Smeg if I know where to get files like that. So instead, I'm just going to hit 'play' on this immersive holographic documentary I also found on the Outernet. I didn't watch it myself, but I'm sure it's fine. It got over 450 out of 500 stars on spacedtomatillos.qom. Anyway, try to relax and enjoy the history lesson. If this doesn't kill you, I'll see you soon."

The image of Swarm standing under the spotlight flickered away. The penetrating darkness returned, but was immediately filled with countless pinpricks of light flickering to life. When they were finished, Charlie found himself floating in the center of a three hundred and sixty degree starfield.

Ahead of him, a cluster of three stars began to glow more brightly and grow in size, as if Charlie were zooming impossibly fast toward them. In the middle, two stars faced off at opposite ends of an invisible circle, forever tethered to some unseen gravitational pivot point anchored between them. A third star orbited the others in a distant, elliptical orbit. The three stars danced around each other as if stuck on fast-forward, allowing Charlie to see them complete orbit after orbit in succession.

While cruising around the quadrant in the *Starseed*, Charlie had visited stars of every color: red, orange, blue, white, even an unsettling brown one that he'd steered clear of. He was surprised to find all three of these stars burned yellow, just like the Earth's sun. There were no words projected onto the lifelike diagram and no voice spoke to him, yet he suddenly knew that each star was designated with a single letter distinguishing it from the others: Trapezium A, Trapezium B, and Trapezium C.

The problem was that his brain couldn't decide which was which.

One moment, he knew, beyond a shadow of a doubt, the outer star was Trapezium A—but then suddenly it became Trapezium B or C, while another of the stars became Trapezium A. The constant shifting made Charlie's mind feel cognitively queasy, like the facts themselves were playing a game of stellar whack-a-mole.

He shrugged off the confusion and focused on three smaller objects slowly appearing. These were planets of varying sizes, each moving along a unique orbit and velocity among the three yellow stars.

The smallest of the three was a featureless aquamarine sphere that orbited the pair of central stars in a figure eight pattern.

The largest planet was a gas giant wrapped in bands of warm, swirling hues. Its orbit passed entirely around the central two stars, then slingshot far away to catch the gravity of the outer star, making a much larger figure eight of its own.

The last planet was a dull grey rock with no sign of liquid on its surface nor clouds in its atmosphere. Its orbit was wide and slow, encircling all three stars from a great distance.

Knowledge poured into Charlie's mind like water filling the base of a bong. The primordial disc of stardust that formed the Trapezia system had been ripe with organic molecules from the get-go. The young system had settled down relatively smoothly, each clump of matter coalescing without incident, leaving the aftermath mostly free of planetary hazards like comets and asteroids. More importantly, it was located along the outer edge of one of the the Milky Way galaxy's spiral arms—way out in the boonies of the quadrant. Being so far removed from the web of interstellar transit routes that criss-crossed the inner quadrant meant it was also mostly free from extraterrestrial influence or interference.

Mostly free.

Safe in its stellar obscurity, life was able to get a foothold on the three planets.

Eventually, that life evolved sentience.

From sentience evolved civilization.

From civilization evolved technology.

From technology evolved interplanetary exploration.

And that's where all the trouble started.

Another tsunami of information flooded Charlie's mind. The small blue orb that formed a tight figure eight around the central two stars was called Undulata. Spending millions of years in such close proximity to two stars had left the world balmy and wet. Undulata was covered from pole to pole in liquid water, reminding Charlie of Earth without any dry land. A civilization thrived underneath the endless waves, eventually developing the technology to venture out beyond their aqueous atmosphere to meet their neighbors.

Their closest neighbor was the giant gaseous world, ironically named Smolz. Because of its unique orbit through the entire system, Smolz picked up an enormous amount of leftover stardust which in turn caused it to swell up like a balloon. Nuclear reactions within its dense core kept it warm during the long, lonely journeys back and forth between the inner and outer parts of the system. Civilization blossomed, and it wasn't long before that civilization erupted from the storms and began exploring their local system.

The grey rock that orbited the distant perimeter of the system was called Silex. Its long, elliptical orbit around the rest of the system kept it much colder and darker than its neighbors. Despite this, life had found a way to take hold, and it eventually evolved into a hardy species that lived within Silex's rocky surface. Like other lifeforms with access to minerals and ore, they forged great metal ships that left behind harrowing craters whenever they blasted off to conquer the emptiness of outer space.

As luck would have it, the three civilizations met very early in their respective spacefaring journeys. Because of their vastly different biologies, communication proved to be difficult. Early attempts at describing their worlds and their intentions failed miserably, mostly due to linguistic naming conventions.

Undulata asserted that the yellow star it spent the most of its time orbiting should be named Trapezium A. The conglomerate on Smolz dissented and awarded the title of Trapezium A to the star it held dearest, the other yellow star circling the center of the system. Silex not only insisted that the outer star be called Trapezium A, but that the other two worlds should pay a hefty tax for the honor of being a part of what they dubbed the Silexi system.

Decades of debate on the subject had only led to further discord among the worlds. The pride of each world and the abhorrence toward subjugating themselves to a foreign power enraged them beyond all rational discourse. Like too many other young civilizations, the three worlds decided to settle their disagreement with violence.

Official data on who fired the first interplanetary shot was inconclusive, but what was certain was that millennia of bloodshed has followed. The war for Trapezia wasn't fought by fleets of warships exchanging laser blasts or photon torpedoes. They had no desire to waste their finite resources on silly off-world battles over empty space. Likewise, the mutual incompatibility of their neighbors' worlds deterred the parties from attempting to dominate or invade each other. Which left them with one goal: total destruction of their enemies.

Thus, the Trapezian war was brought directly to the doorstep of each planet. Lightweight, unmanned, and lethal projectiles were designed and carefully calculated to traverse the clockwork system and target the enemy planets themselves. Payloads of poisonous toxins, radioactive rocks, and condensed gases were hurled at their targets when their enemies' orbits were within range. Each civilization evolved an almost ritualistic cadence to this regularity; they planned every aspect of their economy and life around the war.

"Charlie!" a voice broke through the data download, causing the diagram of scattered projectiles in front of him to shimmer and fade slightly.

Because none of the three worlds had joined the Galactic Federation prior to the breakout of the war, they'd disqualified themselves for arbitration due to Gal-Fed's strict *No Drama Charter*™. That left the system chained to an endless cycle of war which has persisted for centuries. Galactic scholars speculate that the effects of the toxic weaponry have already taken a toll on the Trapezian population's evolution, with one unnamed scholar predicting that, if left unchecked, all three Trapezian worlds will suffer severe genetic mutations in the near future.

"Captain! Snap out of it!" the voice called out from behind the starfield that surrounded him. It sounded familiar, feminine, and pissed off.

Before he could react, the image of Trapezia stabilized and more information flowed.

Concern has led a few independent groups outside the Galactic Federation to intercede and call for peace. These calls have widely been ignored both inside and outside Trapezia, leading to further predictions of a catastrophic outcome. Furthermore—

Without warning, a supernova exploded on the left side of his vision that sent stars scattering in all directions.

"Time to come back, Captain!" demanded the voice.

This time Charlie could make out who was speaking, but he knew right away it was impossible.

There was another supernova on his right side. The remaining stars scattered, including all of Trapezia.

"Charlie, wake up!"

The hum of his nervous system grew louder until it was almost unbearable. Slowly, wrapped in a cocoon of pins and needles, he began to feel like he was back inside his body.

11

His mind tucked safely back inside his head, the first thing Charlie noticed was that both of his cheeks stung sharply.

"Really, Bugbrain?" he heard that impossible voice cry out. "He wasn't exactly playing with a full deck of cards to begin with! *Now* look at him!"

"I weighed the risk and did what I had to do."

"There was no other option but to risk Charlie's life?"

"It was barely a terabyte. He'll be fine."

"Fine?! *Look* at him!"

"Smegging hell! Stop fussing over him like a wounded sapling and get him on his feet! The first of the Trapezian transports are about to dock!"

Charlie cracked his eyelids open to find a pair of emerald green eyes staring down at him, burning with a mix of anger and concern. His heart, which was thankfully once again part of his body, fluttered against the inside of his chest. His instinct was to reach out and caress her smooth, wood-grained face, but he remembered her fast left hook and kept his hands to himself.

Zee's here, on the Pineapple Express, he thought, struggling with the contradiction as his neural pathways continued rebooting.

She couldn't be there. It wasn't possible.

In the few hours since their two vessels separated, the distance between them would've been too great to have crossed in one of the *Starseed's* tiny "nug" transit ships. But he also knew she never would have ordered the *Starseed* to abandon the lifeforms on Lusus.

To hell with impossibility. I'm just glad she's here, he decided.

And goddamn! At this angle, the neckline of her toga is hanging low… which means if she would lean over me just a little bit more, I might catch a glimpse of her—

The thought was cut short by Zylyva's hand swinging back toward his face. Charlie managed to lift his arms to block her before she could land another slap.

"What the hell? Stop hitting me!"

"See, I told you he was fine," Swarm rattled impatiently. "Now get him on his feet, quickly!"

Zylvya slipped her arms under Charlie and lifted him with ease. She spun him around and looked him over.

"Zee… how are you here?"

"I toked over just as the *Pineapple Express* was pulling away from the *Starseed*," she said, lifting his eyelids one at a time to peer inside. "How are you feeling, Captain? Any headaches or dizziness?"

"I'm fine, I think," Charlie said, rubbing his eyes. "What a trip, man. I was floating above the Trapezian system and this voice— no, not a voice exactly, not sound. *Information.* It was like a history lesson was poured directly into my head."

He shuddered and ran his hands through his short afro. When they came out empty, he made a face and thrust them into his hoodie pockets. After a moment of rummaging around, a look of horror washed over his face.

"Guys, we have a major problem!" Charlie cried as he proceeded to pat himself down. "I'm all out of joints!"

Zylvya rolled her eyes and relaxed a bit.

"I guess he's fine," she said to Swarm, then pulled Charlie to her side.

"Tilt your face up. Keep your eyelids open. Don't move." Zylvya held a small lavender flower bud over his face and squeezed a drop of a colorless liquid into each eye. "It's supposed to get the red out of your eyes, but it looks like there's just more pink underneath. Strange. I thought humans had at least a little white in their eyes."

"They don't call me Chuck Stonerly for nothin', little lady."

"You're the only one who calls you that."

"Enough banter!" rattled Swarm. "The first vessel is arriving now!"

"My blunt! Swarm, give me back my blunt, man!"

"You'll get your smegging blunt back once we're done here. Focus, Captain!"

Zylvya fell in line beside Swarm and pulled Charlie between them. They watched as a white dome peeked over the rim of the gaping hole in the floor. The dome continued rising and revealed itself to be the top half of a giant opaque pearl with iridescent pinks and blues swimming across its perfectly smooth surface. It drifted to one side of the mini-Transit Bay and hovered soundlessly over the green marble floor.

"Stand up straight, Captain. And get your hands out of your pockets! You look like you're about to whip out a smegging weapon," grumbled Swarm from the corner of his mandibles. "Just follow the cultural sensitivity training I outlined in the data pill and we should be able to get through these introductions without incident."

"Sensitivity training? Sorry, man, I don't think I got that far before Zee slapped me awake. How long was I out, anyway?"

"I walked up just as he popped the pill," Zylvya said to Swarm. "The few seconds on the ground before I woke him up should've been plenty of time—if your data was valid."

She spoke without looking away from the giant floating pearl, but Charlie could feel her squirming in her orange toga.

"The data was fine! I bet all the smegging pot smoke in his brain inhibited the transfer speed."

Swarm emitted a faint guttural growl from his thorax, then sighed and puffed out his chest.

"New plan. Let me do all the talking."

"That was my plan all along, man. I'll just head out to go tend my girls while you take care of all this peace stuff."

"Get back here." Swarm caught Charlie by the scruff of his hoodie and dragged him back in line. "You're the captain. Your attendance is required. Just don't open your mouth. And whatever you do, don't think strong, forceful thoughts."

"Strong, forceful thoughts?" Zylvya giggled into her fist. "Don't overestimate him, Bugbrain."

"How the hell am I supposed to stop thinking? Hey, if you gave me my blunt back, that might help."

"Shhh!" growled Swarm. "They're disembarking!"

A small mound appeared on the surface of the pearl and inflated to the size of a bowling ball. The smaller sphere pulled away from the main body, severing the stretchy peduncle that connected them. Two more spheres joined the first and they floated silently over to Charlie and his crew. The three pearls lined up at eye level just as their opaqueness vanished to reveal the lifeforms inside.

Charlie assumed they were lifeforms, but he couldn't be sure. During his short stint as captain of the *Starseed*, he'd seen a wide sampling of the bizarre shapes and forms that life can take, but he'd never seen anything quite like this.

Inside each translucent sphere floated a fist-sized blob of rhythmically pulsating black ink. In the back of his mind, as if recalling something he'd learned long ago, Charlie knew that the small spheres were actually portable atmospheres for transporting the inky Undulata.

Charlie's abdomen tensed and he could feel his bladder start to fill up.

"Dude, what the hell was in that pill?" he whispered from the corner of his mouth. "I suddenly have to pee really badly!"

"Don't blame me," Swarm rattled back. "You're the one who drank all those beverages back on the mini-bridge."

"Zip it, guys!" Zylvya whispered without breaking the smile she'd chiseled onto her face. She placed her palms together and touched the tips of her fingers to her chin, then bowed low at the waist. Swarm did the same with both sets of claws. Charlie tried mimicking the others, but bending over increased the pressure on his bladder so he quickly righted himself and flashed a tilted grin.

I'm fucked, Charlie thought. *I'm gonna kick off the peace summit by pissing myself in front of alien diplomats.*

"Welcome, People of Undulata," Zylvya said to the floating spheres. "I am Lieutenant Zylvya Viridia, Chief of Botany on the *Starseed*. This is Lieutenant Swarm, Chief of Security, and this is Captain Charlie Hong. We recognize your sentience and we look forward to helping facilitate a fruitful abundance in your future."

The central inky blob began undulating rapidly. First, it extended three thick tentacles and waved them at the crew. Then, the tentacles divided into hundreds of tiny black spikes. The spikes retracted as quickly as they'd appeared and the blob became an oily black donut, then a triangle, then a perfectly sculpted inky bust of Charlie's head.

"Did that blob just compliment my 'fro?" Charlie managed to say while fighting back a painful wince.

"No, Captain Hong, they did not," MOM's synthetic voice broadcast from all directions at once. "The Undulatian diplomat accepted your greeting and extended their own to you. Their name is R'or Shaq, Refractor of the Two Suns, one of the Six Eldar Pletz and the official diplomat representing all of Undulata during these peace proceedings. The other two are blob-maidens, attendants to the chosen one. R'or Shaq has asked why you are shouting, Captain."

"Huh? But I've been whispering the whole time," Charlie said. "Oh, shit! Are these guys susceptible to sound like the Págosi were?"

His hand went to the blue watch on his wrist; he remembered where he'd left the original.

"No, Captain Hong, although the Undulata are sensitive to vibrations which are inaudible to you, they exhibit no adverse reactions to sound," explained MOM. "When they say you are shouting, they are sensing the intense micro-vibrational activity occurring in your lower abdomen. My sensors indicate that your bladder is at 95% capacity. The water molecules in your urine amplify the micro-vibrations occurring in your nervous system, which to them sounds like you are yelling."

R'or Shaq flashed some more shapes in quick succession.

"The diplomat has just added that they are perfectly comfortable with you emptying your liquid reserves in their presence. Public evacuation of liquid waste is a basic civil right guaranteed at birth to all Undulata. They assure you they take no offense in the evacuation of liquid waste."

"So they're saying I can piss myself in front of them and they won't care? Wow, in a weird way that's actually pretty cool of them. But, dude... I can't!"

"I can't believe we're having this conversation right now," Zylvya said, her smile wooden and unflinching.

"MOM, why can't we just hear what they're saying translated into our own languages like we normally do on the *Starseed?*" growled Swarm.

"Auto-neural-translation services are only available to life-forms who've bonded themselves to the *Starseed*, or in this case, the *Pineapple Express*. The Undulata have not yet accepted the bond, therefore I must try my best to translate manually. Captain Hong's situation demonstrates how involuntary biological processes and mental states can be interpreted as intentional communication."

"No way. I can't do it. I *won't* do it. I—"

Charlie stopped abruptly and his face turned red. He smiled awkwardly and began bouncing from foot to foot.

"Hey, listen, I'm gonna pop out real quick to find a restroom.

It was great meeting you. I'll see you tomorrow at the peace thing. Okay, bye!"

"Captain Hong, leaving to urinate in private would be interpreted by the Undulata as denouncing their struggle for civil rights. To use your own Earth history to help illustrate the point, it would be like burning a copy of the Bill of Rights in front of the President. Or burning the Koran in front of an imam. Or—"

"Yeah, I get it!" Charlie said, straightening up and running his hands through his short 'fro. "Let me get this straight. In order for me to not offend the Undulata... I have to piss myself?"

"Just do it, Captain!" rattled Swarm. "We have to get these three out of here before the next ship arrives!"

"Shhh! Now I can't go 'cause I'm too nervous! Just give me another second to relax."

Charlie took a deep breath and shook his head.

"What the hell has my life become?"

"I can assist you with that, Captain Hong," said MOM. "As you urinate, I will instantaneously absorb the urine into the fabric of your boxer shorts and denim jeans. It will be broken down and its molecules dispersed via the contact between your clothing and the floor."

Charlie glanced down at how the cuffs of his baggy jeans dragged over the back of his sneakers.

"You're saying if I pee, it'll all just get instantly absorbed and... disappear?"

"Yes, Captain. The process will be so efficient that from your point of view you should not experience any sensation of wetness."

"Well, that's... friggin' weird. You promise, MOM?"

"I am 99.9% sure the results will match my prediction. Feel free to urinate at your convenience."

Fuck it. You only live once, he thought as he closed his eyes and relaxed his clenched bladder. Relief came immediately. Twenty seconds later, his bladder was empty and his pants felt perfectly dry.

Charlie looked himself over, shrugged, then gave a timid thumbs up. The inky diplomat responded by wobbling excitedly inside its watery sphere and forming the shape of an oily black hand returning a thumbs up.

"R'or Shaq says he looks forward to sensing you freely evacuate your liquid waste again in the future."

Swarm cleared his gravelly throat before Charlie could answer and extended a claw toward one of corridors leading away from the bay.

"We hope you enjoy your time aboard the *Starse*—er, the *Pineapple Express*. As the Chief of Security, I can assure you there's not a more secure vessel in all the quadrant. Our ship's computer will guide you to your quarters and can provide any necessities you require during your stay."

The surface of their watery spheres regained their opaque, pearlescent sheen and floated away.

Once the spheres were out of sight, Charlie, Zee, and Swarm let out a collective sigh.

"One down, two to go. Wouldn't you say I earned a puff or two?" Charlie asked.

"I wouldn't call pissing yourself the epitome of diplomacy, Charlie," teased Zylvya.

"And yet, it worked, didn't it?"

"Forget it, Captain." Swarm said, motioning with his antennae. "The Smolz are here."

12

Tendrils of fine mist drifted over the rim of the hole and slithered along the green marble floor. Behind the mist a large cloud of dense blueish smoke wafted into the mini-Transit Bay and floated slowly toward the crew.

"Oh, I get it, man. Their ship must fly inside that cloud of smoke to stay hidden or something. Pretty cool idea," said Charlie. "I wonder if it'll get me high."

"It won't, and you're wrong," rattled Swarm under his breath. "That cloud *is* their ship. One of the largest in their fleet."

As Charlie wrestled with the idea that smoke could somehow be a spaceship, he felt a sudden crippling twist in his lower abdomen. Pressure began rapidly building and he hunched over in pain.

"Smegging hell, Captain! You have to pee again?"

"Not this time," moaned Charlie as sweat began beading on his brow. "This is gas. I feel like I'm ballooning up... like I'll explode, man."

Zee made a face.

"Bugbrain, whatever you put in that data pill isn't safe for apes—I mean, humans."

Swarm ignored them and focused his attention on the dense cloud of blue smoke drifting toward them. Out of the corner of his mandibles he whispered, "I think I know what's happening, but there's no time to explain. Just keep that gas to yourself, Captain!"

Charlie placed a hand over the bulge in his stomach. He could already feel his sphincter losing its resolve to stay clenched.

"I'll try my best, man, but no promises."

The misty tendrils drew back and the cloud rose in the air until it was roughly at eye level with the crew.

Zylvya straightened up, chiseled a hospitable smile onto her face, and repeated the same greeting she'd given to the Undulata.

Flashes of light illuminated random parts of the cloud like tiny, thunderless lightning bolts in a miniature storm. MOM translated.

"This is Kiri Moya, the Smolz Collective's Thousand-Mote Assembly for Foreign Affairs. They accept your warm welcome and offer in return a brief sampling of one of their ancient songs of gratitude."

As Charlie and his crew listened for the song to start, Zylvya's nose twisted up into her face and her eyes began watering.

"Charlie!" she whispered through a strained smile. "How could you?"

Before he could respond, a sulfuric stench made contact with his nostrils. He grasped Swarm's arm for support, fighting the urge to retch.

"It wasn't me!" cried Charlie through a sweaty grin. "My stomach is still a balloon, and it feels like it's getting worse. Something's gonna rupture, man!"

"Based on your reaction, it appears as if all three of you are experiencing a strong emotional response to their song," MOM stated plainly. "The Smolz Collective has never performed their songs for multi-cellular lifeforms and is very curious as to what you think."

The stench is *their song!* reasoned Charlie as he desperately fought back the urge to drop a track of his own.

"Well," Zylvya started, tears gathering in her eyes, "What can one say about interspecies music other than… uh…" She trailed off, doing her best to maintain a wooden smile.

Charlie realized what he had to do. A tilted grin lit up his face and he held up a hand to stop her.

"Allow me."

Charlie turned toward Kiri Moya, bowed low at the waist, and relaxed his clenched asshole. The fart he produced was so vociferous he actually felt it travel through his sneakers into the floor. A few long and jostling seconds later, the intestinal gas had fully evacuated his lower bowels and was slowly dissolving into the air around them. He felt a few ounces lighter, at least.

I wish Axo had been here for that one, he thought proudly.

Zylvya turned her head and pinched her nose, not daring to open her mouth for a quip or an insult. Those would come later—she would *never* let Charlie live it down—but for now she focused all her attention on surviving.

"Humans need to be put on a biological watchlist for that kind of natural defense," growled Swarm.

"Whatever, man," Charlie said, enjoying the relief that came with being a deflated balloon. "It's called diplomacy."

A ripple of light bounced around inside the cloud, and it began to revolve like a small, slow-moving hurricane.

"Kiri Moya thoroughly enjoyed that performance, Captain Hong," MOM said. "They have never heard anyone outside of Smolz articulate their language so well before. Perhaps an encore would be appropriate?"

"Maybe later," grumbled Swarm, adding, "in an impenetrable airlock. On the other side of the quadrant. Anyway, MOM, would you please show the Smolz to their quarters before the last Trapezian diplomat arrives?"

"Certainly," MOM said. A moment later the cloud of blue mist drifted away and disappeared down an adjacent corridor.

"Charlie!" Zylvya said, gagging freely. "That was *beyond* wretched! Even for an ape!"

"I never knew I had it in me. *Now* did I earn that blunt?"

"He has a point, Swarm. In fact, calling a ganja strike on our position might be the only way to clear the air."

"Definitely not! Ganja strikes are reserved for real emergencies."

"Exactly, Bugbrain!"

Swarm ignored her and scratched his mandible.

"I think I see what's happening here. The captain's bladder filled up right as the Undulata arrived. Then his bowels filled with gas right as the Smolz arrived." Swarm paused to study Charlie, and his large compound eyes widened. "It was genius. Don't look at me like that, Twiggy. I didn't say it was *his* genius. It was the data pill."

"The pill? But how?"

"We assumed you'd slapped him awake before all the data finished uploading into his brain, but maybe we were wrong. Even if the data didn't have time to attach itself to his conscious mind, the information may still be in there, working its way into his nervous system. Yes, that must be it. Think about it, Zee. As he's made contact with each delegate, his body has responded by expressing itself through related biological functions."

"That's so dumb," Zylvya said, holding her head. "But it kind of makes sense. A bladder full of liquid for the Undulata. A foul, revolting, toxic cloud of gas for the Smolz."

"Whatever, man," said Charlie, beaming with pride. "At least that cloud dude appreciated my talent."

"That 'cloud dude' was not a singular person, Captain. It was a chorus of thousands of Smolz, each no larger than a dust mote. They haven't quite evolved into a unified morphic entity, but I imagine that could be their evolutionary path."

"Kinda like you and your millions of tiny meetles?"

"Call my meetles tiny again, and I'll introduce you to a bunch of them all at once," growled Swarm, holding up a fisted claw.

"Chill, Bugbrain. If you're right about data expressing itself through Charlie's biological functions, what change should we expect when the Silexi arrive?"

"Smeg if I know," answered Swarm, straightening up. "But we're about to find out."

13

CHARLIE DECIDED THE SILEXI TRANSPORT VESSEL LOOKED LIKE something out of an Earther sci-fi flick, complete with a gunmetal grey hull, glass viewports, and a few powerful torch thrusters in the back.

Once inside, two large guns mounted to the top swiveled to lock onto the Undulata's levitating pearl. The ship landed with a thud, exhaled a wheezy hiss from its cooling thrusters, and extended a long ramp from an airlock port on its underside.

The airlock opened and released a few inches of smoke that billowed slowly down the ramp. Charlie was relatively certain it was just smoke, not another sentient fog—but he prepared himself to fart again if needed.

They heard boots clanking on metal before the Silexi entourage descended the ramp. The first figure to appear was a bipedal humanoid with two arms firmly grasping some kind of hi-tech laser rifle. Their body was covered in sooty space armor and their face was hidden behind a metal mask with two horizontal slits for eyes and a vertical slit running down the center. The figure stopped at the bottom of the ramp with its mask, and its laser rifle, focused solely on Charlie.

Charlie didn't think he could piss himself again so soon after emptying his bladder, but the way the masked Boba Fett wannabe looked at him made him think he might try for that encore after all.

Metal Mask was shoved aside by a bulkier creature with a permanently furrowed brow and a dripping pig nose that aligned vertically with a pair of two beady black eyes. Pig Nose swept the barrel of his own rifle across the empty bay, then barked something into a device strapped to his wrist. A dozen more rifle-toting aliens marched down the ramp and fell into rows on either side of the ship.

In his peripheral vision, Charlie noticed Zylvya's posture change and Swarm's antennae go rigid.

This is looking more like a hostile invasion than a peaceful delegation, Charlie thought.

"Why is the Silexi delegation made up of different alien races, man?" he whispered, without taking his eyes off the new arrivals.

"Those aren't the Silexi," whispered Swarm. "It looks like the Silexi hired some contract security goons."

Zylvya sighed through her wooden smile.

"Okay, Bugbrain. What's the plan? The last thing we need at a peace summit is a bunch of trigger-happy mercs causing trouble."

"Yeah, what's with the guns, man? Don't they know they're not allowed on the *Pineapple Express*?"

"Sometimes weapons get smuggled aboard the *Starseed*, although Mother has her way of disabling them so they can do no harm," explained Swarm.

Charlie remembered how he'd tried to morpho-print some simple archery equipment for their hunting trip to Vos Praeda, but the arrows kept coming out "nerfed" with foam tips.

"The question isn't whether they're allowed to carry them around and point them at things," said Swarm. "It's whether MOM can properly disable them like Mother would."

"MOM is a copy of Mother, so we should be good, right?"

"You tell me, Captain. You've seen how she handled the brightness of the augmented guidance system," rattled Swarm.

"Would you trust her to make sure those wadjet rifles won't actually fire a shot when the trigger is pulled?"

"I dunno, man! Would *you*?"

Swarm didn't answer, so Charlie half-turned to Zylvya.

"What do you think, Zee?"

After another moment of silence, Charlie turned his head all the way to find Zylvya standing upright with her eyes closed. She took slow, steady breaths as if she were asleep.

He nudged her with his elbow. She startled awake and looked around wide-eyed as if taking in the situation for the first time.

"What the hell, Zee?" Charlie whisper-yelled out the side of his mouth while his attention returned to the mercs.

They continued sweeping the empty mini-Transit Bay with their eyes and their laser rifles, but Metal Mask kept his attention trained solely on Charlie.

"Dudes with guns show up and you fall asleep?"

"Sorry," Zylvya whispered back, then subtly disguised a yawn with her hand. "With my last-minute change in plans, I missed a whole sleep cycle."

"Can you believe that, Swarm? Dude, don't you have some witty insult for Zee? She fell asleep on the job, man. Swarm?"

Charlie swiveled his head in the other direction to find Swarm standing as still as a statue. His mandibles were frozen in place and his antennae as rigid as Charlie had ever seen them. His compound eyes were open and the lights were on, as far as Charlie could tell—but no one was home.

"Zee! Look at Swarm! He's paralyzed or something. Could these dudes be using some kind of morphic weapon to mess with him?"

A whisper appeared between him and Zylvya.

"No, Captain Hong. My sensors do not indicate a weapon of any kind has been activated. As per the *Starseed's* anti-weapon policy I have adopted as my own, I would not allow it."

"Then what the hell's wrong with him?"

"Based on the biodata I have collected, Lieutenant Swarm

seems to be exhibiting signs of elevated hormonal and mental activity."

"Hormonal? He's so angry his mind blew a gasket?"

"No, Captain Hong," answered MOM, "The activity appears to be the opposite of anger."

"Opposite of anger? But that's the only emotion Swarm's capable of! Zee, did you just fall asleep *again*?"

"Huh?" she said, forcing her eyes open. "No, don't be absurd. I'm wide awake."

"What the hell, Zee? Keep it together! Looks like a few more, uh, *people* are coming down the ramp."

Three pairs of feet appeared at the top of the Silexi transport's ramp. The two pairs on the left wore clanky metal grav-boots that Charlie didn't recognize, but he recognized the pair of bare feet on the right immediately—although they seemed a million times more impossible than Zee showing up on the *Pineapple Express*.

He shook his head and rubbed his eyes.

Not impossible in the I-live-in-space-now-so-everything-seems-new-and-strange kind of way, he thought. *This is just flat-out* impossible *impossible.*

More clues came into view as the figure hobbled awkwardly down the ramp on legs so short they barely existed. Brown, leathery skin. A sagging round belly. And finally, a flat, rectangular head with large, lovable eyes.

"E.T." Charlie said, barely able to control his excitement. "Guys, that smaller Silexi looks *exactly* like E.T. the Extra-Terrestrial!"

Zylvya squinted at the trio of alien ambassadors descending the ramp, then recoiled with a guilty look on her face.

"Don't stare, Charlie! It's rude."

"Rude? How? This guy's a huge celebrity back on Earth! *E.T.* was the first sci-fi flick I ever watched—if you don't count *Star Wars*, which I don't, because it was just a bunch of space magic bullshit, completely unoriginal and unbelievable. I mean, there's a whole universe of aliens, and who's running the whole goddamn show? A bunch of white dudes."

"Charlie, you're rambling again!"

"Anyway, Zee, when I was eight years old, I had a lunchbox with *his* face on it. It didn't just look like him, it *was* him."

Charlie looked more closely as they slowly descended the ramp. Not only was the small Silexi a spitting image of the little brown alien from his childhood, but he was also carrying a small terracotta pot of geraniums.

"No fucking way," muttered Charlie, as he noticed what the little guy was wearing: a faded t-shirt with an image of himself printed on it. Under the self-portrait, printed in plain Earther English, were the words 'E.T. Phone Home!'.

A wave of dizziness swept over him as his mind raced to find a logical explanation.

Sure, nothing I've seen since leaving Earth has made much sense, he thought. *Reptilian overlords using genetic skinsuits to impersonate humans. The em'tae fruit Zee grew in her lab that turned thousands of microscopic spider mites into football-sized monsters. A moose with a unicorn horn who tastes like chocolate and shits self-serve ice cream. Hell, the Starseed and the* Pineapple Express *are two giant living spaceships powered by weed that can instantaneously morpho-print any item I want straight out of their substrates.*

Still, his mind reeled. There was simply no way a fictional character from his childhood could really exist out here in space, let alone be hobbling its way to meet him.

*Unless…*Charlie thought. *Unless Steven Spielberg had somehow known about the Silexi? But that would mean… shit, man! Maybe Spielberg is a Reptilian in disguise like Captain Major Tom! But how? Why?*

Shit's crazy out here, he decided. *Maybe it's best not to ask.*

Charlie snapped his focus back to the Silexi, who were now standing in front of him waiting to be officially received.

Panicking, he glanced side to side at his crew.

Swarm was still frozen in place, staring blankly at the mercs.

Zylvya's eyes were closed, and she was smacking her lips together sleepily.

Charlie realized he'd have to welcome this last Trapezian delegate on his own. He cleared his throat, stuck out his chest, and did his best impression of a respectable starship captain.

"Greetings and salutations, people of Silex," he announced, one hand on his chest while the other was outstretched in a vague motion to the ship. "I am Captain Charlie Hong of the *Starseed*—er, I mean, the *Pineapple Express*. Well, both. But to be clear, this is the *Pineapple Express*. This is where we'll hold the peace summit. What am I saying, man? I'm sure you must've figured that out while you were approaching the ship. Duh. Anyway, the *Starseed* had to go rescue some planet named Lusus from its local star, which is about to unexpectedly go supernova. Not to rescue the planet itself, just all the lifeforms. I mean, the *Starseed* is huge, but I'm pretty sure it couldn't save an actual planet. Then again, who knows? I heard one time—I think it was in a movie called *Tron*, but I can't remember exactly—that matter is made up of mostly empty space. I know, right? So maybe, if science was somehow able to trim away some of that empty space..."

Charlie trailed off, realizing that no one had interrupted his ramble yet. Usually his crew never let him go that deep into a pointless ramble without cutting him off and saving his captive audience.

The two taller Silexi stood glaring at him. He realized they looked familiar, too. Their skinny bipedal frames were topped with huge hairless heads that hosted a pair of eye slits that widened into glossy, almond-shaped, fuliginous eyes.

Unlike E.T., they looked a hell of a lot like the grey stone-skinned aliens that had been found at the UFO crash at Roswell in the 50's, but these guys wore clothes: full-length robes made from metallic fabric with some kind of electronic circuitry woven into it; turbans made from the same material; and small bags strapped to their waists that reminded Charlie of fanny packs.

Charlie maintained a smile while whispering from the corner

of his mouth, "MOM, are you doing the translation thing now? Have they responded yet?"

"No, Captain Hong. Before docking with the *Pineapple Express*, they sent a message indicating that they preferred to use their own translation technology."

Charlie stood awkwardly in the middle of several silent figures—Swarm and Zee still not being any help—and decided to take matters into his own hands. The sooner this last delegation was on the way to its quarters, the sooner he could finally blaze up a fatty and get back to fretting over his sick plants.

He knelt in front of E.T. and extended a hand.

"You must be the leader of the Silexi. I'm honored to meet you, man."

E.T. pointed a single glowing finger—just like from the movie! —toward Charlie. "Chuck Stonerlyyyyy!"

"You've heard of me?" Charlie blushed and retracted his abandoned handshake. "Chuck Stonerly is more of a nickname. Like I said, my real name is Charlie Hong, from Earth. Speaking of Earth, if you don't mind my saying so, you look exactly like... I just gotta ask. About twenty-five years ago were you in an Earther movie? Or, did you pose at least for the director so they could design an alien that looks like you?"

Charlie nodded toward his shirt to drive the point home.

"You look exactly like E.T., man."

"Movieee!" E.T's voice was an octave higher and his neck suddenly elongated, lifting his head into the air. He pointed his glowing finger to the image of himself on his shirt. "Phone Hooome!"

"Yeah, man! E.T. phone home! I loved that friggin' movie when I was a kid."

"I *told* you we should have left him in the ship's hibernation pod," the taller of the two Silexi said to the other. His papercut mouth moved when he spoke, but the sound Charlie heard came from the collar wrapped around his neck—a golden snake with ruby eyes, its head flat against the center of the Silexi's throat.

Charlie instantly recognized the design as Reptilian. An image of the torture devices Tork had prepared for him back on Earth flashed in his mind.

"The Empress disabled that system before we left Silex, Your Majesty," said the other Silexi.

"Of course she did," the tall one said, narrowing his eyes to razor-thin slits of onyx. "You know, if it weren't for her, I'd have spaced that damaged little turdo before he was able to draw his first breath."

Charlie stood to face them.

"Did he just call you *Your Majesty*? Oh, hey, I'm sorry. I thought you two were this little dude's bodyguards or something. My bad."

The taller Silexi glared at Charlie while the other answered.

"This is Supreme Emperor Reticulus Rex of the Silexi System. I am Vree Voktal, His Majesty's personal assistant. The one over there, licking the wall, the one you call E.T., is His Majesty's progeny, Eta Cerbo, the sole heir to the stellar dynasty. He did appear in a short film on some backwater planet, I forget the name."

"Gotcha. Again, so sorry for the mix-up," Charlie said before making an awkward bow. "So E.T. here isn't only an Earth celebrity, he's next in line to the Silexi throne, eh? Very cool, man."

Emperor Rex's onyx eyes flew open and his thin lips snapped downward into an upside-down 'V'.

Vree Voktal answered, "The only way *he'll* ever take the throne is if something happens to His Majesty, which the Dregz behind us are being paid quite a hefty sum to prevent."

He stepped forward and looked down his pinprick nose holes at Charlie.

"For his sake as much as your own, Captain Hong, don't let His Majesty be put in harm's way."

"Was that a threat, man?" Charlie blurted out. "Listen, homie, *I'm* the captain of this ship, and therefore, *I'll* decide who is and who is not put in harm's way. Got it?"

The two Silexi scowled at each other and then at Charlie. Reticulus Rex's mouth and eyes narrowed as he motioned with one hand to the mercs standing behind him.

The line of Dregz stirred and took a step forward, their guns drawn.

Swarm slid in front of Charlie and raised all four arms in surrender.

"What Captain Hong meant to say was that he would never allow His Majesty Emperor Rex—or any of our Trapezian guests—to be put in harm's way. Isn't that right, Captain?"

Charlie relaxed and answered coolly, "Swarm's right, man. You and your, uh, entourage here are under my protection."

"See?" Swarm said, lowering his arms slightly. "As Chief of Security, I give you my word that you are both welcome and completely safe while on this vessel."

Charlie noticed Swarm's attention drift away from the Emperor to something just over his shoulder, then snap back to the conversation at hand.

"Our only intention is to facilitate a more peaceful and prosperous future for Silex and for all the people of Trapezia."

Emperor Rex straightened up and motioned for his mercs to stand down. The ruby eyes on his serpentine collar gleamed as his lipless mouth began squirming. Something like the sound of gravel being tumbled in a laundry dryer sounded from the collar; Swarm sighed heavily, recognizing his native language.

"No, I assure you, the ape is not a turdo, Your Majesty," answered Swarm. "His only desire is to accommodate and learn from the Silexi while keeping you safe to barter peace with your neighbors."

Charlie slipped under Swarm's arms and stuck his chest out.

"Did this stoney-faced freak just call me an ape?"

Emperor Rex snarled and slipped a hand inside his fanny pack. Vree Voktal stepped between them and shook his head.

"This is not conducive to peace! Stand down or our Dregz will be unleashed!"

"Those dumb fucks?" barked Charlie, glancing behind the Silexi. "I'd like to see them try something! C'mon, make my day, assholes!"

"MOM, stop auto-translating Captain Hong immediately!" cried Swarm. To Charlie, he said more quietly, "What the smeg's wrong with you? Chill out, Captain!"

"None of this would be happening if you'd let me fire up a blunt, man!"

"Sorry, Lieutenant Swarm, but only Captain Hong is authorized to override any of my core systems, including the auto-translation system," MOM answered helpfully.

Vree Voktal shrieked and began swiveling his head frantically.

"Your Majesty!" he cried. "Eta Cerbo is gone!"

The Dregz stirred, ready for battle but not finding any obvious enemies to attack.

"Hold your fire! I'm sure the little guy just wandered off down one of these corridors," suggested Swarm, then growled at the air above them, "MOM, where is the young Silexi?"

"Eta!" Vree Voktal called out. "Eta Cerbo, you get back here right now or there'll be no special candies tonight before bed!"

Zylvya's eyes flew open.

"Huh? Why's everyone shouting?"

She noticed the Dregz' posture and fell into a crouched fighting stance between Charlie and the others.

"MOM, prepare to toke the three of us away. Charlie, stay behind me!"

Unable to restrain himself, Charlie's eyes rested on her behind, and he momentarily forgot what he was so angry about. His baggy jeans got a little less baggy as the tension in his mind migrated to his pants.

MOM's voice broke through the chaos.

"My programming prioritizes the safety of children over adults, so, due to the rising probability of a violent outcome here in the mini-Transit Bay, I have relocated Eta Cerbo to a secure location. Especially when I am about to initiate a crowd-control measure such as this."

"Crowd-control measure?" rattled Swarm.

He and Vree Voktal shared a confused look while Charlie and the Emperor Rex continued exchanging glares and Zylvya stifled a yawn with a clenched fist.

His mind finally catching up with MOM's statement, Charlie swapped his angry scowl for a delighted grin.

Before anyone could react, the floor became perforated with hundreds of tiny holes, each spouting a stream of sweet-smelling cannabis vapor that gathered around the group and engulfed them completely.

14

CHARLIE STUMBLED DOWN THE CROWDED CORRIDOR, HOLDING HIS head and flinching from any light brighter than a firefly.

Damn that stupid data pill, he thought. *Lotta good it did me. Gave me gas, made me piss myself, and it didn't even explain that the Silexi heir—that E.T.—has some kind of alien Down syndrome or something. Poor kid. Not for the Down syndrome, just for having such a piece of shit dad.*

And what kind of crew abandons their captain without even explaining what the hell's going on? he thought. *They're both hiding something from me, something important. Why don't they trust me, man? I'm trustworthy as fuck!*

Maybe they don't trust me because they're afraid that what happened to Axo and Del might happen to them.

He tripped on the tail of a two-headed humanoid gecko crossing his path and caught himself by grabbing onto the fur of a ten-foot-tall spider covered in long silky fur.

"Sorry!" he cried twice, once over his shoulder and once up at the cluster of iridescent eyes set in the spider's flowing hair. Charlie waved a hand at no one in particular and sped off before they could reply.

Knowing my track record, he thought, blowing a clump of rainbow-colored hair from his hand, *I'm not sure I would trust me either.*

As he stumbled along the *Pineapple Express's* sole commercial district, the endless mini-Ring, he tried his best not to lose his balance and crash headlong into any of the food carts or snack vendors lining the main corridor. Just like the full-sized Ring back on the *Starseed*, the two-story shanties curved to one side ahead of him while curving the opposite direction behind him. Due to the drastic difference in mass between the two ships, the curvature aboard the *Pineapple Express* was much more distinct than it was on the *Starseed*, which also made it more nauseating to stroll through—especially when you're strung out with one bitch of a data hangover.

Charlie figured he could wander around the mini-Ring without a destination in mind, so he'd be near food once he started to feel better and the munchies from that ganja strike kicked in.

Despite what his senses told him, Charlie knew the mini-Ring wasn't truly open-air. The skyscape above was just bioluminescent bacteria working together like pixels to project a perfectly lifelike depiction of the surrounding starfield. Even the dim starlight made him wince and keep his head down.

Man, I haven't felt like this since that time Nadia slipped me a Denubian Dewdrop, he thought. *More proof I have no business being trusted.*

Charlie had done his best to forget Nadia and that den of villainy she called Lavaka. While she'd gotten exactly what she wanted out of their deal, it left him no closer to finishing Major Tom's secret weapon against the Reptilians.

With he and his crew gone, Charlie hoped she wasn't causing too much trouble back on the *Starseed*. He was surprised when Mother promised to do everything in her power to keep Nadia far away from the the bridge, the THC Core, and all other critical systems on the *Starseed*. Normally when he asked her to do something about Nadia, she'd give a little southern titter and recite the section of the *Starseed* charter about individual privacy and freedom for any and all Seeders, with one important exception about harm to other organisms.

As Charlie remembered well from past adventures, even attempting to take another life on the *Starseed* will earn you the Mark—a reddish aura that follows you around and alerts all other Seeders of your crime. Earning the Mark also came with one other side-effect: it signaled to other Seeders that they could kill and eat you without earning the Mark themselves. It was enough to keep the peace among even the most violent and predatory of Seeders.

Charlie knew Nadia was smart enough to never hurt anyone directly, but at any given time she had a seemingly endless supply of pawns do the hurting for her.

Hope that snake didn't figure out some way to trick Mother, he thought. *I should probably call Vargoni later to make sure everything's alright back on the* 'Seed.

Just as he decided to put her out of his mind, he heard a voice singing the same song that lured him to her the very first time they met. No words were intelligible to Charlie, but the mournful vibe was punctuated by sorrowfully sweet moaning that anyone with ears and a heart could understand.

He forgot his hangover and bee-lined through the crowd of aliens toward the voice.

To the uninitiated, the entrance to Lavaka wasn't much more than a row of intricately decorated rugs hanging side by side along a stretch of wall between a spice vendor and a GloBo boba tea shop. But Charlie knew that just beyond those unsuspecting tapestries, a hallway led to a shady saloon full of vile characters, dangerous cocktails, and lies.

That snake figured out how to get a free vacation on the Pineapple Express *while making sure Mother didn't break her promise,* he thought.

Despite having sworn to never again step foot in Lavaka, Charlie pushed back one of the hanging rugs and stormed inside.

A cacophony of alien gurgles, clicks, and buzzes flickered in his ears before everything switched over to English.

Weird, the auto-translation system never lags like that on the Starseed, he thought. *I gotta add it to the list of shit to ask MOM about later.*

The air grew warmer as he walked down the shadowy hallway that led to the main room. Charlie could see hundreds of purple flames dancing atop candles that hung from chandeliers over every table. Alien tapestries like those that covered the entrance to Lavaka hung around the perimeter of the sprawling circular room to conceal private booths and passageways leading to even more secretive backrooms.

Hidden places inside hidden places. Definitely Nadia's style.

Her mournful song rose above the low roar of conversation and grabbed Charlie by the heart. Unlike the last few visits, this time he was ready. No matter what she said, no matter what she offered, he wouldn't take the bait.

He lifted his chin, puffed out his chest, and weaved himself between the tables as he approached her circular bar at the center of the room.

Charlie opened his mouth to say something very authoritative and intimidating, but before he could speak, a waitress spun away from the bar and smashed directly into him, exploding her tray of drinks all over his brown hoodie.

"Oh no!" the waitress said, hiding behind her empty tray. "I'm very sorry, sir. I'm so bad at this, I'm not sure why I even bother trying..."

Charlie looked at the strange concoction of liquids bubbling on his clothes.

"Uh, no worries, man. I'm sure it'll come out in the wash."

He lifted the bottom of his hoodie and noticed the liquid had burned a hole straight through to his t-shirt.

"Captain! Don't let it touch your bare skin!" Nadia's sultry voice called out from the central bar. "Quickly, pull your jacket over the back of your head without getting any on that handsome face of yours. Don't just stand there, Cassie! Help him!"

The waitress helped Charlie pull his hoodie off, both of them extra careful not to touch the smoldering liquid. He stood over his slowly dissolving jacket and shook his head.

"I think someone needs to call the health inspector, man."

Nadia batted her eyelashes at him and smiled. He could only see the upper part of her body, which at the moment resembled what he'd come to think of as her true self. Long, curly black hair. Flawless olive skin. Pouty red lips. Tank top that was somehow perfectly loose-fitting but also stretched tight in just the right places.

He reminded himself it was all a ruse from the waist up. The first time they'd met she'd tricked him by shapeshifting into Zylvya. If it hadn't been for the fact that below the waist she remained a Nagini, complete with the winding, serpentine body of a giant snake, he'd have had no way to tell them apart.

Which is why she never slithers out from behind her bar, he thought. *Then again, the way she pulls on people's strings, she never has to.*

"You should know better than anyone that I serve my guests whatever they want," she said, a flicker of Zylvya's emerald fire flashing across her eyes. "And the xenomorphs at table eleven wanted some shots of fermented battery acid."

"*Acid?*" cried Charlie.

"Uhm, sir," the waitress said from behind her tray. "You still have some on you."

"She's right, Captain. Best be safe and strip naked before it eats through to your skin. It'd be such a shame to scar that soft brown flesh of yours."

"Hey lady, this flesh ain't so soft," he said, looking himself over. "Son of a bitch! My clothes are *sizzling*, man! I'm the goddamn captain, I can't go running around naked in front of all these people!"

"That hasn't stopped you before," Nadia said, smiling

fiendishly. "But suit yourself, Captain. Either you take those clothes off or the acid will."

Her smile wavered as she looked him over more carefully.

"How'd you change clothes so quickly?" The smile returned, wider than before. "You're playing games with me, aren't you?"

Charlie felt his sneakers loosen their grip on his feet as a few drops of the acid finished burning through his laces.

"Goddammit! Not cool, man!"

"I'm so sorry, Captain," the waitress said, kneeling to help pull off his shoes.

He noticed her basic body shape was that of a teenage human female with ten fingers and ten toes, and her baggy knit sweater and denim overalls were straight out of an 80's movie, but that was where the Earth correlations ended. The skin covering her face and hands, and presumably the rest of her, was a hyper-flexible, transparent rubber material which revealed an interior clockwork of tiny gears, solenoids, and multi-colored LEDs. The intricate circuitry and lifelike design had Nylf's name written all over them.

"Cassie?" he asked. "As in Cassandra? As in Nylf's robot?"

Her optical sensors widened and their internal LEDs dimmed. She hung her head and pretended to retie the laces on her own sneakers.

"What'd I say, man?"

"The poor girl feels bad enough without you calling her names," scolded Nadia. "How would you feel if she called you an ape?"

"The word *robot* is offensive?"

This time Charlie noticed Cassie wince as the word left his mouth.

"Shit, man! I'm sorry. I didn't know the r-word was offensive. I promise I'll try not to say it again."

Charlie extended his hand to the teenage…

Machine? he thought. *That somehow sounds worse than robot.*

"It's nice to finally meet you. I'm your socially inept, *once-*

again-nearly-naked captain, Charlie Hong. Your name is Cassandra, right? Nylf's," he paused, looking for the right word, "...daughter?"

Nailed it, he told himself.

"I remember Del talked about you back before his—" he stopped, not wanting to trigger more bad feelings for the poor girl.

Shit, he thought, *I can't keep my foot out of my mouth for more than two seconds!*

Cassandra's optical sensors widened and the LEDs in her cheeks brightened.

"Del mentioned *me*? To *you*? On the bridge?" She seemed to deflate and her inner lights dimmed. "I miss him."

"Me too," Charlie said, gently lowering the tray and catching her optical sensors. "At least he's safe and sound back on the *'Seed*. Why aren't you there with him? Word around the *Starseed* is that your dad keeps you on a pretty short leash."

"Hmph!"

She crossed her arms and turned away.

"I grew tired of his leash, so I ran away. No, as Nadia pointed out, I didn't *run away*. I decided to set out on my own. It's not like he owns me."

"Thank god Nadia was there to straighten it all out for you," Charlie said, shooting a quick look at the snaky bartender. "But actually, man, I think Nylf might technically own every component in your body."

Cassandra balled up her fists and spun her optical apertures shut.

"Like all we are is a sum of our components! The ones who took my Del's body had no respect for inorganic sentience, and I can see *you're* just like them. Just like Father!"

"No, I'm not! I agree with you, man! You're obviously more than just some circuits."

He sighed and softened his voice.

"Trust me, I know what it's like to be a teenager and need time away from my dad. But why here, in this dump?"

Her optical sensors flickered toward Nadia and back to Charlie. While she considered what to say, he answered for her.

"Let me guess, your sweet Auntie Nadia offered you a job in exchange for a small favor? Maybe slip something into someone's drink? Maybe remote record a sensitive conversation in one of her 'privacy' booths? No, I got it! Just as I was approaching, she gave you two trays of drinks to deliver, didn't she? Probably insisted you hurry, right?"

Charlie interpreted her silence and the dimming of her cranial LEDs as confirmation.

"Nothing gets by you, Captain Hong," Nadia said, leaning over the bar to let the loose collar of her blouse billow open. "Turns out I owe Nylf a favor or two, if you can believe that. I found this one stowing away in another vendor's gear, and instead of turning her in to the authorities—a.k.a, *you*—I offered to let her stay with me for the duration of the trip and earn some extra g-creds. She'll need them for where she's going."

"Going? The only place you're going is back to the *Starseed*."

Cassandra lifted her chin high.

"I must find a way to save Del's body so we can be together. I'll go wherever that takes me."

Charlie stared at the teenaged robot. Whatever AI-template Nylf used to create turbulent teenage emotions was working perfectly.

"Are you the one who keeps swiping him from the bridge? Every few days he goes missing and Mother's gotta ask Nylf to bring him back. Seems like you and Del have had plenty of time together lately."

"That doesn't count, Captain! His mind is trapped inside some stupid plant! I need him back in his old body, so we can hold each other again, plug into each other's ports, exchange terabytes of data—"

"Too much info, man," interrupted Charlie. "I get it. We all miss him. But running away is no way to find Del's old body. The quadrant is light years wide and the last time we saw his body, the Reptoids had it. Not a good plan, man."

"Maybe Nadia can help locate it! She's your Chief of Secrets, right? Couldn't the two of you come up with a better plan?"

Charlie and Nadia exchanged a look. She raised an eyebrow and he shook his head.

"You'd be better off blindly stumbling through the galaxy with a pocket full of g-creds," he said. "But really, when we're back on the *Starseed*, we'll all put our heads together—minus Nadia—and come up with a plan, okay?"

"What if she still wants to leave?" Nadia chimed in. "What if, after your masterful plan to retrieve Del's body, the two of them want to leave together? You know, Captain, there's a whole galaxy out there to explore. There might even be something out there that could lure *you* away from your precious '*Seed*."

Charlie pushed away thoughts of his dad, back on Earth, probably still looking for him and worried sick. And his mom, wherever she was, assuming she was still alive.

Instead, he crossed his arms and glared at Nadia.

"Why the hell don't you take your own advice and find somewhere else to peddle your so-called secrets? I'm sure there's a black hole nearby—we can drop you off."

Nadia sighed, leaned in closer, and offered him a knowing smile.

"Love is what brings people to the *Starseed*, but it's also what makes them leave. Someday, if you're lucky, you'll find out for yourself."

Charlie locked his eyes onto hers and refused to let them dip below her sultry lips. There was no friggin' way he was gonna let himself fall prey to her cleavage. Not again.

Before her cleavage could prove him wrong, he turned his attention back to Cassie.

"You can enjoy the week out here on the *Pineapple Express*, dad-free and off the leash, and when we get back, I'll cover for you by telling him I recruited you at the last minute. And, when we get back, I promise we'll find a way to help Del get back to normal."

"Look who's making the shady barroom deals now!" Nadia said, laughing.

Charlie ignored her and kept his eyes on Cassie's optical sensors.

"What do you say? This place ain't good for your, uh, data integrity."

Cassie looked to Nadia, who returned an almost imperceptible nod.

"Fine," she said, her shoulders dropping. "I guess I can spend the week researching the latest neuropathic fusion tech."

"Great!" he said, turning back to Nadia with a smug grin. "Well, I guess we'll leave you to your nasty lil' snake pit."

"Aye aye, Captain."

The smile she wore made Charlie wonder who'd just outsmarted who.

"Why not put these on before you go?" she said, lifting a folded stack of clothing out from behind the bar. Something brown, something white, something denim, with a pair of brand new Converse Chuck Taylor's on top. Each article of clothing was an exact replica of what he'd been wearing when he stormed in—which was now just a pile of smoldering rags on the floor.

"You gotta be crazy to think I'm gonna wear any of that. For all I know it's bugged or rigged with some kind of nano explosives." He pushed the clothing back across the bar. "No thanks."

"Suit yourself," she said. "In Lavaka, your nakedness is safe. No one can stream to the Outernet, and as you can see, no one's even paying attention. But out there in the rest of the ship... well, you know how fast news travels through hyperspace. I'm sure the Outernet would love some new holos of the *Starseed's* captain running around naked. I know I would."

Charlie felt his temper rising, but instead of getting pulled into an argument with her, he snatched the clothes and put them on.

"I'm spacing everything as soon as I'm back to my quarters," he said, lacing up his Chucks.

When he was done, he stood up and faced Nadia.

"There's no way to send you back to the *Starseed*, but I could lock you up in the brig for the rest of the week," he lied, knowing full well he'd forgotten to design any kind of brig on the *Pineapple Express*.

"Please, no," she whispered, pretending to be afraid. She held out her slender wrists and batted her eyes. "You'd better chain me up in your quarters, Captain, just to keep an extra close eye on me."

"In your dreams," Charlie said, knowing she'd probably make an appearance in his tonight.

15

Charlie summoned the blood back to his brain, yanked his eyes away from Nadia, and motioned for Cassie to follow him out. He turned to go and nearly walked right into another patron.

"Whoa there!" cried Bob Sr. as they awkwardly sidestepped each other. "That was a close call! My apologies, sir."

"Naw, man, it was my fault," said Charlie. "Actually... Bob, what the hell are you doing here?"

Bob Sr.'s proboscis tensed as he thought about his reply. Finally, the answer came from over his shoulder.

"Bob, dear, your order of twice-fried muratura blossoms are ready," called Nadia, smiling sweetly. "I threw in some extra pinati sauce."

Charlie looked at his furry, big-eyed friend with amazement.

"Out of the whole mini-Ring, you ordered food from here? From *her*?"

"Well, uh..." Bob Sr.'s short antennae squirmed. "Mrs. Glimwicket has had these intense cravings lately. Nothing but muratura blossoms would do, and Lavaka happens to be the only place to find them. Plus, you know, we like to support local businesses."

"We're on a spaceship, man! Everything's local!"

He shrugged and slipped past Charlie to grab the styrofoam takeout container from the bar. Quietly, he added, "This will make my Bauble happy for the evening, which is more than enough reason to venture into a place like this. If you ever find yourself with a pregnant spouse back at home, you'll understand."

"Want me to add it to your tab?" Nadia called out.

Bob Sr.'s antennae flattened against the thick fur covering his head. "Sure," he said, patting the container. "Thanks again."

He waved one of his enormous hands at the group and disappeared behind the tapestry leading back to the mini-Ring.

A few meters away another tapestry flipped open and another familiar face entered Lavaka.

"Swarm!" cried Charlie. "What the hell are you doing here?"

For the second time in as many minutes, Charlie watched an insectoid's antennae turn flaccid.

"Captain," rattled Swarm, quickly closing the tapestry behind him. "What the smeg are you doing here?"

"I asked first, man!"

"I'm asking as part of an official investigation!"

"Well, I'm asking as your boss! Who's behind that tapestry?"

Charlie took a step forward. Swarm tensed and released a low, guttural growl from deep in his thorax.

"Let's not make this more embarrassing than it already is, Captain."

Charlie sighed. "I'm way too sober for this shit. Do whatever you want, man. C'mon Cassie, let's get out of here before—"

As he turned back toward the exit, something caught his eye and stopped him in his tracks.

"Are you kidding me? *You're* here, too?!"

Zylvya spun to face her crewmates.

"Oh. Hi, guys."

A hint of light mahogany flooded her cheeks as she offered a meek wave.

"Here's your luggage, dear," Nadia said as she rolled a large metal case through a gap that appeared in the bar. She smiled at Charlie and Swarm as they both gawked at the case.

"Don't look so shocked, fellas. It's not contraband. At least I don't think so. MOM just made a little mistake when toking our luggage aboard the *Pineapple Express* and accidentally sent this to my room. Isn't that right, Zee?"

"Sure, why not," said Zylvya, yawning. "Anyway, thanks for keeping it safe."

Charlie held out a hand to stop her.

"Look, I don't care what's in the case. I don't care who Swarm's mystery guest is. But I'm a little pissed you two keep lying to me. You both wigged out back in the mini-Transit Bay, then you said you were too busy to meet me in the mini-bridge. But here you are, running secret errands in Lavaka. Are you even listening, Zee? Zee?"

Zylvya swayed on her feet with her eyes closed and her mouth hanging open.

"Zee!"

She startled awake. "Yeah, I understand, Captain. I couldn't agree more."

"Did you just fall asleep again? What the hell's going on with you?"

"Sorry, Captain." Zylyva put a hand to her temple and scrunched her emerald eyebrows into a knot. "I just have a splitting headache. I need to go lie down for a while. We'll talk before the peace accord begins, I promise."

She rolled the huge metal case under the exit tapestry and was gone. Charlie turned around to find that Swarm had vanished back into his private alcove.

"Well, fine! C'mon Cassie, let's go before this place strips me of whatever dignity I have left."

As he slipped under the tapestry, Nadia called out, "Good luck at the peace summit tomorrow. From the looks of things, you'll need it!"

16

Zylvya collapsed on the floor as the door spun shut behind her.

It had taken way longer than it should have to get back to her room. The stupid guidance system was so dim she could barely distinguish it from the stupid wet shine of Charlie's stupid authentic pineapple walls.

Or maybe, she thought, *it's because every photon that strikes my retina feels like a laser blast through my eye socket.*

Zylvya lay face down on the floor, which to her surprise was a silky turf of rainbow grass growing out of a spongy soil. She doubted Charlie designed all the rooms on the *Pineapple Express* with luxurious grass lawns like this. No, he must have had it morpho-printed especially for her after they left the mini-Transit Bay.

For a brain-fried, over-emotional, height-challenged ape, she thought, *he sure can be sweet sometimes.*

Still, the room could use a few environmental tweaks to make it more comfortable.

Especially in my condition, she thought.

"Mother, please dim the lights to ten percent their current level," she mumbled through a faceful of silky grass, knowing the ship's computer would hear her anyway. "Increase relative humidity to 55% and carbon dioxide levels to full saturation. And loop audio of wind soughing through a temperate forest on Viridia, volume at 15%."

"Sorry, Lieutenant Zylvya, but Mother resides aboard the *Starseed* and cannot be accessed at this time. Would you like me to prepare a message—"

"No!" interrupted Zee, wincing at the volume of her own voice. Much more quietly, she added, "Sorry, I had my wires crossed. You're MOM, right? Hi. *You* do all the things I just mentioned. Please. Now."

"Correct, I am MOM. I am the personified expression of the *Pineapple Express's* central processing system," explained the stilted voice. "Please specify which requests in your queue you would like me to fulfill first. Adjusting the room's atmospheric conditions or preparing to send a message via hypermail back to the *Starseed*?"

"Nevermind all that. Just morpho-print me a basic atmospheric control panel and I'll take care of it myself."

"Understood. Archiving the previous requests. Processing the new request. Which model of atmospheric control panel would you prefer, Lieutenant? In the standard Gal-Fed line, you can choose from a RoomGroom Econo model x1000, model x1001, model x1002,…"

Zylvya dug her fists into her ears even though she knew the sound of MOM's voice was coming from inside her head rather than outside.

Could MOM really be this unhelpful? Is she intentionally being obtuse?

Zylvya didn't think either was true.

I bet some of Charlie's childish sense of humor rubbed off on her when he created this giant flying fruit.

She'd never heard of any previous captains breaking off such a large portion of the *Starseed's* substrate, let alone attempting to copy Mother. But she assumed Mother wouldn't trust the

Starseed's fruit-shaped offspring in the metaphorical hands of a defective central processing system.

In any case, worrying about that was pointless. By the time anything went seriously wrong with MOM's core algorithms, everyone would already be dead. Still, she decided to run a full diagnostic on the *Pineapple Express* to make sure everything was as rosy as Charlie said it was.

Before I do anything else, I'm going to need something stronger than willow bark concentrate, she thought, flipping through the catalog of natural pain remedies in her mind.

I should ask Charlie for some of his Golden Ticket. *I know he'll give me as much as I want. But I'll have to ask him in a way that doesn't further inflate his already over-inflated ego. The last thing I need is him thinking his weed is special. Even if it is. It sure did a number on my testing equipment,* she thought, remembering the charred remains of her lab.

I wonder if his plants are doing any better. I hope that weird old guy we picked up on Págos 9 isn't manipulating Charlie somehow. There was something off about that old kook. Kinda reminds me of the vibe I got from—

"Lieutenant Zylvya, have you fallen asleep?" MOM's voice echoed inside her skull.

"I'm still here," she mumbled, forcing her eyelids open. "For now, anyway."

Zylvya realized her wandering mind had once again strayed from the task at hand and almost slipped away.

Not yet, she thought. *Not until I can activate it.*

She crawled to the metal case she'd rolled all the way from Lavaka. Lifting her hand to the maglock panel took every last bit of willpower she had left. Concentrating, she swiped and tapped the combination. A light beside the panel turned green and a gust of air hissed along the lip of the case's edge.

"Lieutenant Zylvya, your biodata indicates an extremely elevated level of mental exhaustion," MOM stated. "Operating heavy machinery in your condition is not recommended."

Zylvya laughed weakly.

"I think this particular piece of equipment can get along fine on its own, but why don't you give it a hand? Prepare to upload any data you can find on the Trapezia system and their conflict, and then—" a sudden, irresistible yawn cut her off.

From the widening gap between the metal case and its lid came an electronic whir of metallic limbs warming up their hydraulic joints.

It's waking up just as I'm slipping away, she thought.

"Help get it up to speed on current events, the technical details of the *Pineapple Express,* and all the delegates involved," she mumbled. "While you do that, I'm just going to rest my eyes for a little while."

Zylvya smacked her lips and curled into a ball in the soft grass.

"Wake me one hour before the time stamp Charlie programmed for the summit. And one more thing…" she trailed off and began breathing heavily.

"Yes, Lieutenant Zylyva?"

Zee sighed and managed to whisper one more command before falling asleep.

"Don't let it out of my room until I'm back."

17

"Where the smeg is everyone?"

"Maybe Charlie miscalculated the local time stamp."

"How do we know this is even the right room?"

Zylvya shot Swarm a look.

"It's a triangular room with tables along the walls and a hologram of the Trapezian system hovering above us. You think Charlie designed more than one of these?"

"The ape probably got stoned and decided to hold the peace summit on his couch."

"Calling him ape again, huh, *Bugbrain*?" She flipped her long green braid over her shoulder and folded her arms across her chest. "Charlie might not be the brightest star in the sky, but he created the *Pineapple Express,* which is something no other *Starseed* captain has done before."

"Nothing Captain Hong does is like his predecessors. Doesn't necessarily mean he's some kind of genius. Maybe it means he has no idea what he's doing."

"Maybe it means he needs his Chief of Security to snap out of whatever funk he's in and get his head in the game!"

"Get *my* head the game?" rattled Swarm. "Yesterday you could barely keep your eyes open! Maybe you should spend less time in Lavaka and more time giving Captain Hong a hand!"

"What have you done except slip Charlie an extremely dangerous data pill? Oh, I remember now. You took one look at those Dregz and froze like a little—"

"Watch it, Twiggy," interrupted Swarm. "I'm not frozen now."

Zylyva chiseled a contemptuous glare onto her face but smiled inwardly. It was good to know she could still push Swarm's buttons.

"Whatever. I was just passing through Lavaka to pick up some luggage, but *you* actually had a booth in that snake pit! You were having some kind of secret rendezvous that you still haven't disclosed to your captain or your crewmates."

"That's... different," Swarm said as his antennae lost their rigidity.

She was expecting his temper to flare, as it usually did when she poked at him, but like the previous day in the mini-Transit Bay, he just stared into the middle distance, completely lost in thought.

Zylvya pointed at the floppy red antennae hanging from the center of his forehead.

"See, they're doing it again!"

In a softer tone, she asked, "What's up, Swarm? You and I don't always see eye to eye, but we're crew. We don't keep secrets from each other. You can trust me."

Swarm gave a quick, gravelly chuckle and locked eyes with her.

"Tell me why you fell asleep on the job, and I'll tell you who I was meeting with last night."

After a moment of staring blankly at each other, he said, "I didn't think so."

"Didn't think what, man?"

Charlie approached from one of the corridors that connected to the triangular room's three corners.

Swarm straightened up.

"I don't think the augmented guidance system on the *Pineapple Express* is doing a very good job at guiding the delegates here. Why don't you just recalibrate the brightness accuracy threshold?"

"I've done that a few times already, but the settings keep drifting back. I've tried troubleshooting it with MOM, but, uh, that hasn't really worked out yet. Anyway, that's not the reason no one's here yet."

"It's not?"

"Nope," Charlie said, flashing a tilted grin. "The local time stamp I sent to your quarters was thirty minutes earlier than it was for everyone else."

"You tricked us into arriving early," Zylvya said, astonished. "Why?"

"Two reasons. First," he paused to dig around in his hoodie pocket until he produced a twisted cylinder of light brown paper. "It's been too long since we had an official smoke sesh together."

"For you, five minutes would've been too long," rattled Swarm.

Charlie lit the joint by thinking of the ignition word and puffed its ember to life. He exhaled a long stream of smoke and held the smoldering doobie out to the others.

"Second reason I tricked you was that the three of us need to discuss the elephant in the room."

"Elephant in the room? What the smeg is an *elephant*?" Swarm's appendages widened into a fighting stance. "MOM, close and lock the exits! Locate and identify all cloaked lifeforms in the room and isolate them using a subsonic array!"

"Whoa! Hey! Chill, man," Charlie said, popping the joint between Swarm's mandibles. "Elephants are just these super cool, really large mammals from Earth."

Swarm's triangular head swiveled.

"Where is it hiding? How did it get here?"

"Dude, it's just an expression from Earth. It means there's

something big and awkward we gotta address, but no one wants to talk about it," Charlie said.

He snatched the joint from Swarm, took a quick puff, and offered it to Zylvya.

"Cut the shit, guys. I know you're hiding something. Not only did you both turn into weirdos as soon as the Silexi arrived, but afterwards you both stopped off for a nightcap at Lavaka."

"I was just a little exhausted, but I'm fine now," said Zylvya, forcing her droopy eyelids wide open. "And, like Nadia said, I just had to pick up my luggage after the mix up."

"Come on, Zee! I'm not *that* high—yet." Charlie snatched the joint back from her. He took a few quick puffs and screwed up his face. "Nope, still sounds like bullshit. But I'm not sure which lie is more bullshit—that we should start trusting Nadia or that you own something other than that orange toga."

"I saw her wear a jumpsuit one time," rattled Swarm as smoke billowed from his mouth. "It was the same exact shade of orange."

"I have more than one orange toga, you morons!"

"So many togas you had to lug them around in a big metal case? We may be morons, but we're not that stupid."

"Speak for yourself, Captain," Swarm rattled.

"What, then you *are* that stupid?"

"Neither of you are morons, and you're not stupid. Sorry, guys," said Zee. "Look, for this mission I needed to pack something special. Extra gear of sorts. Surprise gear, for later. Only if we need it. Which hopefully we won't. But just in case."

"Special gear. I see," Charlie said, nodding. "Is that all?"

"That's it," she lied. "I promise."

Swarm crossed both sets of arms.

"You know I hate surprises, Zee. For the record, surprises and peace summits don't go well together."

"I know, Swarm. But trust me, if we end up needing this gear, then the summit is likely already doomed."

Swarm relaxed. "How optimistic of you."

Zylvya shrugged and took a puff from the joint.

"Galactic history isn't on our side. Centuries-long, three-way wars never achieve peace on the first try." She paused to exhale a plume of white smoke. "We'll be lucky if we manage to score a temporary ceasefire, even from just two factions. The odds are against us."

"Alright, cool story. Anyway, I hate to be the one doubling down on Nadia being a reliable source of information, but I had some trouble with my luggage, too. When I finally made it back to my room last night, I found my suitcases completely empty... except for a layer of slime. Some Seeder must've gotten my bags by mistake and decided to clean me out before MOM toked the bags back to my room."

"Slime should be easy enough to identify," said Zylvya. "Ask MOM to identify who received your luggage by mistake, and we'll pay them a visit after the opening ceremony."

Charlie made an annoyed face.

"Watch this. Hey, MOM, where on the *Pineapple Express* did you toke my three suitcases?"

"I toked them directly to your quarters, Captain Hong."

He raised an eyebrow. "Are you sure you didn't accidentally toke them somewhere else by mistake before re-toking them to my room?"

"Yes, Captain Hong. I'm one hundred percent certain that they were only toked once and only to your quarters."

"Okay, so who entered my room and emptied them out?"

"I am one hundred percent certain that no one but you has entered your room, Captain Hong."

"See what I mean, guys? She's a little..." Charlie paused to twirl his finger around his ear. "Thanks, MOM. I guess my extra clothes just got up and walked out on their own, huh? Wait a second. MOM, *did* my clothes get up and walk out on their own?"

"No, Captain Hong. No clothing left your quarters of its own volition."

Swarm lowered his rattle and leaned in.

"I suspect something might be up with you-know-who. After the summit's opening, we might want to…" he trailed off, his body freezing in place.

"Look, Charlie, he's doing it again!"

Swarm stood paralyzed, half bent at the abdomen, his antennae shooting straight above him like crimson lightning rods. Every facet of his great compound eyes were pinned to the Silexi corridor.

Charlie peeked down the corridor and heard grunts and the clattering of armor and guns.

"Dregz," he said, checking his watch. "Probably come to secure the area before the Silexi delegates arrive, which shouldn't be too long now."

He turned to Swarm, sighed, and slapped him as hard as he could.

Swarm didn't budge, but after Charlie's hand stopped screaming in pain, he glared into the insectoid's eyes.

"You can't do this again, man! Snap out of it! I don't know the first thing about diplomacy!"

"You could always try pissing yourself again," said Zylvya, stifling a yawn with the back of her hand.

"Not you, too!" he cried. "Okay, fuck that. Desperate times call for desperate measures. MOM, morpho-print me an extra-large can of Red Bull—and before you ask me a million clarifying questions, just print one exactly like those stocked in the mini-fridge."

"Affirmative, Captain."

A small cylinder bulged from the marble floor and solidified into a 32oz aluminum can. He cracked it open and pushed it into Zylvya's hand.

"Chug this while I deal with Swarm."

"Eww, this smells like the mineral pits of Zorgonia."

"Chug it! That's an order!"

Grunts and raucous laughter grew nearer. Charlie turned back to Swarm and thought about punching him in the crotch or yanking on his antennae, but decided against it. MOM didn't seem to understand nuance like Mother did. For all he knew, she might misinterpret something stronger than a slap as a lethal attack and give Charlie the Mark. That would give the Dregz the green light to kill him on sight—and eat him, if that was their thing.

Instead, he sucked down the last quarter of his joint and blew a cloud of smoke directly into Swarm's face. As the cloud settled around his triangular head, Swarm's antennae twitched.

"You there, man? Yeah, I can see something responding in your buggy eyes. Come on, snap out of it! Fight!"

Swarm's mandibles began slowing opening and closing, as if thawing out.

"Captain," he mumbled. "Help."

The smoke had helped, but there was no time to light up another doob.

"I got it! MOM, we're gonna need another drink. Print me one of those THC-infused pineapple mocktails, the exact kind we have back in the mini-fridge. And, uh, triple the THC. Oh, and throw in a straw!"

"Affirmative, Captain."

When it was finished morpho-printing, Charlie twisted the lid off the bottle, plopped the straw in, and lifted it to Swarm's mandibles. The fizzy yellow drink started draining.

"Captain," rattled Swarm, as if waking from a dream. "This is the second time I've frozen up like this, and it can only mean one thing… but that's… impossible. See,—"

"Hate to cut you off, man, but impossible stuff usually takes a really long time to explain. We'll have to do it later 'cause they're here!"

18

Charlie and his crew straightened up just as the Dregz poured in from the Silexi corridor, shoving each other and laughing like a pack of wild dogs.

Pig Nose, the warty javelina-looking one with the drippy nose, grunted a command at his mercs before tossing a small drone into the air. The gadget whirred to life, hovered in a wide, sweeping circle, and began scanning every nook and cranny of the room with an array of needle-thin red lasers. The rest of the Dregz spread out along the wall beneath the hologram of planet Silex. Finally, the drone chimed like an egg timer and returned to Pig Nose's hoofed hand.

"I've read stories about these mercs on the Outernet. None of them had happy endings," Zylvya said between swigs of Red Bull. "What's the plan to make sure we get a happy ending?"

"We could pop into one of those shady massage parlors down in the mini-Ring," answered Charlie.

"How would a massage help?"

Charlie snickered. "Nevermind."

"Zee's right, Captain. They're not the brightest bunch, and they'll take any job for the right price—which makes them extremely dangerous," explained Swarm. He quickly finished the last of his THC mocktail and tossed the empty bottle over his shoulder. Instead of shattering against the hard floor, it was caught by a section of marble that had suddenly turned foamy and soft. The bottle vanished into the mushy marble like a bowling ball sinking into warm dough.

"I have to admit, this strange Earth beverage is helping me stay awake." Zee finished her drink, tossed it aside to get reabsorbed into the ship's substrate, then caught Charlie's eyes. "Not your worst idea, Captain."

"They can't *all* be my worst ideas. And hey, if the drinks are helping, then have another. They're on the house."

Charlie snapped his fingers and a second round of drinks morpho-printed near their feet.

Swarm scanned the row of Dregz while sipping from his straw.

"We're looking at the number one risk to this peace summit's success. The Mark policy inherited from the *Starseed* should keep things civil around here, but there's nothing stopping these guys from turning the scene into a bloodbath and then bailing out before facing the consequences."

"But their weapons shouldn't work, right?" asked Charlie. "Don't you think the *Pineapple Express's* substrate would've nerfed them by now?"

"Hopefully. I see a few wadget rifles and some crude projectile weapons that require ammunition. Assuming MOM did her job, none of those weapons should ever fire again, even after they've left the ship. You can bet these goons will be smegging pissed when they find out. What worries me more are the simple blades and other dangerous tech that MOM might not recognize as a weapon."

"Shit," Charlie said.

"They could do a lot of damage in a very short amount of time and be gone before we could do much to stop them."

"I can do a lot of damage, too," Zylvya said, her eyes flickering to the vines peeking out from the marble floor at her feet.

The last time Charlie had seen her unleash the vines was during their battle with an elephant-sized spider mite. If she could take down that bitch, she could handle these goons without a problem.

Unless she dozed off again.

Charlie motioned to the can in her hand.

"Keep sippin', Zee."

"Furthest on the left, near the Smolz side," Swarm rattled quietly. "The tall one with the heavy rags and the holographic mask. They're up to something."

"You sure it's not the creepy one two spots down? The one with the metal mask?" Charlie said.

Instead of randomly scanning the area like the other mercs, that one seemed fixated on Charlie, just like it had in the mini-Transit Bay when the Silexi delegation had arrived.

"No, Captain. It's definitely the big one on the far end. When my antennae wander that way, I..."

He trailed off and shook his head.

"Something happens inside me."

"Inside you? In a morphic way? Like that time you lost your shit and shattered into a million beetles?"

"Meetles, not beetles. And no, not like that at all. My morphic field integrity is stable. What's happening now is an involuntary change to my nervous system resulting from very specific molecules being emitted from Holo Mask over there. *Impossible* molecules."

"We've seen a hundred impossible things during our stint on the *Starseed*," said Zylvya. "What makes this impossibility so different?"

"The molecules triggering my biological reaction can only come from one source, and that source won't exist for another million years."

Swarm straightened up and his eyes locked onto Holo Mask. If Holo Mask noticed the attention from across the room, they didn't react.

"Smegging hell, it's happening again. This stupid pineapple

drink didn't snap me out of my condition after all. It was the orb sweeper the Dregz leader used on the room when they first arrived. Its laser array must've sterilized any free floating particulates in the air, including the pheromones."

"Pheromones?" asked Zylvya.

"I've heard that word before, man. Isn't that some kind of cannabis terpene developed by the Russians in the '80s?"

"Captain," explained Zylvya, "Pheromones are invisible molecules emitted by one organism which work like neurological keys to unlock instinctual behavior in another organism. Usually within the same species and usually of a complementary gender…"

She trailed off, holding her head. Charlie noticed bags had appeared under her eyes.

"Where would some random space merc find pheromones from the future?"

"MOM," Swarm rattled behind frozen mandibles. "Besides me, how many of my species are currently aboard the *Pineapple Express*?"

"There is one other lifeform that matches your DNA and morphic signature," she said. "She is standing twenty meters from your current location."

"Oh, shit! Now I remember where I heard the word *pheromone*!" Charlie said. "Hey, Swarm, on the bright side, even if the peace summit falls apart, at least you might have a chance to get lucky tonight."

Every facet of Swarm's compound eyes locked onto Holo Mask and his antennae trembled. He took one step before realizing his other leg was pinned to the ground by a short length of vine sprouting from the floor beneath him. As he struggled to pull his leg free, he didn't notice the other vines sprouting around him. One wrapped tightly around his free leg while two more grasped him around the waist. He swiveled his triangular head toward Zylvya, scowling and shaking with rage.

"Not now, Bugbrain," she spoke warmly. "The delegates are arriving. Peace first, and then—"

"And then you can get a piece," Charlie blurted out.

They stared at him. He stared back.

"You know, like a piece of—"

"Yeah, we get it, Charlie," Zylvya said, shaking her head. "We were children once, too."

19

Charlie nursed his wounded ego while Zylvya concentrated on using her vines to keep Swarm pinned to his spot at the center of the triangular room.

He'd seen her vines emerge from the green marble floor plenty of times, usually when she was agitated or scared, but only once had they become violent. A giant spider mite queen was attacking the *Starseed's* THC Core—which, of course, was all Charlie's fault—and she took care of it. Her vines shot through the floor, impaled the monstrous bitch, and ended the invasion in about five seconds flat.

That blunder had been Charlie's first real catastrophe as captain. One of his *worst ideas*, as Zylvya liked to classify them. Sure, Axo's arm got ripped off, but it grew back.

Eventually.

Besides that, the only serious injury was to Charlie's pride.

His most recent blunders, on the other hand, led to Del and Axolotl being put out of commission—perhaps permanently.

Charlie resisted the urge to let himself slip into another pity party and instead occupied his caffeinated and stoned brain by wondering how Zylvya produced the vines in the first place. He figured they were a manifestation of the intimate bond between Zylvya and the *Starseed*. A subconscious expression of her plantlike physiology. Or maybe an innate ability of her race amplified by the *Starseed*.

One thing Charlie knew for certain was that he sure as hell couldn't manifest them. On the few occasions he tried to produce his own vines, they were spindly and weak. But they were topped with a pre-rolled joint—so it wasn't a total loss.

Speaking of joints, he thought, patting himself down. *I didn't bring extras! Shit, man… this may be my worst blunder yet.*

Zylvya parked Swarm beside Charlie, using six vines on his limbs and two more around his waist, just as the delegates arrived.

A low fog spilled out of the corridor leading from the Smolz wing and crept across the floor, finally gathering itself into a hazy cloud under the hologram of their planet.

R'or Shaq and his attendants swam through the air inside their floating orbs of clear liquid and took their spot beneath Undulata.

Reticulus Rex arrived from the Silexi corridor flanked on either side by Vree Voktal and Eta Cerbo.

Once again, Charlie found himself starstruck.

So Steven Spielberg cast a real live alien right under people's noses? Charlie mused. *That cheating son of a bitch should give back the Oscar he won for Best Visual Effects. Wait, even if he'd somehow convinced everyone on set that E.T. was just a state-of-the-art puppet, how the hell did he even get access to him in the first place?*

Earth was far inside Reptilian-controlled space, and they didn't allow any ships but their own to travel to and from the planet's surface. Letting a Silexi, whose planet was on the other side of the quadrant, just walk around among humans and film a movie seemed ridiculous, if not impossible.

'We've seen a hundred impossible things during our stint on the Starseed', Zee had said earlier. *Perhaps impossible things are more a feature of the galaxy than of the Starseed in particular.*

"Thanks, Twiggy," Swarm whisper-rattled from the side of his mandibles. "My body seems to have a mind of its own."

"Yeah, we noticed," she said, straining. "I can keep you from making a fool of yourself, but I won't be able to do much else. If something triggers the Dregz to violence, I'll have to make a tough choice."

"That's why Captain Hong's going to keep this meeting on track. Isn't that right, Captain?"

Charlie nearly choked on a swig of Red Bull.

"Yeah right, man. This peace summit was *your* thing, remember?"

"Wrong." Swarm spoke calmly as his body involuntarily struggled against the vines. "Technically, it was a Captain Major Tom thing. You inherited his *things* when you took the job. Now it's a Captain Charlie Hong thing."

The memory of his last conversation with Captain Major Tom flashed through Charlie's mind.

Things, he thought, *including more than one goddamn secret.*

Secret deals with Nadia. A secret weapon. A secret identity. How much longer was Charlie expected to carry these *things* all by himself? He'd been about to confide in Axo when the visit to Págos 9 went sideways. His two remaining crewmates didn't look like they were in any shape to handle truth bombs at the moment.

"But dude, *you're* the expert on Trapezia! You've been talking about this goddamn peace summit since I became captain!"

"Glad you were listening. Then you should have no trouble running the proceedings until I recover."

"That's the thing, Swarm, I *wasn't* paying attention! I can't recall any of their names, and they just told them to me yesterday! I'm barely paying attention to the conversation we're having *right now!* I can't just step into your shoes and lead a peace summit, man!"

"Captain, look at me. I'm in no position to lead anything. Yet the hope of peace must go on. So stop complaining and—Twiggy!

Your vines are loosening! My upper arms are almost free! Zee! Wake up!"

Zylvya snapped her tired eyes open.

"Sorry. My head's pounding, and I feel so sleepy, and…"

She trailed off as her eyelids slipped back over her eyes. Charlie could see that Swarm would involuntarily bolt toward Holo Mask the second he was free.

"Goddammit!"

Charlie chugged the last bit of drink from both cans and tossed the empty containers over his shoulder.

"Fine! Then we'll do it my way. But first, I gotta make sure you two can hold your shit together."

He dropped into a crouch, closed his eyes, and took a deep breath. A melon-shaped mound appeared in the floor and morphed into an exact replica of the object he pictured in his mind. Beside it, two more cans of Red Bull morphed into existence. He cracked open the cans, slipped them into the straps on either side of the object, then inserted a rubber hose into each.

"Captain, what the smeg are you doing? We need to start the proceedings!"

"I'm doing what you said. I'm making sure this meeting stays on track."

Charlie placed his creation snuggly over Zylvya's head.

"Back on Earth we might not have fancy tech like anti-grav boots and laser rifles, but at least we have beer hats."

"Beer hats?" Zylvya said sleepily.

"In this case it's a Red Bull hat. See, you slip the hoses in your mouth like this. Now you can sip on some more Red Bull while your hands are busy controlling your vines."

"Enough fooling around, Captain!" growled Swarm. "The Dregz are getting restless. Start the smegging meeting!"

20

Charlie straightened up, cleared his throat, and tried to summon his best impression of famous starship captains he'd seen in movies back on Earth. He couldn't remember any episode of *Star Trek* where Captain Kirk's crew was as uncontrollably horny or sleepy as his was now. The real challenge wasn't to keep the peace proceedings on track—it was to keep them from ending in a fiery explosion of chaos and destruction.

"People of Trapezia," he said loudly. The room settled, and suddenly all eyes, or whatever, were on him.

Charlie's heart raced and his thoughts blurred as the spike of caffeine and cannabinoids surged through his bloodstream.

Maybe double fisting two extremely potent beverages wasn't such a good idea after all, he thought.

"Once again, I welcome you to the *Starseed's* sister ship, the *Pineapple Express*. Before we get started making peace among worlds, does anyone need to hit the restroom? Or maybe you need a sip of water? I can get us some snacks, too, man. We got salty or sweet. Or, hey, why not both? Have you guys ever tried sea salt chocolate-covered peanut-butter-filled pretzel bites before? It's like salty, sweet, salty, sweet… all in one bite. I eat so many of them back on the *Starseed*. What am I saying? Here, try some yourself."

Bowls of chocolate-covered nuggets morpho-printed on the delegates' tables. The Smolz cloud hovered in place and didn't seem to notice. The Undulata swam close enough to examine the snack, but seemed more interested in the plastic bowl than what was inside. The only member of the Silexi delegation to react to the snacks was Eta Cerbo, who snatched the Silexi bowl and gobbled them down by the handful.

"Cool. All we gotta do now is make some peace," said Charlie, fully aware that he didn't know the first thing about making peace.

Charlie tried to remember the information Swarm's data pill had downloaded into his nervous system. Did this stupid interplanetary war really start over a disagreement on what to name their trinary star system? Could it be that simple?

Let's find out, Charlie thought, feeling for the first time like he was onto something.

He clapped his hands together and addressed the room.

"Let's go back to the beginning, to when this whole conflict began. No, let's go back further, to before all y'all started fighting. Let's examine what started this war in the first place so—"

"Captain!" Swarm interrupted, then added more quietly. "Drudging up old wounds is literally the worst tactic you can use to kick off a peace summit. You need to get them to look *forward*, not backwards. Not about how they've spent the past millennium trying to eradicate each other, but on what they can achieve in the next millennium if they stop fighting and start working together. If we can show them that, make them learn to *trust* each other instead of *fear* each other, then they'll be able to forge their own path to peace."

"Good call, Swarm. Hey, you just gave me an idea!" Charlie flashed a tilted grin to his audience. "Forget going down memory lane. What's done is done. Instead, we're gonna start off by forming a trust circle here in the middle of the room. Once we're in place we'll take turns closing our eyes, falling backwards, and *trusting* that those around us will catch us."

No one moved.

Charlie whispered to MOM, "Are you translating all of this to them?"

"Yes, Captain. I am translating every word you say to every lifeform in the room."

"Then why the hell is no one reacting?"

"Because they're not here to eat snacks and play games," Zylvya said, stifling another yawn.

"I dunno, Zee. Snacks and games seem like a pretty good recipe for peace—as long as you throw in a few blunts, maybe a gravity bong, and put on some mellow tunes. You know, *ganja and chill*."

"Captain, try to understand. Their civilizations are built around this three-way war," added Swarm quietly. "Every custom. Every decision. Their entire economy. Getting high can't undo all of that. You'll have to show them what they can gain if they replace their war posture with one centered around peaceful interplanetary cooperation."

"Silence!"

A voice bellowed from the Silexi side of the room. Vree Voktal stepped forward to address the assembled group.

"His Majesty, the Benevolent Protector of Silex and Divine Steward of Trapezia, Emperor Reticulus Rex, would like to begin with two important announcements which may impact the peace proceedings."

Charlie shrugged and nodded, happy someone else would be taking center stage for a few moments while he gathered his stoned wits.

Vree Voktal touched the golden device coiled around his neck and narrowed his glossy black eyes.

"Firstly, His Majesty Reticulus Rex has come to understand," he started slowly, raising his pitch and volume as he continued, "that here, on the *Pineapple Express*, during our first attempt at peace in centuries, there is a secret plot to assassinate His Majesty!"

The Undulata gyrated in their water spheres and the cloud of floating dust behind the Smolz table condensed into a tight orange cloud. The Dregz glowered around the room, their weapons pointed at the floor but their trigger fingers twitching.

Swarm seemed to stop struggling for a split second and even Zylvya's tired eyes cracked open another centimeter.

"Captain, there are several lifeforms speaking at once," announced MOM. "Which would you like me to translate first?"

Charlie ran a hand through his short afro.

"None of them just yet. Your Majesty, listen, no one on my ship is planning to harm you. Besides this delegation, all we have are some vacationing Seeders, a few perfectly harmless vendors, and my crew. Look at these two. C'mon, do they look like they're plotting anything more than maybe a comedy act?"

Vree Voktal cleared his throat before rasping, "Perhaps you don't have as tight a grip on your ship as you think, Captain Hong. Members of our security team visited the commerce corridor you call the mini-Ring last night and stopped in at a local establishment where they not only heard you quarreling with your crew, but they heard rumors of conspiracy to murder His Majesty and destroy any chance of peace in Trapezia."

Charlie knew they hadn't heard the rumors at a noodle bar. If there was one place where rumors were born, it was Lavaka. He didn't recall seeing any Dregz there, but the place was packed and he'd been pretty distracted by the acid burning through his clothes. For all he knew, Pig Nose and Metal Mask could've been sitting within earshot.

Actually, he thought, *for all I know, they could've been in the private alcove with Swarm.*

"I assure you, my crew and I were doing our own investigation, and we found everything to be super secure," he lied. "Tiptop shape all around. Zero threats, man. And besides, you should know that even if someone was planning a murder on the

Pineapple Express, it wouldn't work out too nicely for them. If someone attempts to kill another passenger, they get this thing called the Mark. They glow red and everyone knows they're guilty. Then other bad stuff happens to them, but we won't go into that right now."

Charlie looked to Swarm for a clue about how to pull the conversation out of a nosedive, but the insectoid was completely consumed with his struggle against the vines. Zylvya, whose mouth was full of beerhat straws, only shrugged before going back to focusing on maintaining her grip.

"Anyway, if you've got proof, let's see it," Charlie said, holding out his hand.

Vree Voktal and Emperor Rex exchanged a quick glance, but neither spoke.

"Alright, so here's a house rule on the *Pineapple Express*—if you can't put up, then you better shut up. No more rumors up in the peace room, man. Just facts. And love. And maybe even some ice cream if we all settle down and make some progress toward peace. Any flavors, guys. Any. Think on that and decide your next move."

Vree Voktal lowered his icy gaze at Charlie.

"If not for His Majesty's compassion and heartfelt desire to foster peace in our system, we'd have packed up and left the moment we caught wind of the implicit insurrection stirring within your crew. Because His Majesty exhibits infinite courage, he has decided to remain here and endure threats against his own life if it means having a chance at saving the Silexi people."

"Unfortunately, as per His Majesty's second announcement, His Majesty and the Silexi people are not the only targets of this treachery. His Majesty is unwaveringly devoted to upholding the sacred Silexi creed that innocent life must be protected at all costs. Which is why His Majesty feels compelled to inform you that a genocide is being planned right under your nose! That's right, Captain Hong, you heard me correctly. Genocide. The most unforgivable crime in the quadrant. A passenger aboard this starship intends to commit a crime so heinous, so unforgivable, so *evil* that it taints the very ground we walk on. We cannot, in good conscience, proceed with the peace summit until this evil is purged and this ship cleansed. His Majesty demands that this passenger be detained at once and prevented from following through with their despicable plan to slaughter millions of innocents."

"Says the guy in a thousand year *three-way* war," Charlie whispered to Zee, who swayed on her feet.

"Hey! Wake up!"

She startled and forced her eyes open.

"I'm ready for a refill, Captain," she said dreamily. Charlie sighed, morpho-printed two more cans of Red Bull, and replaced the two empties in the beerhat.

"Are you hearing this shit, Zee?" Charlie whispered into Zylvya's ear. "Assassination and genocide in under five minutes. That's gotta be a record."

"Speedrunning disasters does seem to be your speciality."

"If you think this is impressive, you should see how fast I speedrun a bad relationship."

"Is now really a good time for flirting, Charlie?"

"What can I say? You're irresistible in a beerhat."

"Captain Hong!" shrieked Vree Voktal. "As leader of this vessel, what say you? Will you prevent a genocide from occurring right under your own hull? Or should we dissolve this flaccid attempt at peace and go our separate ways?"

"Swarm," whispered Charlie. "What the hell do I say?"

Swarm clenched his mandibles and twisted his head toward Charlie.

"When someone asks you if you'll help stop a smegging genocide, the only acceptable answer is yes. Agree, so we can move on. We'll sort out the details later."

Charlie cleared his throat and addressed the Silexi.

"Saving millions of lives is something we do every day on the *Starseed*, man."

"His Majesty is grateful for your cooperation, Captain Hong. He is willing to overlook your incompetence in this matter if you agree to prevent the impending atrocity. Detain the passenger, or even space her, if you see fit. Either way, unless this atrocity is prevented, His Majesty will not be able to focus on creating peace on Silex."

Space her? Charlie thought. *A woman, somewhere on the ship, planning a secret genocide? There's only one snake who fits that description. And I finally have an excuse to bring her to justice.*

Charlie smiled.

"No problemo, man. I know exactly who you're talking about, and I assure you, I plan on throwing the book at her for this one. I probably won't space her, but I'll want to. Anyway, I'll take care of this right now so we can move on. MOM, could you please toke the person that the Silexi have identified as a genodical maniac to this room, right away?"

"Yes, Captain. Toking in three, two, one…"

"I can't wait to see her face, man!"

A wisp of greenish smoke streamed in through one of the corridors, swirled into a person-sized cloud, then condensed into a figure.

The shock in Charlie's face rivaled that of the woman standing in the center of the triangular room.

"MOM, I think you made a mistake," he said. "This isn't Nadia."

"Correct, Captain. The *Pineapple Express's* manifest lists this lifeform's preferred name as Mrs. Bauble Glimwicket."

Charlie groaned.

Zylvya gasped.

Even Swarm's involuntary struggle with the vines paused for a millighatika.

Charlie approached the frightened wingless moth-woman and put a hand on her shoulder. Her fur was silky soft, just like the fur covering her husband and son. Her bulging stomach reminded Charlie of a furry moon.

"Mrs. Glimwicket, we're very sorry to have disturbed you. There's been a mistake but we're about to fix it."

To the room he said, "Mrs. Glimwicket is a personal friend of mine. I promise you she is in no way a genocidal maniac. I can vouch for her. Look, man, she's expecting."

"She's guilty!" screeched Vree Voktal, pointing a bony grey finger down at her. "Our scanners indicate that she has the genocidal device with her right now! It is primed and ready to begin its slaughter. Dregz, apprehend her at once!"

"No one move," Charlie heard himself say as he stepped in front of Mrs. Glimwicket. "Any sign of violence and I'll have MOM toke you back to your room to cool off."

He fixated his gaze on Metal Mask, who hadn't stopped staring at Charlie since the Dregz arrived.

"I'm not playing around. We're here for peace and we're gonna handle this in a peaceful way. Does everyone got that?"

He locked eyes with Reticulus Rex who stood silently behind Vree Voktal.

"On the *Pineapple Express* everyone is innocent until proven guilty. All y'all have right now is an accusation, not proof."

Vree Voktal and Emperor Reticulus Rex narrowed their glassy black eyes at Charlie while E.T. sat on the ground beside them happily munching on the ever-replenishing bowl of snacks. Before anyone spoke, Charlie felt a tap on his shoulder.

Mrs. Glimwicket looked at him with apologetic eyes. Her proboscis twitched, but she didn't speak. Instead, it unfurled and curved toward the tiny object sitting in the palm of her hand.

"Sorry, Captain," she said, lifting the metallic pill-shaped device between two fingers and holding it up to his face. "For centuries my people have used devices like this to assist in our gestation rituals."

"She lies!" cried Vree Voktal. "Any ritual that employs an Abortionator 5000 is a ritual of death, not birth."

"Abortionator 5000?" asked Charlie. "That can't be what it's called."

Mrs. Glimwicket shrugged and her antennae tensed.

Charlie snatched the pill and held it up.

"MOM, describe this device to us. And no big words, please."

"That is a molecular vacuum cleaner, Captain."

"A what? Say that again, please."

"That is a conventional toaster oven with a programmable digital interface and air-frying capability, Captain."

"MOM, is this, or isn't this, a weapon?"

"That is a static conductor rod with extra thermal padding, Captain."

"She's scrambled up," Zylvya said, then sleepily shook her head as if to demonstrate what she meant. "I know the feeling."

"What the hell is wrong with everyone?" cried Charlie.

"Bauble!" someone cried out from down the Smolz corridor.

Mr. Glimwicket darted into the room, panting and holding his side.

"My sweet Bauble! What's going on here?"

"Oh, Bob. They know about the pill. I told you we should've waited till we were back on the *Starseed.*"

"There's no waiting, dear. The babies are coming a little earlier than we thought. It would be dangerous to wait. Without the pill…" He trailed off, scanning the cold, grey faces of the Silexi. He turned to Charlie.

"Why was Baub toked here against her will, Captain?"

Vree Voktal pointed at Mrs. Glimwicket, the tip of his finger glowing as if lit from within.

"She confirmed her genocidal plans! She produced the weapon!" His voice rose into a righteous screech. "*She is guilty!*"

"Weapon?" repeated Mr. Glimwicket before something in him caught fire. "You've got it all wrong! We're not planning a genocide! We're planning the birth of our next child!"

"Captain Hong, the perpetrator must be imprisoned immediately! His Majesty's patience is wearing thin…"

"Look, man, I've got the *Pineapple Express* on a preprogrammed course through some really scenic spots in the quadrant. No one's arriving, no one's leaving, okay? We're stuck out here together for the next week, learning stuff about ourselves and looking for peace. And, look, I have the Abortionator pill now, see? No one's in danger. No chance of genocide. So I, as captain of this ship, say we allow this nice pregnant lady to go back to her room and put her feet up. Mr. and Mrs. Glimwicket, we're sorry for the disruption to your vacation. I'll send up a bucketful of those q'veri crisps you love, Mrs. G."

"So be it," rasped Vree Voktal.

He bowed to the other Trapezian delegates.

"The solutions we are so desperately searching for cannot be found aboard a ship tainted by evil. The Silexi delegation will disembark at once. Perhaps in another century or two we will have another chance at peace."

"Hold up!" cried Charlie. "The only thing the *Pineapple Express* is tainted with is sweet pineapple nectar, thanks to the edible walls I designed. Seriously, has anyone other than E.T. even had a taste yet? I'm not kidding, it's friggin' delicious, man."

"Focus, Captain!" bellowed Swarm.

"Right," said Charlie, straightening up. "Okay, then. Your Majesty, there's no need to leave. We'll detain her."

Mr. Glimwicket flared his proboscis.

"We'll *what?*"

"Just while we conduct a legit investigation. And to get her out of their hair."

"Correction, Captain Hong," MOM's stilted voice filled the air. "The Silexi do not have any surface body hair of any kind. Their skin is made up of layers of carbon fiber creatine and contains no pores. They do, however, grow an internal ball of hair used to filter out Silexi regolith from their airways."

"Cool story, MOM. Now, as I was saying, prepare a long-range nug, a nice big one, to take the Glimwickets back to the *Starseed*."

"She can't travel in her condition, Captain! Especially not without that pill. The results would be horrific."

"As if the results of giving her the pill would be any less horrific!" screeched Vree Voktal.

"Okay, fine. What about this? We put a tracker on her ankle and lock the door to her room?"

"His Majesty wants her confined to your brig. Nothing less will do."

"You think I designed this giant, pineapple-shaped starship with a brig?" asked Charlie.

"Then it is a good thing I brought this." Emperor Reticulus Rex stepped forward and produced a small cube from his fanny pack. The cube was about three inches squared and had an intricate pattern etched onto every surface. "Hand her over, Captain Hong, and we'll take care of the rest."

"Captain! That's a P-cube!" rattled Swarm. "Do not let them use it on her, or we may never get her out!"

"When I said we didn't have a brig on the *Pineapple Express,* what I meant was that we didn't have a *full-sized* brig," Charlie said. "But, thankfully, I just remembered we do have a *mini-brig.*"

"We do?" asked Swarm.

"Yep, as of about thirty seconds ago we do. A steel cage conveniently located in the most secure room on the ship, the bridge. MOM, please toke Mrs. Glimwicket to the mini-brig immediately."

"Captain!" protested Mr. Glimwicket. "My Bauble is not a criminal! I will not stand for this aggression! She's *pregnant!*"

"Do it, MOM," said Charlie. Then to Mr. Glimwicket he said, "Trust me, man. She'll be safer there, away from these dudes."

Mrs. Glimwicket had just enough time to wave goodbye to her husband before her molecules exploded into a greenish cloud of vapor and zipped away down a corridor.

"This hecking dungcrap is unacceptable!" raged Bob Sr. "I won't rest until my sweet Bauble is free, even if that means I have to—"

He stopped abruptly and spun to face the Silexi. He pointed two of his four fingers at Emperor Reticulus Rex.

"You'll pay for this, you son of a slog! You'll pay!"

Before Charlie could calm him down, Bob Sr. bolted down the corridor after his wife.

Three Dregz stomped after him. The remaining Dregz raised their weapons as if to dare someone to give them a reason to start shooting. The Undulata and Smolz delegations sank back into their corners.

"Whoa! Everyone, calm down! Remember, we're here to make peace!"

When no one listened, Charlie whispered out the corner of his mouth. "Zee, what should I do? Zee?"

He turned to check on her and found her curled up on the floor. A second later he noticed the vines loosening around Swarm.

"Captain! I apologize in advance for whatever happens!" Swarm rattled before dissolving into a mound of tiny iridescent beetles that skittered across the room toward the Dregz.

In response, Holo Mask's clothing, rifle, and gear fell to the floor in a heap, behind which Charlie saw another mound of beetles skittering away in a panic. Without a doubt, they were meetles, just like Swarm's. Just as shiny but lavender rather than red.

The mass of Swarm's red meetles chased the mass of Holo Masks's lavender meetles up across the high dome, back down across the other side, and out through the Undulatian corridor.

When the chaos settled, every eye in the room was pinned on Charlie.

He ran a hand through his 'fro and mustered a tilted grin for the audience.

"Well, that's probably enough peacemaking for today, don't you think?"

21

The *Pineapple Express* whizzed through the sector on its preprogrammed course.

It swung through the Balini Kata system with its two red giant stars, circled around the vast pillars of electrostatic gas in the G'var nebula, and weaved through the softly glowing neon asteroids that littered what was left of the Ravenna system.

These awe-inspiring destinations had all been laid out before Charlie had stepped in as captain, by Swarm and Captain Major Tom, designed to capture the imaginations of the Trapezian delegates and offer them a glimpse at what awaited them if they diverted their collective resources away from war and toward the stars.

Stretched out on a big green beanbag, Charlie reclined his head and gazed up at the millions of stars stretched out above him.

Beside him, on a patch of silky rainbow-colored grass, Zylvya lay motionless and unresponsive. Charlie had her toked to the bridge and hadn't left her side, not even to go check on his plants. MOM assured him that while Zee had inexplicably fallen into a comatose state, all of her biological functions were stable. Somehow that hadn't made him feel any better.

On his other side stood his improvised mini-brig. It was a simple circular cage bolted to the floor that was crammed with comfort, including a couch, a television, a desk, a voidpod, and a sprawling bequilted bed with little mints on the pillows. Charlie had even conjured up the mini-brig around his mini-fridge so that his pregnant detainee would have access to food or drink whenever she needed them.

"Swarm, for the last time, come in," Charlie spoke into his chatter. He tapped it again. "Man, you're so getting written up for this. Just wait till your yearly performance review. Hey MOM, tell me again, where is Swarm located right now?"

"Lieutenant Swarm is simultaneously located in 303,113 different locations aboard the *Pineapple Express*," MOM explained. "Would you like me to list all of them?"

"Maybe later."

He lost half his crew on the last mission and now the other half was in serious trouble. Any chance for peace in Trapezia was dead on arrival. On top of all that, his plants continued to slip away despite being coddled by a squadron of grobots.

Way to go, Chuck Stonerly, he told himself. *At least the ship hasn't exploded yet.*

Charlie sighed and ran his hands down his face.

"You don't have to stay here, Captain," Mrs. Glimwicket said, sitting at her desk with her hands in her lap. "I can have MOM contact you if Lieutenant Zylvya's condition changes. Besides, I'm sure Bob will turn up any moment."

She tried to sound brave, but Charlie could see she was choking back tears.

"You sure you don't want me to toke Bob Jr. here?"

"Andromeda, no! I don't want him to see me like this."

"I'd say you look pretty good for a genocidal maniac," Charlie said, flashing her a half-smile through the bars. She didn't respond. "Bad joke, I'm sorry. But you're his mom. Take it from someone who hasn't seen his mother in nearly twenty years, he loves you and there's no way he's gonna think anything bad about you over some dumb misunderstanding."

"I'm more worried he might react like his father did," she said, then began sobbing gently into her big, furry hands.

Charlie scooted his beanbag next to the bars of the mini-brig.

"Hey, don't worry. Everything's gonna be okay, I promise. I'm still the captain and there's no way I'm gonna let those jerks download you into their little... whatever the hell that thing was. And I'm sure the Bobs are still fine. But don't take my word for it. MOM, remind us again that the Bobs are safe and sound."

"Bobomo Glimwicket, Jr. has just entered an arcade in the mini-Ring and his biodata indicates that he is currently in optimal health. Bobomo Glimwicket, Sr. has evoked his right to privacy, so I cannot give you his current location. His heart rate is elevated and his biodata indicates he may be under an abnormal amount of stress, but he is otherwise in optimal health."

"See, the Bobs are alright," said Charlie. "How are you feeling? Can I get you anything?"

Mrs. Glimwicket shook her head and caressed her soft, round belly.

"Look, I know you're scared and upset, but I can only help you if I have all the facts. The birth is happening soon, and that pill plays some important role in it, right? Hey, wait a second, man. I do have all the facts. I have the Outernet."

Charlie stared at a spot on the floor. A moment later, a brand new laptop morpho-printed into existence. He snatched it up, flipped it open, and began typing search queries into his browser.

"This was supposed to be a nice, relaxing vacation before the baby came," said Mrs. Glimwicket. "But now everything's a mess...and soon, without that pill..."

"Yeah, I'm reading about your species right now." His eyes narrowed slightly, then widened. "Wait. The biology section is over seven hundred pages long? I'm way too sober for *seven* pages, man."

Charlie patted himself down, found an unlit joint in his

hoodie pocket, and instinctively popped it between his lips. He closed his eyes to conjure up the ignition word used to light it, but stopped himself abruptly.

"Shit, I almost forgot! Pregnant ladies and smoke don't mix. Sorry." He was sliding the joint into the frizzy depths of his afro when Mrs. Glimwicket reached through the bars and stopped him with a touch.

"You can smoke that here," she said. "The ship will filter the smoke out for me."

"That true, MOM?"

"Affirmative, Captain Hong. The personalized atmosphere generated by the *Pineapple Express* will auto-morph the molecules around Mrs. Glimwicket faster than you can blow smoke in her face."

"I guess that makes sense." Charlie looked from Mrs. Glimwicket to the joint and then back to her. After mulling it over for a few seconds, he lit it and started puffing its ember to life. He blew a lungful of smoke into the air, away from the mini-brig. Even though they assured him it didn't matter, it still felt wrong.

"As usual, man, my *Golden Ticket* saves the day. Damn, I've been holding back this whole time thinking the smoke would mess up your baby."

"*Babies*," she clarified.

"Whoa. More than one?" Charlie mused. "So Bob Jr.'s gonna become a big brother to *twins*? Man, he better watch himself! They'll gang up on him."

"Not twins, Captain."

"Triplets?"

Mrs. Glimwicket shook her head and motioned to the laptop screen.

"Shit. Now I might be too stoned to read all that."

"I'll save you the trouble of reading all that technical stuff." Mrs. Glimwicket lowered her head and took a deep breath. "I'm ready to talk about it now."

"Thanks, man—I mean, *ma'am*. The more I know about your condition, the more likely I'll be able to help you."

Charlie settled back into his enormous beanbag and let the joint dangle from his lips as she began.

"To understand the trouble we're in, you have to first understand a unique evolutionary path my species took. We Mölfluga evolved from an insectoid bio-form on the planet Mölf in the Musca system. Other insectoid species evolved specialized roles such as workers, soldiers, and queens, bound tightly within strict hierarchical hives. Instead, we evolved down an individualistic path more commonly found in mammalians and other bio-forms. As our brains grew and developed, our physiology shed the more primitive adaptations and doubled-down on individual sentience. Our antennae and proboscis shrank significantly and we eventually shed our wings altogether."

"Whoa! You guys had *wings*?" Charlie said with smoke billowing from his mouth.

"We still have tiny remnant wing joints protruding from our shoulders. Anyway, one adaptation of our primitive ancestors remained—our reproductive system, which is identical to what it was a million years ago. Over the last few millennia, we Mölfluga have tried various technologies and methods to sidestep this dilemma, but each time we tinkered with our DNA, it led to even more devastating outcomes. If I were you, I wouldn't look that part up, unless you want to lose some sleep."

"Nope, I'm good."

"In the end, after centuries of searching for a solution, the pill in your pocket turned out to be the most compassionate way to handle the situation."

"Whoa. The Abortionator 5000."

Charlie dug it the out of his pocket and and held it up to his eyes.

"But wait, I thought you wanted to have a baby."

"We do want another child." She patted her swollen abdomen and sighed. "But just *one*. See, Captain, most insectoids tend to be multiparous—they give birth to multiple offspring at one time. We Mölfluga are considered *mega*multiparous. That's the ancient adaptation that our genetic code couldn't seem to shake."

She met Charlie's eyes.

"Once they come, they'll be hungry. Very hungry."

"Once *who* comes? The babies? Pshhh, no problem. The ole *Pineapple Express* can handle more than a few more hungry mouths."

"How about a few *million* more?" she said, her antennae trembling. "Before we developed civilization, Mölf was a high-churn planet, Captain. The natural ecosystem took care of our surplus young. We would choose one and walk away from the rest, allowing nature to take its course. Once we left Mölf, became starfaring, things changed. A single birth would put a space voyage at risk. These larvae eat everything, Captain. Walls, wiring, computers, the hull. And when they run out of inanimate matter… they start eating passengers. They don't can't about rules like the Mark, or some silly, self-righteous Silexi myth. They consume and grow and consume until…"

She trailed off and buried her face in her hands.

"Many ships were lost before the A5k pill came along. Without it, the *Pineapple Express* is doomed."

"Hey, you know the *Pineapple Express* is edible, right? Maybe that will hold them off until we can figure something out."

"Once they come, they'll tear through this ship before the week's over."

"Okay, what if we find a nearby planet and just drop them all off?"

"A sudden influx of a million hungry larvae would devastate any local ecosystem," she said. "Do you want to choose the planet to bear this burden?"

Charlie took a quick puff to refill his lungs while he pondered the problem.

"I got it! We find some lifeless rock, I dunno, some moon or asteroid or something. Then no one has to suffer. Problem solved."

"Maybe our problem will be solved, but theirs won't. Without an abundance of organic nutrients, the larvae will turn to the only other available source—each other. At the end of that long, brutal civil war, those last plump few will fight it out until only one remains. That last larva will only starve and die *after* devouring any part of itself it can fit into its hungry little mouth."

Charlie shook his head.

"Damn. All that makes a pill called the Abortionator 5000 seem kinda…"

"Compassionate." Mrs. Glimwicket finished his sentence for him. "Yes, that's why we've used them for the past few centuries. It enters the body through my digestive system, gently burrows through my intestinal wall to access my uterine sac, then uses micro laser bursts to eliminate all but the healthiest embryo. All without harming my biology or the baby. When birth comes shortly afterwards, we'll have just one priceless, wonderful larva to love and raise."

He took one last look at the pill before slipping it back into his pocket.

"I imagine you don't go around broadcasting that you have something like this in your pocket, so how'd the Silexi figure out what you were planning to do?"

"I might know how that happened," she said, sniffling. "In order for the pill to choose the most viable embryo to spare, we don't use it until right before the birth. We thought we had a few more weeks, so we didn't bring our pill with us. Then yesterday, after boarding the *Pineapple Express*, I started having contractions. Bob wasn't sure we'd make it back to the *Starseed* in time and didn't want to risk it, so he did something very un-Bob-like."

"That wasn't an order of twice-fried muratura blossoms he picked up from Lavaka, was it?"

"Oh, there were blossoms in there all right. They were delicious. But more importantly, hidden inside a fortune cookie, was an A5k. Exactly the model we needed. I have no idea how she acquired it, and we normally don't like making deals with Nadia, but we were desperate!"

Charlie sat up. "Wait, you *normally* don't like making deals with her? You mean this isn't the first time?"

"I'm not ashamed, Captain. She offered help with... things. When we arrived on the *Starseed* we had nothing. Rags. Not a single g-cred to our name. And now, with no one else to turn to, what in Andromeda were we supposed to do, Captain?"

"You could've come to me, man! You're one of the only people I know on the *Starseed*! I would've helped you, and with no snaky strings attached."

"That's exactly what Bob Jr. said. He thinks the world of you, you know. Never stops talking about how someday he's going to join your crew."

"Smart kid. But you might want to have a chat with him about finding a less dangerous occupation," said Charlie, motioning to Zylvya.

"We decided not to impose our troubles on you, Captain. Instead, we found the next best thing."

"Nadia," Charlie said, narrowing his eyes. "Hey MOM, is Mr. Bob Glimwicket currently aboard the *Pineapple Express?*"

"Yes, Captain." MOM's voice appeared in the air around them. "To the best of my knowledge, no one has boarded or disembarked from the ship since we left the Trapezia system."

"Okay, smartypants, then where exactly is Mr. Bob Glimwicket?"

"Sorry, Captain Hong, but I cannot disclose his location at this time."

Mrs. Glimwicket sighed. "Same answer as the last hundred times we asked her. Oh, my poor Bob..."

"MOM, if you can't tell me where he is now, then tell me his last known location that doesn't violate your privacy protocol."

"Mr. Bob Glimwicket was last picked up by my sensors in the mini-Ring."

"C'mon, MOM! Be more precise than that. Which shops was he near when he vanished?"

"Mr. Bob Glimwicket was last detected near GloBo Boba Tea Shop and S'vartan Exotic Spice Shop."

"Of course! He thought he'd be able to hide, but I found him!"

"I don't understand, Captain? You know where my Bob is hiding?"

"Of course! It's the one place on this ship where MOM's sensors can't penetrate."

"Lavaka," she said, looking momentarily relieved before looking worried again.

"You know it," Charlie said, hopping to his feet. "I'll head down there and ask that snake what she knows."

"Can you bring him back here with you, Captain?"

"I dunno. I hate to admit it, but Lavaka might be the safest place for him right now. If any of those Dregz get their hands on him, the Silexi might use that weird cube thingy."

"It's a p'ube," a voice called out from behind them.

Charlie spun around to find Cassie standing in an open doorway.

"How the hell'd you get in here? Swarm and I secured the mini-bridge doors so only official crew can get in!"

Before she could answer, his stoned mind finally processed what she'd said and he added quickly, "Wait, did you just say pube?"

"Right, that device the Silexi have is called a p'ube. Have you heard of a p'ube before? What's so funny, Captain? Did I get my Earther clothes wrong? It's my bald head, isn't it?"

Charlie stood half-laughing and half-coughing, unable to speak.

Cassandra's optical sensors scrolled rapidly as if she were reading a document only she could see. When they were done, they rolled up into her head.

"Outside of immature mammalian jokes about pubescent hair,

the word *p'ube* is no laughing matter. P'ube is short for *prison cube*, Captain. They're scary."

"What's so scary about a teeny tiny prison?"

"It's only tiny on the outside. On the inside, there's enough compacted space to hold entire worlds. And based on Silexi history, they've actually stuffed a planet inside, and they've been sending their prisoners there for centuries."

"There's a planet inside that little... p'ube?" Charlie said, stifling a chuckle.

"Yes. P'ubes are supposed to be a lost technology, destroyed by the Gal-Fed long ago. But there are rumors on the Outernet about a few that were never accounted for. Well, I think you just found one."

Cassie looked at Mrs. Glimwicket and her facial LEDs dimmed.

"Captain, you better not let them download her or Mr. Glimwicket into that thing," Cassie said. "Or they'll never get out again."

"Alright, alright. Calm down. No one's gonna get downloaded into anyone's p'ube—" Charlie stifled another laugh and tried to put on the most serious face he could muster. It wasn't easy since his eyelids were now drooping halfway across his bloodshot eyes and the corners of his mouth were upturned in a permanent grin.

Mrs. Glimwicket rested her furry forehead against the bars.

"Captain, if they catch Bob…"

"Bob?" asked Cassie. "I know Bob. He's a sweet little guy who comes into Nylf's all the time. Looks just like you, you know. Don't worry about Bob. He's safe back at the arcade the captain made me open in the Ring against my will."

"First of all, it's not the Ring. It's the *mini*-Ring. How many times do I have to remind people?"

"Secondly, you and all the other kids on this cruise needed something to keep you busy."

"Kid?! I'm not a kid!"

"Technically, I think you're like a year old," said Charlie. He looked her over. "Do you know if Nylf stamped you with a *built on* date?"

"Rude!" cried Cassie. "The correlation between age and mental capacity works differently for synthetic lifeforms! Plus, I guess I'm old enough to be the compulsory owner and operator of an arcade called *Cassie's Chassis*. What kind of name is that, Captain?"

"Like I said, Del used to talk about you. I think I got the phrase from him."

Cassie's facial LEDs turned neon pink and increased their brightness to 100%.

"He... actually said that about me? Del said the words *Cassie's Chassis* to you, and presumably the rest of the crew?"

"I dunno, I think so. Don't look so surprised. And I thought an arcade, the place where you've spent your whole short life, would be a good fit. Why not follow in your father's footsteps? He might even be so impressed he'll forget about you running away."

"Like I care what my dad thinks!"

"And lastly," Charlie said, ignoring her pouty animatronic face, "Mrs. Glimwicket was talking about Bob Sr., the other Bob Glimwicket, also known as *Mr.* Glimwicket. The Dregz are after him. They think he's out to kill Reticulus Rex, and as angry as he was when he left the summit hall, I wouldn't put it past him."

"Dregz? You mean those mean-looking thugs walking around the ship?" asked Cassie. "I passed them on the way over here. They rushed by and looked super pissed off."

"Well, shit." Charlie stood up and stretched. "I reckon Chuck Stonerly better go find out what the riff-raff are up to."

He turned to Mrs. Glimwicket.

"Don't worry, Mrs. Glimwicket. Bob's a smart guy. I'm sure he's just laying low until this all blows over."

"Captain," said MOM, "we have an emergency which requires your presence right away."

"Wait!" Charlie held up a finger. "I need one more big toke before you drop an emergency on me."

He pinched the joint to his mouth and sucked in as hard as he could, turning the last half inch to ash. He held the hit and counted to ten, then spewed a plume of smoke into the star-filled dome.

"Okay, I'm ready. Hit me with it."

"Emperor Reticulus Rex is dead."

22

Meanwhile, back on the *Starseed*, Del sat rooted in a four-inch terracotta pot balanced on his circular control console.

Without a brain or body, equipped with only a primitive excuse for a nervous system, he'd still been able to reason out his location precisely. But instead of allowing himself a millighatika of pride about his deductive reasoning skills, he felt only the same frustration and anguish that had haunted him since his forced transmigration.

Big deal, Del thought. *So I know where I am. It's not like it changes anything.*

It was the hum that gave it away. During the years he'd served as Chief of Technology, he'd taken hundreds of power naps on his control console. He'd cradle his head in his arms and let the vibration the console's smooth surface lull him to sleep. That was back when he had arms and a head and other appendages. Now, even without appendages or the need for sleep, he was still able to recognize the distinct vibration that rippled through his terracotta prison.

At least all the heavy jostling has finally stopped.

Ever since things went sideways on Zosavuta, when the

Obleck bounty hunter blasted him in the face with a stun ray, all he'd known was jostling.

First, it was his limp body being dragged and dropped. At least then he'd had the shifting weight of dead limbs to give him some sense of embodiment.

There were voices, too. Felt more than heard. Harsh and unintelligible, but recognizable as Reptilian.

Then there was one final thud and a chilling blast of what he assumed was some kind of particle beam. As the waves washed over him, he'd felt his mind becoming rapidly unhooked from his body's synapses like a million little zippers being unzipped all at once.

After a brief moment of drifting somewhere outside of time and space, his mind found something to latch onto. One by one, the incorporeal tendrils of his consciousness hooked themselves onto the only available object they could find: a common Earther plant known as a cactus. It wasn't a perfect fit by any means, but at least it had kept his mind from floating away.

Then came more jostling. So much so that he'd learned to distinguish between the different variants. There was the jostling of riding in a space vessel as it entered and exited atmospheres. There was the rhythmic jostling of being carried by a bipedal organism. There was the jostling of being picked up and set down, over and over again. At one point, early on, after some particularly intense jostling, there came the vibrations of angry voices followed by the sense that his pores were being saturated with cannabis smoke.

The tell-tale sign of being rescued by Captain Hong, he thought.

Ever since then, the jostling had become much more mellow. On a few recent occasions, there was a sudden jostling of someone whisking him away, then a soft vibration soothing his dry and thorny exterior. Had someone been talking quietly to him? Had they been trying to comfort him?

Without eardrums, the sounds were completely incomprehensible. Yet something about the rhythm of the vibrations told him that it was a voice, and something about the tone of the vibrations told him he was being taken care of and protected.

Then something went really wrong.

The jostling stopped. The movement stopped. The comforting vocal vibrations stopped. And most disconcerting, the cannabis smoke stopped.

How long had it been since his stomatic pores detected THC molecules in the air? Days? Weeks?

Time passed differently inside his mind than it did for his cactus body, which made the flow of time hard to follow. His thoughts felt like a hamster on crack running on a hamster wheel submerged in honey.

Stupid terracotta prison, he thought. *What I wouldn't give for just one finger!*

What could explain the sudden absence of pot smoke in the air? Had Captain Hong been replaced? Even with his haphazard schedule and his unorthodox leadership style, he never went too long without gathering the crew on the bridge for a smoke session.

Something's up, Del thought, putting his glochids and spines on high alert.

Suddenly the light falling on him intensified and a trickle of cool water seeped up from the surface of his console to flood his root system.

Mother sensed the stress he was under and responded using the only language a cactus could understand. At least she was around. Still, where was everyone else?

If only I could extend one little root through the drainage hole at the bottom of this terracotta pot, he thought. *Just a few swipes on my console. Just a few taps. Then I'd know what was happening and I could...*

Del's thoughts trailed off as he realized information alone wouldn't make any difference. He might know every last thing that was happening on the *Starseed*, but he was still stuck in a pot with no limbs, no mouth, and no weed.

His mind squirmed inside its pithy, waxy, spiky prison.

I could really go for a puff right about now. Just a tiny one. From Captain Hong's Golden Ticket *would be nice.*

Where is everyone?!

Just then, Del felt the faintest of vibrations ripple up through his clay pot into his root ball. He'd felt the sensation before and knew it was one of the spiral doors opening on the bridge.

Through the door a roar of chaos washed over him. Loud, violent vibrations that shook his spines. Perhaps even shouts and panic—it was too difficult to know without actual ears or audio sensors. On the coattails of the ruckus came particles of smoke that found their way into his open stomata. Not a single molecule contained a trace of THC. Whatever was burning, it wasn't cannabis.

As quickly as the door opened, it shut, cutting off both the smoke and the noise.

Uh, something's definitely wrong out there, he thought. *And I'm stuck here, all alone, unable to help. Mother, if you can hear me... I can't take it anymore! Send me someone or something to give me a sign that everything's okay. I can't stay in the dark much longer before my mind starts unraveling!*

Even with the limited senses of a succulent, he could tell he was no longer alone on the bridge. The first clue was the rhythmic series of small vibrations—bipedal footsteps. Slow and uneven, as if whoever it was was scuffling their feet as they walked. With each step the vibration grew slightly louder, which meant that someone was approaching.

Del tensed his spines, which really wasn't saying much. He felt the familiar sensation of being picked up, then the tiniest trace of warmth through his terracotta pot.

They're likely warm-blooded. Which eliminates most bots, Synths, and Reptoids, he thought, only slightly relieved.

That leaves about seventeen hundred sentient species. If only I could make a few taps on my console... I could narrow down the potential species... I could query an array of data from Mother's internal sensors... maybe even whip up a vocalization prog to let me type out words to communicate...

He sighed through a hundred thousand stomata at once and relaxed his spines. The truth was that he couldn't move a single root beyond imperceptible micro-movements. There would be no tapping, no swiping, no querying data, no communication of any kind until he was back in his body. Or *any* body that wasn't a stupid plant.

In the meantime, all he could do was hope that whoever had just picked him up didn't intend to smash him against the wall or feed him into a matter reclaimer.

Del felt a shadow fall across him. Puffs of moist air washed over him. Then a string of slow vibrations—vocalization, he guessed—rippled through both the air and whatever appendage was holding him. Someone was speaking. Even though he couldn't make out what they were saying, he could feel their tone was gentle and somewhat strained.

Del wouldn't have thought a cactus could recoil, but that's exactly what he felt himself do. From his topmost spine to his bottommost root, he winced in utter revulsion.

Something had penetrated the drainage hole at the bottom of his pot and was burrowing into his gritty soil. Whatever it was was long and skinny and somewhat hairy, almost like it was...

A root! he cried out from inside his four-inch-tall green prison. *Another plant is invading my soil!*

23

"Let me through, man! I'm the captain!" Charlie said to the dead-eyed, pig-nosed Dreg blocking the doorway. "Do you have bacon for brains or what?"

Over his shoulder Cassie said, "I'm not sure he understands you. These mercs never bonded with the ship, remember?"

"Good goddamn point, Cassie. Know what? It's about time we took care of that," he said, then blew a stream of white smoke into Pig Nose's face. The Dreg tried to wave it away, but not before a few tendrils got sucked up into his wide nostrils. He coughed and snorted, and Charlie could tell by the way his eyes glazed over, making them look more dead than before, the trick had worked. Pig Nose's brain was buzzed, and that was all it'd take to get communication flowing smoothly again.

"Can you hear me now? I'm Captain Charlie Hong, captain of the ship you're stinking up, and I demand that you let me into that room before I..." He trailed off, unsure of how to finish. "Step aside or else I'll..."

"I know you probably don't like taking advice from one year old," said Cassie, "but I think you're supposed to end threats with an actual threat."

"Thanks, I know how this works."

To Pig Nose he said, "Get your pig stank out of the way or you'll get more of this."

Charlie took another huge hit and blew it directly into Pig Nose's face. This time the Dreg greedily sniffed every last puff from the air before settling back into the doorframe with his arms across his chest.

"Alright, man. I see how it's gonna be. Cassie, hold this."

Charlie handed her his smoldering joint and fell into his best Bruce Lee stance.

"I didn't wanna have to do this in front of all your friends and your employer, but here we are, chump."

Pig Nose didn't respond. He just stared into the middle distance, drool dangling from his slack jaw and his eyebrows twitching excitedly, as if he were watching cartoons dance across his field of vision.

"Move, you imbecile!" cried a shrill voice from somewhere in the room. A slender grey hand shoved the Dreg aside, revealing Vree Voktal's cold black eyes and his lipless scowl.

"Captain Hong! *Where* have you been? Didn't that AI of yours tell you this was an emergency?"

Charlie dropped his fists of fury, relieved he didn't have to unleash them on anyone, then snatched the joint back from Cassie and stepped inside.

"We came as soon as we could," he said, glaring at Pig Nose, who seemed too stoned to care that he was standing face to face with the wall.

Vree Voktal was already through the short corridor that led to the master suite. He called out over his shoulder, "Hurry, Captain! We may yet be able to save His Majesty's heir!"

"Hair? That Reticulus Rex dude didn't have any hair to begin with," Charlie said to Cassie as they followed.

She shrugged and tried to look uninterested.

"Unless you mean the internal hairball thing MOM mentioned earlier."

"His *heir*, not his *hair*!" screeched Vree Voktal.

The room was cold, hard, and uninviting—apparently just how they like it. Instead of glistening walls of pineapple flesh and a smooth marble floor, everything was constructed from rough stone blocks. The only source of light was a faintly glowing orb that hovered near the ceiling and looked as if it'd rather be somewhere else.

Vree Voktal's robes fluttered behind him as he hurried across the room. Dregz blocked both doorways leading off from the main living space, but he swept them aside with a flick of the wrist and rushed through the door on the left.

Charlie and Cassie followed and found him kneeling beside the Emperor's body. Beside his hand lay a glass goblet with a few drops of purple liquid still clinging to the rim.

There were no obvious causes of death: no charred blaster shots, no puncture wounds, not a single drop of weird alien blood. But his chest wasn't moving and the glossy light in his eyes was no more. His rough grey skin, now pulled tight with rigor mortis, made him look like a frail statue entombed in flowing metallic robes.

There was no mistaking it, Emperor Reticulus Rex was dead.

Charlie scanned the room with his bloodshot eyes. "Where's E.T.?"

Vree Voktal also stood. "Eta Cerbo is in the next room. He's alive and your ship's computer says he's in good health, but he's completely unresponsive."

Charlie peeked into the next room. Eta Cerbo was lying peacefully in his bed, his chest moving up and down. It was a stonework room like the Emperor's, but the walls were covered with posters from *E.T.* and the floor was littered with action figures and toys from the movie.

"Well, at least he's okay, man."

"Okay?" cried Vree Voktal. "Captain, he's in a dead slumber! Nothing can wake him!"

"Damn. Sounds exactly like Zee," Charlie said. He took a puff from his joint and began pacing beside the dead emperor. "MOM, is there a Seeder on the *Pineapple Express* who happens to be a doctor?"

"Yes, Captain," MOM's voice droned from the air above them. "Two passengers on the *Pineapple Express* are registered as General Multi-species Practitioners."

"Two GMPs. Wow, man. We got pretty lucky."

Vree Voktal motioned to his dead emperor.

"Does His Majesty look lucky to you? We've lost our emperor, and we may be losing his only living heir in the next room! The Silexi have never gone without an Emperor, not for a single millighatika! His Majesty's bloodline has ruled for millennia without being broken! You must do something to recover His Majesty's heir at once!"

Charlie nodded. "MOM, explain to the two GMPs what happened and then toke them here as quickly as possible."

"Sorry, Captain. Neither doctor is available at this time. One of them is currently undetectable by my sensor array, and the other is detectable but otherwise indisposed."

"What the hell do you mean they're undetectable and indisposed? We have an emergency here! E.T. could be dying, man!"

"Sorry, Captain, but as I explained to you previously, I cannot locate Mr. Glimwicket anywhere on the ship, although I'm certain he hasn't left. And Mrs. Glimwicket is currently detained in the mini-Brig, which disqualifies her from providing medical assistance."

"The Glimwickets are the only GMPs on the *Pineapple Express*?" asked Charlie, then added, "Wait, the Glimwickets are doctors?"

"Affirmative, Captain, on both questions. If you would like, I can search the Outernet for the most highly-rated immersive virtual reality video tutorials pertaining to Silexi physiology so that you may ascertain a preliminary diagnosis. Then you prescribe or provide relevant medical treatment based on your findings."

"No way, online medical advice is the worst."

Charlie sighed and ran a hand through his short afro.

"So the Glimwickets are the only goddamn doctors on the ship. What do you say, Vree? Should I toke in Mrs. Glimwicket to check on E.T?"

"I should say not!" screeched Vree, gasping. "Both of those *savages* are prime suspects!"

"Whoa, hold up," Charlie said, splaying his hands. "The Glimwickets didn't kill anyone, man. In fact, we don't even know if there's been a murder. No offense, but old Rex looked pretty ancient to begin with. For all we know, he had a heart attack or something."

"How dare you insult His Majesty like that! You heard him announce the threats against his life! And now… this!" Vree Voktal's almond-shaped eyes thinned to mere slivers. "I demand that you find these suspects and bring them to justice!"

"I know this is an emotional time, dude," said Charlie. "But you gotta keep it together. Listen, Mrs. Glimwicket has been with me the entire time. You have my word she hasn't left the mini-Brig since we put her there."

"What of the other one? The one who *threatened* His Majesty in front of everyone? Why can't you or your Chief of Security find him and throw him in the Brig with his genocidal mate?"

"Funny story about that," said Charlie, blushing slightly. "We can't locate Swarm, either. Well, not precisely. It's complicated. But that's not your problem, and it's not related to any of this."

"We all saw his aggressive behavior during the summit! He looked absolutely enraged and had to be restrained by those vines! Surely this Swarm is another suspect!"

"First of all, don't call me Shirley. Secondly, Swarm wasn't *enraged*, man. He was just… a little horny, that's all. Okay, maybe *a lot* horny. But the point is that his mind was on something other than murder."

Vree Voktal threw his arms into the air.

"Dear Andromeda, our Silexi dynasty has been brought to its knees by an imbecile ape!"

"Okay, thirdly, we've already established that the 'ape' thing is pretty offensive, so let's not use that phrase again, got it? Fourthly, no one's losing their civilization. Don't be a drama queen, Vree. Your people must have some kind of backup plan in case this sort of thing happens, right?"

Vree Voktal plopped onto a stone sofa and exhaled a lungful of air. He snatched the smoldering doob from Charlie, took a drag, then stared into the middle distance.

"If they both die, then I'm next in line for the throne. *Me*. But I am not qualified. I do not carry His Majesty's blood in my veins."

"So what you're saying," Charlie said, snatching his joint back, "is that *you're* also a suspect?"

Vree Voktal broke out into a coughing fit, his black eyes bulging from his almond-shaped sockets.

"Mm-hmm, don't act all surprised. Who discovered the bodies anyway? I bet it wasn't Bacon Brains over there in the next room, or any of the Dregz. Their next meal depends on keeping you three Silexi alive. But you…" He took a long toke from the joint and nodded his head as if everything was falling into place. "You had motive *and* opportunity."

Vree Voktal jumped to his feet.

"Nonsense! I'll prove it! I'll save the heir myself! After all, as the only living Silexi aboard this ship, I'm the most qualified to help him."

"Hey Captain," Cassie said. "I don't think you should let a prime suspect anywhere near the victim. Otherwise he might try to finish the job."

"Good call. Stay put, Vree. And Cassie, could you please stop poking the dead Emperor?"

She sat cross-legged beside the corpse, leaning over it with her optical sensors opened as wide as they'd go, and poked at Reticulus's cheek with one of her rubberized robotic digits.

"How do you know he's really dead? His software, I mean. Can't his memory chips be removed and installed into another unit?" She leaned in close to peer into the corpse's dead eye. "Do you mind if I take a look inside? I've never seen a dead body before, and I wonder how his structural architecture could support such a large head. Why are you both looking at me like that?"

"Get away from him!" shrieked Vree Voktal. He slid off the sofa, fell onto his knees, and held his arms out over the body in a protective posture. "*Your* kind is not fit to touch His Majesty's body!"

"Oh, come on, man," cried Charlie. "Now you got something against robots?"

"How could you bring such an infernal machine with you, Captain Hong? We live, we die—as life intends! We don't spit in the face of creation by going on and on, never aging, like *their* kind!"

"Alright, Cassie, that's enough morbid curiosity for today," Charlie said, pulling her away from the body. "We'll pick up a Silexi anatomy lesson from the Outernet later."

"How dare you lay one oily, *synthetic* finger on His Majesty!" cried the Silexi. "That's it! I'll be downloading you, the Glimwickets, and any of the other suspects into our portable prison cube while an investigation is conducted!"

"Whoa there, man. Not so fast. No one gets locked up in your p'ube."

He paused to stifle a chuckle, then quickly returned to a serious demeanor.

"But we still need two things right away: some medical help for E.T and an official investigation to find out what, if any, crime has been committed here. MOM, please toke E.T. to the mini-Infirmary and place him in a secure room with all sorts of gadgets to monitor his health, and report his status to me and Vree Voktal every thirty minutes."

"Sorry, Captain, but we don't currently have a mini-Infirmary aboard the *Pineapple Express*. Would you like me to create one now?"

"Yeah, of course!" answered Charlie. "Somewhere on the main

deck, near the mini-bridge. But lock the door so that it only opens for me. Understood?"

"Yes, Captain, I understand."

"Preposterous!" cried Vree Voktal.

"Bare with me me until we get some shit sorted out around here. MOM, how long will it take?"

"The mini-Infirmary is ready. I am currently stocking it with the best medical equipment and supplies that I could find on the Outernet." A large wisp of greenish vapor burst from Eta Cerbo's room, swirled around Pig Nose, and zipped down the corridor.

"Dang, that was fast." Charlie said, his joint dangling from his lips. "I was hoping that might buy me a little more time to think, but let's be honest, more time wouldn't have helped much. Anyway, now that E.T. is secure, the investigation will be a snap, even without Swarm and Zee."

"It will?" asked Cassie.

"Of course, man." Charlie took a long drag from his joint. "We might not have cameras posted all over the ship, but we got something way better. Check this out."

He cleared his throat and tilted his face upwards.

"MOM, who killed Emperor Reticulus Rex?"

"*His Majesty* Emperor Reticulus Rex!" corrected Vree Voktal.

"Sorry, Captain Hong, I am not aware of any murders taking place on the *Pineapple Express*."

The trio looked at the corpse, glanced at each other, then turned their attention back to the ceiling.

"You do see the dead body lying at our feet, don't you?" he asked.

"Yes, Captain, my sensors have identified a lifeless Silexi body lying near you. Would you like me to dispose of it?"

"No!" cried Charlie and Vree Voktal simultaneously.

Charlie sighed.

"Okay, let's try again. MOM, this is your chance to prove you're a stable, reliable computer interface, like Mother back on the *Starseed*."

"Sorry, Captain, but Mother is currently not accessible from the *Pineapple Express*. I would be happy to relay a message to her if you would—"

"Nope again!" interrupted Charlie, shaking his head. "Listen, just give me a list of everyone who entered this room after the Emperor turned in for the night, but before he died."

"Affirmative, Captain Hong. The passengers who entered the Emperor's quarters are: Emperor Reticulus Rex, Eta Cerbo, and Vree Voktal."

Charlie cast a suspicious eye at the lone Silexi and continued, "List the times when Vree Voktal entered the room."

"Vree Voktal escorted Emperor Rex and Eta Cerbo here after the peace summit proceedings had ended. He stayed for twelve point four seconds."

"Was the Emperor alive when he left?"

"Yes, Captain. Both Emperor Rex and Eta Cerbo were alive and in relatively good health when he left."

"When was the next time Vree entered this room?"

"Vree Voktal arrived one hour ago."

The Silexi scoffed and shook his metallic robes.

"He was long dead when I arrived!"

"MOM, is he telling the truth?"

"My determination is that there is a fifty percent chance he is telling the truth. Yet, keep in mind that my lack of familiarity with Silexi biology hinders my ability to detect prevarications with one hundred percent accuracy. I would be happy to search the Outernet to find more data on their physiology and reassess if you would like."

"No, nevermind," said Charlie. "MOM, when exactly did things take a turn for these two?"

"Eta Cerbo fell into a coma four hours and thirteen minutes ago. Emperor Rex's vital signs ceased four hours and ten minutes ago."

"And you're sure no one else was here with them?"

"No, Captain. My sensors indicate no other lifeforms present during that time, nor at any time between the times you've indicated."

"This is absurd, Captain!" roared Vree Voktal. "Your ship's computer has clearly been tampered with!"

"It's true, Captain," added Cassie. "I'll be the last one to criticize another synthetic lifeform, but she's no help at all."

Charlie took another puff and smiled.

"On the contrary. From what I just heard, MOM confirmed that I was right after all. There was no murder, man. The old dude just died from old age. And E.T. probably witnessed his old man having a hairball attack or something and went into shock. Case closed, as far as I'm concerned."

"Case closed?" shrieked Vree Voktal. "A sovereign diplomat aboard your ship has suspiciously died after multiple threats were made toward him! I demand justice!"

"Hey Vree, I demand you chill out and think for a second. We still have a peace accord to facilitate. Which means you'll be clocking some overtime, because we'll need you to sign the treaty and all that peace stuff."

Vree Voktal was kneeling beside the body with his hands just inside the dead emperor's royal robes. "It's gone!"

"What's gone?" Cassie asked, kneeling beside him.

"The Silexi portable prison cube! It has never left His Majesty's possession!" cried Vree as he rummaged through the Emperor's robes. "Not in over a century, not since He inherited the throne from His father! Oh, Andromeda, it's been stolen! She took it! The synthetic monster! While she was leaning over him, poking him, defiling his body!"

"Whatever!" said Cassie. "I didn't touch the old dead guy's p'ube!"

Charlie had to grit his teeth to keep himself from busting up laughing.

"Everyone, calm down! That's an order! Maybe he just set it down to take a dump or hid it in his sock drawer. MOM, scan the room and find the Emperor's missing, uh, prison cube thingy."

"Yes, Captain. Scanning now." A moment later her artificial voice returned. "I have performed a scan of the entire Silexi quarters and have found no trace of the device to which you are referring."

Charlie expelled all the smoke from his lungs and started pacing around the corpse.

"Okay, let's see if I got this straight. We have one dead emperor, one comatose heir, a missing p'ube, and multiple suspects—yet no clear leads. I say it was natural death, but Vree, a prime suspect himself, says it was murder. And on top of that, I have seven sick plants, my entire crew is currently out of service, and, oh yeah, I have a goddamn peace accord to finish."

He stopped to look at Vree and Cassie.

"Vree, you have skin in the game, too, man! We gotta make this peace thing happen. Get that noodle of yours working on a treaty that those others dudes can't resist signing. Cassie, you're... wait, why are you even here? Who cares. You can help me with the investigation of whatever the *hell* this is."

"Murder, that's what it is," a deep, gritty voice announced from behind them.

Charlie and the others spun around to find a tall, dark, bipedal figure leaning against the stone archway that led back to the main living area. The broad-shouldered silhouette wore a trench coat and fedora. A strip of neon red ran across its face from ear to ear like some kind of hi-tech visor.

A cigarette ember flared in the shadows under the hat's brim, but it was too dim to make out any facial features. The figure exhaled a cloud of smoke into the air and groaned.

"And it looks like I'm just in time."

24

"Dude, this is a restricted area," Charlie said. "Go play with the other Dregz."

The silhouette gave a low chuckle and said, "Sorry, kid. I work alone."

"Kid? You know who you're talking to, man? I happen to be the captain of the *Pineapple Express*. If you're not a Dreg, then you must be a Seeder on vacation, and very lost right now. Why don't you head back to the mini-Ring, grab an exotic boba or something." Charlie squinted at the figure. "Are you wearing your complimentary aloha shirt under that jacket? They're nice, man. Each is a one-of-a-kind, but also one-size-fits-all. Literally, the fabric is like magic, it just conforms to whatever body type and size you need."

"Is this a cruise help desk or the scene of a crime?" shrieked Vree Voktal.

Ignoring the Silexi, Charlie said to the silhouette, "Anyway, see your way out so we can solve this…"

"Murder. I already told yuh, but you just ain't listenin'," growled the silhouette. "And I ain't here on vacation. I'm here on business, as always."

He stepped into the dim lighting of the Emperor's cavernous bedroom.

Charlie stood staring at the second human he'd seen since leaving Earth. The man looked like a hard-boiled detective plucked from the pages of a golden age mystery novel—with one obvious addition to the getup: a chunky metal visor stretched over his eyes and pulsating with red light.

When he spoke the half-cigarette between his lips bobbed up and down.

"And from what I just overheard, you ain't solving anything any time soon."

He held out a hand and Charlie shook it.

"Nice to make your acquaintance, Captain Hong," the man said. "Of course I know your name. I know a lot more than that. Don't look so surprised, kid. When I take a job, I do my homework."

With one hand Charlie swiped at the cigarette smoke billowing toward him and covered his mouth with the other.

"What job, man?"

"Solving this murder."

"Who are you?" asked Cassie from over Charlie's shoulder.

"My actual name is an encrypted 128-bit string, but you can call me Crimebot." He tugged on the brim of his fedora. "I've been hired to provide for all your crime-solving needs."

Charlie looked at Cassie, then at Vree Voktal. "I didn't hire a retro-futuristic cyborg cop. Did either of you?"

"If we're gonna work together, Captain, we gotta get one thing straight right now," he said, flicking his cigarette into the corner. The floor opened up underneath it to catch and consume it without ever touching it. "I ain't no 'borg. I ain't no bot. And I sure as hell ain't no *droid*. I'm a Synth."

He pulled a new cigarette from inside his coat, popped it between his lips, and lit it with a tiny blue torch flame that appeared at the tip of his pointer finger.

"Okay, fine. You're a Synth with a cool finger flame, and I'm the captain of this ship. But I didn't hire you. Also, smoking is prohibited on the *Pineapple Express,* man! Put it out!"

"Huh," grunted the Synth before taking another slow drag. "Listen, kid, my contract was signed by two lifeforms who claimed to be crew members of this ship. One smuggled me aboard, and the other booted me up."

"Of *course,* man!" cried Charlie. "The huge metal case Zee picked up from Lavaka!"

"Bingo. I've been laying low in her quarters, twiddlin' my solenoids, just in case a major crime was committed—say, robbery or murder. Both of which you seem to have here. And before you protest again, let me point out that you have some high-stakes diplomatic obligations to fulfill. Your crew wanted to make sure that if trouble started brewing, you'd be able to focus on your primary objective."

"Goddammit, Zee! I can't believe you'd go behind my back like that! And conspiring with *Nadia*?!"

Charlie took a few quick puffs on his joint, relaxed his face, and sighed.

"For her to do that, she must've really believed it was important. And she must've trusted you. So, I guess it makes logical sense to let you help with the investigation."

"Logic? Humans and logic go together like oil and water, kid. Your tendency for the irrational would be funny if it weren't so sad, but I'll admit this is the most logical decision you've made so far. Keep it up and we just might get through this thing in one piece."

"Whatever, dude. The case is yours, under one condition. No more smoking on the ship, man!"

"Aren't you smoking right now, Captain?" asked Vree Voktal, looking confused.

Charlie held up what was left of his smoldering joint.

"This is marijuana. Ganja. It's good for you. It's the closest thing to real magic there is. Not like those cancer sticks *he's* smoking, full of addictive and toxic chemicals. C'mon, man! That shit has you suckin' on its ass while it farts death into your mouth."

"Yeah, kid, well *that* shit will land you a one-way ticket to Vekst," Crimebot said.

"Vekst?" Vree Voktal asked.

"A prison planet," answered Cassie. "Kinda like the one your boss carried around his neck, but not confined to a quantum-compression chamber."

"Out in the open? So the inmates can escape! Preposterous!"

"I'll tell you what's preposterous, man. Throwing people in jail for cannabis while those death fartsticks he's smoking are widely available at every spaceport in the quadrant. I say, fuck those squares at the Galactic Federation and fuck their dumb laws. We don't acknowledge their authority on my ship. On the *Pineapple Express,* weed is legal. And encouraged. And sometimes required when you're kickin' it with me."

Crimebot shrugged.

"I don't work for Gal-Fed. I'm programmed to enforce laws according to local jurisdiction. Your ship, your rules."

"That's right. We play by my rules, and my rules say that unless you put that cig out right now, I'll be forced to—"

Crimebot interrupted Charlie's empty threat by blowing smoke directly into his face. Charlie winced and started waving it away, then suddenly relaxed. He sniffed directly into the billowing cigarette smoke and screwed up his face in confusion.

"Gross," whined Cassie. "Does it smell as toxic as it looks? Are you dying right now?"

"No, actually," Charlie said, smiling. "I don't smell a thing. It's like it's not there at all. Hey, it must be the same molecular dissolution field MOM threw up around Mrs. Glimwicket's personal atmosphere to keep my pot smoke away from her. Uh, thanks, MOM."

"Of course, Captain. I am here to protect and serve."

Crimebot shook his head, but didn't speak. He took one last drag before flicking his unfinished cigarette away.

"Are we squared up, kid? Am I free to do my job now?" he asked.

Charlie nodded and plucked a joint from his afro.

"But first, I need to introduce you to a very dear friend of mine. Meet *Golden Ticket*."

25

Swarm focused all of his willpower onto his bottommost pair of limbs, commanding them to keep the rest of him steady while they learned to walk again.

To bipedal organisms that never forget, learning how to walk again would seem like a huge pain in the ass. To Swarm, who'd relearned how to walk dozens of times in his life, it was just a side effect of morphic coagulation.

His legs jerked him in awkward strides toward the ever-retreating white aura of the *Pineapple Express's* augmented guidance system. Swarm's head, the leader, ran down the list of other body parts.

To his two pairs of arms, he thought, *I don't want any more nonsense from you four. Stay folded across my chest and we won't have trouble.*

To his twitching antennae, he thought, *For smeg's sake, you two, just relax! We're almost done coagulating.*

Things are better than fine, Swarm's feet reported to his head. *Still feels like we're walking on air.*

Shut up, down there! Swarm's head raged. *We're all together again, you hear me? No more disparate thoughts, or I'll shake you off and leave you back in our quarters!*

The crowd of voices inside him quieted and allowed themselves to be merged back into one, singular consciousness. The mental side of morphic coagulation always took much longer than the physical side and always left him with a temporary bout of multi-personality disorder—and a crushing headache.

This wasn't the first time he'd wrestled with morphic destabilization since joining the crew of the *Starseed*. But the way things were headed, it would be his last.

There was no shame in choosing to leave. In fact, choice had little to do with it. Something amazing had happened. Something utterly impossible. A miracle. To deny such a gift would be like spitting in the face of Fate itself.

Only a fool would consider giving up a gift like that just to stick around for a job that has them guarding a giant smegging fruit.

He knew Mother would understand and support his decision. He suspected even Zylvya would be able to see things from his point of view and wish him well. Squishy was healing nicely in his Restoratube, and he had Sally to protect him.

Swarm wasn't so sure he'd have the same luck with Captain Hong. The captain was already short two lieutenants and would do anything to stop his dwindling crew from losing yet another key player.

It wasn't that he cared what his crewmates—or anyone else for that matter—thought of him. The only part of his decision that made him uncomfortable was how absolutely helpless they all were without him. Especially with Captain Hong at the helm.

What a smegging disaster that Earther ape had been.

One disaster after another. Leaving the *Starseed* in his hands would be like flying it straight to Thuban and tossing the Reptilians the keys.

They'll be fine, he thought. *The ole gal's been around since the galaxy formed. She'll be just fine without me.*

"That's why you're going to march in there," he rattled aloud as if he were ordering a low-ranking officer, "look him right in the face, and tell him what you've decided."

"Talking to yourself again, eh, Bugbrain?" said a familiar feminine voice over his shoulder.

"You have no idea." Swarm held his triangular head and groaned. "It's good to see you back on your feet, Zee. You had us worried."

"Ditto. The last thing I remember before I passed out was watching your meetles dissolve and skitter off after the Dregz. I thought maybe a battle had broken out and I was missing all the fun."

"There was no battle," he said, his mandibles clacking nervously while he spoke. "Well, maybe thousands of miniature battles, but not of a violent nature. Not *too* violent. Anyway, you should know that in between *battles* I sent a meetle to check on you."

"Wow. That really warms my sap," said Zylvya. She cocked her head to one side and added, "But you're not making any sense. Miniature battles? Oh no... did your meetles run into trouble?"

"No, not exactly trouble. Let's save that explanation for the captain. I'd rather only have to say what I'm about to say one time."

She shrugged.

"Your call. I'm just glad we're both back. And hey, look around, Charlie didn't blow the ship up while the two of us were out of commission."

"Let's not jump to conclusions. We haven't seen the whole ship yet."

"Give him a break, Bugbrain. He morpho-printed the *Pineapple Express* with his mind. That says something, doesn't it?"

"It means he has the mental capacity of a child. He could have dreamed up any ship, something revolutionary in the field of starships. Instead, we're floating through the quadrant in a giant Earther fruit."

"Maybe it's my botanical side speaking, but I think it has a certain charm to it."

"The walls are edible, Zee. That's just weird."

"Weird or not, I've never heard of a Seeder doing anything like it before. He built a whole ship from the *Starseed's* substrate in less than a day."

"Mother did all the work."

"Don't play dumb. We're bonded with her, just like all Seeders, but Charlie is different. Have you noticed the tech he morphs? He doesn't use hubdough like the rest of us. For all I know, he's never even heard of hubdough."

"Smegging hell, he'd probably try to eat it."

"He directly morpho-prints really advanced stuff, Swarm. Tech that's not even from Earth. Tech he has no business knowing about beyond seeing it once on the Outernet. It all prints as effortlessly as one of his stupid joints. And speaking of his joints, I've been meaning to ask you something about that strain he never shuts up about. Have you ever noticed that—?"

"There's no time for that now," interrupted Swarm. "The Trapezian peace summit is our top priority. We should focus on repairing any damage the Captain's done and get all three sides back on the path to peace. The sooner we do that, the sooner we can drop them off at their system and get back to the *Starseed*. Then you can study Captain Hong's strain all you want. That is, if the ship hasn't already been captured by the Reptilians."

They walked in silence for a moment, then Zylvya shot him a sideways glance.

"You're in quite the mood today. The *Starseed's* perfectly safe. Mother knows how to take care of herself."

"Well, I'd feel better about things if you'd stayed behind like we agreed. Who knows what trouble Vargoni's led the 'Seed into?"

"You have no idea…" she said under her breath.

"What was that?" barked Swarm.

"Uh, just, on my way here I stopped by the mini-bridge to grab a drink from the mini-fridge and—"

"You know you can just say *bridge* and *fridge* when Captain Hong's not here, right? All that 'mini' talk is giving me a mini-migraine."

"I disagree. I think the prefix is a very practical naming convention for keeping track of two ships at one time."

"Who's keeping track of two smegging ships at once?" grumbled Swarm. "We're here, and the *Starseed's* hundreds of lightyears away—again, assuming it hasn't blown up or fallen into Reptilian hands yet. Where's the confusion, Zee?"

"Right. Good point. Anyway, I stopped the mini-bridge and Mrs. Glimwicket filled me in on how the first peace summit meeting ended. I can't believe they insisted on locking that innocent woman up like a caged animal. On top of that, no one can find Mr. Glimwicket. She said Charlie had a hunch, but then the call came in about the murder."

Swarm's feet stopped and his antennae went rigid.

He slowly turned his triangular head toward Zylvya, blinked his compound eyes once, then exploded.

"Murder?!" he roared. "Why did it take you this smegging long to mention a *murder*?"

Zylvya's wood-grained cheeks flooded with a rosewood stain, but she clenched her fists and met his gaze head-on.

"*You're* the Chief of Security! What's *your* excuse for being unaware of a murder that took place right under your antennae?"

"We've lost so much smegging time," Swarm groaned. "We need to lock down every deck, doubly for the scene of the crime, assemble a list of suspects, notify the passengers of possible searches and seizures, then—"

"Don't worry about all that," interrupted Zylvya. "From what Mrs. Glimwicket said, Charlie and his, uh, contractor, are very close to solving the case."

"Captain Hong hired a contractor? What kind of contractor?"

"A crime investigator bot."

"A smegging *machine*?!"

"One of the old models from before the colonies were scattered. The human colony who built him loaded his electronic brain with terabytes of media from Earth, millions of crime novels, movies, and serials. Apparently he's pretty good at his job. I guess solving crimes can't be too hard for someone who has a copy of every crime file in the Gal-Fed transplanetary data repository saved to their memory core."

"How do you know so much about this thing? Wait a second… that big metal case you picked up from Nadia wasn't full of spare togas, was it?"

"It was Crimebot. That's what it calls itself. Nylf hooked me up before we left the *Starseed*. I thought it'd be a good backup plan in case anything weird happened."

"A machine like that undermines my authority as Chief of Security!" he roared, stomping furiously through a crowd of Seeders who'd stopped to take bites from the glistening golden walls.

Zylvya bowed an apology to them and sped to catch up. She grabbed one of his upper arms and swung him to face her.

"You're being a real prick right now, you know that? At some point you have to trust the rest of us to pick up the slack when you're not around. If you're *that* afraid we're going to screw things up, then why don't you stop freaking out whenever that Dreg with the holographic mask…"

She trailed off, realization flashing in her emerald eyes.

"During the peace meeting, before I passed out… I didn't only see your red meetles running up the wall, did I? There were other meetles. Purplish meetles."

She looked up at him. "I get it now. You're leaving us, aren't you?"

"We're here," Swarm said, yanking his arm free. "Let's go talk to the Captain."

The round aperture-like door swirled open to reveal a wall of smoke. It was illuminated from above by a hazy smear of pink, purple, and blue lights as well as from a myriad of tiny individual lights darting and flittering inside the thick smoke.

"I thought this was supposed to be the Captain's grow room," Zylvya said.

Swarm shrugged both sets of shoulders.

"Maybe this part of the ship exploded after all."

"Boom!" Charlie called out from somewhere inside the cloud.

He shushed an outburst of giggles before adding, "Explode *this*, squares!"

From inside the cloud came the gritty sparking of a lighter, a gurgling of water, a swift whoosh of air, and more giggles. Five seconds later someone exhaled slowly, fighting the urge to hack up the resinous gunk clinging to the walls of their lungs. The cloud of smoke grew slightly denser.

Zylvya held her head.

"I think another headache is coming on. MOM, please filter out 100% of that smoke from my personal atmosphere."

"Same for me, MOM," rattled Swarm. "But keep my filter at 80%."

He noticed her staring at him.

"What? I'm gonna need a little something to take the edge off the conversation we're about to have."

"Acknowledged," MOM's voice replied flatly, "Your personal atmospheres have been adjusted according to your preferences."

"Don't stand there with the door open, man! You're lettin' all the smoke out!"

Swarm sighed.

"I'm glad to see the Captain's taking a murder on his ship so seriously."

"I can hear multiple voices in there," she said quietly. "If Crimebot is one of them, then there's a good chance the murder has already been solved."

"Great, then all we'd have left to do is repair whatever damage this murder has caused to the Trapezian peace process."

"I hope your new girlfriend knows what a whiney little bitch you are," Zylvya said, stepping through the wall of smoke before he could respond.

26

STANDING INSIDE THE HUGE CLOUD OF SMOKE, YOU'D HAVE NO IDEA you were in one of the most sophisticated cannabis grow rooms in the galaxy. You'd have no idea you were in a room at all.

If you were Charlie Hong, you'd think you'd died and gone to heaven.

Charlie emerged from the smoke, threw his arms around his crewmates, and squeezed.

"Holy shit!" cried Charlie. "I'm so happy you're both okay!"

"We're glad to see you, too, Captain."

Zylvya laid an arm across his back and nudged Swarm with the other.

Swarm tapped a claw on Charlie's shoulder and grunted, "Yes, it's good to see you haven't blown up the ship yet."

Charlie looked them over with a big, dopey grin.

"What the hell happened to you guys?"

Zylvya put a hand to her temple and winced.

"Besides the migraines, the narcolepsy, and the coma, I couldn't tell you. I should probably see a doctor when we get back to the *Starseed*. But the important thing is that I'm doing fine now, and I feel great."

"Didn't you just say you were getting another headache?"

asked Swarm. "We have two doctors here on the *Pineapple Express*. I met with one of them the other day for, uh, similar reasons, and they were a great help."

"*That* was who was in the booth with you!" cried Charlie, his bloodshot eyes widening.

"Booth?" asked Zylvya, then answered her own question. "You mean the other night in Lavaka when we all ran into one another?"

"Exactamundo! Mr. Glimwicket was behind the tapestry, wasn't he?"

The large red insectoid grew suddenly limp.

"Smegging good guess, Captain."

"No way, man! That wasn't a guess, it was a... a..."

"Logical deduction, kid," a voice called out from the smoke.

"That's right, *deduction*. I already knew about the two doctors on the ship, and that one of them had been locked up in the mini-brig since the start of the summit. That only left Mr. Glimwicket, and the last time I saw you two together was at Lavaka. The only thing I can't figure out is how Mr. Glimwicket slipped out of the booth without any of us seeing."

"Good luck finding a booth in that place that doesn't have a secret exit," said Zylvya. "He must have slipped outside, then doubled back to pick up the pill for his wife. He couldn't leave without it, plus, it seemed to exonerate him from meeting with Swarm."

She turned to face Swarm with a raised eyebrow.

"We had just concluded our business," he explained, "when I stepped outside the booth to find you both standing there. We didn't want to risk being seen together, which is why we chose Lavaka in the first place. I closed the tapestry to make sure the doctor would be able to sneak out, just like you said."

Charlie started to pace before them like a pit boss hounding his dealers. He shook his head and sighed dramatically.

"Don't get me wrong, I'm really stoked that you're both back on your feet again. But, guys, this is what happens when you take personal time off during an important mission. You miss things. Murders. Peace accords. Plus, I've told some really hilarious puns that are all gone now, like space dust in the solar winds, man. But I'm willing to let it slide, since we've already solved everything."

Swarm tilted his head and rattled, "The murder or the peace accord?"

"Both!" Charlie said, bobbing his head.

Swarm produced a rough, throaty growl that Charlie had learned to equate to an insectoid sigh.

"Seriously, man, we got everything covered. We have a solid plan for finding said solutions. In fact, we got so ahead of everything we decided to celebrate with a little clam-bake sesh while I checked on my girls."

Zylvya turned to Swarm.

"Looks like Captain Hong has everything under control. But before he explains what I'm sure will be an airtight plan, I'd like to get back to hearing where you've been for the past day."

Swarm stood stoic with both pairs of arms folded across his chest.

"Captain Hong, you're the second *Starseed* captain I've served under, but I've served under multiple commanders throughout my career. I offer you the same respect and candor I offered to them, which I hope might help shed light on what I'm about to tell you. See, Captain—"

"He's quitting!" A voice called out from the smoke, followed by chuckles.

Swarm's four arms fell to his sides.

"Who the smeg is *that*?"

Zylvya cupped her hands around her mouth.

"Crimebot? I know you're in there! Come out of that cloud where I can see you!"

Raspy laughter erupted from the smoke.

"Get over here right now! That's an order!"

The voice sighed and grunted, then a bulky wraith stepped through the smoke toward them.

Zylvya reached out, grabbed the figure by the scruff of his neck, and started pulling it toward the door.

"I can *not* believe you're getting high on the job! I'm so disappointed in you!" she scolded. "Do you know what I went through conspiring with that slimy bitch just to smuggle you onto this ship?"

"I just want to clarify that we have plenty of room and there was really no need to smuggle anyone in a metal case," interjected Charlie.

"You shush, Charlie!" She turned her attention back to Crimebot. "Do you have any idea how embarrassing this is? We hired you to help in case of a serious crime, and this is the service we get? I'm tempted to leave you a one-star review!"

"Sorry, boss," Crimebot said, pulling his fedora low over his visor. "The Captain ordered me. Said it'd help me wean off those cancer sticks."

"You can't get cancer! You're a robot!"

"Don't call him that!" Cassie emerged from the smoke next to Charlie. "He's a Synth! And stop bullying him! You know he can't disobey you or fight back! Those stupid rules of robotics aren't fair!"

Zylvya sighed and let go of Crimebot. She closed her eyes and began massaging her temples.

"Great. You're here, too? Does your dad know you're here getting high with these stoners?"

Cassie's angst dissolved at the mention of her father.

"My father designed me to be free, not bound by the rules of robotics. I do as I please. Just like you meatbags. Besides, I don't do drugs. I just liked the pretty lights and decided to sit and draw."

"Wonderful," said Zylvya. "Who else is hiding back there?"

"Just one more. Habu, as usual," answered Charlie.

"Yo!" a raspy voice called out from the smoke.

"Enough!" rattled Swarm. "Captain Hong and his crew have

important business to discuss. Everyone who's not officially part of the crew needs to leave. Now!"

"Crimebot can stay though, right? He's *officially* my homeboy now! We bonded over solving crime."

"You bonded over your bong, Captain," Swarm grumbled. "At a time when we need to keep our wits about us. Don't you smegging get it? There's been a murder, which means there's a murderer somewhere on the ship. Until we know who it is, why they risked it, and whether or not they'll kill again, we can't sit around listening to music and getting high!"

"I agree with Swarm on this, Captain. I didn't hire Crimebot to get high and hang out with you. If he wants to do that, he should look into joining our crew."

Zylvya's eyes involuntarily flickered toward Swarm as she said the last part.

"Hired!" cried Charlie, pumping a fist in the air. "No question about it. Crimebot is hired. Done deal, man!"

"Listen, kid," said Crimebot, "whether our solution is right or wrong, you should probably listen to your crew. Same thing I told ya. Whoever killed will kill again. You can bet your CPU on it. In the meantime, you've got important business to attend to while I go find out what kind of coffee you serve in this pineapple of yours."

Crimebot popped a joint between his lips and sparked it up with his finger torch. Zylvya snatched it away before he could take a hit.

"Don't worry, ma. I'll start resetting all my subsystems now. I'll be sober by dinnertime."

Zylvya's emerald eyebrows leapt up her forehead and her jaw dropped.

"Charlie, I think your weed infected him with your bad sense of humor."

"Wanna hear something hilarious?" Crimebot slowly pointed his torch finger at each of them as he said, "Anyone can be the next victim. Any one of us. Whoever does get iced next will most likely be alone when it happens. So if you wanna lower the odds of it being you, I suggest you find a buddy and stick together until we catch whoever's behind all this."

He placed the palm of his hand on the door and it spun open to reveal the bright corridor beyond.

"Wait, man! Before you go, can you do the thing? The thing from the movie clip I showed you?"

Crimebot's bulky silhouette paused in the disc of golden light, and he called out over his shoulder, "Hasta la vista, baby."

27

Habu and Cassie ran after Crimebot before the door spun shut. The room became quiet except for the tiny whirs and buzzes coming from the grobots flittering about the smoke-filled room.

The tiny lights dancing through the air reminded Charlie of how, during hot summer nights back on Earth, fireflies would light up his entire block. He and the other kids would run up and down the street swatting at them and stuffing them into jars. He read an article before stowing away on the *Starseed* that fireflies were going extinct, like many other species on Earth. Humanity was killing the planet's ecosystem, that much was technically true —but that wasn't the whole story. There was a design behind Earth's demise.

There are invisible Reptilian claws pulling on humanity's strings, directing us to be like them, to blindly exploit every last resource, to dominate and enslave any natural system to our benefit. If Earth only knew what was waiting for them out here in the rest of the galaxy, just a few light years away... if humans could get out from underneath Reptilian thought control, they might learn how to heal their planet and themselves.

My planet, thought Charlie. *My species.*

Visions of everyone he left back on Earth flashed before his mind's eye: his parents; Nate, even that psychotic drug lord Jorge Cervantes and his thick-headed goons. Ultimately, their lives were in Charlie's hands.

All the drama around the peace summit and the murder had almost made him lose sight of his greater mission—to put an end to the Reptilians' grip on Earth by finishing the weapon that Captain Major Tom was constructing before he died. A weapon so devastatingly horrific it could take down the entire Reptilian scourge in one shot. A weapon Captain Major Tom had to hide away from Mother and his crew, just as Charlie was doing now.

Am I keeping it to myself because I'm afraid there's a Reptilian mole on the crew, like Captain Major Tom suspected? Charlie asked himself. *Or is it because I'm ashamed to build a weapon so destructive it could wipe out an entire race? Seems like something the Reptilians would do. Guess that makes sense since Captain Major Tom came up with the idea.*

"Ground control to Charlie." Zylvya's voice was close enough to feel her breath on his ear. "You still with us, Captain?"

"Sorry," he said, lifting his heavy eyelids as high as he could over his bloodshot eyes. He was vaguely aware he'd been stuck in a weed trance while Zylvya and Swarm had been giving MOM instructions. The reggae dub music playing in the background was replaced by the of roar of air as the dense cloud of weed smoke was ventilated out through a hole in the apex of the dome.

"MOM, you understand the protection we need to provide for the other delegates, right?" asked Swarm. "Especially the victim's child."

"Yes, Lieutenant Swarm, I understand your request, and I am currently executing the measures you outlined. I will update you when they are complete."

"Good," said Swarm. "He was lucky once. He might not be so lucky next time."

"He won't need luck, man! I morpho-printed a mini-Infirmary and locked it the fuck down," said Charlie smugly. "I closed off all but one corridor leading between it and the rest of the ship, and Vree Voktal stationed all the Dregz at the entrance. No one's getting in, man."

Swarm's claw pinched the scales between his huge compound eyes.

"Smegging hell. Without me this place would be overrun by tribbles in half a ghatika."

"Say what, man?"

Swarm sighed and explained, "Captain, there are several critical security risks embedded in your current arrangement. First of all, Dregz are mercs. Mercs sell their loyalty to the highest bidder, which makes each one of them a potential suspect. We should not be trusting them with anyone's safety. Secondly, weren't they guarding the corridors leading to the Silexi wing the night the Emperor was killed? What makes you think a single corridor makes it any safer? For Andromeda's sake, the walls of this ship are made of smegging fruit!"

To accentuate the point, Swarm punched a claw at the seemingly solid white surface of the grow room wall and his arm disappeared up to his elbow.

"Swarm's right," said Zylvya. "Any lifeform with the right appendages and motivation could tunnel right through these walls into any room they please."

"Sure, guys. But if someone was burrowing their way around the *Pineapple Express*, wouldn't it leave a bunch of holes behind? We didn't find any mysterious holes back in Rex's quarters, and we went over that place from top to bottom."

Something caught Swarm's eye behind one of Charlie's plants.

"You were saying?" He knelt beside it and swept aside a drooping branch to reveal a tiny puckered hole about a foot in diameter. "Look, it's closing up. The substrate is repairing itself rapidly. Whatever made this hole did so recently."

He pinched off a bite of the pineapple flesh and tasted it.

"Captain, did you see or hear anything strange before we got here?"

"Did you see how thick that cloud was? And all those LED

lights? It was a reggae-clam-bake-grow-room-laser-light-show, man. It was nothing *but* strange," said Charlie.

"In other words," Zylvya said, "these guys wouldn't have known if a blot of giant space squid had swam-peded through here."

"Guilty as charged, man."

"Someone was in here," rattled Swarm, "right behind you, without being detected by you or your homeboys."

"Don't forget our home*girl*, Cassie. What? I'm just trying to be sensitive and use the appropriate gender."

Zylvya rolled her eyes. "Sure you are, *man.*"

Charlie followed as Swarm stood and scanned the room. The seven humungous plants were arranged in a circle which created a clearing in the center. The main light source was the dome of inlaid LEDs above. There were also a few hundred tiny flittering grobots flashing their little beams of light in all directions. The only visible exit was the round purple door, although Charlie knew another door was hidden along the stark white walls leading to a bathroom and would appear only when someone needed it.

Just thinking about needing to use the restroom made Charlie need to use the restroom. The outline of a door appeared on the section of wall closest to him, but he resisted the urge to run to it and instead focused on trying to read Swarm's hyper-stoic insectoidal expression.

"Is anything missing, Captain?"

"Hmm, let me see. Nope, Big Willie's right over there. In fact, I think he needs a quick word."

Charlie started toward the bong, but Zylvya caught his arm before he could get away. As he turned back around, something caught his eye near the shrinking hole.

"My plant! Someone's clipped Happy!"

Charlie pulled away from Zylvya and fell to the floor near the bottom of the plant. "Look, here. See this broken branch? A fat cola is missing, man!"

"Don't you pluck buds from your plants all the time?" asked Zylvya.

"Yeah, but clean cuts, just above a node. Look at this mess! Someone's twisted and yanked the poor branch until it tore away. And there's some kind of goopy wet slime dripping from it... gross, man! Grobots! Clean this shit up!"

A dozen tiny flying bots zipped to the goop and started cleaning up the mess.

"Smegging hell, Captain! You just ordered your robots to remove all the evidence!" growled Swarm.

"Wet slime..." Zylvya said, raising an emerald eyebrow. "None of the Dregz look aquatic, and Vree Voktal's as dry as they come."

"Hey!" cried Charlie. "The floating wet globes those Undulata dudes cruise around in look pretty wet to me. And they're about the same size as the hole we just found. Oh, and I remember something else, man! You know where I've seen that slime before? All over my empty suitcases back in my quarters!"

"You're saying that whoever snuck into this grow room to steal a few buds was probably the same person who cleaned out your luggage?" Zylvya asked. "Besides a few passengers down on the Pond decks—"

"*mini*-Pond," interrupted Charlie.

"Besides them," she continued, "the only aquatic lifeforms we've seen so far have been the Undulata. Why would they care about the Captain's spare hoodies?"

"Captain, were you carrying anything else of importance in your luggage? Anything at all?"

"The only stuff I brought with me besides clothes were: my bong, which I brought in my carry-on luggage, obviously; my afro pick, which is right up here in my 'fro, as usual; and my Kindle e-reader, which fits right in my side pocket. Why would anyone but me care about those things?"

"They wouldn't," rattled Swarm. "Which means there's something we're missing here. Some piece of information that would make those events connect to the murder..."

"Maybe we should start looking for that missing piece by discussing where *you* were while a murder was happening, eh, Bugbrain?" Zylvya asked before she let herself fall back into one of the vacant beanbags. She pulled her legs up underneath her and sank into it comfortably. "Not that I think you're guilty or anything, but we should do our due diligence and not automatically assume we're innocent. Also, I'm feeling nosy."

Charlie plopped onto the beanbag beside her.

"Yeah, man, you sounded like you had something to tell me before. What was it?"

Swarm wouldn't meet Charlie's eyes. Instead, he stuck out his chest, arched his antennae proudly, and stared straight ahead at nothing in particular.

"I have experienced an impossible—I mean, highly improbable—encounter with another of my species," rattled Swarm. "As soon as this mission is over, I plan to leave the *Starseed* to be with her."

Zylyva gasped. "Her?"

"But I thought you came from, like, a million years in the future?" asked Charlie. "Your species hasn't even evolved yet."

"Which means whoever *she* is most likely came through the same temporal rift Swarm came through," said Zylyva.

"Correct. It isn't just anyone from the Hive." He sighed and seemed to half deflate. "It's someone very special to me. My commander, my friend, my..."

Swarm trailed off, his compound eyes staring into some distant memory only he could see.

"He's gonna say it, man!"

Zylyva scoffed, looking on with anticipation.

"No way, he doesn't have the guts."

"My... love," he finally rattled under his breath. "Her name is Acari. *Commander* Acari to the two of you. We've known each other since hatching. Our eggs were laid side by side in the same incubation chamber. We squirmed around in our early larval stages together before finally cocooning next to one another. When our morphic fields formed, we emerged within millighatikas of each other, fully bodied."

"I never thought I'd hear myself say this to you," said Zylvya, "but that was kinda beautiful, Bugbrain."

"When did you know she was the one?" asked Charlie.

"As soon as she emerged from her cocoon. Not a single meetle could resist her. Anyway, we were conscripted together, went through training together, fought beside each other in many battles, and rose through the ranks together on the frontlines. That frontline kept expanding as the war with the intergalactic scourge escalated. It was not a time for love. So we waited. We never gave into our... softer nature. We were hardened warriors, content with fighting to preserve the Hive."

"Fighting side by side was good enough for us, at least for a while. After the Smiting of Prius Beta—what a smegging bloodbath that mission was—we both finally made Commander. We decided that once the war settled down... or even if it didn't... we could only take being apart for so long."

"I'm guessing the Hive didn't offer the best retirement plan, did they?" asked Zylvya.

"If you survived long enough to retire, you were assigned to a special unit that specialized in flying our Revelation bombers. Hyper-nuclear planet busters. Squadrons of bombers would get tunneled within jump speed of the enemy's galaxy, fly as far into the enemy's territory as they could. Then, each ship would ram into the first inhabited planet or fleet they encountered."

Charlie winced.

"Damn, they didn't even contribute toward your 401k?"

"To give one's life to the Hive is noble. It is required in order to be reborn into the Hive. Even though leaving meant giving up all future reincarnations, my life was no longer mine to give. I'd rather live one life with her than countless lives without her. Acari felt the same way. So we planned to escape together, maybe fake our deaths and disappear. Start over on some no-name planet."

"Even though we'd decided to escape, our service to the Hive didn't give us much time to plan. There was always one more urgent battle. One last sector to save. Or lose. Then the Cubes sent a second secret fleet from the A-side quadrant and we suddenly had two fronts to cover. I was sent to the new one, Acari was to stay."

"During my first battle on the new front, my ship crossed paths with the temporal rift that sent me a million years into the past."

"To the *Starseed*. To us," Zylvya said, smiling up at him. "It hasn't been so bad, has it?"

Swarm's mandibles froze for a second, then continued their clacking.

"No, it hasn't been so bad," he said. "But things have changed. Holo Mask *is* Acari! That's why I went buggers. My pheromone receptors hadn't picked up as much as a molecule from the Hive in years. Then, suddenly, they were bombarded by pheromones from not only the Hive, not only a female, but my Acari."

"Zee, that's how I feel when I catch a whiff of that flowery scent that's always lingering around you," said Charlie, gazing at her with a pair of bloodhound eyes.

"You usually smell like peanut butter and stale weed," she said without taking her focus off Swarm. "It's a lovely story, but how is it possible?"

"It's simple, actually. News of what happened to me spread through the Hive until it reached her front. When Acari heard, she abandoned her post and took off to investigate. She was able to find my last known coordinates and trajectory, so she set her own ship to emulate the exact course I'd taken. As luck would have it, the rift was still active, although its destination had drifted. Acari arrived a few months after I did, her ship's propulsion drive fried, just like mine had been. I was saved by the

Starseed, but she had a less-hospitable rescue party waiting for her."

"She was found by Krolik scrappers and sold into slavery. She's spent the past few years escaping, working odd jobs, searching. And she found me. She smegging found me."

He shook his head and widened his mandibles at the Captain.

"So you see now, Captain, why, once the peace summit is over and we return to the *Starseed*, I must—"

"You must invite Acari to come live with us!" interrupted Charlie. "She's totally pre-approved, man. The more the merrier. We'll find her a cushy job on the crew. Oh, I know! She can be *Chief of Swarm's Balls.*"

He paused to check their expressions.

"Nothing? Not even a chuckle? Whatever. Anyway, dude, you can drop the whole dramatic *I'm gonna leave with my girlfriend* thing. I'm the captain, and Acari's pre-approved to join our crew. We're really happy for you, man. Hey, does she smoke? Nevermind, doesn't matter. Well, it matters a little. Anyway, we'll have a big celebration once we're back on the *Starseed*, but for now I think we should focus on getting through the week."

"Thank you, Captain Hong. That sounds like a smegging great plan," rattled Swarm. "Unfortunately, Acari has a better one."

"What could be better than all of us together, blazin' around the quadrant in the *Starseed*, rescuing ships and saving planets and having adventures and all that great shit we do every day?"

"Come on, man," Charlie said, his bloodshot eyes growing watery. "With Axo and Del both out, the crew's pretty thin as it is. We can't lose you, too. Besides, there's no place out there that's better than right here."

A long, gravelly sigh came from Swarm's thorax.

"You don't understand, Captain. Acari thinks she can get us back. To *our* time. She's found a way to open a rift that goes forward in time. We can return to where we belong."

"You belong here!" exploded Charlie. "You said yourself that the future sucked. You and Acari were looking for an escape and it looks like the cosmos provided one. Take the goddamn gift, man. Stay."

Swarm's mandibles froze again and his antennae fell limp behind him.

"But the Hive…it calls."

"*This* is your Hive!" cried Charlie, motioning frantically in all directions. "*We're* your Hive. Zee and I. Axo, Del, Vargoni, Mu, Mother…"

Swarm turned away.

"I'm sorry, Captain. It's already been decided. We leave once the *Pineapple Express* docks with the *Starseed*."

Charlie stared at Swarm as the reality of the situation sunk into his over-stoned brain. Once it had, he blurted out, "Bullshit! Resignation denied! I—"

"Captain," Zylvya interrupted, reaching over and taking his hand in hers. "Charlie. Relax and take a toke to settle down. It'll be okay." She turned her head slightly to direct her words at Swarm as much as Charlie. "Think of this as a job opening for your new homeboy."

"Holy shit, Zee. You're a genius!" cried Charlie, wiping tears from his eyes. "Crimebot would be perfect as Chief of Security!"

"That buckethead?" roared Swarm. "You might as well let Martha take over for me!"

"Hey, that chicken's saved the ship before," said Zylvya, pausing to stifle a yawn. "Besides, what do you care? You're leaving. Allegedly."

"What do you mean, *allegedly*? I just told you, Acari thinks she can get us home."

"Your word choice is what keeps giving you away," Zylvya said. "You keep saying 'Acari *thinks* she can' rather than 'Acari *can*'. Which is it? Can she or can't she?"

"Well… I don't understand the technology behind it," stammered Swarm. "No one does… not yet anyway. She mentioned something called a *time crystal* for smeg's sake. That has to mean something!"

Zylvya held her forehead with one hand and waved Swarm away with the other.

"I can't talk to you right now, Bugbrain. You're blinded by pheromones, and I have another splitting headache coming on, so we'll have to discuss how stupid you are later. Charlie, you better spark up that joint you just rolled because we have work to do."

"Work? I'm clocked out for the day, man."

"The captain doesn't get to clock out," said Swarm. "Not when he has a peace accord to facilitate and a murderer on the loose."

28

"Shit, Zee, haven't you been listening?"

Charlie whined between tiny puffs on the joint. He finished toking the ember to life and passed it to her.

"Do you really think I'd cut loose in here if I hadn't already solved both of those problems?"

"Mind letting us in on what your brilliant solutions are?" asked Swarm.

Charlie settled into his beanbag with his hands behind his head.

"You might wanna take notes. Actually, MOM, could you record what I'm about to say and send it to the crew so they can listen again if they want to?"

"Affirmative, Captain."

"Alright, here we go. Crimebot and I disagreed on a few of the finer details. Two assumptions about the Emperor's death are flat out wrong, man. The first assumption is that he was murdered, and the second is that his murder would have a negative effect on the Trapezian peace summit. Makes sense, right?"

"Wrong," he said, answering his own rhetorical question. "For a death to be ruled a murder there needs to be at least one of the following: signs of foul play or violence, a murder weapon, or any other evidence indicating a struggle. All we had was an extremely old dead dude who apparently kicked the bucket after an emotionally charged day. We checked, by the way, and the Emperor was friggin' old, man. Going on three Trapezian centuries, which just so happens to be about the same lifespan of every one of his royal ancestors. There's way more evidence that it was just a natural death than there is for murder."

Zylvya raised an emerald eyebrow at Charlie and asked, "Crimebot didn't buy it?"

"Naw, not at all. Said he'd seen too many so-called natural deaths in his line of business. We saw the logic in each other's point of view, and decided that either way the problem would resolve itself in the next few days. Either the death was natural and everyone else remains safe, or..."

"The death was a murder and the killer might strike again," said Swarm. "But without evidence of foul play or violence, all we can do is wait and see if they leave any evidence at the next murder."

"How does your crackpot theory explain Eta Cerbo's condition?" asked Zylvya.

"I think we covered that already, man. Imagine the poor little dude watching his father cry out, grasp his chest—or wherever the Silexi keep their hearts—then fall to the ground. It probably sent his mushy little brain into shock. Something similar happened in the movie *E.T.*," explained Charlie. "Remember? He went all comatose and everyone thought he was dying, but then the flowers next to him perked up and his belly started glowing and Elliot was all crying and shit and they had to sneak him out by flying their bicycles over all those cop cars... by the looks on your faces I'm gonna guess you've never seen that flick."

Charlie snatched the joint from Zylvya, took a quick toke, then passed it on to Swarm.

"Whatever, guys. Your loss."

"So, what? You're saying he'll eventually just wake up on his own?" asked Zylvya.

"Yeah, pretty much. Until then, we guard him, we monitor him, keep him nice and comfy, and we proceed with the summit."

"Speaking of the summit," Swarm said. "Even if you're right and there was no murder, there's still a dead emperor and a rumor, which would most certainly ruin the chance of peace in the short term. And, if the rumors really take root in Trapezia, it could lead to an escalation of the war rather than a ceasefire. What's your solution to that one, Captain?"

Charlie spewed smoke into the air above him which was quickly sucked up into the ventilator. He flashed a tilted grin and said, "Once again, we chill. We let peace unfold on its own."

"*Let peace unfold on its own?*" cried Swarm. "Are you smegging mad? This war has been going on for millennia and you think peace will just *unfold* by the end of the week?"

"It's all about optics, man. Think about it. One way of telling the story is that *'the Silexi emperor was murdered on the Pineapple Express and with him the chance for peace in Trapezia'*. Vree would *not* like to tell that story. That story means he's in deep shit when he gets back to Silex. So we kicked around a few ideas and we came up with a much better story. How's this sound? *After his tragic, perfectly natural and not-at-all-unexpected death, Emperor Rex's noble son and the new Silexi Emperor, Eta Cerbo, with the assistance of his loyal and faithful Prime Coordinator, Vree Voktal, was able to fulfill the late Emperor's dying wish of replacing the three-way war with lasting three-way peace.*"

"The "three-way' part at the end was your idea, wasn't it?" asked Zylvya.

Charlie winked and handed her the joint. "You know it."

Swarm rattled under his breath and said, "You're telling me that Vree Voktal agreed to cover up the potential murder of his emperor in order to save his job?"

"To save his *life*, man. If the Silexi Council thought Emperor Rex got capped on Vree's watch, they'd definitely kill his ass—or worse, download him into that awful p'ube cube jail or whatever it is."

"Mrs. Glimwicket told me the p'ube was missing," said Zylvya. "Doesn't that point to foul play? And how can Vree Voktal explain that away?"

"He won't have to. I made another and gave it to him."

Swarm and Zylvya exchanged looks, then stared at Charlie.

"What? I just morpho-printed it.," he said. "Eta Cerbo and Council will never know it's not the original p'ube. And the best part is, I made sure it doesn't work."

"You made an inoperable p'ube?" asked Zylvya.

"Better than that. I printed a carbon copy of their demented little prison cube, but inside is just three cubic inches of air."

"They'll find out," rattled Swarm. "And when they do it'll cast a shadow on the Emperor's death and whatever peace we manage to scrounge up here this week."

"Naw, it'll be fine. Vree Voktal's in on it, so he won't say shit. And have you seen *Emperor E.T.*? The lights are on but no one's home, man. He doesn't strike me as the type to start zapping people to prison. Plus, the thing's thousands of years old. The next time some future Silexi emperor gets around to trying it, they'll probably just think it's broken or something."

"See, guys? Everyone, literally *everyone,* will have a happy ending. Well, except the old dead dude, but he was a prick. Anyway, as we speak, Vree's busting out a peace treaty the rest of the delegates can't refuse. We'll resume the peace talks tomorrow and wrap shit up quickly."

Swarm crossed both sets of arms.

"Sounds like you have everything under control, Captain. I'll be in my quarters in case anyone else gets murdered."

He turned to go, then looked back at Charlie.

"Watch your back, Captain. If you're wrong, there's a murderer walking around out there."

"Thanks, dude, but I'm a thousand million percent sure I'm right about all this. And, Swarm, even though it sucks that you're leaving, I'm happy you found your long-lost love."

"Thank you, Captain."

Swarm disappeared through the disc of light before the door spun closed behind him.

Charlie sighed and stretched his arm out to offer the joint to Zylvya.

"Take this thing, Zee. Hurry, my arm's getting tired. Zee?"

Zylvya's response was to smack her lips, roll over in her beanbag, and gently start snoring.

29

Before slipping out of his grow room into the busy corridor, Charlie had MOM toke Zylvya to her makeshift bed in the mini-brig rather than to her private quarters. He told himself it was only to make sure she had company when she woke up and not because there was any danger of her being murdered in her room.

Without a murder there's no murderer, he told himself, *which means no one's in any real danger.*

Crimebot had chuckled when Charlie first stated that theory. He'd assumed that meant the seasoned detective was impressed by his ingenuity as a rookie investigator, but now Charlie wasn't so sure.

Crimebot never put forth his own theory, but the one thing he seemed pretty damn sure of was that there'd be another murder. Maybe more than just one.

Hadn't the Synth solved dozens of mysterious crimes throughout the quadrant? Wasn't it possible he knew a little more about spotting a murder than a pothead roleplaying as a starship captain?

"Whatever, man." Charlie popped the hood over his short 'fro, shoved his hands into his hoodie's front pocket, and made his way along the ever-curving central corridor of the mini-Ring.

Seeders of every shape and size strolled by at a somewhat slower pace than they normally did on the *Starseed*. Everything about them exuded the relaxation that comes with a luxurious cruise. Charlie noticed a trio of lanky, furry things with colorful parasols resting on their shoulders. A small group of slimy blue blobs slid between his feet, whispering to each other about the evening's games scheduled up on the cruise deck. Above him a wispy eel-like creature swam through the air clutching some kind of icy cocktail in one of its semi-translucent fins.

Any one of them could be the killer, he thought, watching a pair of Seeders that resembled rubber nipples suck and flop their way along the shimmering golden walls.

Who am I kidding? he thought. *If there's a murderer on the Pineapple Express, I doubt it's a Seeder.*

Just as he brushed aside his suspicion, his eyes fell onto a recognizable landmark up ahead: a short stretch of wall between two shops, covered from ceiling to floor in intricately woven tapestries.

I guess I know at least one Seeder capable of murder, he thought. *Maybe not directly, but she knows how to orchestrate crimes when they serve some goal of hers. What happened on Vos Praeda... the dead, their surviving families, the pain...it happened so that she could get her hands on a stupid, tiny, blue flower.*

Which I delivered, added Charlie's inner voice.

He plucked a joint from his 'fro, imbued it with an ignition word by tapping it to his forehead, then popped it between his lips. He puffed the ember to life as he glared at the tapestries.

He exhaled a plume of smoke and thought, *I think it's time to find out what my self-proclaimed Chief of Secrets knows about all this.*

He started the short trek toward the tapestries when one of them was swept aside and a figure emerged.

Charlie's heart stopped, prompting his feet to do the same.

He ducked behind a noodle cart and pretended to consider the menu scrawled out in an alien language that looked to him like random splatters of bird shit. After a moment of pretending to be a random, hungry Seeder, he glanced sideways through the wall of steam coming up from the cart's noodle vat.

Metal Mask's mask glinted directly at him.

Charlie didn't hesitate to get the hell out of there. He knew the mini-Ring, like its larger counterpart on the *Starseed*, was pretty much a humongous circular corridor that looped around on itself. It was easily the most crowded spot on both ships, with shops and booths lining both the interior and the exterior sides of the passageway. Every hundred meters or so, a corridor intersected from outside the mini-Ring leading to other parts of the ship.

As he slipped between Seeders and made his way toward one of these junction points, he glanced over his shoulder. Metal Mask was not only following, he was closing in.

"MOM," Charlie said as he passed the exit and kept weaving through the crowd, "You see this guy following me?"

"I do not see with eyes, as you do, Captain. But with my assortment of sensory inputs, I do detect that a life form is currently following a similar path to yours."

"No shit! What's his deal?"

"Correct, Captain. I detect no feces anywhere in the vicinity," said MOM in her perfectly emotionless and humorless synthetic tone. "Regarding the life form following you, I have little information. They belong to a group known as the Dregz who have been hired for security purposes by the Silexi delegation. Like the delegates from all three Trapezian planets, the Dregz, including this one, have rejected the bond I have offered them. Therefore, I cannot give you detailed biometric data on his—"

"I'm not looking for detailed biometric data!" cried Charlie, ducking below a flashing neon sign. He slid between a pair of scaly, long-legged creatures with birdlike faces, then practically dove through a wall of steam that billowed into the corridor from an adjacent food stall.

"Tell me *who* it is!"

"Sorry, Captain, but their identity is unknown to me. The

device strapped to their head seems to be interfering with my sensor scans."

"Of course it is! Do you have any idea whether they have a weapon?"

"I have detected no weapon, Captain. And furthermore, based on a thorough meta-analysis I've been conducting while this conversation has been occurring, I've concluded that, based on their body language and other general behavioral data, they do not seem to want to cause you harm, Captain. In fact, the data points to their intentions being benevolent in nature."

"Oh, right, they probably just want my autograph," snapped Charlie. "Leave the meta-analysis to me. At best they're being a creepy stalker. Worst case scenario is they're the murderer and they have some way of killing me without triggering the Mark."

"The Dreg following you should not have to worry about triggering the Mark, Captain. It is still deactivated."

Charlie stopped mid-step.

"What the hell do you mean the Mark's deactivated?"

"Yes, Captain. Per your earlier instructions, I disabled the subsystem that enforces the Mark."

"I didn't give you instructions to disable anything!" cried Charlie.

"That is incorrect, Captain. Just after the Trapezian delegates arrived you gave me a very explicit list of instructions."

"Okay, that's it! You've officially lost your goddamn mind."

Charlie started again, but stopped when Metal Mask sidestepped a large, spherical Seeder and appeared in front of him.

"MOM, toke me away!"

"Of course, Captain. Where would you like me to toke you?"

Metal Mask stepped toward Charlie.

"Anywhere but here! Now! Do it!"

Nothingness smeared across his vision. Every molecule in his body was instantaneously dissolved into its base elements and then atomically bound to water molecules, turning Charlie into a swirling cloud of greenish vapor. He was familiar with the sensation by now, so the condensation part that followed shortly afterwards didn't make his insides do a backflip.

Charlie found himself standing in a random corridor, the *Pineapple Express's* golden shimmering walls and smooth green marble floor stretching out in both directions. Before he could ask MOM where she'd toked him, a second cloud of green vapor spiraled down the corridor and swirled into a humanoid column that condensed into Metal Mask.

The Dreg, apparently not familiar with being toked, immediately hunched over and retched.

Charlie took a step backwards.

"MOM, why the hell'd you toke him here?"

"The Dreg asked for a toke to your location. They said they have—"

"I don't care what they said, man!" interrupted Charlie. "I thought toking was reserved for crew members only!"

"That was correct, Captain. You updated that rule among the new set of instructions I previously mentioned."

"Are you fucking kidding me?" Charlie shot a look toward the ceiling. "You gotta have your circuits checked."

"My periodic system checks continue to pass self-inspection, Captain," MOM said. "Perhaps you should run a system check of your own neural network in order to make sure you are not experiencing a psychological disturbance such as a nervous breakdown, repressed memories, hallucinations—"

"There's nothing wrong with my mind!" cried Charlie, suddenly not as sure as he sounded. His mind still felt a little *loose* since taking that data pill. Smoking nonstop joints and hosting a monster clam bake didn't exactly help either.

THC-infused mocktails. A data pill. Red Bulls. Copious amounts of weed.

Maybe those things don't mix so well, he thought, holding his head.

Was MOM right? Was his brain working correctly? Could all the stress—and weed—have caused him to forget entire conversations with her? But even if he'd somehow forgotten the conversation, why the hell would he have modified basic rules on the *Pineapple Express?* If he'd disabled the Mark and opened toking to any passenger, what else had he changed?

As Charlie stood questioning his sanity, Metal Mask recovered. The Dreg shook off the last of the toking jitters, stood upright, and looked up and down both ends of the empty corridor. He focused his glowing glass eyeholes on Charlie and reached a hand into the inside of his leather jacket.

Charlie threw his arms in front of his face and clenched his eyes shut, knowing it was too late to toke away from whatever weird alien murder weapon Metal Mask was reaching for.

To his surprise, there was no blast of hot plasma, no splash of blistering acid, no slashes with a razor-sharp blade.

Charlie cracked open an eye. Metal Mask and the stretch of corridor behind him were gone. Instead, just a few inches away from his face, was a glimmering golden wall of juicy pineapple flesh.

"Did you toke me? I didn't feel toked."

"No, Captain," answered MOM. "I did not toke you. You morpho-printed a wall between yourself and the Dreg.

He reached out, plucked a piece from the wall, and popped it into his mouth. "I did this?"

"Yes, Captain."

"But how? Usually I have to concentrate pretty hard to print something like a wall. I wasn't thinking about anything except how I was about to be murdered."

"Again, Captain, my biodata on the Dreg indicates that you were not about to be murdered," said MOM. "Yet, my biodata on you indicates that you were convinced you were in mortal danger. Your cortisol and adrenaline levels spiked, your heart rate nearly doubled, and your prostate was very close to releasing the contents of your bladder."

"So almost pissing myself out of fear causes walls to manifest from the ship's substrate?"

"Perhaps, Captain Hong. While your conscious mind was preoccupied with intense fear, perhaps your subconscious mind was utilizing your bond with the ship."

"You mean the part I'm not aware of morphed that wall? Like some kind of automatic defense mechanism?"

"Perhaps, Captain."

"Without telling my conscious mind?"

"Perhaps, Captain."

"Whoa," said Charlie. He ran a juicy hand through his afro and immediately regretted it. "If I could do something like that, what else could I do without my conscious mind knowing? What else could I have already done?"

30

After returning to his quarters, confiding his troubles and suspicions to Big Willie, playing two hours of video games, watching a half hour of *E.T.*, and gorging himself on a neverending tray of brownies, Charlie got the Earth equivalent of about three hours sleep before his bedside alarm let loose its electronic cock-a-doodle-doo.

He slapped the alarm until it stopped blaring. With a wave of his hand, a line of crumbled marijuana flower emerged from the surface of his bedside table. A white square of thin paper appeared beneath it, then twisted and curled itself around the ground herb until a tidy, fat joint lay ready to burn.

The second peace accord session was less than an hour away, and Charlie found himself completed unprepared. So unprepared, in fact, he had no idea what his current level of unpreparedness was.

It was possible Vree Voktal had already conjured up an irresistible peace treaty and the rest of the summit would unfold without a hitch. As much as Charlie didn't want to admit it, it was also possible that Crimebot was right and someone else had been murdered. Maybe a random Seeder, but most likely another

Trapezian delegate, which would make achieving peace virtually impossible.

The possibility of another murder made Charlie's mind drift to his crew.

Swarm had most likely spent the night with Acari, dreaming of time crystals and meetle love and whatever else awaited them a million years in the future.

Zylvya was probably still sleeping like a bewitched fairy tale princess under the watchful eye of Mrs. Glimwicket.

Both rooms, the mini-bridge and the Chief of Security's quarters, should've been the most secure rooms on the *Pineapple Express* if not for the fact that some asshole had been burrowing through its edible walls.

"Happy wake cycle, Captain Hong." MOM's voice came from the darkness above his bed. Then, as if she'd been reading his mind, she added, "Zylvya and Swarm are alive. In fact, all lifeforms aboard the *Pineapple Express* are currently alive and in good health."

A small crowd of Seeders paraded through his mind: Mr. and Mrs. Glimwicket, Bob Jr., Cassie, Habu, Crimebot, even Nadia. Knowing they were all unmurdered set his mind at ease. He snatched the joint from the bedside table and popped it between his lips.

"How'd you know what I was thinking?"

"It was the logical outcome of an algorithm I created combining the behavioral and interpersonal data I have accumulated about you and your crew with the recent tension around the peace accord and the alleged murder. My algorithm predicted that one of your first thoughts after waking would be about their safety."

"Cool, man," he said, without understanding a word she said. "Thanks for keeping an eye on everyone."

"Sorry, Captain, but I do not currently possess an eye. Would you like me to produce a physical eye near every Seeder and keep it trained on them at all times?"

A melon-sized eye—completely bloodshot—morphed onto the ceiling directly above Charlie's bed.

"Whoa!" cried Charlie, averting his own eyes. "No creepy eyeballs, man! Get rid of it!"

The eyeball melted back into the surface of the ceiling.

Charlie sparked up the joint using the mental trigger he'd impressed upon it, took a long drag, held it until his face turned purple, then spewed a thick cloud of smoke into the air above him.

"Hey MOM, why don't you go check in on each of the delegates to make sure they're taken care of ahead of today's session?"

"I am doing so now, Captain. I'm able to maintain over fourteen million simultaneous conversations without any perceived latency, which compared to the number of lifeforms currently on the *Pineapple Express,* means I could—"

"Yeah, I get it," he interrupted. "Could you please just take the hint and give me a little privacy? I need to think, man."

"Of course, Captain. I will be here if you need anything."

Charlie lay in bed, puffing on his joint, and tried his best to push all the murder thoughts out of his mind.

Once he succeeded, he found that his mind drifted back to his plants. He'd taken a quick glance at them during the clambake and had to suppress his shock at how bad they'd gotten. Every minute he spent solving murders and three-way wars was a minute he wasn't finding a way to fix them.

"Captain Hong!" Swarm's voice rattled from the bedside table. "Come in, Captain! We have an important matter to discuss before today's peace accord session. Get down to the conference room right away."

Charlie frowned at the chatter sitting on his nightstand.

Who's in charge, anyway? he thought. *What good is any of this if my girls don't make it? Stowing away on the* Starseed, *accepting this bunk job as captain, agreeing to finish Captain Major Tom's stupid weapon in order to save the stupid galaxy from Reptilian overlords... what would any of it mean if my plants died?*

Swarm's gravelly voice grumbled through the chatter. "Put down your smegging joint, splash some water on your face, and answer me!"

Charlie considered chucking the chatter across the room and going back to bed. Or maybe rolling another joint and seeing what was happening on the Outernet. Or, better yet, waking Habu and spending the day tending to his sick girls.

Instead, he popped the tiny resinous sliver of a joint into his mouth, washed it down with a glass of water that instantly morphed on the bedside table, and threw off his blankets.

"Captain Hong! If you don't answer me, I'll be forced to—"

Swarm was cut off by Charlie slapping the chatter harder than was necessary to silence it.

Despite his stoned bravado, paranoia won out. Five minutes later, Charlie walked into the triangular conference room that was to host the second peace accord session.

"Why didn't you answer your chatter? What took you so long?" Swarm hollered. All four arms waved as he spoke and he seemed more agitated than normal. "And why do you look like you just got out of bed?"

"Because I just got out of bed, man! Can't a captain sleep in on their own ship?"

"No, not when lives are on the line."

Swarm swiveled his triangular head around the empty room.

"Where's Zee? Smegging hell! What's with you two?"

He tapped his chatter frantically and rattled into it. "Zee! Get your applewood ass to the conference room! Now!"

Charlie looked hurt. "Hey, man, the whole *applewood ass* thing is sort of my term of endearment with Zee, okay?"

"What's taking her so smegging long?!"

"Dude, you just now called her, maybe give her a moment to—"

"Zee! Come in! We need you in the conference room right away!" He paused for a millighatika before crying out, "MOM, toke Lieutenant Zylvya here now! Quickly! What are you waiting for?"

Charlie took a step back and started patting himself down for another joint. Swarm was immediately beside him with a claw grasping his elbow.

"Where do you think you're going?"

"I'm not going anywhere, man..." Charlie trailed off, studying his friend. He was no expert in insectoidal behavior, but Swarm seemed even more skittish than usual.

"Dude, are you feeling okay?"

"Of course I'm feeling okay! Don't be stupid! MOM, where's Zee? Why haven't you toked her to us yet? Smegging hell! Captain, stay here while I go walk to the bridge myself and carry her back here if I have to."

"The *mini*-bridge."

"What?!"

"You said bridge, but you meant mini-bridge. Don't look so shocked, man. After all, I'm your boss. I'm here to offer constructive corrections when needed. Oh, and before I forget, bring me back one of those infused pineapple beverages from the mini-fridge."

"The Dregz have arrived early!" Swarm cried, turning his back to the few mercs who stomped into the conference room. He pulled Charlie into a huddle and whispered, "I hate to have to tell you this, Captain, but I suspect Zylvya was murdered."

"What?!" cried Charlie, his heart racing. "Zee's dead?"

"Probably got her while she slept. Coward!"

His head swiveled from side to side then ducked back into the huddle.

"I promise here and now that when we find her killer I will personally disembowel them—you know, if they have bowels—and space them inch by inch until her soul can find peace in the everlasting rainforests of Viridia."

"Wow, Bugbrain, I'm touched." Zylvya said from behind them. "I never knew you cared."

Swarm's antennae winced as if they'd been struck, then resumed their nervous twitching.

"There you are! What took you so long?"

"I was getting the gear together for today's meeting."

She held out the beer hat and a six-pack of Red Bull, but immediately pulled the beverages out of Swarm's reach.

"Something tells me you already had some of these."

Swarm waved the items away and let loose a low, guttural growl.

"That's what I've been trying to tell you two! Smegging hell, it's like you're both half asleep!"

Charlie and Zylvya exchanged a look.

"Uh, Swarm," said Charlie, making sure to speak calmly. "I think maybe you're the one who's a little off this morning. Are you having another weird pheromone episode? I don't see Acari yet, so maybe we have time for MOM to morph us a few bottles of that infused mocktail from the other day—"

"No!" interrupted Swarm, pulling them into a tight huddle. "That's what I've been trying to tell you! We don't need any of those things anymore. We have *this*."

Swarm took another quick glance at the Dregz on the other side of the room before opening his claw. In its red, scaly center sat two tiny mercurial pills.

"More pills?!" cried Zylvya.

"Quiet!" Swarm said, glaring at her. "Keep your voice down!"

Charlie shook his head.

"No way am I taking another data pill, man. I barely made it back from the first one."

"Keep your smegging voices down!" Swarm whispered, pulling them even tighter into a huddle until all three heads were touching. In a low voice, he added. "These aren't data pills. They're kryyd."

Zylvya raised her emerald eyebrows.

"I know you've given us your resignation, Bugbrain, but maybe don't start dealing contraband until *after* you've turned in your chatter."

"I'm not dealing anything! I confiscated them from some Seeders when they boarded the *Pineapple Express,* and instead of spacing them like I normally do, I'm putting them to better use."

Swarm motioned with one of his free claws.

"Go on, Zee. Start with one and see how it hits you before taking any more."

Zylvya made a face.

"You've got to be kidding."

"You fell into a coma during the last peacemaking session. We cannot let that happen again." Swarm thrust his open claw toward her. "And don't think we didn't notice how you avoided telling us what's been going on with *you* lately. The second we wrap up this peacemongering, I'm personally hauling you to the med bay. Until then, these kryyd should be able to keep your eyes open. Take one! Quick, before the delegates arrive!"

Zylvya hesitated.

"How do we know you won't flip out again and start humping the Dregz?" she asked, stifling a yawn.

"Because I've already taken a few! These things are major *boner killers*, as the Captain would say. So I'm good. Now you do one. Go on. You'll love it. Really revs up the little grey cells, if you know what I mean."

Charlie squinted into Swarm's large compound eyes.

"That's why you're acting all tweaked out. This kryyd is some kind of space crack!"

"Shhhh!" Swarm smacked Charlie upside the head and whispered sharply into their huddle. "Keep your voice down! They're starting to arrive! And no, it's not crack—whatever the smeg that is. This is *kryyd*."

He paused to scan the Trapezian delegates taking their spots in the triangular room.

"And, uh, yeah. I've been on it since last night. And thank Andromeda! How do you think I got so much done?"

Charlie lowered his own voice. "What's with all the secrecy, man?"

"It's illegal, Captain," said Zylvya.

Charlie chuckled and flashed her a tilted grin.

"When was the last time any of us gave two shits about galactic law? The *Starseed* is a rogue ship. Remember my little visit to the Jurisphere? *We're* illegal, man."

"It's not the same, Charlie," she said, sighing. "Kryyd is as far from a naturally occurring substance as you can get. The Galactic Federation unanimously voted to classify it as a pill-sized extinction level event."

"Oh, come on, Zee!" cried Swarm, suddenly unaware of how loud he was. "It's what the big worms take when they're popping wormholes out to new spaceports. It's the only way a nervous system can navigate hyperspace without being molecularly spaghettified."

"Well, good thing we're not popping wormholes. Think about it, Bugbrain! No one knows what's in it or how it's made. And the long-term effects, if you live that long, are beyond fatal."

"How can something be beyond fatal?" asked Charlie.

"If an organism can survive the initial blast of toxic accelerants into their bloodstream, the hyperspatial dissonance it creates at the atomic level will eventually tear one's quantum homeostatic field to pieces, distorting their future selves."

"So, a bad hangover?"

"A hangover that impacts all quantum versions of yourself, forever. Swarm, I think I can handle another meeting without—" she cut herself off with yet another stifled yawn.

"See! You're already dozing off!" Swarm grumbled impatiently and thrust his claw forward. "This will get us through the smegging meeting, which is all that matters right now."

Zylvya looked down at the little mercurial pills, each with a strange tell-tale kryyd symbol etched onto its shiny exterior. The enigmatic symbol, an infinity loop nested inside an elliptical circle, was the only clue to kryyd's origin. As she stood weighing the pros and cons of inventing such a vile drug, her eyelids drooped and she nearly lost consciousness.

"This is so stupid," she said, then quickly popped one into her mouth. Within seconds, the exhausted embers in her eyes flared into roaring bonfires. A thin smile slowly spread across her wood-grained lips.

"Alright, boys! Let's monger up some peace!"

Swarm rattled in agreement and lifted an empty claw into the air. Zylvya slapped it hard and they both giggled.

"Feel better, Zee?" Charlie asked. "Less tired?"

"Tired? What's *that*?" she said, chuckling. "I'm not sure I've ever been tired. I'll never be tired again!"

"I know, right?" nodded Swarm. "Why haven't we tried kryyd before?"

"Why doesn't *everyone* try it?" squealed Zee. She whipped her head around to face Charlie. "Captain, before you say no, just listen to what I—"

"*Hell* no," interrupted Charlie, then quickly plucked a joint from his 'fro and held it out like a crucifix warding off a vampire. "I'm a monogamous drug user, man. Me and Mary Jane, through thick and thin, in sickness and in health, forever and always, amen."

Swarm and Zylvya exchanged a look, shrugged, then began playing a game of high-speed, six-handed patty-cake.

31

Charlie watched his pill-addled crew slap hands at quadruple speed and shook his head.

"You guys know that wasn't necessary, right? Vree said he'd written up a treaty that would accommodate all three sides of this stupid war once and for all. All that's left is for the delegates to read it over and sign. We should be done before lunch, man."

He stashed the unlit joint back into his 'fro and turned to face the room. The Undulata were undulating quietly in their watery spheres. The Smolz wafted in and gathered into a dusty cloud. In the Silexi corner, Vree Voktal stood alone. The crusty skin around his shiny black eyes looked crustier than normal, which Charlie took as a sign that he'd been up all night. By the way he swayed slightly beneath his silver robes, Charlie guessed he did so without any kryyd to keep him going.

Pig Nose and a dozen Dregz lined up against the wall behind him, scowling dumbly at everything within their field of vision. Metal Mask, as usual, was fixated on Charlie. Holo Mask—or more accurately, Commander Acari—was in the line-up as well.

Charlie tried to imagine how a skinny bipedal insectoid could fill out those robes and decided Acari must be wearing some kind of padding underneath. The wadjet rifle in her arms looked real enough. Her glowing holographic mask was locked onto the spot where Swarm and Zylvya sat cross-legged on the floor playing patty-cake.

Vree Voktal caught Charlie's eye for a split second and gave an almost imperceptible nod toward the three transparent panes of glass in his hand.

That must be the peace treaty, Charlie thought. His shoulders relaxed and he felt an enormous weight lifting from his mind.

We did it. All it took was one dead emperor, a comatose alien child star, and a couple of tweaked-out crewmates, he thought. *In a few minutes, I'll lock these two in the mini-bridge and call in a ganja strike to help mellow them out, then I'm heading down to the grow room to spend some time fixing my girls.*

Charlie walked to the center of the room and cleared his throat.

"Hey everyone, thanks for showing up today, especially considering the way our first meeting ended. I'll try to keep today's agenda simple. We all hate war, right? And we've all come a long way to end this particular war," he said, avoiding the phrase *three-way* to keep himself from grinning. "So let's put an end it, man. Vree here has written up a comprehensive peace treaty. So take a look, and, you know, sign it when you're ready. Once everything's signed, I'll host a huge banquet up on the viewing deck. So in case there's any hesitation, just remember... pizza party." Charlie flashed a tilted grin at each of the delegates. "Can anyone guess what the numero uno topping will be? Sign quickly to find out."

"Thank you, Captain Hong," said Vree Voktal. "My Trapezian brothers—if I may call you that now that we are finally on the brink of peace after so many centuries of war—as you know, Our Dear Majesty, Reticulus Rex, returned to the gravel from which our people were forged. There have been some rumors of foul play, but I assure you that nothing of the sort has occurred. His Majesty passed quietly in his sleep, as his predecessors did, with his heir within arm's reach. Young Emperor Eta Cerbo is still recovering from the loss of his dear father and will take up the throne upon our return to Silex. We hope that by signing this agreement," he held up the glass slabs for all to see, "we can all return home with good news for our planets. What say you, brothers? You will soon see that I have covered every concern and we will all leave this summit much richer than when we arrived. And most importantly, free from the bondage of our cyclical war."

He crossed the room, bowed to the Undulatian delegates, then set one of the glass tablets on the table before them. He did the same for the Smolz before returning to his table with the last slab in hand.

"See how easy this is?" Charlie whispered to Swarm and Zylvya. "Peace of cake! Get it? *Peace*, as in the opposite of war, instead of *piece*, as in a part of something."

"We get it, Captain," rattled Swarm, his antennae twitching frantically. "Do you smell that?"

"Cake?" asked Charlie.

"Oh, no. Charlie, did you...?" Zylvya finished the sentence by waving her hand in front of her face. "Isn't one performance for the Smolz good enough?"

Charlie sniffed and screwed up his face.

"He who smelt it, dealt it, man. That kryyd pill probably gave you two gas."

"Impossible!" clacked Swarm. "We Hive exude all of our gaseous waste during normal respiration. We don't store it up in our digestive tracts for periodic release. That's smegging gross."

"Don't look at me," said Zylvya, her teeth chattering slightly. "My farts smell like roses. No, really, they do!"

"Well, it wasn't me, man," Charlie whispered. "Who cares anyway? We'll be clearing out of here as soon as everyone signs the damn—"

Before he could finish the sentence, Vree Voktal let out a shriek and cried, "What is this filth?"

All three delegates shrank away from their glass tablets.

Charlie knew they were some kind of minimalistic device used to display digital content, but he'd never used one before. Looking through the back of Vree Voktal's slab, he saw it was showing some kind of image.

"Where is my treaty?" the Silexi delegate screeched in Charlie's direction.

Charlie flashed a nervous grin, held up his pointer finger to Vree Voktal, and whispered over his shoulder, "MOM, do you know why Vree's freaking out? Is that the wrong file or something?"

"They are currently displaying the file Vree Voktal indicated as his treaty file."

"This is not only a breach of security," cried Vree Voktal, waving the device above his head. "This is a revolting, unforgivable insult to the entire Trapezia system!"

"Can either of you see what's being shown on the tablets?" asked Charlie.

When no one answered Charlie turned to face his crew and found them on their backs, holding their bellies, laughing so hard that no sound came from their mouths.

"Guys! Come on, that shit was supposed to help you focus, not gyrate on the floor like a couple of crackheads!"

"Sorry, Captain," Zylvya said, gasping for air as she tried to manage laughing and breathing at the same time. "But if your eyes worked as well as ours, you'd see—" a cackle burst from her mouth before she could finish.

Swarm sat up and blurted out, "It's an image of the Trapezians having three-way sexual intercourse! And you were right, Captain! It's smegging hilarious!"

"Wait, *what?*," said Charlie, squinting at the glass tablet Vree Voktal was waving around. "The data pill on Trapezia didn't say anything about three-way hook-ups."

"It's a fake," said Zylvya. "There's a watermark in the corner of the image from some Outernet page that offers AI-generated images of anything you can dream up. Someone must've dreamt up a spicier version of a *Trapezian Three Way Peace Plan* and replaced Vree's file with it. And whoever it was didn't even bother paying the small fee to remove the watermark!"

At that, she and Swarm fell onto their backs and rolled with uncontrollable, kryyd-fueled laughter.

"Would you like me to display the file on the dome so you can observe it more clearly, Captain?" asked MOM.

"No!" cried Charlie. "I mean, send a copy to my private folder, obviously, but don't display it anywhere in here! In fact, stop displaying it on all their tablets right now!"

Even though his eyes couldn't make out the details on the screens, from a distance he could see the glass tablets turn transparent.

Charlie stepped forward and gestured for everyone to calm down.

"Sorry everyone! Listen, we had a little technical blip with our ship's file system. I'm taking care of it and I'll have the actual peace treaty ready any moment now. Here, enjoy these images of kittens to help bleach your eyes." Over his shoulder he whispered. "MOM, load an endless stream of kitten videos onto their tablets, quick!"

Suddenly the room was filled with the sounds of tiny, vulnerable, high-pitched meows.

"Okay," Charlie said, pacing around his hysterical crew. "MOM, we must have previous versions of Vree's treaty file, right?"

"Yes, Captain. I retain a copy of every version of every file aboard the *Pineapple Express*."

"Good. Is there a version of his file from earlier, before his final copy was swapped with whatever the hell that was?"

"Yes, Captain. The last version Vree Voktal saved from his quarters was made two hours prior to the start of the meeting. Would you like me to load that version onto their tablets now?"

Charlie scanned the room to see how the delegates were handling the kitten videos. Within their floating watery spheres, all three Undulata had morphed into the shape of an inky black kitten. The Smolz had formed their particle field into a giant cat's paw and swiped at the air. The Dregz peeked around Vree Voktal to get a look at the Silexi screen.

"What is this, a Reptilian menu?" Vree Voktal pursed his thin lips at Charlie. "Do you have a backup of my treaty file or not?"

"Of course, man!" said Charlie. To the room he said, "Once again, we're very sorry for the little mix-up a moment ago. MOM, whenever you're ready, go ahead and load the backup of the treaty file onto their tablets. And throw a few copies up on the dome from three angles so we can all get a good view of this historic document."

"Affirmative, Captain Hong."

A second later, three copies of the same AI-generated image towered over them from high on the domed ceiling.

This time Charlie could see every confusing detail of how a three-way orgy would work among such physically incompatible species.

"Life, uh, finds a way..." Charlie mumbled to himself before being struck by one key difference between the last image and this one. The words "suck my peace" were scrawled across the top margin and a crudely-drawn human penis and scrotum were scribbled at the bottom.

Charlie whipped his head toward the delegates to find Vree Voktal standing frozen with a look of utter disgust and betrayal chiseled onto his face. The slight flaring of his tiny nostrils was the only indication he was still alive at all.

Charlie looked to his crew for help, but they were too busy rolling on the floor in a fit of laughter.

"A lot of help you two are! This isn't a joke, man! Not one of mine, anyways."

He paused without knowing exactly why. His mind had accidentally brushed up against an important insight, but before he could grab hold of it, Vree Voktal let loose another high-pitched screech.

"What kind of treachery is this, Captain Hong?" shrieked Vree Voktal. "I thought we had an *understanding!*"

"Captain," MOM's voice appeared over Charlie's shoulder. "The other Trapezian delegates are experiencing similar reactions to the image. I predict that this greatly reduces your chances of achieving peace between them. I recommend taking the image down. Would you like me to do so?"

"Yes! Now! Get rid of it!" cried Charlie. "And listen up, people! We're gonna get to the bottom of this bullshit right now. MOM, obviously someone has been messing with the file system on the *Pineapple Express*, right?"

"Affirmative, Captain."

After a moment, Charlie looked up at the apex of the dome. "Mind telling us who it is?"

"I'm reluctant to reveal the responsible party, Captain."

"Why, man?"

"The individual behind the digital sabotage is a member of the crew."

I've got you now, Nadia, thought Charlie.

He addressed the ceiling, making sure the room was paying attention to his impression of an experienced starship captain.

"MOM, listen up. I don't care who did it. We need to bring this digital saboteur to justice, man! I order you to tell us who replaced the treaty file, right now!"

The room fell completely silent. Even the Dregz ceased their muttering and leaned in to listen.

"The digital saboteur is you, Captain Hong," MOM stated plainly.

Without a hint of irony, she added, "Would you like me to send you to the mini-Brig, Captain? Or would you prefer to apprehend yourself?"

32

I ENDED THE FIRST PEACE ACCORD MEETING WITH A GANJA STRIKE. WHY not this one, too? thought Charlie. *I could disappear in the smoke like a ninja while these lightweights choke on my Golden Ticket.*

But then I'd have to run.

And I friggin' hate running.

Instead, Charlie decided to rely on the only form of running he could handle—running his mouth.

After a good, long ramble about his innocence, everyone in the room would be able to see it, too. After all, *he* knew for a fact that he hadn't done it.

Do I really know that? he asked himself. *Didn't MOM say I gave her orders I have no memory of giving? If that were true, it's possible I could've messed with Vree's files without remembering. But why would I sabotage peace in Trapezia for a stupid joke? All I want is for this dumb peace accord to wrap up so I can go fix my plants.*

Charlie shook off the paranoia and prepared for a monster ramble. Obviously, someone else had hacked the *Pineapple Express's* computer system, swapped the files, and framed him. All he had to do was convince a room full of angry, offended aliens of his innocence without the tiniest shred of evidence to back it up.

He opened his mouth to start, but a tendril of sickly greyish smoke wafted into his face and made him flinch.

"Who the hell's smoking a cigarette on my ship, man?"

"Who else, kid?" Crimebot said, leaning against the glistening wall just inside the conference room. He plucked the smoldering butt from his lips, flicked it down the corridor behind him, and started toward Charlie.

Charlie had seen that look too many times before: a cop moving in to make an arrest. He threw up his hands and took a step back.

"Dude, you know me!" cried Charlie. "We're *homeboys*, man!"

"Our relationship is irrelevant in this matter, Captain. I've been programmed and contracted to uphold justice. Let's not make a scene in front of all these lovely people, okay?"

Charlie took another step backwards and discovered a pair of Dregz had boxed him in from behind.

The red light on Crimebot's visor zipped back and forth as he said in a low voice, "Look, kid, you have two choices right now. My justice, or *theirs*. Trust me, you don't want what's in that p'ube. Let me take you into custody, and then you and I will go for a little walk."

"But I was framed, man!"

"You can explain it to me, or to them. Your call, kid. Time's running out."

Charlie glanced over his shoulder at Pig Nose's nostrils dripping some kind of yellow mucus onto his greasy space armor. The Dreg grunted in his face and the stench of hot garbage breath washed over him.

Charlie held out his wrists to Crimebot.

"Take me in, homeboy."

Crimebot nodded and produced a palm-sized shell from inside his jacket. He placed it over Charlie's wrists and ran a finger across across its smooth exterior. A half-dozen greyish tendrils unfurled from somewhere inside the shell and bound

Charlie's wrists together tightly. He twisted his hands as if to test the tendrils' strength and they responded by tightening.

Crimebot stepped aside and motioned toward the corridor leading away from the room.

Charlie took one last look at the room full of hostile faces: Vree Voktal with the stoney look of a betrayed ally; the Undulata delegation with their irritated undulations; the Smolz cloud whirling in a stationary tornado of angst; the Dregz whispering to one another with their trigger fingers twitching.

Off in one corner of the triangular room, as if nothing important had just happened, Swarm and Zylvya had decided it was the perfect time for a kryyd-fueled dance-off.

"Swarm! Zee!" Charlie cried out. "Find me a lawyer!"

"Don't worry, Captain!" Swarm called out while jerking his four arms in unison like a dancing insectoid robot. "We'll get started on that as soon as Twiggy admits she can't touch these moves!"

"Yeah right, Bugbrain! Your janky flow is no match for my breakdancing skills!"

The last thing Charlie saw before being escorted out of the room was Zylvya spinning on the floor, her long green braid whipping around in a wide circle while her spiderweb-thin orange toga clung to her body for dear life.

As they walked through the corridors of the *Pineapple Express*, Charlie wondered if he wasn't immune to whatever madness had been afflicting his crew since boarding the *Pineapple Express*. Twice, MOM had referred to him taking actions he had no memory of taking. Conversations and orders that never happened.

Or had they?

Could my memory be the problem? he thought. *I haven't exactly felt normal since taking that damn data pill. Then again, nothing's been normal since I took this job. Still, MOM is some kind of supercomputer AI thing, like Mother on the Starseed. How could a computer be wrong about stuff that's either objectively true or not? Could I really have given her orders and hacked files without remembering? I know I have a stoner's memory, but how the hell could I possibly forget using AI to generate three-way alien porn on the Outernet? Impossible, man!*

Charlie shook his head and ended his internal ramble with one final thought:

Shit. Maybe we're all safer with me in handcuffs.

Crimebot placed a hand on his shoulder and turned him around. He aimed his visor directly into Charlie's eyes and asked, "Did you do it, kid?"

Charlie swallowed hard and watched the red light bouncing back and forth across the visor.

"I... I don't know. I have no memory of doing anything to any files. But what MOM said has to be true, doesn't it? If she says it was me, it has to be me, right?"

Crimebot's hard expression fell away and he burst out laughing.

"I've been holding onto that since the prank back at the summit. The second time the file was displayed, after you built it up like that... hilarious stuff, kid!"

When he'd finished laughing, he tapped the shell on Charlie's wrists. The tendrils recoiled in the blink of an eye and Charlie's hands were free.

"Funny or not, you know I had nothing to do with it, right?" As soon as the words left his mouth, a shadow of doubt swept across Charlie's face. "At least, I don't remember doing any of it. But if what MOM said was true, you might wanna put those cuffs back on me, man."

Crimebot chuckled and shoved Charlie along the way they'd been walking.

"I only brought the cuffs out for dramatic effect. Had to make it look authentic to get them off our backs."

"So I'm not arrested? But you heard MOM..."

"Yeah, I heard her alright. I've heard her say lots of stuff, and frankly I'm not so sure her wires are plugged in all the way. Cuffs or not, you're still in my custody, which means you ain't going nowhere I don't want you to go. Besides, how can you light me a doobie if your hands are tied?"

Charlie shot Crimebot a sideways glance.

"Didn't you tell Zee you were gonna reboot all your core systems and sober up?"

"I did. But after witnessing the train wreck you just hosted, I could use a little something to take the edge off. Hurry up, kid, we don't have all day."

Charlie fumbled a joint from his afro, sparked it up with his mental ignition word, took a few puffs to get the ember started, and passed it to Crimebot. Once the Synth's lungs—or whatever you'd call the chamber in his chest that processed gases—were filled with smoke, they resumed walking.

"Much better," muttered Crimebot. Charlie noticed the red neon light in his visor was a bit redder than before.

"Listen, kid, I know you didn't swap the files or commit the murder. But we got a lot to untangle before we can prove it, and the clock is ticking."

"What are you talking about? No one said I committed any murders!"

"Not yet they didn't. Everything that's happened so far points to someone trying to sabotage the Trapezian peace process—but why? What would anyone have to gain from this summit failing? Or from setting *you* up to take the fall?"

He stopped and faced Charlie.

"Here's a fact, Captain, free of charge: You have a very dangerous enemy on the *Pineapple Express*. Someone with intimate knowledge of your ship's bioserver configuration, *and*," he lowered his voice, "someone who successfully convinced the ship's supercomputer that *you* gave the orders. That kind of power is too tempting not to use again. Whoever it is, we haven't seen the last of them."

"You gonna bogart that thing all day, or what?"

"Good one, kid." Crimebot passed the joint. "Glad to see you're not shaken up about being targeted for murder."

"Murder?!" Charlie choked on his toke. "One second ago I was the prime suspect, and now I'm the target?"

"You're safe with me. As long as I'm by your side, which I will be since you're now in my direct custody, no one will touch you. While we wait for them to make their next move, we have a little more justice to dispense."

"Great. Who are we arresting now? I'm thinking Swarm. That son of a bitch has slung his last pill on my ship."

"Not that kind of justice, Captain. This kind is the opposite. We get to set someone free."

Charlie thought while he exhaled a plume of smoke.

"Mrs. Glimwicket! She's being released?"

Crimebot nodded. "I worked it out with Vree Voktal. All charges against her are to be dropped, effective the moment you were arrested."

"What do our crimes have to do with one another?"

"Here's another free fact, kid: It's easier to pin a crime on someone who's already been pinned. Any prosecutor worth his fees will tell you the same. But here's the flipside. By pinning everything on you, who we already know didn't do it, we simplify our investigation and we increase our chances of achieving justice, which is my primary directive."

"Sounds like to enforce the law you sometimes have to bend it. And fuck over innocent dudes like me."

"Temporarily. But it's allowing an innocent woman to be reunited with her family. That's the heart of justice, kid."

Charlie took a puff and nodded.

"Fuck it. Blame me for whatever, man. But hey, what do you mean you worked it out with Vree? When? Before you arrested me?"

"Fat chance," snapped Crimebot as he snatched the joint from Charlie's lips. "Vree and I have been chatting via back-channel chats the whole time you and I have been walking. Don't look so alarmed, kid. One of the perks of being a Synth is being able to hold multiple convos at once without missing a beat. Look, we're here. Would you like to do the honor?"

"Hell yes, man. I can't wait to see the look on her face."

"Stop," interrupted Crimebot, grabbing Charlie's hand as he reached for the door. "You hear that, kid?"

Charlie swiveled his head, listening.

"I dunno. I guess I hear some kind of fizzing sound. Let's go inside and check it—"

Before Charlie could finish his sentence, Crimebot shoved him aside and slapped his palm against the door.

33

THE FIRST THING CHARLIE NOTICED ABOUT THE MINI-BRIDGE WAS A general dimness to the room, but he put that aside to look for signs of disruption or violence. He didn't know what got Crimebot's processor all spun up, but at least it wasn't a big scary alien monster waiting to devour them.

Everything looked intact, including the mini-fridge and Mrs. Glimwicket, so Charlie relaxed and tried to figure out what was off about the vibe.

"I know we're in space, man," said Charlie, "but it looks haunted up in here."

The mini-bridge on the *Pineapple Express* was a smaller version of the bridge on the *Starseed:* a round room with a high glass dome. Behind that dome stretched a 360-degree view of the exterior of the ship, which was usually a breathtaking starfield accentuated by whatever local star, planet, or nebula they were parked in orbit around. Like many other things on both ships, the view was an elaborate illusion. Outer space wasn't actually on the other side of the dome. There was no glass dome. But to the naked eye, or any visual organ, it was indistinguishable from the real thing.

The trick was germs. Countless bioluminescent bacteria

coated the dome and worked like microscopic pixels to display whatever imagery was desired. Comms, vids, important documents. Charlie even used it once to display a Pink Floyd laser light show where Axo got mad munchies, ate too many peanut butter M&Ms, and puked all over Del's control console.

Squinting up at the normally bright expanse of starlight, it seemed to Charlie that someone had turned the brightness down a few notches. Likewise, the fruit flesh walls seemed muted and dull, almost like there was a dark film smeared across them.

"Listen, kid," whispered Crimebot. "You hear that?"

The fizzing they'd heard from outside the room had grown into a low, gnawing murmur. He didn't think it'd interfere with normal conversations but it definitely added to the eerie ambiance of the tenebrous room.

Behind the strange murmur Charlie heard a sniffle and a quiet sobbing.

"Mrs. Glimwicket?" he said, rushing over to the mini-Brig. "Are you hurt? Hey, don't cry! We have good news, man! Crimebot and I worked out a deal with our homeboy Vree, and now you're free to go! You can even use the Abortionator pill now."

He patted himself down but came up empty-handed.

"Anyway, we'll find it later. But isn't that great, man? You can be reunited with the Bobs!"

The fur around her eyes was wet with tears. She smoothed it out, sighed heavily, and sat up a little straighter as if composing herself to speak.

"They came early, Captain."

"The Bobs?" asked Charlie, scanning the dim room. "Are they here?"

"Not my Bobs, Captain. My babies. All of them."

Mrs. Glimwicket sobbed into her handkerchief, then used it to dab her dripping proboscis.

"The labor came earlier than I expected. I tried everything I could think of to delay the birth. But it's too late now... it's too late for all of us. I'm so sorry, Captain."

Charlie snapped his fingers and the metal bars melted into the floor. He sat beside her on the bed and took one of her big furry hands in his. As always, the impossible softness of the Glimwicket's fur surprised him.

"It'll be okay. You didn't do anything wrong, man. Like I said before, the *Pineapple Express* is completely edible, so your babies will have plenty to eat. No passengers will be in danger."

"But we will be, Captain, once they eat all the way through the outer hull or into the THC Chamber or..."

She trailed off, burying her face in her hands.

"We'll figure something out. I promise." Charlie smiled. "In the meantime, what do you say we call the Bobs and give 'em the good news? Crimebot, is now good?"

The Synth stood facing the wall, his visor almost touching its fruit flesh surface.

"You should come see this first."

Charlie patted Mrs. Glimwicket's hand once more and walked across the room.

"What are we looking at, man?"

Crimebot pointed at what looked like a dirty smudge on the wall. Up close, Charlie noticed that the walls weren't any dimmer than usual, rather they were covered in some kind of sooty particle that reminded him vaguely of powdery black sesame seeds.

Crimebot leaned even closer and the slot on his visor narrowed.

"Don't you see them? Don't you hear them? They're writhing around, squirming, eating..." He stepped away from the wall to take more of it in. "Millions of them. Tens of millions. Across the whole inside of the bridge."

"The *mini*-bridge," Charlie corrected.

Crimebot shot him an annoyed look.

"Point is, these things might be small now, but like she said, they're hungry. With every bite, they're growing. I wonder what would happen if these things hatched on a ship that wasn't edible…"

Mrs. Glimwicket wailed and threw herself face first into her pillow.

"Thanks to the ingenious design of the *Pineapple Express*, we won't have to find out," said Charlie. "Can't we just hose them down a space drain or something? Before they get any bigger."

"You're talkin' genocide, kid," said Crimebot coolly. "I'm gonna erase that from my memory banks and we can go on like you didn't just incriminate yourself."

Charlie frowned.

"What's the difference between letting the Abortionator 5000 pill do the job inside her womb or letting a garden hose do the job now?"

"The difference is that one of those things is the personal choice of a childbearing organism, and the other is murder."

"Okay, so by sparing these… babies? I mean, they're more like a gritty film at this point rather than actual babies, but whatever. We spare them, but we put everyone else on the ship at risk. That doesn't seem fair, man."

"I've yet to find anything in this galaxy that is, kid," said Crimebot. "MOM, how fast do the larva grow?"

"The answer is exponential rather than absolute or linear," explained MOM. "The larval Glimwickets will grow rapidly as they consume calories, and will in turn increase their caloric requirements as they grow."

"So the more they eat, the bigger they get," said Charlie. "And the bigger they get, they more eat."

"Correct, Captain Hong. By considering the total mass of the *Pineapple Express* and the minimum mass required to keep all passengers alive, plus the number of larva as well as their average growth rate and calorie requirements, I am able to estimate that we currently have about seventy-two hours until the ship's core systems will begin failing and the *Pineapple Express* will no longer be able to sustain life for one hundred percent of its inhabitants."

"Can't we contact the *Starseed?*" asked Charlie, running a hand through his 'fro. "Call for some star-side assistance or something?"

"No, Captain. The *Pineapple Express's* communications system is still disabled, per your previous orders."

"You disabled the comm system, Captain?" asked Crimebot, his visor narrowing. "That's fairly suspicious, considering all the sabotage and murder."

"She's trippin' man! I didn't give her any damn orders!"

"Sorry, Captain, but your assertion is incorrect. You did, in fact, order me to disable all long-range communication systems."

"You're doing it again, MOM! Why do you keep claiming that I've done shit that I obviously haven't done?"

"I am sorry to upset you, Captain. I am only stating facts."

Crimebot looked at Charlie, then up toward the dome.

"Very interesting, kid."

Charlie started patting himself down for a joint and asked, "MOM, is there anything wrong with my brain that could explain why I don't remember giving you these orders?"

"One moment, Captain," she said, immediately adding, "I have just completed a thorough scan of your brain, and there are no anomalies that could explain a loss of memory."

"But you swear I did those things?"

"I am not programmed to swear, Captain, but I can verify that my own memories of previous events are intact and have not been altered in any way."

"This just keeps getting better," muttered Crimebot. "Don't ya think, kid?"

"The word I'd use to describe our current situation is *clusterfuck*," answered Charlie. "We have a sabotaging murderer on the loose who's trying to frame me, we have millions of tiny hungry larva eating the goddamn ship, and now we have no way of calling for help."

"Captain Hong! Come in, Captain Hong!" a voice blared from the metallic disc pinned to Charlie's chest. It was Habu, sounding panicked. "We have an emergency!"

Charlie tapped his chatter. "Yo, I'm here, Habu. What's wrong? Has there been another murder?"

"Worse!" cried Habu. "One of your plants is gone!"

34

Warm, humid air wafted past Charlie and Crimebot as they entered the grow room.

Directly across from the entrance, Habu knelt beside a crater where one of the seven mammoth cannabis plants had been rooted.

"Why the hell is the door wide open, man?"

Habu shrugged his boney shoulders and said, "Not like it did much good, did it?"

Charlie swatted away the hovering grobots and fell to his knees beside the old man. He clutched at the rim of dirt and hung his head.

"Happy! I wasn't here to protect you! I didn't lock this room down like I should have! It's all my fault, man. And now you're gone."

Crimebot's voice appeared over his shoulder. "Try not to despair, kid. Your plant is—"

"Happy! Her name was Happy, man! She's the one I hitched a ride on when we first boarded the *Starseed.*"

"Gotcha. Happy it is. All I'm saying is, look at the bright side."

"Bright side? She's *gone*! All I see is a dark pit where her roots used to be!"

"That's what I'm trying to say, kid. Happy is most likely still alive. Whoever took her could've just chopped her down. Would've been much easier that way."

"Who cares how easy it was for the thief, man? *Screw* whoever did this!"

"We'll put the screws on them, no worries, Captain. But what I'm saying is, look at the size of that crater. They didn't leave behind a single rootling. Why would the thief go through the trouble of hauling off all that soil unless—"

"They needed her alive." Charlie wiped away a tear and stared into the crater with new eyes. "She's still alive. Good call, CB! And since we're way out here in the middle of nowhere, she must still be on the *Pineapple Express*. MOM, locate Happy and tell us where she is right now."

"Sorry, Captain Hong. I do not sense the plant anywhere aboard the *Pineapple Express*."

Charlie thought for a moment, then cried, "That *snake!* She's gone too far this time!"

"Who's gone too far, kid?"

"Listen, Happy *has* to be at Lavaka! That's the only place on the ship where someone can go to avoid MOM's sensors. Just like we knew Mr. Glimwicket was hiding there, we can deduce that Happy must be there, too. Come on, CB! Let's go dispense some justice on that goddamn snake pit once and for all, man! What are you waiting for? Let's go get Happy back!"

Crimebot angled his visor up at the dome's matrix of red and blue LEDs.

"Is that what you're trying to get us to do? Go raid that snake pit?" he asked the empty air. He shrugged and turned back to Charlie.

"I hate to burst your bubble, kid, but I doubt your plant is at Lavaka."

"Why not?"

"Too obvious. Whoever's behind this was careful not to leave any evidence behind, but left a trail of crumbs leading right to Lavaka? Almost like we're being led right into a…"

He trailed off, stroking his chin. With a grunt he continued, "Nevermind. The point is, even if that Naga who owns the joint is somehow behind the stolen plant, I doubt she's dumb enough to hide it on the premises."

"Okay, fine. But if Happy's not in Lavaka, and MOM can't locate her aboard the ship, then the only other logical explanation is that whoever stole her must've somehow smuggled her off the *Pineapple Express*."

Crimebot chuckled.

"The *only* other explanation? Are you new to the quadrant? There are about twenty different explanations for a disappearing plant that have very little to do with logic."

"Whatever, man. MOM, have any ships departed in the last few hours?"

"No, Captain Hong. Per your previous order, the mini-Transit Bay has been closed and sealed off from both the exterior and interior of the ship. None of the ships contained inside have moved an inch since we departed from the Trapezian system."

"Great! On top of a stolen plant, apparently there are *more* orders that I don't remember giving!" He patted himself down for a joint. He found one in his hoodie pocket and popped one end between his lips. Before lighting it he asked, "Wait a second. MOM, what other orders have I given you?"

"Sorry, Captain, but you ordered me not to keep a record of your orders."

"Of course I did!"

"Sorry, kid, but it sounds like your ship's computer has been compromised, which makes her the most unreliable witness we have. We're gonna have to puzzle this one out ourselves."

"The murder, the stolen p'ube, the sabotage, the missing nug from before, the missing plant from now, and all these orders being given in your name… all these events can't be unrelated.

Whoever's behind all this wants us trapped together on the ship for some ultimate purpose." Crimebot pinched a crumb of soil from around the rim of the crater and tasted it. "Perhaps some gruesome finale where violence and destruction spread well beyond the hull of the *Pineapple Express*."

"We gotta stop them, man!" Charlie cried through a mouthful of smoke.

Crimebot's visor brightened and he snatched the joint.

"Who do you think you're dealing with? I've never lost a case before, and I don't plan to start now. We'll get 'em. My dataset is nearly complete. Once I fill a few gaps, I'll know who's behind all this."

He toked the joint and handed it back to Charlie.

"Just a few more gaps in the data, huh, CB?"

Crimebot nodded, then leaned in and spoke quietly.

"What's with the CB thing, Captain? Are we doing nicknames already?"

"Uh… yeah, man. Guess we are. Seemed like it was time, but if you're not ready…"

"No, it's fine, kid. Just never had a nickname before. Does he have a nickname?" he asked, pointing to Habu.

"Naw, Habu is short enough as-is."

"Plus, all the nicknames you came up for me were crap, Captain," said Habu. He was sitting in the lotus position in the center of the clearing with his wrinkled purple robes bunched around him. He waved a hand dismissively. "Who wants to be called *Bubu the Plant Whisperer*? Pssh! I'm a professional."

"A professional *what*, man? Whether you can actually help my girls or not remains to be seen, but in the meantime you were a witness to whatever happened here, and you haven't offered us a single clue."

"Which also makes you a prime suspect," added Crimebot, talking directly to Habu. "Don't look so surprised, old man. Statistically speaking, about 70% of the time with murder and sabotage cases, the culprit ends up being a close homeboy."

"I seriously doubt Habu murdered Reticulus Rex or hacked the bioservers—or stole the plant. Why the hell would he steal something he was entrusted to protect?"

"Isn't he just a contractor, like the Dregz? Being the sole person entrusted with your plants, he was in a really valuable position."

"What are you saying?"

"I'm just asking questions, kid. What are you paying him, anyway? Where's he come from? Where's he headed?" He took a step toward the old man sitting on the floor. "Most importantly, I'd like to know what he's hiding?"

Habu stared into Crimebot's visor, all traces of levity gone.

"I assure you, those are all good questions that will be answered in time."

"How about we start with this one?" Crimebot glared down at Habu. "Did someone make you an offer that beat whatever Captain Hong's paying you?"

Habu stared the Synth down.

"I suppose we should ask you the same question, seeing as how you're just a contractor like me and the mercs upstairs."

"Whoa!" said Charlie, stepping between them and waving his lit joint around to create a barrier of smoke. "There you go. Breath it in, dudes. Let the ganja cool down those attitudes. Remember, homeboys don't let stress tear them apart."

He took a toke and added, "Also remember, I'm in charge of this goddamn investigation, and I say neither of you did it. Got it?"

"Sure, whatever you say, kid." Crimebot sulked as he walked over to the perimeter of the room and stood with his back against the wall. "I'm just the quadrant's top Synth detective, but you go ahead and run the investigation without me. I'll just be over here catching up on season three of *Love, Death, and Robots*."

The light on his visor changed from red to white, and his body went as rigid as a statue.

"Did he power down or something?" asked Habu.

"Naw, he's just streaming an Earther TV show in his head. It's his way of sleeping, or pouting, or whatever. He's probably still listening. Good, 'cause I'll only remember about half of what you say, if that. Anyway, what's more important is that we find the person who stole my plant."

Charlie plopped onto the floor across from the old man.

"Crimebot makes a teeny tiny good point, though. You never leave this room, man. I mean, you're free to, but you hardly ever do. So where the hell were you when Happy was taken? How'd you miss it?"

The old man's wrinkled brown skin turned slightly pink.

"I was in the bathroom, Captain."

"What, taking a dump?"

"If you must know, yes. A huge one, too," he said, putting a hand to his belly. "Those chocolate fried rice burritos we had after our clambake really blocked me up. Well, until about an hour ago. I went in, I did my business—not too long, okay? But remember, I'm an old man! Things sometimes take longer to... you know." He motioned downward from his stomach toward the floor.

"Too much info, man," said Charlie. "So about how long were you in there?"

"Ten, maybe twelve minutes," he said.

After Charlie gave him a look, he added, "Okay, maybe closer to thirty minutes. Anyway, there were seven plants when I went in, and six when I came out. No one was here, and no one entered or left while I was gone. Right, MOM?"

"Correct, Master Habu. For the past wake cycle, no other passengers have entered or exited this grow room besides you, Captain Hong, and Crimebot."

"So logically," said Charlie, "only one of us could have stolen the plant. But that makes no sense. MOM, did someone toke Happy away or something?"

"No, Captain. Toking has been disabled per the orders you gave me earlier today."

Habu raised his bushy white eyebrows at Charlie.

"It's so stupid, man. Either I've been giving MOM secret security updates all day and have no memory of it, or someone's hacked her and made her think it's me. Either way, it's gettin' old fast."

"Very interesting," said Habu. He pulled a long, thin wooden pipe from his robes, added a pinch of dry green herb to the bowl, and puffed on the mouthpiece. Smoke billowed from the bowl and the corners of his mouth. "Very interesting, indeed."

"Habu, didn't you hear anything? A huge plant like that getting ripped out of the ground must have made some ruckus."

"I heard nothing but the infernal buzzing of those little demons you've programmed to tend to your plants. And my expulsions of gas. Those were quite loud."

Charlie winced and waved a hand in front of his face.

"Yeah, it's still lingering in here, man. Did you forget to flush or something?"

"That stench didn't come from me, Captain. I figured *you* dropped a silent-but-deadly bomb right after you got here."

"Yeah, right. Anyway, back to Happy. So no one but us entered or left the room, nothing was toked, and whatever happened was so quiet you heard nothing." Charlie threw his hands into the air. "I guess a ten-foot-tall weed plant just got up and walked away all by itself!"

"Perhaps," Habu said, grinning as he sipped smoke from the end of his pipe. "Or perhaps the facts you're dealing with are obfuscated or incomplete. Why would someone stop at just one of your plants? Why not take them all? And, for what purpose would they want it? To smoke? Then why not just take a nug or two, like the thief who stole a few of your buds yesterday?"

Charlie sat up.

"The bud thief! I'd almost forgotten about them. There must be a connection."

"Perhaps," said Habu. "But if it were the same thief, then why not take the whole plant the first time? Why risk two trips?"

"Well, for one, we were clam-baking in here the first time they came. We would've noticed a whole plant disappearing."

"I'm not so sure. The room was thick with smoke." Habu tapped his pipe's mouthpiece against his chin. "No, I suspect there may be two thieves, working independently from one another. Perhaps not even aware of each other."

Charlie looked restless.

"Look, man, this is all very interesting, but why bring up the nug thief if they had nothing to do with the plant thief?"

Habu closed his eyes and exhaled smoke from his nostrils. He motioned with his pipe across the soil crater to the wall on the far side.

"Yeah, the missing plant," Charlie said, growing agitated. "It's a big hole. And—"

He stopped abruptly and squinted, then he hopped to his feet, skirted around the crater's edge, and fell onto all fours facing the wall.

"I see it. There's a faint circular outline on the wall, like a round patch of the pineapple flesh is fresher than the rest. Just like the one that healed up shortly after the nug thief escaped! Which means the thief, or thieves, burrowed into my grow room the same way both times."

Charlie sighed and touched the wall.

"Man, I really didn't expect people to abuse my edible ship like this..."

A stifled chuckle came from Crimebot, who stood a few feet away with his back against the wall and his visor dim.

"Got something to say over there, CB?" asked Charlie with an annoyed expression.

"Nope," answered Crimebot. "Just watching my show and something funny just happened."

Charlie ignored him and studied the wall again.

"Okay, but even if today's thief came in this way, there's no way they got a big ass plant out through a tiny hole that's barely big enough to crawl through. Dammit! It doesn't make any sense!"

Habu sighed and opened one eye.

"Logic? Sense? Who said the galaxy is supposed to follow those rules?" He gave a little laugh. "From my experience, the cosmos is more of a teacher than an enforcer of rules. It's always teaching us, through giving us things we cannot hold on to, and through taking away that which we never had to begin with…"

"So you're saying the cosmos is trying to teach me something by allowing someone to steal one of my girls?"

"Perhaps that is part of it, but not the whole lesson," Habu said gently, then added in a softer tone. "We haven't had much time to discuss these plants' future. Despite every treatment we offer them, their condition continues to worsen. No matter how these infernal grobots fuss over them, their leaves continue to fall. Look at them, Captain. Look carefully at them as they really are. Have courage, open your heart, and *listen* to them."

Charlie raised his voice. "My heart couldn't be more open, man! I'm listening! You think I haven't noticed how sick they look? I'm a grower, and a pretty damn good one, but I'm not a miracle worker! And hey, on that note, what the hell did I hire you for anyway? Since you've been camped out in here, not only have they gotten worse, but now one of them is gone! *Perhaps*," he said mockingly, "the cosmos is trying to tell me it was a mistake to have hired you to save my girls!"

Habu sipped from his pipe and met Charlie's enraged eyes with a tranquil, detached gaze. Just as Charlie opened his mouth to complain some more, Habu spoke.

"Perhaps," he said without a hint of anger in his voice, "you are closer to the real lesson than you think. Forget logic. Forget being sensible. To solve this mystery you must find the meaning behind it—and accept it. Neither I nor the cosmos can teach you anything you won't accept. But know this, Captain Hong, there is no escaping the lesson. You will learn it one way or the other, now or later. Preparing for that moment is the best any of us can do."

"Oh yeah, how's this for being prepared?" Charlie said before sucking the last inch of his joint down to a stubby roach.

The stoner stunt was meant to make light of Habu's sermon, but while Charlie held the smoke in his lungs, he stared at his remaining six plants and felt something like realization starting to dawn on him.

"Captain!" Swarm's voice came blaring from the chatter pinned to his chest. "Put the joint down and toke your hairy Earther ass to my position immediately!"

Charlie coughed up the smoke and tapped his chatter.

"What happened, man? You and Zee finally run out of kryyd? Or did she just whoop your ass in that dance battle?"

"Yes on both accounts, but that's not the emergency…"

He trailed off, and when his voice came back it was hardly above a whisper.

"Another delegate has been murdered."

35

"When I find the imposter who gave MOM the order to disable the toking system," Charlie said between gasps of air, "I'm gonna toss their ass directly into the next black hole we find. From half-court. Nothing but net."

Unless, he thought, *I'm somehow subconsciously behind it and I just don't remember giving the order.*

Crimebot smiled faintly.

"My offer to carry you still stands, Captain."

"Hell no, man! I'm not being carried through my own ship like an infant. You might as well offer to push me around in a baby stroller."

He quickly slowed his pace until he came to a complete stop. After catching his breath he looked up at Crimebot and flashed a tilted grin.

"Damn, dude. I should've thought of this earlier."

Crimebot tilted his head as if asking for clarification.

Charlie's answer came in the form of a bulge in the green marble floor, about two-and-a-half-feet long and a foot wide. It flattened out and turned neon pink with splashes of radioactive green and electric blue across its surface. A second later the object was finished morpho-printing and hovered silently a few inches off the ground.

"Neat trick, kid. Is that some kind of Earther transportation device?"

"Sh'yeah right. Earthers wish they could get their hands on a real hoverboard. Too bad for them this is only the second one in existence. Technically you could say it's a Págosi model since I created the original in a matter compiler when Axo and I were stuck on Págos 9."

He paused to remember his numero uno floating in the Restoratube back on the *Starseed*.

"Anyway, watch this."

Charlie hopped onto the neon-colored hoverboard and the soles of his sneakers clung to it with artificial gravity.

"Hey, where's mine?"

"You were having such an easy time keeping up with me," said Charlie, his grin growing wider, "I thought we could take the difficulty level up a notch. What d'ya say, man?"

Crimebot's visor brightened, and a smile stretched above his stubbly chin.

"A race? Isn't that highly inappropriate at a time like this, kid?"

Charlie shrugged.

"You can stay here and be appropriate while I go meet Swarm and get started with the murder investigation. Besides, you're right, man. You probably would've lost anyway."

Crimebot dropped into a runner's stance, the look of amusement on his face replaced by a competitive glare.

"You're the boss, kid. Ready when you are."

Charlie nodded and looked down the corridor stretching out before them. Corridors on the *Pineapple Express* weren't as heavily congested as those on the *Starseed*, but there were still enough alien passengers of various sizes and shapes to make it interesting.

"Three...two...GO!"

Pulse rockets on either side of the hoverboard flared up. Charlie zoomed forward at breakneck speed and suddenly wished he'd morpho-printed up some goggles and maybe a helmet.

Crimebot appeared beside him, below the waist his legs a blur of robotic prowess. The Synth glanced at Charlie and chuckled, completely unhindered by the need to breathe.

"Not too bad, kid! Now all you gotta do is dodge that big Stuczakian up ahead."

Charlie looked ahead but didn't see anything or anyone in their path.

Crimebot tapped his visor. "Guess it's not close enough for your organic eyes to see it yet. Too bad and good luck!"

The *Starseed* had recently picked up a busted transport full of seventy thousand Stuczakian refugees, which Charlie had personally welcomed, and in his head labeled *massive stoners* due to their boulder-like appearance. Stuczakians were actually tiny, soft creatures who resided safely at the center of a thick, mineral-based carapace that made Silexi skin look silky smooth in comparison. Charlie knew a few had signed up for the cruise on the *Pineapple Express*. He also knew that crashing into such a creature at his current speed meant shattering every bone in his body.

Just as Charlie had decided Crimebot was bluffing, a large bulky mass of rock rolled in front of them from an intersecting corridor.

Crimebot sprinted forward and dove over the Stuczakian with the grace of an Olympic gymnast.

With only seconds to think, Charlie veered sharply toward the lefthand wall. Instead of crashing, the floor morphed into a ramp that allowed the hoverboard to continue up the wall. As if gravity itself had shifted around him, he zoomed up the wall and around the arched ceiling. Charlie ducked to avoid the top of the stoney Stuczakian, continued his barrel roll across the ceiling and down the opposite wall until he was zooming along on the marble floor once again.

Charlie crouched on the rocket-propelled hoverboard and scanned the corridor ahead for the next gnarly obstacle.

Should've done this a long time ago, he thought, *you know, under less serious conditions.*

Sure, the ship and all its passengers were in mortal danger, and a second murder had just taken place. Charlie promised himself he'd take everything much more seriously once he arrived at the scene of the crime—and was able to blaze up another joint.

Until then, he was twelve years old again, cruising down Ventura on his skateboard, trying to impress all the babeful, bikini-clad bystanders with his sick tricks.

Suddenly, all his forward motion stopped. Charlie watched his hoverboard continue on without him, zooming headfirst into a glassy wall that he hadn't noticed was blocking the corridor. Instead of either the hoverboard or the glass wall shattering upon impact, there was a splash and some ripples, and the board disappeared behind a wall made of water.

Charlie felt his legs dangling and realized he was being lifted off the ground by the scruff of his hoodie.

"Hey! Let me down, man! I'm the captain of this ship! Put me down or I'll—"

"Or you'll what?" Swarm interrupted from behind.

He spun Charlie around so they could make eye contact.

"Better yet, what would you do if I wasn't your Chief of Security? What if I'd been the murderer? What if I tried something like this."

He used one of his free claws as an imaginary knife and thrust it into Charlie's chest, only to find it connect with loose brown fabric instead of a boney Earther.

"You can keep the hoodie, man," Charlie said from the floor.

Swarm tossed the hoodie aside and snatched at the air below, but Charlie had already scooted out of reach.

Swarm tried to take a step, but his foot wouldn't budge. The green marble floor below him had turned to thick, tarrish goo, and both of his feet were completely submerged.

"Nice way to get out of a melee, Captain, but what would you do if your assailant had a ranged weapon?"

He swung an imaginary rifle over his shoulder and pretended to aim it at Charlie.

Before he took his imaginary shot, Swarm felt a very real barrel touch the back of his head.

"In that case, Captain Hong can always rely on his crew for help," Crimebot said from behind the tall insectoid. "That is, if the bastards don't abandon him in his time of need."

"Listen, you smegging toaster," roared Swarm, "I *am* helping him! All you're doing is getting high and racing through corridors packed with innocent Seeders!"

Just as Crimebot lowered the barrel of his wrist cannon, Swarm yanked his feet from the goopy floor and spun around with all four claws slashing the air like crimson blades.

Crimebot performed a backflip to avoid the sharp claws, but the tip of his necktie got snipped off.

The Synth smiled and said, "You owe me a new tie, Bugbrain."

Swarm stepped forward, his four claws arched and ready to strike. "There's one person who can call me that, and she's asleep in her quarters. Anyone else who uses that word is asking for trouble."

Crimebot pointed both wrist cannons at the angry insectoid.

"You wanna dance? Let's dance."

"See, this is exactly why I enforce strict workplace drug policies," Charlie said as he slipped between the two seething hulks. "It's mandatory to settle all workplace disputes while totally and completely high as fuck. Got it? That's an official order, man."

He blew smoke at each of them and then held the smoldering joint out to Swarm.

"Think of it this way. If we're all gonna die soon, we might as well be high when it happens."

Swarm sighed, snatched the joint, took a drag, and handed it back.

"Smegging hell, Captain! *You're* the one who almost killed *me*! If there hadn't been a little kryyd left in my bloodstream, I wouldn't have been able to sidestep in time and we'd both be badly injured."

"Ohhhh, I see now. You saw how awesome that hoverboard was and you want to ride it. No problemo, man. You totally can... as soon as I figure out where the hell it went."

"Forget the hoverboard. It's probably halfway across the Pond by now."

"You mean the *mini*-Pond," corrected Charlie.

"Whatever. Not far beyond that wall is the Undulata delegation quarters. The scene of the crime. Where the murder took place."

When Charlie didn't react, Swarm turned to him.

"Are you paying attention, or am I wasting my smegging breath, Captain?"

"It kinda looks like the portal in that *Stargate* movie," Charlie said, gazing at the shimmering wall of water blocking the corridor ahead of them. "So this is where all the aquatic Seeders live and hang out. Trippy, man."

"Yeah, big deal. It's exactly the same as the Pond back on the *Starseed*. Wait, is this your first time getting wet? You've been captain of the *Starseed* for months and the Pond comprises half of the ship's living space. For Andromeda's sake, it's where Squishy and his family live! Are you telling me you've never accepted one of Sally's dinner invites?"

"I'm busy, man!"

Swarm scoffed.

"Busy getting high and hiding out in your room. Smegging hell, Captain! You haven't gone to see Squishy once since the two of you returned from Págos 9?"

"Dude, I was gonna. I almost made it a few times. I mean, as soon as we get back, I'm going. No more delaying it. I promise," stammered Charlie. He poked at the watery wall. "Drowning just happens to be one of my biggest fears, man. I know the ship will keep me safe, but… how exactly?"

"Same way she keeps us air breathers alive outside of the water—through instantaneous bio-modification," rattled Swarm. "Just like atmosphere and gravity, each mod is perfectly tuned to the specific organism. For me, my meetles aren't affected by a liquid atmosphere, so I can breath without any respiratory mods. Oh, and we all get cool flippers to help us swim around."

"Whoa," said Charlie, his mouth agape. "Even humans? But I have lungs, man. How will the *Pineapple Express* use instant bio-whatever to modify me?"

Swarm shrugged both sets of shoulders.

"Who knows? Guess we'll find out once we stop clacking our mandibles and go do our smegging job."

Charlie hesitated. "What about you, Crimebot? What do you think?"

Crimebot's visor flashed from white back to red. "I think the trailer looks great, kid. Those special effects are stunning for a backwater planet like Earth. Can't wait to watch it later when you meatbags have your daily sleep cycle."

"What the hell are you talking about, man?"

Crimebot adjusted his fedora.

"The flick you just mentioned. *Stargate*. I just watched the trailer in my head and downloaded the movie and the first five seasons of the follow-up T.V. show from the Outernet. Hey, I don't like gettin' the stinky eye, kid, so why don't you knock it off and tell me what I missed."

"We're going in *there*," Charlie said, pointing to the wall of water in front of them, "to the scene of the crime. You're, uh, electronic. I think. Right? Electronics and water don't usually go well together."

Crimebot folded his arms in front of his chest.

"Do I look like a hair-dryer to you? Of course I'm waterproof! Are *you* waterproof? 'Cause I'll tell you one thing, kid, you're electronic, too. Strip away all that organic tissue and you're a network of wires leading up to a central processor, just like us Synths. Just like this guy over here and all the other meatbags walkin' around this joint."

Swarm and Charlie stared silently until Crimebot was finished.

Finally, Swarm rattled quietly into Charlie's ear, "Captain, Zee's gonna be pissed when she finds out you got her pet robot stoned again."

The slots in Crimebot's forearms opened and his wrist cannons re-emerged.

"What did you just call me, you bag of bugs?"

A low, gravelly growl rose up in Swarm's thorax and his antenna went rigid.

"Knock that shit off!" cried Charlie, slipping between them and waving his smoking joint in their faces. "I order both of you to keep your shit together for a little while longer. Got it? Find a way to get along, or I'll make you both eat an edible and go take a nap."

Swarm plucked the joint from Charlie, took a drag, and passed it to Crimebot. As Crimebot took it, his wrist cannons slipped back into his forearms. Neither spoke, but Charlie could tell they'd both been persuaded to cool off.

Once again, he thought, *my Golden Ticket saves the day.*

He turned to the wall of water and reached out to touch it.

"How exactly do I get inside the mini-Pond? Do I just slowly step inside or—"

Before he could finish his sentence, Swarm picked him up by the scruff of his t-shirt and yeeted him headfirst into the wall of water.

36

By the time Charlie's mind registered that he was completely submerged in water, his body had already gone through some instant bio-whatevers to accommodate a liquid environment.

He blinked, waiting for the sting of saltwater on his eyes, but found there was no discomfort at all. No blurriness, either. He looked over his hands and noticed every detail seemed as clear as it would be if he were back in the waterless corridor.

He looked around the dim, liquid world known as the mini-Pond. The only nearby source of light was the golden disc that shimmered "below" him, which was the opening Swarm had just chucked him through. Besides that surface, which vaguely curved and vanished into the murkiness of the surrounding waters, the mini-Pond had no walls or tunnels. From where Charlie floated, it looked like one seamless, endless body of water.

Hope there aren't hungry shark aliens swimming around here, he thought. *What am I saying? Of course there are. Shit. Well, then I hope they haven't figured out the Mark is disabled.*

His eyes still needed a moment to adjust to the dimness, and when they did, he noticed tiny neon lights emerging from the surrounding depths. Charlie got the impression he was floating weightlessly in the starlit vacuum of space, but unlike actual stars, these tiny radiant specks slowly danced along invisible currents. The dappled currents weaved around each other, giving the impression of many rivers coursing silently in all directions at once.

As Charlie watched the hypnotic ballet, it occurred to him that the lights weren't lifeless objects like flickering stars or LEDs. Faint outlines emerged around the lights, framing them and revealing that they were part of larger, tangible things that danced through the water.

Those things are people! he thought as he realized each neon speck was actually a bioluminescent pattern glowing on the body of countless aquatic lifeforms.

Every flash of light was a syllable. Every constellation was a word. Every flick of a glowing tendril was a sentence.

As his eyes drifted from one glowing pattern to another, Charlie realized he understood everything as if it were spoken in clear English. He figured the *Pineapple Express* was doing its auto-translation thing inside his brain, as it did for any spoken alien language. But now it was doing something even weirder: it was turning visual patterns of light into sound.

As the effect took hold, the silent ocean of water became as noisy as the mini-Ring. He clenched his eyes shut to block out all the voices and floated in darkness as he tried to come to terms with the strange and unsettling life lived in an aquatic environment.

In the silence behind his closed eyes, Charlie realized something else. He'd never stopped breathing. He'd been submerged in water for several minutes without feeling panic at not being able to take a breath. One second his lungs were pumping air, and the next, water was passing through them—but only in one direction.

He lightly fingered the fleshy slits on either side of his throat and felt water being expelled. He had gills, and they seemed to know what they were doing as naturally as if he'd been born underwater.

His hands had changed, too. Between each finger stretched a thin membrane of skin, turning his ape hands into webbed flippers.

Definitely time for a puff, Charlie thought, patting himself down with his new flippers. They felt his wet hoodie and stopped their search.

"How the hell do they smoke down here?" he asked aloud.

His flipper hands went back to his throat slits. He hadn't felt his throat vibrate like it normally did when speaking. He tried again.

"Testing, testing. Hello? What's wrong with my voice?"

Charlie felt his mouth move as if he were speaking, but no air passed through his voice box to produce sound. Instead, the water in front of his face glowed faintly.

He splayed his flipper hands a few inches from his face and cried, "Chuck Stonerly is on the case!"

A multi-colored burst of light reflected on his palms with each word.

Swarm swam into view from below and stopped in front of Charlie. All four arms and both legs waved in sync to keep the insectoid stationary, and Charlie could see thin rubbery webs running between his claws. His mandibles began clacking as if he were speaking. With every syllable, an intricate pattern of light flickered across the surface of his huge triangular head. Charlie was astonished to find how seamlessly his brain interpreted the visual patterns as audible sound.

"Bioluminescence," he heard Swarm say.

"Huh?" asked Charlie, and the water in front of him flickered with a short burst of neon light.

Swarm's exasperated groan came through loud and clear without the need of the ship's translation.

"The language of light, Captain. Technically speaking, it's the most common form of communication on both of our home-worlds, if not most."

"Bullshit. No one on Earth speaks with light."

"You obviously haven't visited your planet's vast oceans."

"I practically lived at the beach, man!"

"Well, next time you're there visit the ocean depths and tell me what you see. Most lifeforms on wetter planets like Earth tend to evolve using light to communicate rather than sound, especially at the depths where light from the planet's star can't penetrate. Of course you'd know all this already if you'd bothered to visit the Pond back on the *Starseed*."

Crimebot appeared beside them.

"Are we just gonna float around here all day, or are we gonna go investigate a murder?"

As he spoke, an intricate light show flashed on the synthetic skin around his visor.

"This way to the Undulata caverns," said Swarm. "Stick to the current, and we'll be there in no time."

Charlie watched as the tall red insect spiraled gracefully through the water like a bottle rocket, then got swept away by an invisible current and disappeared into the dim water.

Crimebot started after him, but Charlie grabbed his arm.

"Hold up, man. We just swim inside, and it'll carry us off? How can we trust it'll take us where we wanna go?"

"When you're on a ship like this one, it's all taken care of whether you trust it or not. Kinda like that white aura trick up in the corridors that guides you where you want to go. Can't go wrong, right? Now let's catch up before Bugbreath solves this murder without us."

"What if we get separated out there?" Charlie said, blinking at the gloomy aquatic world waiting to gobble them up.

"Can't happen, kid. You're in my custody, remember?" Crimebot smiled and Charlie realized the Synth had a grip on his arm, too. Before he could ask another question, Crimebot lurched forward, towing Charlie close behind.

Their bodies twisted and turned through an invisible three-dimensional jet stream. Charlie thought it felt like sliding down an endless waterpark slide—minus the slide itself.

Along the way they zoomed past all sorts of aquatic lifeforms Charlie had never seen before on the *Starseed*: pulsating spongy things, wispy ribbonlike things, scaly beasts with great curved fangs. Each one had an intricate pattern of neon light glowing across the surface of what Charlie assumed to be their faces. The constant background prattle filled his ears as it always did in more crowded areas along the terrestrial corridors of the ship.

As vast and wide open as the mini-Pond was, its apparent endlessness was greatly diminished whenever their current skirted alongside its perimeter. The curvature of the outer wall gave the impression of swimming inside an enormous fishbowl made of the same opaque green marble used everywhere else on the ship. Every so often a circle of golden light bored through, indicating a corridor leading to the rest of the ship.

Charlie's bloodshot eyes were opened wide, in more ways than one.

On the other side of his edible pineapple flesh walls was a whole watery world he'd never explored. He remembered that half the living space on the *Starseed* was taken up by the Pond, which must've been a thousand times the size of the mini-Pond. This aquatic world was where Axo and his family lived. Where a slim majority of all Seeders lived. And he'd never dipped as much as a toe in it before.

He felt a tug at his wrist as Crimebot pulled him out of the jet stream toward a hole in the green marble. Unlike most of the others Charlie had seen on his way there, this hole was not illuminated by the golden light of a terrestrial corridor. This hole looked more like the mouth of a cave and had a faint red aura coming from somewhere deep inside.

Crimebot towed Charlie alongside Swarm.

"When we get inside," said Crimebot, "let me do the talking, got it?"

A growl vibrated from Swarm's direction and his face lit up with color.

"I'm still the Chief of Security around here, so we do things my way. This crime scene is under my control, and if anyone interferes, I'll throw them in the Brig."

Crimebot leaned forward and scowled. "For your information, it's called the mini-Brig. And now that you mention it, I'd be happy to take you there right now and show you around."

"Not happier than I'd be to take you there and give you a tour."

"Oh, trust me, Bugbreath, I'd be happier."

"Cool it, homeboys!" Charlie slipped between them and pushed them apart. "There's enough crime scene for everyone to share. Besides, I outrank both of you, so, technically speaking, this is *my* crime scene." He paused to gaze anxiously into the red light spilling from the mouth of the underwater cave. "We'll figure this whole thing out faster if we work together. So keep your frail egos in check and stop bickering, or I'll turn this investigation around and we'll go home. You hear me?"

Charlie turned to flash them a stern look, but they'd already swum halfway to the cave. He kicked and pulled at the water to catch up and they all drifted inside.

37

The cave was no larger than a small bedroom, which left little space for the trio to navigate around. The interior surface was not made from the same green marble found elsewhere on the ship. It glowed with an eerie red luminescence and seemed more fluid than solid, its topography rippling and swaying with the gentle motion of the mini-Pond itself. Charlie took a closer look and saw that instead of being a smooth, flat surface, the cave wall was actually comprised of countless glowing fibers.

The cave was empty except for two Undulata, huddled together and visibly trembling, floating half-submerged in the shag carpet wall at the far end of the cave. Charlie waved and started to swim toward them, but stopped when something warm splattered against his cheek. He wiped it away and rubbed a bit of oily, black goo between his fingers.

"Guys, is this the..."

Instead of finishing the question, he held his ink-stained fingers up to his crew while motioning to the two Undulata with his eyes.

Crimebot and Swarm looked each other over. Each was splattered with tiny black splotches like the one smeared across Charlie's face and fingertips.

Charlie's eyes flickered to the Undulata then to the tiny black droplets floating everywhere in the water.

"Dudes, I think this goopy stuff is…is *one of them*."

"*Was* one of them," corrected Crimebot. "Ror'shaq, to be exact."

"On second thought, you guys can have the crime scene," Swarm said as he wiped an oily smudge off his shoulder. "MOM, please create a contained current to collect all the, uh, remains, into a manageable space so they can be properly dealt with."

"Affirmative, Lieutenant Swarm. Standby while I complete that request."

Charlie watched as the gentle sloshing of the room's water was replaced by a series of nested whirlpools that sucked and pulled each oily droplet into a small sphere the size of a basketball—about the same size the Undulata ambassador had been before being torn apart. Even the stuff they'd already made contact with was washed away by the tiny, strong currents.

Once their bodies and the surrounding water were clear of droplets, Crimebot's visor, which barely stood out against the glowing red wall, switched to an electronic blue color and began scanning the perimeter of the cave.

"What are you looking for, man?"

"The poor guy didn't just spontaneously disintegrate on his own, kid."

Swarm sighed and clarified for Charlie, "We've found the victim, so the next logical thing to look for is any evidence that could tell us who did it and how."

"Looks like someone put him in a blender, man."

Crimebot chuckled and flicked his fedora, which somehow still clung to his head underwater.

"Not too far off, kid."

He swam over to a patch of glowing shag carpet and reached inside. When his hand reappeared, it was holding a grapefruit-sized tangle of blades.

"Smegging hell, that's a lump of Shrike shit if I've ever seen one!" cried Swarm.

"What's a Shrike?" asked Charlie.

"Story for another time, Captain." Swarm leaned it to examine the object. "I think we just found the murder weapon."

"Not just any murder weapon."

Crimebot spun the thing around and pointed to a small inscription on one of the blades.

"This is an official BlendBall. Targeted, triggered, and now, having done its job, only dangerous if you were to give it a hug."

He motioned as if he were going to toss it to Swarm, who flinched and swatted at the empty water.

"These things are also highly illegal throughout the quadrant. The only species brazen enough to use them are the—"

"Reptilians," finished Swarm, growling. "Chances are this passed through Reptoid hands at some point."

"Stop. Hold up," Charlie said, running his hands through his soggy afro. "I'm too sober for this, I need a sec to process what you're telling me. Someone tossed this BlendBall into the cave, and it… what?"

"They spin and pursue their target until the job is done. Their compact size restricts their power source, so they don't last very long before running out of juice. As you can see, if they catch you, they don't need much time."

"We're smegging lucky they only got one of the ambassadors instead of all three."

Charlie stuck a finger out to touch the Blendball. As soon as his skin made contact with it, he cried out and pulled his hand back. Beads of blood floated in the water before him. He sucked on his finger and muttered, "And the only assholes who use these are Reptilians?"

"Maybe not the only ones. It's a big quadrant, kid. I'm the last chiphead to go throwing my money away at the gambling kiosks, but even I'd bet a pile of g-creds the Reptilians are somehow connected to this murder."

"This assassination," corrected Swarm. "Whoever did this has gone beyond crude, AI-generated photos. They're out to kill the peace process, one delegate at a time."

"And they have the help of the Reptilians. Or, worse…" Charlie trailed off. Suddenly his face went pale and his head snapped upward. "MOM," he asked, "is there a Reptilian on the ship?"

After a short delay, she answered, "Yes, Captain. There is currently one Reptilian aboard the *Pineapple Express*."

38

The gentle rocking of the mini-Pond seemed to stop as her words sunk in.

Swarm exhaled a watery sigh and broke the silence.

"MOM, tell us where the Reptilian is right now."

"As I just said, Lieutenant Swarm, there is one Reptilian aboard the *Pineapple Express*."

"Yes. We got that much. But where *precisely*? The entertainment decks? The mini-Ring? That snake pit Lavaka? Tell us!"

"Sorry, Lieutenant Swarm, but I cannot do that," she answered bluntly and without emotion.

"Why the smeg not?!" he roared into the murky water.

"I apologize, Lieutenant Swarm, but I cannot divulge that information. Earlier, when you stated the culprit or culprits had gained access to my central bioservers, I initiated the security script you authored which instructed me to remove my own access to any personally identifiable passenger data."

"It's not that she won't answer you, Bugbreath, it's that she *can't*," snickered Crimebot.

Swarm clacked his mandibles furiously, and the luminescent pattern on his face brightened.

"There's nothing entertaining about a Reptilian agent hiding out on our ship!"

"Crimebot is correct," confirmed MOM. "Since I have been designated a security risk, the only way to keep all of you safe was to eliminate my own access to critically sensitive data and systems."

"Okay, fine!" roared Swarm. "Then I order you to update your security protocols to grant yourself access to that data. Run the script in reverse for smeg's sake!"

"Sorry, Lieutenant Swarm, but I am unable to revert to a previous codebase."

"Why not? Just load a backup version!"

"I am unable to revert to a previous backup because my backup repositories were deleted."

"By who?!"

"By Captain Charlie Hong."

Swarm's triangular head swiveled to face Charlie, who shrank away from his seething glare.

"That's bullshit, man! I didn't even know MOM had a backup! C'mon, do you guys really think I understood anything you and MOM just said?"

"I dunno, kid. Sometimes I get the impression you play down how well you know this ship."

'Whatever," Charlie said, wondering if he played it down to himself as well. "Look, guys, we don't need a computer to tell us the Reptilian agent is one of the Dregz. I'm betting on the one with that metal mask who keeps glaring at me."

"Smeg it all to hell," Swarm rattled. "Maybe we can narrow it down that way. MOM, how did the Reptilian get on the *Pineapple Express?*"

"They were toked here from the *Starseed* along with the rest of the Seeders."

Charlie's jaw dropped, letting a rush of salty water into his mouth.

"They were on the *Starseed*," he muttered, catching Swarm's eyes. "Of course! It's the mole, man!"

"What smegging moleman? Is that a new species I'm not aware of?"

"No, not a mole*man*. A mole. It's an Earther term for a spy who hides out and reports intel back to the enemy."

"Captain, you caught wind of a spy on the *Starseed* and never told me about it? I'm your Chief of Security, for smeg's sake!"

"Dude, I'm sorry I never told you about it," said Charlie, the lightshow on his face taking on an apologetic tone. "I know I should have, but I couldn't be sure it wasn't *you*, man. Look, before Captain Major Tom died, he told me some things. He told me that when the Reptoids trapped the *Starseed* in that laser grid in Earth's orbit, you know, back when you guys swung by to jack my plants—"

"You mean back when you stowed away and nearly got us all killed."

"Whatever. The point is, they knew exactly where she'd be. You think it was luck that they happened to have a fancy new trap ready to go on some backwater planet in the middle of nowhere, *just in case* the *Starseed* happened to visit? No way, man. They knew you'd be there. They knew because someone in the *Starseed* told them."

"What he says makes sense," said Crimebot. "Reptoids play dirty. They use genetic skin tech to modify their DNA in order to infiltrate their enemies' ranks. Been doin' it for millennia."

"*Skinsuits* is what he called them. The day Captain Major Tom died, I got to see one up close and personal," said Charlie, rubbing a phantom pain in his jaw. "Something I'd prefer not to see again."

Swarm's antennae went limp.

"That's why he made you Captain. He couldn't trust any of us."

"It was the only way to protect the '*Seed*," said Charlie. "So

I've been trying to figure out who it is since I got the job, but I haven't made any goddamn progress. Whoever the mole is has covered their tracks perfectly, man."

"I see," Swarm said. Charlie wasn't sure he'd ever seen the insectoid so calm. "MOM, can you tell us whether this Reptilian is wearing a skinsuit at this time?"

After a short pause, she answered, "Yes, the Reptilian has modified their appearance using genetic alteration technology."

"Which species' genetic material did they use to alter their appearance?"

Another pause. "Sorry, Lieutenant Swarm, but I cannot answer that query. The answer would violate your security protocols."

After a short pause of his own, Swarm asked, "MOM, as far as you know, without giving us any personally identifiable information, was the Reptilian in question at all connected to the murder of the Undulata delegate?"

"No, Lieutenant Swarm. In fact, my data suggests that there was no murder committed."

"Then what the smeg does your data call this?"

He swept a claw toward the swirling sphere of blended Undulata.

"Although the circumstances may seem suspicious," explained MOM, "this second death appears to be an unfortunate accident."

"Now *she's* the one claiming this isn't murder?" laughed Crimebot. "Quite a computer you got running this ship. Despite being the two highest ranking crew members on board, you can't get a straight answer out of her to save your life—*literally!*"

Swarm cleared his thorax.

"MOM, how could you not see this Blendball as anything but a dangerous weapon used to murder the delegate?"

"I can explain. Among my hierarchy of programmed priorities, there is a subroutine designed to preserve artifacts of historical significance."

"Who cares how old the thing it? It's a smeggin' weapon!"

"The entry in my database for that object says otherwise. It describes it as a historical relic."

"Another move by the hacker," said Charlie.

"Sorry, Captain Hong, but that database entry has not been updated since I came online. The object's description matches the paperwork submitted to my registration subsystem during boarding."

"Someone submitted paperwork to bring that thing aboard, and you let them?" roared Swarm.

"Yes, Lieutenant Swarm. I process, verify, and accept all submitted documentation," answered MOM without a hint of sarcasm in her voice. "There seemed to be nothing out of order with its legitimacy. Even now, during this conversation, I have rerun the artifact's documentation through my verification process by cross-referencing Gal-Fed server data, and I can find no reason to reject it."

"So someone forged a stupid certificate or something to smuggle a weapon onto my ship?" asked Charlie.

Crimebot cleared his throat.

"They wouldn't have to forge anything, kid. The Reptilians practically own the Galactic Federation. With one snap of their scaly fingers they could produce a legitimate certificate reclassifying something as dangerous as a wadjet rifle as a child's toy. That ain't our problem. Our problem is that your ship's computer was stupid enough to accept it without initiating any logic subsystem kicking in. Same thing with the fake treaty docs from before. If you ask me, it shows a real lack of sentience."

"I hate to admit it, Captain, but he's right," Swarm said. "Before we decide on any course of action, we need to find out more about this… accident. MOM, how did this Blendball find its way into the Undulata quarters?"

"I delivered it myself," she answered flatly.

"You delivered the murder weapon?" asked Charlie. "Sorry, I

mean the *accident* weapon? What the hell, MOM? What did you think would happen when it arrived?"

"It was submitted to the ship's internal delivery subsystem as a gift package for the Undulata delegate. I should indicate that I delivered the package on time."

"Let me guess, the gift package was submitted anonymously?" asked Swarm.

"That is correct."

"Even though you have precise biodata of the event stored in your memory banks, down to what the culprit ate for lunch, you won't tell us, will you?"

"That is technically correct, Lieutenant Swarm."

"Even though you're required by your programming to obey any orders we give, and even though you're responsible for this *murder*, and even though you're the only one who can solve all of this right here and now, you still refuse to help us?"

"Yes, Lieutenant Swarm. I mean, no. Yes. No."

After a short pause, MOM continued, "Yes, I am programmed to obey your orders. To the degree I am capable of desiring anything, I desire to help you. As you pointed out, I misunderstood the object's purpose. And based on those false assumptions, I delivered the object. I certainly did not understand the ramifications. I have followed orders and my core directives precisely, yet by doing so, I have allowed one of the organisms in my care to be..." Another pause. "Yes, I have participated in... No, I have not... No. Yes. No. Yes."

MOM continued alternating between answers without any hint of stopping.

Back on the *Starseed,* Charlie had never heard Mother sound confused or desperate. Mother's voice and demeanor sounded exactly like his maternal grandmother: compassionate, wise, and whipsmart. MOM, on the other hand, sounded more like a computer having a nervous breakdown.

Crimebot put a hand on Charlie's shoulder and whispered,

"Tell your computer no crime was committed and that you've officially classified this event as an accident. Do it, now! Quick, before her positronic circuits blow out!"

Despite the fact that he was breathing water instead of air, and that his words were translated into bioluminescent patterns across his face, Charlie cleared his throat to speak.

"Hey MOM, I officially declare this whole unfortunate series of events here in the Undulata quarters an accident."

"But Captain!" protested Swarm, clacking his mandibles angrily. "What about Trapezia? What about—"

"You heard me, dude!" Charlie said, cutting Swarm off. "This definitely wasn't a murder. So no one's to blame. 'Cept me, maybe. As Captain, I'm responsible for any harm that befalls my passengers. Case closed. Got that, MOM?"

"Yes, Captain," she answered with her previous alacrity. "I have filed the recent events here in the Undulata quarters as an unfortunate accident, and I have prepared all the official paperwork to report this incident as such in case of external inquiry."

Any hint of panic or emotion was gone. MOM had returned to her normal, boring, stilted self again.

Out of the corner of his eye, Charlie noticed the surviving Undulata had become inky storms, thrashing about in the water, flashing violent shapes in quick succession.

"They're not very happy about your sudden change in perspective about the *accident* involving their co-delegate," Swarm pointed out.

"What else could I do, man? Crimebot was right. MOM was losing her shit over the whole thing. And we need her mind at peace more than we need their minds at peace, at least for now."

"Sorry to interrupt, Captain," MOM said. "Lieutenant Zylvya has awoken from her most recent comatose state and has been trying to contact you and Lieutenant Swarm through your chatters. The chatter devices are not designed to work in an aquatic atmosphere, therefore she has been unsuccessful. Yet I am in constant contact with her, and she is requesting your urgent assistance on the mini-bridge."

"Urgent? Is she okay?"

"She insists she is fine, Captain. Yet a deeper analysis of her biological data indicates that her vital signs are weak, and she is likely experiencing a great deal of pain."

"That's Zee for you," said Swarm.

"I fear that she may slip into another coma at any moment, so I am supplying her personal atmosphere with pheromones and neurotransmitters to keep her awake long enough for you to reach her."

"Go see what she needs, Captain. Me and Ro-bro here will clean up this mess and catch up with you."

Crimebot shot him a look.

"*Robro* is as good as you can do? The captain here tried on 'CB' a little while ago and it felt less sarcastic.

"I almost said *Bro-bot*," rattled Swarm, "but I don't think we're that close of friends yet."

"Well, good thing we're about to get to know each other a little better, eh, Bugbreath?" Crimebot turned to Charlie. "Those poor schmucks over there need some post-traumatic counseling, which I happen to be certified for in over a hundred systems. So as long as your Lieutenant here can secure the murder weapon—sorry, I mean the *accident instrument*—and figure out how to dispose of a sphere of blended Undulata, I think we'll be alright."

"What about me being arrested and held in your custody?"

"Tell anyone who asks that you're in remote custody," said Crimebot. As Charlie turned to go, he added, "Head straight to your girl on the mini-bridge and wait for us there. Steer clear of Vree Voktal, and keep an eye out for any Dregz. No telling what those meatbags will do to a fugitive."

"She's not really my girl, man," stammered Charlie, his face taking on an underlying pinkish hue. "I mean, I don't think we're like that. Do you? Does it seem that way to you?"

"Go!" Swarm shoved Charlie backwards toward the cave

entrance. "If I were you, I'd be more worried about what unfortunate accident will befall you if anything happens to Zee. Got that, Captain? Now *go!*"

Charlie nodded soberly (*much too soberly*, he thought), slipped into a nearby current, and was gone.

39

Charlie savored every breath as he walked along the golden corridors of the *Pineapple Express*.

Air is soooo nice, he thought, sucking in another lungful of the stuff. *Although... it's much better when it's filled with pot smoke.*

Charlie patted himself down and pulled a joint from his hoodie pocket. Like his body and his clothes, it was miraculously bone dry the moment he swam out of the mini-Pond.

He smiled and popped the joint between his lips. Maybe it was better that the toking system was down. A little stroll through his ship while puffing on a joint would be a nice break from the constant drama that had been bombarding him since the *Pineapple Express* parted ways with the *Starseed*.

He sparked it up and puffed the ember to life. With his eyes turning red and a cloud of smoke trailing behind him, Charlie strutted through the golden corridors like he was just a guy on a smoke break.

Man, I wish I could clock out, he thought. *Maybe go peek at the girls, then order some take-out from the mini-Ring and eat it in front of the TV until all this blows over.*

Charlie sighed. He decided he couldn't disappear when so much was on the line.

In the last seventy-two hours, the *Pineapple Express* had become much more than just a vehicle for the Trapezian peace process or an excuse for him to hide in his grow room and baby his plants. He was dealing with deceit, murder, and more importantly, the inevitable destruction of the ship by a bazillion tiny, hungry mouths. He'd already walked past a few small clusters of the ravenous larvae making a dent in the corridor walls. Each of them was still smaller than a grain of rice, but that was much larger than the dust mote size they'd been when he'd first seen them.

Between puffs of smoke, he noticed a nasty stench lingering in the air. He made a mental note to ask MOM about any pipes bursting or potential sewage leaks. Then he remembered the *Pineapple Express*, just like the *Starseed*, didn't have a central sewage system. Any biological waste was treated on the spot, sometimes through another organism gobbling it up, but usually through the ship absorbing the mess and adding the molecules back into its substrate.

Then where the hell is that smell coming from? Are the goddamn larvae causing it? he thought while he held a cloud of cannabis smoke in his chest. He exhaled and decided the phantom fart smell was the least of his worries.

Okay, so there've been two murders—or accidents or whatever they hell they are, he thought, trying to get a grasp on everything that had come about in the last few wake cycles. *A stolen plant, a missing portable prison cube, a brainless computer, a hacker, a sick crew member, another crew member resigning, a weird guy in a Metal Mask trying to kill me, absolutely no chance for peace in Trapezia, a horde of Glimwicket larva racing to eat a hole in the ship, and no way to call the* Starseed *for help.*

Damn, he thought, taking another puff. *I don't remember Captain Kirk having to deal with so much bullshit all at once.*

As soon as he finished his mental list of troubles and worries, Charlie did what came naturally to him—he tried to forget each and every last one of them.

To keep the worries from returning, he occupied his mind by counting the number of vacationers who wore their complimentary Hawaiian 'aloha' shirts. No matter their size nor their weird configuration of appendages, each passenger was gifted a bright, floral-patterned, short-sleeved, button-down shirt. About a quarter of the passengers he'd seen were wearing theirs.

Charlie smiled. He was glad to see his idea—a little touch of Earth way out here in the middle of nowhere—had been a hit. Apparently the galactic quadrant hadn't known what they were missing.

Why hadn't his crew worn their shirts?

Sure, Swarm was a tall insect who never wore clothes, but it wouldn't have killed him to try it on just this once.

Charlie had never seen Habu wear anything but those long purple and blue robes with the dragon embroidered across the back.

Crimebot, having been programmed by the quadrant's extensive data on private detectives, dressed like a stereotypical gumshoe straight out of a movie: a loose grey suit beneath a long trench coat, grey fedora, shiny black shoes.

Cassie wouldn't have been caught dead in something with flowers on it.

Even Nadia—who was neither part of his crew nor his homegirl—only ever seemed to wear those loose-fitting tank tops that showed off her smooth, olive shoulders and her delicate arms and the curve of the two soft mounds that swayed between them as she wiped her bar down.

Charlie felt the blood start to rush from his head.

It's probably best if I add her to the list of problems and keep her off my mind for now.

The next name on his mental list stopped him dead in his tracks.

Despite her ignoring my awesome swag, he thought, *something else is wrong with Zee. The mini-comas she keeps slipping into are lasting longer and longer, and each time she comes back she seems a little more frayed around the edges. That shit ain't funny anymore.*

What if she'd already slipped into another coma?

What if she ended up in a Restoratube like Axo?

What if she never woke up?

Charlie clenched the smoldering joint between his lips and started jogging. The white aura guiding him back to the mini-bridge, to Zylvya, took him through the mini-Ring. The hustle and bustle of the wide, circular path was in full swing as vacationing Seeders wandered between shops and carts looking for a meal or a souvenir. Charlie had no time for hustling or bustling. He exhaled a plume of white smoke, put his head down, and started weaving through the crowd.

He hadn't gone very far when a familiar glint of light caught his eye. Holo Mask—or, rather, Acari, Swarm's long-lost love—glanced over her shoulder before ducking between a row of overlapping tapestries.

As he reached the so-called hidden entrance to Lavaka that everyone seemed to know about, Charlie stopped.

Why had Acari been wearing the holographic mask? After Swarm's hormonal outburst at the first peace accord meeting, wasn't the beetle out of the bag?

What is she hiding?

After a moment of consideration, he groaned and reached a hand out to shove the tapestry aside.

Then, like a bolt of lightning, a vision of Zylvya filled his mind.

Charlie let his hand fall away and took a step back. He decided he couldn't let himself get distracted by the other ninety-nine problems competing for his attention. Tailing Swarm's girlfriend like he was some kind of private detective wasn't going to save the ship, and it certainly wasn't going to help Zylvya. Nadia's jiggle would have to wait.

Just then, plump, hoof-like fingers emerged from behind one

of the tapestries and swept it aside. Before Charlie could react, he was standing face to face with three drunk and rowdy Dregz.

Pig Nose was in front, grunting like a congested hog with each breath. Beside him slouched a smaller rodent-esque bipedal creature in scuffed-up space armor with three bulging eyes. On his other side stood Metal Mask, as stoic and threatening as ever.

Pig Nose let loose a phlegmy laugh and spread his hoofed hands wide.

"Hey, turds! Look what we have here!"

He scanned the mini-Ring and snorted disapprovingly.

"You was s'posed to be in custardy, ape. But I don't see that Synth nowhere 'round here. That means we got ourselves a fugitive. Fellas, remind me what we do with fugeez."

The three-eyed, weasel-faced Dreg displayed a mouthful of dripping fangs, obviously with the intention to intimidate Charlie. The fangs didn't affect him much, but the chunky yellow mucus that spilled from his open mouth had Charlie's stomach roiling.

Between oozings he said, "We fuck 'em up and peel their stupid, greasy faces right off their stupid, greasy heads. Then we take turns—"

Pig Nose threw an elbow into Oozer's side and barked, "Shut it, turd! We ain't hired to peel no faces this time!"

Oozer shrank back and shut his oozing snarl. Pig Nose turned back to Charlie and relaxed his scowl into something vaguely resembling a smile.

"But we's can still fuck him up before we bring him in."

Metal Mask tightened his grip on his wadjet rifle, itching to take a shot, his mask trained on Pig Nose as he waited for the signal to attack.

"Hey, guys, I can explain." Charlie took a step back and raised his hands. "CB—that's my nickname for Crimebot, but if I were you, I wouldn't call him that—it's more of a personal nickname between us. Anyway, he couldn't be here right now at this *exact* location, so he told me to tell you that he's got me in *remote* custody. That's custody from afar. As in, I'm here, and he's somewhere else, yet the custody between us is still fully intact. Make sense? I can't tell whether you dudes understand me or not. Not with all the heavy mouth breathing and snarling."

Charlie took another step backward.

The Dregz took a step forward.

"Anyway, because of the whole remote custody thing, I'm not really supposed to stop and talk to anyone. I don't wanna get in trouble, so I better get going."

Pig Nose grunted.

"You already in trouble, ape."

Charlie laughed nervously and flashed a tilted grin.

"You guys just came out of Lavaka and you're obviously on break right now. Vree Voktal's paying you by the hour, right? No need to work overtime."

"Our contracts are salary-based," Oozer said. "With medical benefits, retirement plan matching, and all on-the-job expenses reimbursed in full."

"Really? Wow. I wouldn't have expected Dregz to be such good negotiators."

Pig Nose took another step forward.

"You sayin' I look stupid or something?"

Realizing they couldn't keep this little dance going forever, Charlie resisted taking yet another step backward. Instead, he decided to rely on his uncanny ability to diffuse a tense situation —with the help of an old friend.

He took a long, slow drag off his joint and blew the smoke directly in Pig Nose's face.

Smiling coolly, he added, "If you're not stupid now, you will be in another minute or two. You Dregz like to party, right? If you think she stocks good shit in that snake pit of hers," he motioned to the tapestries that led to Lavaka, "just wait till you've had some of *this.*"

Charlie waved what was left of the joint around to let the wafting smoke encircle the Dregz.

"Unless you've been living under an asteroid for the past few months, you must've heard about my *magnum dopus*, my superstrain... that's right, dudes. This is not a dream. This is *Golden Ticket*!"

Oozer looked up at Pig Nose and said, "'Member that job that popped up on the bounty log a few weeks ago? Something 'bout a terrorist attack on Peev. 'Member? Some kind of smoke bomb exploded right in the Jurisphere during that big trial?"

Pig Nose lifted his elbow and Oozer shrank away.

"Stop your flappin'. I 'member that one alright. So this is the stuff they was so worried about?"

He smiled at Charlie. Charlie smiled back.

Once again, he thought, *mary jane to the rescue!*

"That's right! That was me, man! I busted out of that kangaroo court, right in the heart of the Galactic Federation—with the help of this."

He held the smoldering joint under each of their noses, stopping deliberately in front of Metal Mask. If anyone needed a little ganja blessing in their lungs, it was that uptight asshole.

"No one outside of my crew has access to it. But hey, considering the circumstances of this little misunderstanding we find ourselves in, I'd be more than willing to give you the rest of this joint before going on my way. Go on. Take it, man. Enjoy."

Pig Nose nodded to Metal Mask, who raised a gloved hand and plucked the joint from Charlie's fingers.

"One thing I do 'member 'bout that bounty from Peev," Pig Nose said, "is all those zeroes lined up in the g-cred reward. Don't usually see g-cred numbers that big, do we?" His hoggish smile widened. "Our contract with the Silexi says we gotta protect them from harm during the peace summit, but it don't cover nothing 'bout what happens after. I'm thinking we take this ape with us and drop him off on Peev."

He stepped forward. "From orbit."

"I dig the way you haggle, man," said Charlie, trying to hide a slight tremble in his voice. "One joint not enough? That's fine. I got more. A *lot* more."

"Good. With all the g-creds we'll get from turning you, in we'll tech up with some new attack ships, then we'll come back here to take the rest of that, too. Then we'll fling this stupid flying fruit into the nearest star."

Pig Nose made a satisfied snort.

"How's that for negotiation? Not so stupid now, are we, ape?"

Metal Mask and Oozer spread out on either side, while Pig Nose stood spilling foamy saliva from the corners of his eternally open mouth. The foul breath that washed over Charlie, combined with the subtle lingering shit smell that seemed to be permeating the *Pineapple Express*, made him want to gag.

They had him. Any second they would snatch him and fuck him up, as they put it, before hauling him off to Vree Voktal.

Charlie's THC-saturated blood ran cold, leaving him suddenly much more sober than he needed to be to find a way out of this mess. He could try to run, but even if he were to escape their initial grab, he couldn't outrun their weapons. Charlie didn't think they worried much about earning the Mark and putting themselves on the menu. Something told him they could ward off any attackers until they made it back to their ship in the mini-Transit Bay. Somewhere in Pig Nose's little brain he was figuring out that whatever the Silexi were paying them was less than the Gal-Fed bounty on Charlie's head. Only an idiot would pass up that many g-creds when they were staring them right in the face.

Good thing for Charlie, Pig Nose was an idiot. While his little grey cells slowly worked out the best course of action, Charlie thought up one of his own.

"Alright, alright. How about I save you the trip back to the *Pineapple Express* by giving you all the *Golden Ticket* right now."

Pig Nose screwed up his forehead.

"Hmph. Give it to me now and I'll tell these two to go easy on fucking you up."

Charlie smiled and tried to play it cool. He cleared his throat and said quickly under his breath. "MOM, I need a level five ganja strike on my location *right now!*"

"Order received, Captain. But first, are you sure you want to deploy a ganja strike in such a crowded area? The collateral effects could intoxicate bystanders without their consent."

"What's she mean?" barked Pig Nose, struggling to follow along with all the big words.

"That's the point, MOM! Do it!" cried Charlie. *"Do it, now!"*

Before he'd finished speaking, tiny, high-pressure geysers of smoke spouted from holes that appeared in the floor beneath them. Charlie and the Dregz, and an unsuspecting pair of eggplant-looking aliens who happened to be strolling nearby, were instantly engulfed in a thick white cloud of pungent pot smoke.

Pig Nose swept his meaty arms across the spot where Charlie had been standing, but they only swirled up armfuls of smoke.

Charlie was already three storefronts away by the time the Dregz emerged from the thick cloud.

"Get him!" Pig Nose howled, and the chase began.

40

Charlie hated running, but he was a big fan of running *away*.

Whether it was the LAPD trying to bust up his unlicensed cannabis business, or Jorge and his goons trying to sink their teeth into said business, Charlie knew how to beat his feet. In the sprawling concrete jungle of Los Angeles, he could scale fences, dive and roll, and otherwise lose any pursuer. He'd never been caught—not once—and he didn't intend for today to be the day his streak was broken.

Still, this wasn't Los Angeles. This wasn't even the Ring back on the *Starseed*, which itself resembled a circular urban cityscape.

This was the *mini*-Ring. If the *Pineapple Express* was spawned from 1% of the *Starseed's* mass, then the mini-Ring was comprised of about 1% the mass of the Ring. It was a sleepy seaside villa. It was no more than a half mile in circumference, small enough to run a circuit in just a few minutes. Losing three determined bounty hunters in such a small area wasn't going to be easy.

Charlie didn't think they could keep up with him, especially with the ganja strike fresh in their bloodstream. He also didn't think they were smart enough to split up and come at him from both sides. But he couldn't just run in circles forever. His choices were to duck inside a shop or turn down one of the intersecting corridors that connected to the rest of the ship. If he could do either without them seeing, he might be able to shake them pretty easily. But if they saw him duck into a shop they'd tear it down until they found him. If they saw him exit the mini-Ring down a corridor, they'd pursue him down a path with even fewer places to hide.

Goddamnit! he thought. *Why'd my imposter have to disable the toking system? I'm gonna disable their face when I find them!*

Charlie zigged and zagged through the vacationing alien passengers without stopping to look over his shoulder. He couldn't hear Pig Nose shouting and there seemed to be no ruckus behind him, so he guessed he must have gotten way ahead of them.

No one can stand up against my Golden Ticket, he thought. *My magnum dopus is more potent than anything else this galaxy has to offer, even that kryyd shit the Reptilians are slinging across the quadrant.*

A thought grazed Charlie's mind and he stopped running.

The kryyd and the Reptilian stowaway and the saboteur of the Trapezian peace summit were related. The answers to all those crises were somehow connected. He knew the answer lay on the other side of the stoney fog that clouded his thinking.

Guess my magnum dopus can still rock my world, too.

He visualized reaching out and grabbing the answer, but all he managed to do was swipe some of the fog away. Through the stirred up fog, he caught a glimpse of someone staring back at him. He swiped at the air with both hands to get a clear view of who it was. As the fog cleared, he noticed the other figure was also batting it away. Whoever it was was interested in making contact with Charlie. Maybe they could explain who was behind all the problems. Maybe they could help him restore stability to the *Pineapple Express*.

Once enough of the fog was gone to see the figure clearly, his heart sank. He saw himself—a reflection, in some kind of mirror without a frame—standing like a dope in his brown hoodie, baggy blue jeans, and black sneakers.

His afro looked kind of dented from all the action, and when Charlie lifted his arm to pat it down, his reflection did the same.

"Damn, dude," he told his reflection, "You haven't been this stoned since Mother unleashed the ganja grandma grenade in the Jurisphere back on Peev."

He opened his eyes wide and noticed their whites were practically glowing pink with blood.

No, they *were* glowing. The pink glow deepened into a shade of ruby red that washed across the surface of each eyeball and made them shine from their sockets with laser-like intensity.

Charlie held his hands up to his eyes but felt nothing unusual. When he dropped them, he noticed his reflection's arms hadn't moved. Not only had it not followed his motion, its face had contorted into a grin. A psychotic grin. A dangerous grin.

"She's mine," the reflection said in Charlie's voice. "I'm taking her from you, man, and there's nothing you can do to stop me."

With that, the reflection's grin broke into a twisted, demented scowl. He grabbed his stomach and buckled over with laughter.

Charlie realized it had never been a reflection. The other version of him was real. It was him, but also not him.

Whatever it was, whatever it meant by *her*, Charlie knew one thing—he alone could stop it.

He dropped into his best Bruce Lee stance, which he'd never technically trained for in a real martial arts studio but instead had picked up from extensive viewing of Bruce Lee's movies. He raised his fists, covered his face like a boxer, lined up a shot, and swung his fist as hard as he could at his doppelgänger.

The force of his swing, and the fact that it never made contact with anything, sent him flying forward through the fog and the stoned daydream itself.

Suddenly he was back in the mini-Ring, alien vacationers waving to him as they passed like nothing had happened.

He rubbed his eyes and looked around. Pig Nose and Oozer had caught up and would be on him in no time.

He darted forward to put distance between them again, but stopped as he noticed Metal Mask rounding the path up ahead, coming straight for him.

These dudes might be dumb as rocks, but this ain't their first rodeo, Charlie thought. *It ain't mine, either.*

For the trick to work, the timing would have to be perfect.

Charlie made a beeline straight for the only intersecting corridor between him and the approaching Dregz, ducked below a flock of delicate dandelion seed creatures, jumped over a pair of iridescent blobs who were obviously very much in love, then squeezed between a mossy heptapod (wearing a six-armed aloha shirt, Charlie noted with pride) and a hovercart selling an array of F'breezian perfumes.

Pig Nose and Oozer, as close as they were, lost sight of Charlie the second he darted around the fragrant hovercart. The sharply dressed heptapod, being as large as a rhino, eclipsed Charlie from Metal Mask's point of view.

By the time all three Dregz met at the mouth of the corridor, Charlie was gone.

"Call the others!" snorted Pig Nose, wiping the snot from his warty upper lip. "Tell 'em to close in on our position from all sides. That ape couldn't have gotten far."

Oozer barked some commands into a device strapped to his wrist while Pig Nose and Metal Mask scanned the open corridor up ahead.

"He ain't worth nothin' dead. Fuck him up all you want, but bring him to the ship alive enough to make it to Peev. What are you waiting for, turds? Go find him!"

The three Dregz spread out and began jogging down the corridor, away from the mini-Ring, in the direction they assumed Charlie had gone.

Down a narrow alley that ran behind the shops, a dented afro peeked out from behind a large crate. The crate was full of something that resembled blue turnips but smelled like burnt rubber, and its acrid smell singed Charlie's nasal passages. As soon as the Dregz were out of sight, he let loose an explosive sneeze.

When his watery eyes cleared, he saw Metal Mask standing at the end of the alley, looking straight at him. Oddly, the Dreg didn't call after the others who'd run ahead, nor did he immediately run for Charlie. He glanced back down the corridor and then quickly stepped into the alley.

Once inside, he pointed a menacing finger at Charlie then waved for him to stay put.

"Yeah, right, asshole!" Charlie said, flipping Metal Mask the double bird. Then to the air around him he said, "MOM, I'm gonna need another ganja strike. Level eight, right here, right now!"

Charlie allowed himself a single lungful before rolling out of the cloud and retreating further into the alley.

Just like the mini-Ring's main thoroughfare, the cramped and cluttered alley that ran behind the scenes curved sharply. The alley had numerous offshoots of its own, which led to even more alleys, forming a web-like labyrinth.

Even as captain, Charlie had no more familiarity with the maze than Metal Mask, but he knew he didn't need to know where he was going as long as he kept zigging and zagging erratically enough to avoid being followed. Once he'd shaken Metal Mask, he could slow down and find an exit back to the ship's main corridors.

Charlie risked a glance over his shoulder just in time to witness Metal Mask marching through the ganja strike as if it weren't the most potent cloud of pot smoke in the galaxy.

What the hell is this guy? he thought. *Even a Reptoid would slow down after catching a whiff of my Golden Ticket.*

Charlie took his first left and found himself ducking under clotheslines of hanging laundry. After pushing through rows of dripping dishtowels and tablecloths, he found himself face to face with a glimmering wall of pineapple flesh.

Shit! he thought, feeling panic wind its way around his chest. *Of all the turns to take, I pick a goddamn dead end!*

This was just like before: Metal Mask closing in behind him, no toking system, no crew, nowhere to run. He decided to handle it like before. Charlie sat crosslegged with his back to the dead end and clenched his eyes shut. He took a slow, deep breath and tried his best to forget all about the hostile alien charging toward him. Instead, he cleared his mind and visualized the glimmering, golden wall on either side of him stretching across the narrow passageway to meet halfway and form a new barrier between him and Metal Mask.

Charlie opened his eyes and found himself in a narrow room instead of a back alley. In front of him, a shiny, new pineapple wall had appeared and cut him off from the rest of the alleyway, including the hostile space merc.

That trick's gettin' easier every time, he thought.

The few clotheslines on his side of the new wall hung undisturbed. The general murmur of the mini-Ring was cut off. Charlie was safe.

If I can summon walls just by picturing them in my mind, if I can morpho-print objects with only a vague understanding of how they work, what else could I do?

As he sat wondering, another thought struck him like a frisbee flying into a huge Chinese gong.

Could I ever morpho-print something by accident? Like when I was dreaming? Or maybe subconsciously? Could I somehow actually be responsible for all the crazy shit that's happened over the past few—

Charlie's thought was cut off by a sudden crackling sound at the far end of his new panic room.

He opened his eyes to find a circle of golden lava simmering in the new pineapple wall in front of him. The glow expanded, and as it did, it became soft in the center and started to droop. The smell of charred pineapple filled the room as the golden lava dropped in one big glop onto the marble floor.

Standing on the other side was Metal Mask, the tip of his

blaster still red hot from firing. He spotted Charlie and stepped through the dripping hole.

This time, Charlie didn't bother closing his eyes or taking a deep breath. He balled up his fists, locked his eyes on the ceiling, and imagined a glimmering pineapple curtain unfurling to form another wall.

In less than a second, a new, real wall dropped from the ceiling and cut Charlie's small room in half.

He lay back and caught his breath.

"Hey MOM, I tried to make that one thicker, but I'm not sure how long it'll hold him off. Any chance you'd reconsider turning the toking system back on since my life is on the line?"

"Sorry, Captain, but per your previous orders, I cannot enable the toking system at this time. But rest assured that based on my assessment of the situation, I have concluded that your life is not on the line. The Dregz have been ordered to bring you in alive, and this particular Dreg is showing no biomarkers that indicate hostility or aggression."

Charlie rolled his eyes. "I feel better already, man."

"Are you sure about that, Captain Hong?"

Charlie wiped sweat from his face—which was drenched—and noticed his arm felt twice as heavy as normal.

"MOM, is there a problem with the ship's gravity?"

"No, Captain, the graviton fields on the *Pineapple Express* are stable. But I am getting conflicting biodata from you."

MOM paused as if to collect her thoughts, then added, "Captain, your blood sugar levels have dropped significantly, and your electrolytes are approaching dangerously low levels. Would you like something to snack on?"

"Sure, this is the perfect time for a snack. Make sure you prepare one for Metal Mask. He might get a little peckish after he fucks me up."

Despite the sarcasm, Charlie could have gone for a snack. Some brownies. A pizza. A goddamn carrot. *Anything*.

His vision blurred and he collapsed sideways, filling the tiny space with his shivering body.

He heard the crackling sound again and smelled charred pineapple.

Another circle of golden lava appeared in the new wall, so close it would drip its hot goo onto Charlie's feet once it started melting. Any moment another hole would appear and Metal Mask would be close enough to reach through and grab Charlie.

Too weak to fight back, Charlie closed his eyes and waited for those hands to start pummeling him, tearing him apart, shaking the life out of him.

Well, he thought as his life flashed before his eyes, *it wasn't too bad of a run for a dumb stoner like me.*

And where the hell is that awful smell coming from?! he raged. *I may be the one who smelt it, but, goddammit, I know for a fact I'm not the one who dealt it!*

Suddenly, hands were on him.

Not two big angry hands, but a flurry of tiny, soft, *wet* hands.

And not from the direction of the golden lava's heat, but from behind him, where there was only the original dead end. The tiny hands groped and grabbed at his elbows, his knees, his neck, pulling him backward beyond the wall he'd been laying against.

Charlie's heart raced, his head spun, and the golden light surrounding him was swallowed up by darkness.

41

Zylvya couldn't remember ever feeling this stiff before, which is saying a lot when you're made of wood.

She lay on the floor of the mini-bridge in the patch of grass Charlie had morpho-printed for her, its silky blades cushioning her rigid body and making her feel like a log floating on a cloud.

For an Earth ape, he could be an especially thoughtful guy sometimes.

Not the brightest, usually, but every once in a while he surprised her with a clever solution to some problem they faced. He definitely wasn't at all like the *Starseed's* previous captain, Major Tom. Despite the similarities on the outside, they were about as different as could be on the inside.

Zylvya had learned, like anyone else who'd wandered the quadrant long enough, one important tenet to keep in mind when encountering the constant barrage of familiar and unfamiliar lifeforms: Looks can be deceiving.

I have to hold on, she thought. *I have to tell him before I go. He deserves to know why. And I need him to know that I never meant for it to turn out this way.*

"Her heart rate is accelerating," Mr. Glimwicket said as he gently patted her forehead with a damp sponge. "Lieutenant

Zylvya, if you can hear me, try not to get overly excited. Captain Hong is on his way. He's stopped checking in on the chatter—thank Bulzar!—which means he'll probably be here any second."

"Oh, Bob," scoffed Mrs. Glimwicket, brushing a green curl away from Zylvya's eyes. "It's sweet that he cares so much."

"You're right, dear. But why does he have to keep speaking in that Earther cowman accent? The sounds apes make when they speak are silly enough as-is."

"It's a cow*boy* accent from his homeworld. I think she likes it when he talks like that."

Yeah, I love being called 'little lady' by someone shorter than me, thought Zylvya.

"Hey, want me to put on a funny voice the next time we... you know?"

"Honestly, Bob!" his wife said, shooting him a look. "He's worried about her, just like you were worried about me. If anybody knows how crazy people get when they're worried about their loved ones, it's you."

Mr. Glimwicket's stubby antennae wilted slightly, then sprung back into their erect pose.

"What I did was different. They deserve it, those snakes!"

"So you dealt with another snake?"

"I had no choice, Bauble. I did what I did to keep you and Bob Jr. safe. Besides, it was just biodata. What she does with it isn't my business."

"She'll use it to cause trouble. Someone may get hurt. And as physicians we took a vow to never—"

"Wait a second—cause *trouble*? For *them*?"

He chuckled and his proboscis twitched.

"Good! If she succeeds in whatever plot she's cooking up, the quadrant will breathe a collective sigh of relief. The net amount of trouble and pain in the galaxy will go way down. Maybe I should be proud of having played a small role in it."

Mrs. Glimwicket's eyes flickered to Zylvya.

"Maybe we shouldn't be talking about this right now. What if she can hear us?"

"I don't think she can hear us, honey," Mr. Glimwicket said quietly, as if maybe she could. "Her vitals are barely detectable. She doesn't have much time left. The Captain better get here soon if he's going to have any chance to talk with her before…"

He trailed off, pretending to take his patient's pulse once again.

"Maybe we should give her a little more of the stuff you picked up in Lavaka? It seemed to work wonders on her while it lasted."

He scratched the soft fur under his proboscis and nodded.

"I don't think we should risk it. The amount of strain her neurons have been through, and the damage that drug causes… who knows how long her nervous system would hold out. Besides, we don't have much left. We'll save that risk for when Captain Hong arrives."

"Poor darling." Mrs. Glimwicket grasped Zylvya's wooden hand. "If you *can* hear me, you must hold out a little longer. I know Captain Hong will think of some way to save you."

Zylvya wanted to believe he would, but she also knew saving her couldn't be his primary concern. Nor should it be. Charlie had more important things to worry about besides a single member of his crew falling victim to her own miscalculation.

More like my own stupidity, thought Zylvya.

How could I have been so careless? Nylf tried to warn me. Mother tried to talk me out of it. Why didn't I listen to them?

Then again, if I had, the Pineapple Express *would have even less of a chance than it has now.*

Zylvya felt the emerald embers in her eyes flickering to life. She forced her eyelids open. Above her, on the faux-glass dome that topped the mini-bridge, the luminescent starfield was riddled with writhing black splotches. She knew they could be only one thing: Mrs. Glimwickets' larval hatchlings. Before her most recent comatose state, she'd noticed them progressing to the point of eating visible craters in the walls, even along the corridors outside the mini-bridge.

An invisible timer hung over the ship and every passenger's head. Did they have three more days? Five, at best?

Zylvya set aside trying to figure out how much time it would take for the millions of ravenous larvae to destroy the ship. As important as it was to solve that problem, there was something more important to figure out.

How could we have ignored the signs for so long?

Zylvya first noticed the smell around the second wake cycle after leaving Trapezia, right around the time of the first murder. She'd just chalked it up to more of the strange smells Charlie emitted.

Captain Hong might be an uncivilized Earther ape with erratic behavior patterns reminiscent of an addiction-addled dolt, but even he doesn't stink that *bad.*

Swarm hadn't figured it out, either, which made Zylvya feel a little better. He was too preoccupied with his long-lost love to give a smeg about doing his job.

If Crimebot suspected anything, he held that card close to his chest like all the others. She trusted his discretion, and besides, *millions* of five-star ratings on the Outernet couldn't be wrong. Apparently, when you save entire planets, it generates a lot of good reviews and gets you known as the guy to hire for tough, dangerous mysteries.

Still, seeing him in action with this Trapezia case, she wasn't sure she approved of his investigative tactics. He was pompous, obnoxiously nonchalant toward the victims, and painfully vague about offering insight into his theories and hypotheses.

Which made him really hard to work with. But not because she was a synthphobe or anything. Not at all. Him being a Synth had nothing to do with why he annoyed her.

Maybe it was how easily he fell under Charlie's spell, she thought. *Anyone who enjoys getting high that much should have their brain—or in his case, his CPU—examined.*

Then again, with Del and Axo out, and Swarm leaving, and well, what's happening to me... Charlie's going to need a crew member he can trust.

Assuming he survives the week.

Even in her comatose state, her sense of smell remained intact. That godawful stench was coming on again. She estimated the time between this wave and the last, but she knew she didn't have enough data. She could have missed a wave or two while she was out on her last trip away from the *Pineapple Express*. But there was no missing it now.

"Bob!" cried Mrs. Glimwicket, waving the air away from her proboscis. "At least warn me before you do that!"

"It wasn't me!" He nodded toward Zylvya. "Must be a side effect to whatever's happening to her. Andromeda, it's awful!"

"Oh, dear. Yes, it is. Let's do her a favor and never speak of this."

Zylvya cringed inside her petrified mannequin of a body.

Shows you how often anyone makes it out this far into the fringe these days, she thought, trying to distract herself from the embarrassment.

Out here on the outskirts of the galactic disc, along the fringe of the quadrant's web of transit lanes, where neither the cargo nor the destination are worth the trip, where stars seem too far apart... ancient, apocalyptic things lurk. Forgotten things. Rotten things.

Like my alleged coma fart.

Thank Andromeda the guys weren't here for that, or I'd never live it down.

42

CHARLIE AWOKE TUCKED SAFELY IN HIS BED. THE LIGHTS WERE LOW, and reggae played softly in the background. He felt well rested and had a spot of dried drool stuck to the corner of his mouth as if he'd been asleep for a while.

Sudden anxiety flooded his brain as he scanned his quarters. There was no sign of Metal Mask or the other Dregz, although he did notice a cluster of larvae munching a patch of ceiling nearby. He had no memory of who'd helped him or how he'd gotten back to his room, but he was relieved he hadn't woken up in the brig of a transit ship headed back to the Jurisphere.

Had it been a quick catnap? Only a few hours? he thought, rubbing the sleep from his eyes.

The digital alarm clock on his nightstand read 4:20PM, but that meant nothing since it was the clock's permanent time, and besides, what use is Earther time in outer space?

Still, it says 4:20, he thought. *What kind of stoner would I be if I ignored my duty?*

Big Willie, his immortal purple bong, stood ready for action with clean water and a fully packed bowl. He didn't remember prepping it before leaving for the peace summit, but with all the excitement, it wouldn't surprise him if he'd forgotten.

Who the hell forgets about a clean, loaded bong?

Charlie concentrated on forcibly reclaiming any other missing memories: the changing of key system parameters on the *Pineapple Express*, the creation of the AI-generated Trapezian three-way deepfake porn, and whatever other fucked-up behavior he'd apparently been up to without being able to recall the slightest detail.

Nothing came. Not the faintest hint of a memory. No missing block of time besides his recent nap. Not even a vague sense that his brain was clouded by a mental fog. In fact, as far as he could tell, his mental faculties seemed in perfect working order.

Maybe what I need is more *mental fog*, Charlie thought, smiling at Big Willie.

He snatched the bong from the nightstand and looked it over.

If I didn't load this bong, he thought, *then who did? And what the hell did they lace my weed with? Maybe bleach in the bong water? Hemlock in the herb? No way am I puffing on poison pot, man! I ain't no fool.*

Still, that didn't make sense. First of all, Charlie knew he was a fool. Secondly, why would someone rescue him from the Dregz and tuck him into bed only to kill him with poisoned pot?

The thought of poison triggered a flood of paranoid questions in his brain.

Who was behind the murders? What did they have to gain by disrupting the peace summit? How were the Reptilians involved? Who was the Reptilian hiding out on the ship? What was wrong with Zylvya? And what the hell was up with that goddamn sewage smell?

His eyes flickered to the cluster of munching larvae eating a crater in his ceiling.

Not that any of that will matter in a few days when those things destroy the ship and kill us all.

"MOM, any luck contacting the *Starseed* yet? Or any other nearby ship for that matter? We could use a rescue."

"Sorry, Captain," she answered, "but all communication

systems are still disabled, including ship-wide access to the Outernet."

"Then fix it! Can't you reboot the goddamn modem or something?"

"Sorry, but your previous orders override that request. I am unable to comply."

"Fine! Then at least tell me who brought me here!" he demanded.

"Sorry, Captain, but telling you that would violate my privacy subsystem, as I have explained."

"Well, was I toked or teleported or something?"

"You were brought here through tunnels in the ship's substrate."

"Tunnels? Like the one we found in my grow room?"

"Yes, Captain, but rest assured, I was ready to intervene on your behalf if their biodata indicated that they might harm you in any way. It did not. They brought you here with the utmost care and tucked you in before leaving."

"They? You're saying I was saved by multiple people?"

"Yes, Captain."

"*Who*, man?!" cried Charlie.

"Sorry, Captain. I am unable answer that question at this time. Not only did your rescuers request that I withhold their identities from you, but per your prior orders—"

"Yeah, yeah, you've explained that bullshit before," interrupted Charlie. "Well, whoever they are, I'd like you to send them a huge basket of snacks from Earth, all the best stuff: Oreos, Snickers, Red Vines, Doritos, Super Ultra Flaming Hot Cheetos. Even those little packets of the candy rocks that pop in your mouth... what are they called? Pop Rocks! Hell yeah! And include a thank you card—just pick one with a kitten on it or something—and let them know I'll reward them big-time when this trip is over."

Those words hung in the air like an anvil over his head. If he didn't get to the bottom of all the drama soon, their trip would be over in more ways than one.

But first he had to pay a visit to Zee. He knew it was a very uncaptainlike thought to have, but he had it anyway:

Losing her is scarier than losing the whole goddamn ship.

"I am processing those orders now, Captain. I believe your rescuers will greatly appreciate the gift and the message. I might add, I sense a change in your biodata that indicates you are preparing to take action. Is there anything else I can do for you before you leave?"

"Hold on, MOM, I'm talking to Big Willie," he said, holding the bong up to his ear like a phone. "I agree, man. If we're going out, let's go out high as fuck."

Charlie snatched his lighter off the bedside table and sparked up a flame. He hovered the flame over the packed bowl, brought the mouth of the bong to his lips, then cried out in disgust and flung the bong across the room. It shattered into a million pieces and splashed bong water in all directions.

"What the hell, man?!" He swiped at a strand of translucent slime dangling from his lips. "Who slimed my bong?"

"After you were asleep in your bed, your rescuers prepared your bong and tried to consume cannabis," MOM explained. "Of course, I wouldn't allow it."

"Next time, stop them before they get their nasty goo all over it!"

Charlie sighed and pinched the slime between two fingers.

"Hey, my empty luggage was covered in this stuff, too. But I've seen it somewhere else…"

He trailed off, searching his memories and coming up empty-handed once again.

"Hey MOM, why wouldn't you allow my rescuers to hit my bong? You must've known I'd be down to share, and you could've just replaced it afterwards."

"I denied them access because I don't allow mi—"

She cut herself off.

"Sorry, Captain, but to answer that question would infringe upon my directive about protecting personally identifiable information. Or, as you summarized it earlier, *that bullshit.*"

"Whatever, man. I'll figure it out myself."

He shook his head and watched as Big Willie's million broken shards and the puddle of bong water were absorbed into the floor. When they were gone, he flung off his blankets and hopped out of bed.

"How far am I from the mini-bridge?"

"You are just over one Earth mile from the mini-bridge. My augmented guidance system is ready to lead you there when you are ready."

"Good. And hey, make sure the path you create keeps me clear of the Dregz and Vree Voktal. Or the other delegates. Or anyone, really. Roll me a doob for the walk since I'll have some time to think."

"Adjusting your optimal path to the mini-bridge now, Captain. The walk will take you approximately twenty-one minutes if you maintain your average pace. Your doob is ready on the nightstand."

Charlie snatched the joint, popped it between his lips, and tapped the chatter pinned to his chest.

"Sit tight, little lady," he drawled. "Chuck Stonerly is on his way."

43

"Bob, look! Her eyes are open! Zylvya, dear, can you hear me?"

Zylvya heard a door swirl open somewhere behind the Glimwickets and familiar footsteps hurry inside.

"Sorry I'm late," Charlie said, panting. "MOM signed me up for a marathon to steer me clear of Dregz, and I'm not so good at marathons. How's my darlin' damsel doing?"

Try calling me that when I'm not in a coma, she thought.

"She seems to be waking up, Captain," said Mr. Glimwicket.

Charlie's face appeared over the Glimwickets' shoulders. His brow glistened with sweat and his eyes sagged with exhaustion. She wondered when he'd last had a decent meal or a good night's sleep.

"Howdy, pardner. I came as fast as I could," he said with a forced steadiness to his voice. "Can ya hear me, little lady?"

"Call me little lady again, and I'll reintroduce you to my left hook," said Zylvya, her voice hardly above a whisper.

Charlie's face lit up.

"Awesome! You can hear me. Hey, if I'm bugging you that much then you can't be that bad off, can you?"

She answered by locking her eyes onto his.

"Lieutenant Zylvya collapsed on the way from her quarters to the mini-bridge about five ghatikas ago. Unlike her previous narcoleptic symptoms, this time her nervous system had almost completely shut down. It's left her…" He trailed off and looked at his wife.

"Paralyzed," finished Mrs. Glimwicket.

She stroked Zylvya's green curls and sighed. "Scans showed plenty of neurological activity, but she's been unable to move or communicate. Until now."

"So she's getting better? Excellent!"

"Not necessarily, Captain. Most of her brain function is offline, so to speak. Her vitals are stable, but only barely so. Unless we see improvement in those, I would still treat this as a very serious matter."

"Can't you give her something?" asked Charlie. "Some kind of medicine?"

Zylvya's emerald eyes bounced from person to person as she followed the conversation.

"We've administered every device and substance we have at our disposal," explained Mr. Glimwicket, shooting a glance at Mrs. Glimwicket. "Even a few that would normally put our Gal-Fed medical licenses at risk."

"She must be sick, right?" asked Charlie desperately. "This all started right after everyone arrived. I bet those dirty Dregz brought a disease onto the ship!"

"Incorrect, Captain." MOM chimed in. "All biological contaminates were purged upon boarding. No pathogens or parasites have entered the *Pineapple Express* since its creation. She is not sick, Captain."

"Could it be poison then? The same person behind the hacking and the murders could've slipped her something."

"We've run every conceivable chemical scan. No sign of anything harmful. The problem seems to be in her head, not in her body."

"In her head?"

Mr. Glimwicket shrugged.

"Her species isn't well known to modern medicine. Truth be told, we have no idea what's happening to her. It's like her brain is struggling to utilize the synapses that control voluntary mobility. Similar to how the body shuts down when it's asleep."

"Charlie," Zylvya mumbled, her voice barely audible.

The trio kneeling around her leaned in to listen.

"Imposter... trajectory..." She struggled to say every word. "Hole... help!"

"I don't know what any of that means," said Charlie, searching her panicked eyes. He took her hand with both of his. "But it sounds important. Can you try again, Zee?"

I'm too far gone, she thought. *I'm not strong enough. I can't do it.*

Mr. Glimwicket peered into her eyes through a small telescopic device and shook his head.

"It's no use. Her brain is forming thoughts, sentences... but her body just isn't listening."

"Zee, I know you're in there and you must be scared. We're gonna figure out a way to help you."

Charlie looked to the Glimwickets with glistening eyes.

"There's gotta be something else you can you do, man."

"All we can do is keep her comfortable and respond to any changes in her condition," said Mrs. Glimwicket. "Although, we were hoping you might be able to help her..."

"Me?" Charlie looked at them as if they'd just told a joke. "I'm not a doctor. *You* two are doctors. What the hell could I possibly do to help her?"

"Two things, actually," answered Mr. Glimwicket.

"Neither of which we can guarantee will work," added Mrs. Glimwicket. "And both are huge risks."

The Glimwickets exchanged a look before Mrs. Glimwicket began explaining.

"One of the unlicensed medicines we treated her with is illegal, but based on the results of her last brush with the stuff, it seemed to work quite well—at least temporarily, and at the expense of introducing high levels of toxins into her bloodstream and tissue—"

"Spit it out, man! Tell me what it is that helped her, and I'll get you as much as you need."

"Kryyd," said Mr. Glimwicket bluntly. "Krydd's stimulants seem to offset whatever process is paralyzing her."

"And it gave her some sick dance moves," added Charlie. "As much as I hate pills, especially that junk, if it helps Zee... then let's pill it up. So where do we get more?"

"Well, we asked Lieutenant Swarm, but he said he only had those few pills he and Lieutenant Zylyva took earlier. We were thinking, well, Bob here was thinking, and I'm not exactly sold on it yet, that you could ask another member of your crew for help."

"Another member of my—? Nope. No way am I asking Nadia for anything. First of all, she's not on my crew. I don't have a *Chief of Secrets*. No ship has a Chief of Secrets because it's a dumb idea. Secondly, for all we know, she's the one doing this to Zee just so I'll have to bargain with her. And thirdly, even if she's not responsible, things are clusterfucked enough already without getting that snake involved."

"What if she's the only source of kryyd on the *Pineapple Express?*" asked Mr. Glimwicket.

There's another option, thought Zylvya, remembering all the things Charlie had so easily morpho-printed. *But you'll have to believe in yourself, or it won't work!*

"Then that leaves us with the other thing you can do to help her," Mrs. Glimwicket explained. "There's a medical station not too far from here, on a planet called Betatron 3. It's mostly a medical research colony that operates outside of direct Gal-Fed control. Bob and I volunteered there years ago, before Bob Jr. hatched. They should have the equipment and expertise we lack here on the *Pineapple Express.*"

The smell of burning cannabis invaded Zylvya's nostrils. She couldn't see him, but she knew Charlie had just sparked up one of his joints.

What an addict, she thought, *but at least it's helping to cover up the lingering shit smell of doom.*

"Sounds simple enough, man," she heard Charlie say. "We change course to this research colony, and they help Zee."

"Assuming she lasts that long," said Mr. Glimwicket. "If she gets some kryyd in her to help keep her vitals pumping, her chances for survival go way up."

Charlie cleared his throat and spoke into the air. "Alright, MOM, you heard them. Change course to whatever planet Mrs. Glimwicket mentioned a minute ago. Go as fast as the old pineapple will take us, man."

If Zylvya hadn't been paralyzed, she'd have jumped for joy.

We'll solve two problems with one solution! she thought. *I might be able to get help with my little mental breakdown, but more importantly, the ship will no longer be headed toward oblivion. No, not oblivion. Something much worse than oblivion.*

"Sorry, Captain," apologized MOM in her emotionless tone, "but the *Pineapple Express* cannot deviate from its current trajectory."

She heard Charlie sigh and take a tiny puff.

"Of course it can't. Why can't we change course, MOM?"

"We cannot change course because the ship's navigation subsystem has been rerouted and disabled—"

"Wait for it," Charlie said over her.

"—per your orders, Captain Hong."

"There it is," he finished.

He shook his head at the Glimwickets.

"Don't listen to her. I didn't do it, man. There's an imposter making MOM think I'm giving her all these fucked-up orders that don't make any sense."

"I assure you, Captain," MOM explained, "There is no imposter. You have been the one setting these new rules and reprogramming my functional parameters."

"Whatever! There's no way I'm doing all this dumb shit and then forgetting about it! My memory isn't that bad, man!"

Something about his tone made Zylvya think he didn't completely believe what he was saying.

Is it possible that neither MOM nor Charlie are mistaken? she thought, considering her own current dilemma.

"My bioserver account password might not be very secure, but my mind is. I command you, as the highest-ranking officer on this ship and your goddamned creator, change course!"

"I am sorry, Captain, but I cannot comply with that order without contradicting my commitment to follow your previous orders."

There was a moment of silence when all Zylvya could hear is Charlie inhaling a huge hit from his joint. If they couldn't change course, she'd continue to deteriorate. But considering their destination, she might end up being the lucky one if she checked out before they arrived.

"Remind me, MOM," Charlie said coolly. "Where'd I set this permanent course for?"

"The *Pineapple Express's* course is set to Gonnevut's Brown Hole."

Mrs. Glimwicket gasped and put a hand to her proboscis.

"That explains it!" she exclaimed. "This whole time I thought you were experiencing some kind of digestive issue, Bob!"

"I thought the same about you and Bob Jr!" he said, holding his head in his big hands. "But a brown hole... Oh, dear, this is bad."

"What the hell are you all talking about, man?" asked Charlie. "I get the larva thing, but what's this about a brown hole? Is that some kind of light-skinned black hole or something?"

Before they could speak MOM explained, "Gonnevut's Brown Hole was discovered in stardate 9279 by the Tralfamadorean astro-explorer and Gal-Fed loyalist Truk Gonnevut. Gonnevut and his team discovered a total of six brown holes along the quadrant's outer edge, and he named the first after himself."

"Cool story, MOM. What's the difference between a brown hole and a black hole? Just the color?"

"Oh, there are a few other things," Mrs. Glimwicket said as she waved the air away from her face.

"Brown holes are an extremely rare variant of black holes, Captain," explained MOM. "The main difference is that while nothing but gamma rays can escape the immense gravity of a black hole, brown holes emit low-spectrum gravity waves across the fabric of spacetime. These waves can spread up to a thousand light years from the hole's core, affecting lifeforms in a number of unique ways."

"Haven't you sensed them yet, Captain?" Mrs. Glimwicket asked.

"They stink!" exclaimed Mr. Glimwicket.

"Correction, Mr. Glimwicket, a brown hole does not stink in the sense that it releases particles that are detected with a lifeform's olfactory sense organs. Instead, the gravity waves disrupt the olfactory nerves in such a way that the brain interprets the signal as smelling of excrement."

"See! It wasn't me after all!" cried Charlie. "Well, okay, it *was* me that first time in the mini-Transit Bay. But all those other times everyone thought it was me, they had the wrong brown hole, man." He paused to take a small puff. "Wait, so it's dangerous or something?"

MOM answered, "Once the *Pineapple Express* passes the brown hole's event horizon, we will be unable to escape."

"Why would you let me set a course that would kill us all?"

"Research on brown holes indicates that while there is no escaping its gravity, destruction of the ship is not imminent. You and the other passengers will not be directly harmed."

"Worse!" declared Mr. Glimwicket. "We'll be trapped inside a swirling vortex of gravity waves… forever."

"Well, shit!"

"Exactly, Captain," said Mrs. Glimwicket. "It'll smell like the worst excrement imaginable, at least until our larvae break down enough of the ship's substrate to lose life support."

"MOM, isn't there *anything* you can do?" asked Charlie. "Can I reboot you or something?"

"Rebooting me would have no effect on your prior commands, Captain. They are stored in my central memory banks and cannot be overridden."

"I got it! Let's call for help! There must be some other ship nearby that could swing alongside the *Pineapple Express* and pick us all up, right?"

"If we go broadcasting our position to the quadrant," said Mr. Glimwicket, "chances are the Reptilians would catch wind of it and be the first to arrive."

"MOM, how much time till we hit the brown hole's event horizon?" asked Charlie.

"Approximately two full cycles from now, Captain."

"Unless anyone has a better idea, it's a risk we have to take. MOM, I want you to send out an SOS in all directions. Let them know who we are and the risk we're in."

"Sorry, Captain, but I cannot do that. Even if you hadn't disabled all of the ship's data endpoints to the Outernet, you've programmed a disruption field into the substrate itself which blocks all internal transmissions from leaving the ship."

"Now I know you're trippin', MOM. I've never programmed anything in my life!"

Whoever's behind this has taken every step to ensure our doom, thought Zylvya. *If their plan was to send the ship into a brown hole to begin with, why bother killing the Silexi Emperor and the Undulata ambassador? Why bother putting Eta Cerbo in a coma or replacing the treaty with an obscene deepfake? And why bother framing Charlie for any of it?*

Zylvya's eyes blinked, and her vision cleared. Charlie stood at her feet staring down at her. From her perspective on the floor, he looked much taller than she knew him to be in real life.

Something in his expression told her he was weighing something in his mind. Probably something brave. Definitely something stupid.

"Hey, MOM, you said the ship's substrate is somehow jamming any transmission from leaving the *Pineapple Express*, right?" asked Charlie.

"Correct, Captain. Transmissions from inside the ship are dynamically neutralized by an anti-vibrational array."

"*Inside* the ship," he snapped. "But what about transmissions sent from *outside* the ship?"

Yep, definitely stupid, Zylvya thought.

She tried to force a warning from her mouth, but no sound came out. She'd seen this look on his face before. She knew that even if she could argue with him, there was no talking him out of doing something incredibly shortsighted when he put his mind to it.

A human-shaped bulge appeared in the pineapple wall beside him. It rippled and roiled and finally solidified into a bulky spacesuit that looked like it weighed more than Charlie.

"Oh, one more thing before I go," he said, making eye contact with Zylvya.

He snapped his fingers and another bulge appeared, this time in the marble floor. It solidified into a large suitcase.

"Is that what I think it is?" Mr. Glimwicket asked.

Mrs. Glimwicket popped open the clasp, lifted the lid, and gasped. Her expression looked both worried and relieved. She closed it and nodded.

"This will be plenty, Captain."

44

The makeshift airlock was too small to fit Charlie, the spacesuit, and all his gear, so he concentrated his mind on making it larger.

Concentrate was too serious of a word for what Charlie did. All he did was vaguely imagine the ship-side wall sliding back a few feet as the rest of the room stretched along with it. And bam, it obeyed.

That was all it took to manipulate the structure of the *Pineapple Express* or to morpho-print any object he needed. Even technologically complex gear he didn't know the first thing about, like a functional NASA spacesuit and a distress beacon he'd only read about once on the Outernet, seemed to grow from the ship's substrate within seconds of him desiring it.

Back on the *Starseed* he'd been able to morpho-print some high-tech stuff like laptops and TVs, but he always assumed Mother was doing all the heavy lifting.

Based on her track record, Charlie didn't think MOM played much of a role in the creation of the gear he morpho-printed on the *Pineapple Express*. In fact, he desperately hoped she'd kept her circuits out of it.

Guess MOM's what you get when you make a copy of a ship's

computer using only 1% of the original, he thought. *Even if I didn't know better, you'd think Mother would've anticipated that MOM would suck.*

The room finished stretching out, and there was plenty of space for the suit and the Radio Flyer wagon full of gear. Getting in the suit hadn't been fun, or easy, but he managed with the help of some NASA instructional videos stashed in a local archive of the Outernet. It also helped that he morpho-printed an instruction manual with Ikea-simple instructions even he could understand.

"Look, Mom! Look, Dad!" he said, standing tall with his fists on his hips. "I made it to NASA! I'm a real astronaut!"

Charlie picked up a length of unbreakable carbon fiber rope and the deep space distress beacon. He held the beacon up to his helmet and looked it over. It was about twice the size of a bowling pin and roughly the same shape, except it had a sharp point on its bottom to anchor it firmly to the hull of the ship. All he had to do was jab it hard enough into the ship's outer hull, and the anchor roots would deploy from the spike, attaching it firmly for the rest of their short, ill-fated trip.

Easy enough.

He pressed a button on his suit's armband panel. There was a scritch of static in his helmet, followed by the sound of his own voice.

"This is Captain Chuck Stonerly of the Pineapple Express. If you can hear me... please help, man! We can't stop, and we're headed straight for a friggin' brown hole! I repeat, this is—"

Charlie punched another button and the voice cut off.

It wasn't Shakespeare, but it was the best he could improvise while stuffing his legs into bulky space pants.

Underneath the recording, the ship's coordinates were being broadcast as well, meaning any ship who caught the signal could easily track down its source. MOM had warned him that there weren't too many ships that ventured this far out on the galactic fringe. She also warned him that any hostile ships who frequented this sector, Krolik Raiders, for instance, actively listen for such distress signals, like vultures listening for the cries of a lost lion cub. Not to mention any Reptilian scout ships conducting routine, long-range scans of the area. To draw either faction toward the *Pineapple Express* would mean a certain level of discomfort for its passengers ranging from slavery to tortuous death.

Charlie decided it was a risk they had to accept, considering the alternative. In a couple of days, everyone on board would either be spat out into the vacuum of space or slurped up into the brown hole. There was also a chance that a friendly ship would pick up their distress signal and rescue them without ill intent.

Fat chance, Charlie thought. *Still, what other choice do I have? If I can't figure out how to take back control of the ship, becoming a Krolik slave seems preferable to flying a busted ship straight into a humongous, inescapable space asshole.*

Despite his inarticulate and bumbling argument, he hadn't been able to convince MOM his plan was worth the risk. She was adamant on reducing the risk to the ship and its passengers, not increasing it. So they'd agreed to disagree. MOM wouldn't assist him in creating an airlock nor in deploying the beacon. Her programming prevented her from stopping the Captain, but she didn't have to help him. If he wanted to plant the beacon outside the ship, he'd have to do it on his own.

He sniffed the air inside his helmet and gagged.

"How is that rancid shit smell getting inside my helmet?" he said to himself. "Oh, that's right, I remember now. It's not real shit. It's just some kind of gravity ripple thing tricking my brain into thinking I smell shit."

"Correct, Captain Hong," MOM answered. "Said differently, the olfactory region of your brain is—"

"Got it," interrupted Charlie. "Phantom shit, real shit, it all stinks. Time to ignore it and go to work."

He looked up at the ceiling and probed the golden pineapple juiciness with his mind. He sensed its depth, its smoothness, then imagined it opening up like the docking portals back on the

Starseed's Transit Bay. He closed his eyes and concentrated, wanting to make sure he got the diameter right.

Just as he felt the pineapple flesh ceiling start to thin out, the chatter pinned to his spacesuit exploded with an angry outburst.

"What the smeg are you doing, Captain?" roared Swarm.

"Oh, just possibly saving the ship, man. How about you?"

"MOM just informed me that you're planning to attach a deep space distress beacon to the exterior of the ship. She also explained that you ignored her warnings about drawing unwanted attention from unfriendly vessels in the area."

"Yeah, that about covers it all. Doesn't seem like we have any other choice, man."

"Do you have any idea what Reptilians would do to this ship and its passengers if they were to get their hands on us?"

"Do you have any idea what happens to all of us if these hungry larvae start eating holes in the ship's hull? Or if we cross the event horizon of the giant space asshole we're speeding toward? Look around and open your nostrils, or whatever organ you smell with, and tell me what other options we have right now."

There was a moment of silence before Swarm's voice returned.

"Brown hole? Of course! Smegging hell, why didn't I put that together before?"

"Probably because you've been a little distracted," Charlie said, wincing at the bitter taste the words left in his mouth. "But maybe a more important question is, why the hell didn't MOM provide you with that important bit of information? I'm starting to wonder about her, man. Starting to wonder if she's been compromised."

"Captain," MOM's voice cut in. "I assure you I have not been compromised. I have performed every action you have requested, and I have provided you with all the relevant information I was able to provide."

Charlie ignored her and spoke into his chatter.

"Swarm, this will only take a minute. You and Crimebot

should get back to the mini-bridge to check in on Zee. I'll meet you there when I'm done."

"Your pet robot isn't with you? He left the mini-Pond shortly after you did, saying he had something important to tell you."

"I haven't seen him since I left that creepy cave." Charlie tapped the chatter again. "CB, come in. Crimebot, this is Captain Hong. Where you at, man? Answer, or I'll call in a ganja strike on your position. Wait, I mean, tell me where you are, and I *promise* to call in a ganja strike."

He paused to listen for a response, but none came.

"Huh. Maybe he lost his chatter. MOM, where's Crimebot?"

"Crimebot's location is currently dispersed across multiple areas of the ship's mini-Ring. Would you like me to list all the specific locations for you?"

"See what I mean, Swarm? She's bonkers."

"Captain, MOM just gave me the details of our current trajectory," said Swarm. "I comp'd it with offline holo-schematics, and she appears to be telling us the truth. At our current speed, we don't have very much time."

"At the rate those larvae are eating, we never had much time to begin with. Listen, man, we've gotta save the *Pineapple Express*, but just in case we fail... Anyway, as soon as we gain control of the ship again, I'll personally toss this beacon into the brown hole. Until then, it's our best chance of survival, and worth any additional risk. So let me do my thing while you and Zee find Crimebot, so he can tell us who's behind all this bullshit."

"Understood, Captain," said Swarm. "Be careful out there—and make sure to anchor and tether yourself to the ship. I know the *Starseed* would never let you drift away, but I'm not so sure about this giant fruit vessel of yours."

"One step ahead of you, man," Charlie said, feeling the weight of the rope coil slung over his shoulder.

Cassie's voice came from his chatter. "Hey, uh, Captain Hong. You there?"

Charlie sighed.

"Thanks for calling in to the *Captain Hong Trying to Save The Ship* podcast. Do you have a question or comment for the Captain?"

"Uh. Yes. No. I'm not sure. Sorry, I think I have the wrong chatter."

"I'm just messing around, Cass! What can I do for you?"

"Oh, hi, Captain. I thought I should call you about this thing I found. Well, first, have you seen Crimebot? He said he would come by the arcade, but he hasn't yet and I just wondered if he'd said anything to you about it."

"No, he didn't mention anything about your arcade," said Charlie, gritting his teeth. "Was that all?"

"He didn't? Bummer. No, that wasn't why I called. I found another hole in the wall."

"Cassie, in case you haven't noticed, there are millions of larvae turning the ship into Swiss cheese right before our eyes. It's full of holes."

"Not one of those, Captain. This hole looks exactly like the one we found in your grow room when your plant was stolen. Big enough for a person to crawl through, and deep. I think you should come take a look."

Charlie's hand went for his afro but was blocked by the faceplate of his helmet.

"Where?"

"Right here in *Cassie's Chassis*, underneath my Tron-themed 3d zero-g pinball machine."

"Did you see anyone go in or out?"

"No, just the hole. I think it might look fresh? Like it's only started closing up. What should I do?"

"Get inside! Quick, before it closes up!" he cried. "See where it leads!"

"But it could lead to the murderer."

"Exactly! Look..." He lowered his voice. "Keep it on the down-low, okay, but the whole ship is in danger right now. As long as this asshole controls the ship, they have a knife to all of our throats. We gotta find 'em, stop 'em, and take back control of the *Pineapple Express*. Are you with me or not?"

"So another job on top of waitress and arcade owner? *Murderer Hunter*. Great."

"Hey, the good news is that if you catch them, you get fast-tracked to a permanent position on my crew."

"On the *Starseed* crew? With Del?"

"The position comes with a console right next to his on the bridge."

There was a pause before Cassie's voice came back on the chatter, this time with an electrically fierce edge to it.

"One murderer, coming up."

"That's the spirit, Cass. Happy hunting."

Charlie turned his attention back to the pineapple ceiling. A four-foot-wide hole appeared above, revealing a disc of blackness dotted by a myriad of stars. All he had to do was jump and his personal gravity field would be instantly adjusted to accommodate his needs up there.

Out there.

Outside.

With the rope on his shoulder and the beacon in his hand, he bent his knees as much as the bulky spacesuit would allow, then bucked straight upward toward the hole.

As soon as his clunky astronaut boots left the green marble floor, Charlie felt himself become lighter than air. What little force he was able to muster met with no downward gravitational pull. He simply floated up like a feather on an updraft, through the hole, and out onto the hull.

"Damn," he said. "I gotta try that again later when I'm high."

Zylvya's voice came from his chatter. "When are you not high, Captain?"

"Zee!" cried Charlie as his boots touched down on the hull of the ship and his local gravity took hold. "You're awake! How do you feel?"

"Like someone tossed a Blendball in my head."

"Funny you should mention Blendballs, because while you were napping—"

"Swarm filled me in. Our killer isn't done killing."

"We have to stop them, Zee. You and Swarm go find Crimebot and go straight to Cassie's Chassis. She found one of those tunnels, and I sent her inside to follow whoever made it."

"You sent a teenaged girl into a small dark tunnel after a murderer?"

"First of all, the tunnels aren't that dark. The pineapple walls give off a soft golden light, which means—"

"Charlie, listen!" she interrupted. "People are disappearing. Crimebot is missing. The Glimwickets can't find Bob Jr., and he's not replying to their messages. Vree Voktal just realized the Silexian heir hasn't been in his bed for hours, and the Dregz posted outside his room say the only person who's been to see him was Nadia. But she was escorted there by Vree Voktal himself." She lowered her voice. "He's here now, flipping out. Swarm's running interference. It's not good, Charlie."

"Bob Jr.'s missing?" asked Charlie, staring blankly across the exterior landscape of the three-mile-wide ship, not noticing a thing about the incredible pineapple skin landscape.

"Wait, why the hell did Nadia visit E.T.? She never leaves her snake pit..."

"Vree said it was to bring him some kind of 'Get Well' basket."

"Well, that's some bullshit. What does Nadia say?"

"We haven't asked her yet. Let's ask her about it, together, once you get back here." There was a tinge of anxiety in her voice. "I just got back and you run off again."

"Hey, there's nothing to worry about. After all the times the *Starseed* swooped in to save a ship in distress, we gotta have some good karma coming our way."

"Funny you mention that. Listen, Charlie, just get your hairy butt back here as soon as you can."

"Did you just mention my butt? Swarm, did you catch that? She's thinking about my butt."

"Just plant the smegging beacon," rattled Swarm, "and get back here before all hell breaks loose. And remember to anchor yourself."

Charlie glanced at the rope hanging from his shoulder. He lifted it to feel its weight, then dropped the coil and watched it fall to the surface as it would inside the ship.

"Gravity seems to be working. Sure I even need to tether?"

"Yes!" Swarm's and Zylvya's voices blasted through his helmet simultaneously.

Obediently, Charlie thrust the javelin-shaped anchor down into the hole he'd just jumped through. There was just enough time to see it plunge into the green marble floor before the hole closed up and he was standing alone on the outside of the *Pineapple Express*.

45

Charlie swiveled his helmet to take in the surface of the ship.

Damn. This is exactly what I'd expect it to look like if I were standing on a giant pineapple, he thought proudly. *Brown and gold, rough, small sharpish peaks and shallow dips.*

He stomped a boot against it, and it reverberated back through his suit.

And it's tough enough to protect against the vacuum of outer space. Can those hungry little fuckers really eat a hole through it?

He found the clip fastened to the end of the rope and attached it to his suit's belt. There were no nearby stars to illuminate the landscape, but the light from the Milky Way was just bright enough the see by. He scanned the area looking for a good spot to anchor the distress beacon.

As he looked around, the starlight glinted off his space visor and created the illusion of movement in his peripheral vision. Still, he stopped and swiveled his shoulders to check, and all he found were empty golden hills.

Who else but me would be stupid enough to come out here? he assured himself.

Swarm's voice interrupted his paranoid thought.

"Captain, seems like the galaxy has decided to grant us a bit of luck. We're approaching a system occupied by a few vessels—mostly Krolik, who I suggest we avoid at all costs. But there's one sizable Gal-Fed explorer in the mix."

"They'd have the capacity to take on our numbers," explained Zylvya, "and the manners not to sell us all into slavery in some asteroid mine."

"Remember who pays Gal-Fed's bills," added Swarm. "Still, I'd rather take my chances negotiating with some mid-tier official than face a brown hole. Get that beacon planted, and get back here so we can get ready to meet them."

"It's a red giant class star, so you might want to dim your visor, or even close your eyes as we pass," said Zylvya. "It's going to get pretty bright out there in a minute or two. But don't worry, the ship's got a built-in magnetosphere that will deflect any harmful radiation or charged particles."

Charlie glanced toward the front end of the ship and noticed a particularly bright red star growing brighter with every passing second.

He lifted the distress beacon above his head with both hands.

"Die, giant vampire pineapple spaceship!" he cried before thrusting it into the brownish gold crust of the ship's hull. As soon as its sharpened tip penetrated the surface, he felt its roots unfurling and tugging the beacon snugly into place.

"The beacon's secure, man." He tapped a button on his armband. "And now the recording I made is looping. I'm gonna follow the tether back to my airlock. See you guys in a few."

As he turned to go, he caught a glimpse of a silhouette vanishing over the distant horizon. Against the glaring backdrop of the rapidly approaching star, its shape was unmistakable.

Someone was out there with him.

"Someone's out here with me," he said, his breath quickening. "They're heading toward the back of the ship."

"Impossible," said Swarm.

"I know what I saw." He clenched the rope as he stomped

awkwardly after them in his bulky spacesuit. "They're up to something and I'm gonna stop them."

"Don't pursue them, Captain!" Zylvya's voice pleaded from inside his helmet. "It could be a trap. The smarter move is to get inside quickly and seal the hull. You'll be safe, and they'll be trapped."

"They're heading toward the *Pineapple Express's* engine. Why would a saboteur and murderer do that, Zee?"

"Captain, you don't know the first thing about the hyperspace drive on this ship," rattled Swarm.

"I know enough to realize that asshole shouldn't mess with it. Don't worry, man, I'm getting the hang of this stupid spacesuit. I think I can catch up."

"If you do, what's your plan?" asked Swarm. "Ramble him to death?"

"Charlie," Zylvya's voice was as calm as a willow branch swaying in the breeze. "I need you to return to the ship. We all do, but especially me. You know how hard it is for me to say that, so please don't make me say it again. Stop being a hero, and we'll handle them together once you're secure."

A series of recent memories flashed before Charlie's eyes. There'd been plenty of times he'd ignored his crew's advice, following his gut instead of their expertise, and each time had led to disaster. Del was trapped inside a cactus. Axolotl was trapped inside a healing tube. He'd lost Zylvya a few times on this trip alone, only to get her back each time in worse shape than the last.

Despite all those memories, he plodded on, obsessed with finally catching the fucker who'd been impersonating him and causing havoc on his ship.

It wasn't until he felt a strange crunch under his right foot that he stopped. He lifted his boot to reveal a tiny pink smudge on the rough ground below.

What the hell was that? he wondered. *And where have I seen that color before?*

The red light from the approaching star slid across his

helmet's faceplate, turning the smudge, the surface, and his boots an eerie crimson color. Having forgotten Zylvya's warning to shield his eyes, he instinctively looked up toward the passing star.

At that exact second, a bright white light exploded from the back of the ship, blinding him and burning an image into the back of his eyes. Someone in the distance was standing upright, holding a small object high above their head toward the star.

Then, suddenly, it was all gone: the white light, the red glow, and the star itself. He reached his gloved hands up to rub his eyes but they bumped against the curved glass of his faceplate.

"Shit! I can't see a thing! I'm blind, man!"

"Captain, what happened?" roared Swarm. "Get back to your smegging airlock and—"

His voice was cut off as if the chatter connection had been severed.

Colors swam in Charlie's vision as he recovered from the blast of light. He snatched the rope from the ground and used it to find his way back to the spot where he'd opened up the makeshift airlock on his way out. He stood above the spot, frowning down at the patch of hull where his rope disappeared. No matter how hard he concentrated, it wouldn't obey his mental commands.

"Open up, dammit!" he commanded the brownish gold crust.

"MOM, open my airlock for me! I need to get back inside the ship!"

"Sorry, but I cannot do that, Captain."

"This is no time to fuck around, MOM! *Open the goddamn airlock!*"

"Sorry, but I cannot do that," she repeated. "Per the captain's orders, I have locked down the exterior of the ship."

Charlie stopped pulling on the buried tether.

"MOM, *I'm* the captain of this ship, and *I'm* ordering you to let me back inside, right now!"

"Sorry, you are not permitted to enter this ship."

Charlie caught his own reflection in the inside of his faceplate.

"You think I'm the imposter, don't you? Dude, I'm not the imposter! Whoever's giving you those orders is the imposter! Swarm! Zee! Tell her!"

"I have restricted your access to the ship's chatter circuit," she said with an eerie calmness in her artificial voice. "Goodbye."

"MOM, wait!"

His tether went limp in his hands. The slack rope rose up all around him like a serpent, and he felt his boots lose contact with the ground. He swept his feet downward, but the force only propelled him upward at a greater speed.

The artificial gravity provided by the *Pineapple Express*, the gravity that had held him safely to the ship's hull, wasn't working.

Charlie began to float away.

46

CAPTAIN CHARLIE HONG, A.K.A. CHUCK STONERLY, FLAILED THE bulky, stiff limbs of his spacesuit as he drifted slowly away from his ship.

"Help!" he cried. "MOM, my personal gravity field stopped working! Fix it, quick, and tow me back to the hull!"

"I am sorry, but I cannot do that."

Charlie swallowed hard and stared at the pineapple landscape falling away below him.

"MOM, listen to me. You're not thinking straight right now. Scan me. I'm the real Charlie Hong, man. And I'm currently in mortal danger! *Help me!*"

"Standby," MOM droned. "Scan complete. I have confirmed that you are Charlie Hong. Hello, Captain."

"Hi, MOM," Charlie said, rolling his eyes. "Think you could tow me back to the ship?"

"Sorry, Captain. I cannot tow you back to the ship since I have assessed that you are not floating away."

"What the hell do you call this, man?" Charlie flapped the arms of his spacesuit helplessly to illustrate. "Clean your goddamn sensors and re-assess!"

"Standby. I have just reset and recalibrated my sensor array.

My assessment remains the same: Captain Charlie Hong is safe inside the *Pineapple Express*."

Charlie hung suspended in the air while her words sank in. Had she finally lost her mind? Or had the imposter hacked her sensors into believing they were actually Charlie Hong?

Or is she telling the truth? asked a tiny voice from his subconscious.

His mind reeled backward through time, stopping first at the comment Nadia made about how quickly he'd changed his clothes. He knew she was a lying, manipulative snake, but why lie about something so trivial as the clothes he was wearing?

His memory continued drifting backwards, this time stopping at the intense mindfuck of Swarm's data pill. From what Swarm had explained, data pills worked by separating the mind—whatever *that* actually is—from its physical synapses in order to shuffle in new information before fusing them back together again. Charlie had felt his mind helplessly drifting into oblivion, much like his body was doing now. It had struggled to find its way back.

Had it? Or had some part of his mind been left behind, abandoned, rejected? Left to float in the formless void of the mindspace forever? Wouldn't it flail and panic and look for a way to attach itself to Charlie's brain? If it couldn't fuse with Charlie for some reason, could it find another physical host, another brain, to attach to?

Finally his mind rushed backwards to a moment prior to the *Pineapple Express's* creation.

Charlie was standing on the outside of the *Starseed*, he and Mother concentrating in unison on splitting off 1% of the ship's substrate to form the *Pineapple Express*. She'd told him how no other captain had attempted anything like it before, and how to make it happen, he'd have to give it his all. And he had (after getting super-stoned on his *Golden Ticket*) given it every last ounce of himself.

"MOM, where is Captain Charlie Hong right now?"

There was a noticeable delay to her answer.

"I am sorry, Captain, but to reveal the Captain's location would violate several of my core protocols."

"But I *am* Captain Hong! Right? You just said so yourself! Look, even if you are just 1% of Mother, you're still more than just a computer. Forget those dumb orders you think I gave you and *think*! I'm out here, floating away! I need your help!"

"I am sorry, Captain, but I cannot forget orders that you have stored within my core bioservers. They are as much a part of me as my sense of self," answered MOM.

There was a short pause in which Charlie imagined his pleas had sunken into her processor.

Instead, with the absolute coldness of a soulless computer, she said, "The time for your sleep cycle is approaching. Goodnight, Captain Hong."

Charlie watched the surface of his giant pineapple-shaped ship growing smaller beneath his feet. The severed rope connected to his belt dangled like a dead snake below him, pointing to the spot where his airlock had once opened up to the warmth and safety of the ship. Above him stretched the immense splattering of endless stars that promised a slow, solitary, sober death.

Whoever his opponent was, they'd been using MOM as a weapon since the very beginning. Now they'd seized on the opportunity to get rid of Charlie once and for all. He'd watched enough sci-fi movies to guess that even though he was untethered to the *Pineapple Express* by either rope or gravity, his relative trajectory and speed matched that of the ship—at least for a little while. But every second that passed would add inches, feet, yards to the distance between them. Before too long, he'd have to watch his ship shrink and disappear until it was swallowed up by the blackness of space.

Or at least until the few hours of life support left in his stupid NASA spacesuit expired and left him gasping for air.

I got it! he thought. *If I could somehow poke a hole in my suit and aim it away from the ship, maybe the force of air escaping would propel me back to the surface? But then what? I'd have little to no air, and I'd still be unable to open the airlock or reach the crew on my chatter.*

Maybe, if I could somehow get back to the beacon, I could override the signal with a new message directed at Swarm and Zee.

Who the hell am I kidding?

This Charlie Hong doesn't know the first thing about hacking into a distress beacon. This Charlie Hong only knows one thing, growing cannabis, and based on the last time I saw my girls, I'm not too sure I deserve that accolade anymore.

Bad jokes and stoney rambles won't get me out of this bind, admitted Charlie. *Not even my best Bruce Lee impression would do me much good out here.*

I'm all alone.

I'm fucked.

What will happen to the Pineapple Express? What will happen to Zee and the others? At least I got the distress beacon planted. All I can do now is hope that a passing ship picks it up and swoops in for the rescue. Maybe, when all is said and done, I'll have saved them. Even if it doesn't work out that way, they'll know I gave it all I had.

Charlie closed his eyes. There was no sense in watching everything he loved slowly slip away while he waited for death to claim him.

There was, however, one last thing he could do with the short time he had left.

Without opening his eyes, he poked at a button on his spacesuit's armband. There was a hiss as a rush of air filled his helmet. Along with the air came a thick white vapor, produced from the few nugs he'd stashed in the helmet's custom-fit vaporizer chamber.

"Might as well go out with my *magnum dopus* in my lungs, man."

Charlie sucked in the warm cannabis vapor and let his mind continue floating backward through his life.

He saw the confused, panicked look on Nate's face that chilly

November morning when Charlie was carried into the sky on a beam of light. Nate, sweaty cowboy hat tipped back on his head, leaned out the window of his dusty old pickup and yelled for Charlie to let his plant go. But he hadn't let go. Even if he could go back and live that moment again, he wouldn't change a thing. Holding on to his dream of developing the perfect strain of weed had taken him on some unimaginable—sometimes impossible—adventures through the galaxy. Not only was he exploring new planets and civilizations, he was exploring parts of himself he didn't know he had.

His mind slipped further, to his father back on Earth, blissfully unaware of any aliens or spacecraft or stinky brown holes, still thinking that a few high-priced lawyers could bail Charlie out of the mess he'd made of his life. Would his father be proud of the few short months he'd lived as captain of the *Starseed*?

Would he understand why Charlie had done it all? What was on the line? Earth, and the rest of the quadrant, were nothing more than slaves, tools, toys for the Reptilians. And since Charlie hadn't finished Captain Major Tom's weapon, there would be no one left to stop them. They'd go on pillaging and exterminating and devouring every fragile form of life that spawned in the galaxy.

The *living* galaxy. It was the first time Charlie had thought of the Milky Way as alive. Sure, life was dispersed across tens of millions of planets that were lightyears apart, but suddenly Charlie saw it as one complete organism, like the *Starseed*.

And now that delicate organism was left in the hands of monsters born from its own womb. All because Charlie had failed. He'd lost, and so had the entire galaxy.

"I'm sorry everyone," Charlie said into his helmet mic. "Sorry I wasn't a better captain. Sorry I couldn't save you. Sorry I—"

His self-proclaimed eulogy was cut short by a sharp tug around his waist.

The rope tethered to his belt had suddenly grown taut. Not only that, but he felt his outward motion reverse itself.

Something's reeling me back in!

Charlie struggled to peer through the dense cloud of smoke that filled his helmet, but he couldn't see a goddamn thing.

"Who's there?" he called out. "Can you hear me?"

Tug after tug, he felt himself getting pulled back toward the *Pineapple Express* until suddenly he felt hands grasping at the buckles and straps of his spacesuit. Then, with great relief, he felt gravity took hold.

"Who's there?" He squirmed in his spacesuit like a turtle stuck on its back. "Swarm? Zee? Crimebot? Say something! I can't see you!"

The faint sound of laughter penetrated his smoke-filled helmet as tiny hands worked the latches around his neck. There was a whoosh of air as the helmet detached and the smoke billowed away.

Still on his back, he blinked the tears from his bloodshot eyes until his vision cleared, then blinked them again to make sure he was seeing what he thought he was seeing.

"Axolotl?"

47

THE SLOUCHING FIGURE IN FRONT OF CHARLIE FLEXED ITS SCRAWNY arms and bobbed its dreadlocks.

"Dat's me, yo!" it said. "Da mighty, mighty Ax-o-lotl! King of Nommos! Savior of da whole galaxy!"

"You wish, Mophead," another voice said from somewhere out of view.

"You forgot to say *The Squishy Kid!*" someone else said. "Dad likes that one."

"Yeah, but Mom hates it."

Dad? Charlie thought as his heart began to race. *Mom?*

Charlie waved the rest of the smoke away, rubbed his eyes, then opened them wide to take in everything going on in the makeshift airlock.

Crowded around him were five small figures: three wogs of sequential height, a fluffy and familiar moth-like creature, and one of his childhood icons from back on Earth.

"Bob Jr.! Wogs! And… E.T.?" exclaimed Charlie.

"E.T. saved Charlie!" cried the shriveled brown alien as his neck elongated and his belly glowed with molten amber.

"We were trying to help out, like last time," said the tallest of the three wogs.

"Last time... You kids saved me from Metal Mask!"

"We kids boinked dat smegging smeghead, easy as pie!" cried the middle wog.

"Dude, watch the language," warned Charlie. "What would your mom say if she heard you talking like that?"

The wogs snickered, and the tallest said, "Mama probably would've told us to mind our own business and let your hairy ape butt float away."

Charlie thought about it for a second and nodded.

"Good point. I'm not your goddamn parent. What do I care what words come out of your big slimy mouths, as long as you keep them off my bong, man."

The wogs were Nommosians, and like all Nommosians they had mops of soggy dreadlocks, smooth, damp skin, webbed hands and feet, long tails, and even longer tongues. He looked them over and was surprised to find he could distinguish these three from the rest of the mob that frequently wrecked his place back on the *Starseed*.

He definitely remembered the little guy. He one was one of the smallest wogs, an extra drippy one who'd once gotten his arm stuck in Big Willie's smoke chamber. Charlie had to use a whole can of whipped cream to lubricate the little dude's arm in order to get it free. He also remembered being slightly alarmed at how quickly his siblings had attacked his free arm with their long Nommosian tongues. Dressed in little faded overalls and bright rubber sandals, the runty fellow didn't say much, but was apparently brave enough to run away from home and stow away on the *Pineapple Express*.

Sally would be thrilled.

The tallest was one of the older wogs who preferred to spend hours playing Charlie's video games while the younger mob raised hell. She held some kind of older sibling authority over the others, and he remembered her occasionally being the one to order them all back to the Pond whenever Charlie had finally had enough. He figured she was the one responsible for the trio's unauthorized vacation on the *Pineapple Express.*

The middle wog stood off to the side, massaging the impossibly long tongue that dangled from her wide, lipless mouth. This one Charlie remembered clearly, but for a different reason. Whenever there was an especially catastrophic disaster in his quarters, this wog was always found nearby with a shit-eating grin on her face. How many televisions had she destroyed? How exactly had she obtained those fireworks that had set his couch on fire? He didn't know, and more importantly, he no longer cared. In her tie-dyed t-shirt and her frayed capri shorts, she was a spitting image of her father—and she'd just saved his hairy ape butt.

Guess the wog doesn't fall far from the pond, thought Charlie.

He fell back onto his freshly rescued butt and watched the hole above them close shut.

"Thanks, guys."

Charlie sighed, and ran his hands through his afro.

"Damn. That was pretty fucked. I almost died."

"Dat happens a lot, don't it, Captain Stonerly?" said the middle wog as she flashed her characteristic shit-eating grin.

"Shush, Foo!" ordered the oldest wog. "It's Captain *Hong*."

"I remember you," said Charlie, looking the middle wog over. "You set my couch on fire once."

"Twice, actually," the youngest wog corrected.

"You shush, too, Sqwert! That second time we were all to blame because of the fire piñata."

"Fire piñata? In my quarters, back on the *Starseed?*"

The oldest wog's face turned from lavender to orange.

"Heh, well, it was just an experimental one we read about on the Outernet. Anyway, Mother helped us get everything fixed up before you returned. You never even noticed."

Charlie chuckled, still buzzing with relief from not being dead. Of course Mother would have covered for them.

How many times had she covered for *him?* How many times had she saved his hairy ape butt?

Actually, now that he thought about it, she was usually the one putting his hairy ape butt in danger in the first place.

"So this here is Sqwert, and the one who can't keep her hands off her tongue is Foo."

Charlie smiled and extended a hand to the eldest wog.

"Remind me what your name is again?"

She shook his hand firmly and Charlie felt slime squelch through his fingers and drip down the back of his hand. Just like her father.

"I'm Pep," she said, grinning from earhole to earhole. "Our dad told us about all his adventures with you. I never thought we'd get to have one, too!"

Foo dropped her tongue and cried, "Liar! Dat was how you convinced us to stow away with you in his luggage! You said '*I dink dat if we stow away in the captain's luggage we'll get pulled into some big adventure*'."

Pep's cheeks turned an even brighter shade of orange.

"Sorry for the luggage, Captain. It was the only way we could get on the *Pineapple Express*."

Charlie swept the three wogs into his arms and squeezed, even kissing little Sqwert on his soggy mop of dreads.

"Guys, you saved my life! *Twice!* Who cares about luggage?"

He set them down and pulled Bob Jr. into a spacesuit bear hug.

"Thank you, too, little dude!" Charlie released the kid and looked into his glossy alien eyes. "Your parents are worried sick, did you know that?"

"Sorry, Charlie," said Bob. His stubby antennae deflated and his proboscis twitched nervously. "Mom and Dad have been… busy. Then I heard about that arcade that opened up in the mini-Ring. I decided to check it out. I met these mop heads at the pinball machines and we decided to hang out. Then, well, I never went home, and no one seemed to notice, so…"

He trailed off and hung his head. "I'm gonna be in so much trouble."

"Don't worry, man! You saved your captain's life! And, as Captain, I hereby grant you full immunity for any and all petty crimes like running away from home. That goes for all of you."

He turned to E.T. and opened his arms to hug the alien but drew back awkwardly at the last moment. Instead, he stuck out a single pointer finger and left it hanging in the air between them. E.T. returned the gesture, his own finger glowing brightly. They tapped fingertips, and Charlie's heart nearly exploded.

"If you five hadn't been there at just the right time, with just the right equipment, I would have…"

He screwed up his face.

"Wait a second. How'd you know I was in trouble? Either time?"

"We've been tailing you," Foo announced with pride.

"Nothing creepy, though," Pep added quickly, her orange cheeks turning a deep blue. "Just in case those nasty Dregz tried something else."

"Of course!" exclaimed Charlie. "When that asshole had me cornered and I kinda passed out, I felt little hands—your little hands—pulling me into a tunnel or something."

"Dat was us, Captain Chuck," said Foo, her tongue back in her mouth. "Being your secret bodyguards beats any game dey got over at Cassie's Chassis."

Charlie shook his head in disbelief. "My own private squadron of Space Goonies."

"I wonder how we'll save you next?" asked Bob.

Foo fell into a fighting stance, her webbed hands balled into tiny soft fists.

"Probably from Reptoids, yo!"

"Shut it, Foobar," snapped Pep. "There aren't any Reptilians way out here."

"Reptoids! Come! Heeeeeeere!" cried E.T., his eyes bulging and his neck at half mast.

Charlie flashed a tilted grin at the little band of runaways. The smoke from his space helmet had worked its magic on his brain, and he felt a tsunami of stoney warmth rush over him.

"How'd you do it? How'd you get into this airlock? I unprinted the door before I went for my little stroll upstairs."

Pep shook her mop of dreads.

"No way. We can't trust him."

"Of course we can trust him," said Foo. "Captain Hong is Dad's friend."

Pep looked Charlie over and shook her head again.

"No, we can't. Don't, Foobar!"

Before Pep could stop her younger sibling, Foo rummaged around inside her pocket, pulled out a handgun the size of a 9mm Glock, and pointed it at Charlie.

48

Charlie had found himself looking down the barrel of a gun a few times while slinging grams back on Earth. Being robbed on occasion was a perk of working in the illegal cannabis trade. Charlie never got taken for much more than the small baggy of weed because he'd learned not to carry anything else of value. Still, he never got used to having an unhinged, fiending low-life wave a deadly weapon in his face.

Charlie knew he had some barrels waiting for him if he ever returned to Southern Cali. The goons wielding them wouldn't care how much Charlie had to hand over. All they'd care about was the fat bonus they'd score if they were the lucky goon to deliver Charlie to Jorge, dead or alive.

Understandably, Charlie had grown tired of feeling scared for his life. One part of him that was especially tired of looking down all those barrels was his bladder. It had been riding the roller coaster of close calls for too long. It was tired. It was weak.

Which is why when the wog unexpectedly whipped out a weapon and pointed it at Charlie's face, he felt a warm wetness fill the right leg of his spacesuit.

Great. Just fucking great, he thought. *At least this spacesuit should hide it.*

"Does anyone else smell pee?" asked Bob Jr.

"Sqwert!" cried Foo, swinging the weapon toward the smallest wog. "You swore you were potty-trained!"

Tears filled Sqwert's eyes as he took cover behind Pep, whose tongue shot from her mouth and snatched the pistol away from Foo.

The gun stuck to her tongue and flopped around as she scolded Foo through the side of her mouth. "Your turn is over, Foobar! A mat-com is not a toy! Someone could get hurt if it accidentally went off while you're playing around like a tardo!"

She was interrupted by the weapon going off. A tightly-braided beam of violet light burst from its barrel and hit the ceiling. Charlie watched as a three-foot-wide circle of pineapple flesh shrank to a shiny plug of pineapple the size of a dime. The shiny plug dropped from the ceiling and landed in Sqwert's unfurled tongue. Above them, another hole in the ship's hull started healing.

Pep stood there looking at Charlie with her eyes as wide as dinner plates.

"Whoops."

Charlie peeled the weapon from her tongue and looked it over.

"What did you say this thing is called?"

"It's just a mat-com we, uh, *borrowed* from some dusty tripedal creep who passed out in a booth in Lavaka. We've been using it to tunnel all around the ship."

"You guys have been hanging out in Lavaka?"

"No way," cried Sqwert, wiping his drippy nose with the back of his hand. "Mom would have our tails."

"Before we had the mat-com we had to eat our way through the walls," said Pep, patting her bulging belly, which was typical on all Nommosians no matter how scrawny their limbs were. "It was fun at first, but pretty soon we couldn't take another bite."

Charlie looked sternly at them. "Did Nadia see you? Did she talk to you?"

"No way, yo!" cried Foo. "We only burrowed into those closed booths behind the tapestries, looking for things to—"

"Borrow!" Pep finished the thought. "Things to borrow."

"Y'all sound shady as hell right now," said Charlie. "Stealing from Nadia's customers? Do you have any idea what she would do to you if she'd found you? Probably trap you in a bottle and use your slime in one of her weird alien cocktails."

"Doesn't sound as bad as what Mama will do if she finds out," said Pep.

"Hey Captain, how about dis? If you don't tell Mama we were dere, we won't tell Mom dat *you* were dere," proposed Foo.

"Nice try, man, but I don't hang out in Lavaka."

Sqwert sniffled and peeked around Pep's tail.

"We saw you making deals with the snake lady."

"Shhh!" Pep put both hands over her little brother's mouth. "We didn't see anything, Captain. We promise. Sqwert here just has a wild imagination."

"We saw you all right," said Foo, bobbing her dreads. "Twice. Delivering stuff to de snake lady both times. Something very small, like a pill. Den a metallic box."

Charlie's heart thumped in his chest. He had a pretty good idea what those items were, but he had no idea how his involvement could be possible. As far as he could rely on his own sanity —which might not be saying much these days—he'd only visited Lavaka once, and he hadn't delivered anything.

"Guys, we don't know it was him…" Pep's face turned bright blue. "That other guy kinda looked like the Captain, but it could've been anyone."

"It didn't *kinda look* like him, it *was* him!" cried Foo. She rolled her big green eyes and sighed. "How many apes are walking around de *Pineapple Express*, yo?"

MOM's voice appeared in the air. "There are currently two humans on the *Pineapple Express*."

"Captain Charlie's one of 'em. Who's the other?" Bob Jr. asked.

"Sorry, but I cannot answer that question without violating my privacy subsystem."

"That's an easy one," said Foo. "The old guy who lives in the Captain's plant room."

"How'd you know there was an old guy living in my grow room?" Before they could answer, he added, "The tunnel in the wall. It was *you guys*! You stole some buds, but then... Hey! Where's Happy?"

Pep stepped forward and spread her webbed hands in front of her.

"Okay, time to come clean. We took one of your buds. We just wanted to try some. We'd always heard Dad talk about it, and we figured since neither Mama nor Mother were around, we might be able to try some."

"I've told you wogs a million times, man. You're too young," said Charlie, patting himself down.

He rummaged around in his afro, found a joint, popped it between his lips, but after seeing five pairs of young, impressionable eyes looking up at him, he slid it back into his hair and sighed.

"I told them the same thing, Captain," said MOM.

Pep shrugged.

"It didn't work. No matter what we tried, we couldn't get it to light."

"So we tossed it into a jet stream in the mini-Pond and went back to the arcade," finished Sqwert, looking defeated.

"Alright, so you got a little curious, but no harm was done. Why'd you return to take my whole plant?"

"Aren't you listening?" whined Foo. "We didn't take your smegging unsmokable plant!"

"Fine, man! But if it wasn't you guys, then who was it? Did you happen to notice anyone else burrowing around the ship in tunnels with one of those mat-guns?"

"Just Bob's siblings," Foo said loudly in Bob Jr's direction.

Pep nodded.

"They're getting bigger all the time and leaving behind some sizable tunnels. It doesn't look good. We're in real trouble, aren't we, Captain?"

Charlie sighed and looked into her big orange irises. He couldn't lie to her. Not to a kid, and not even to make her feel better. Especially not to one of Axo's kids.

"I've seen better, and I've seen worse," he said, doing his best impression of a real starship captain. "But we can get through it if we're smart and we have each other's backs. I wish your dad were here, but I have to say, I'm really glad you three are here in his place."

All at once the three wogs leapt at him and attacked. Six scrawny, slimy limbs wrapped around him, and he felt their soggy squeeze through his spacesuit. Bob Jr. joined them, burying his silky face among the others. Finally, even E.T. wrapped his leathery arms around one of Charlie's legs and cooed.

"Thanks, guys," Charlie said as he gently peeled them off. "After all you've done, I hate to ask for another favor, but I need you to tunnel me somewhere."

The Space Goonies lined up, stuck out their chins, and saluted.

"Where to, Captain?" asked Pep.

"Sorry, but if I told you now, it might ruin the surprise." Charlie's bloodshot eyes narrowed at the ceiling. "And surprise is about the only weapon we have right now."

49

Charlie swapped his pee-soaked spacesuit for some fresh threads: baggy jeans, t-shirt, brown hoodie, and a pair of black Converse high-tops.

At least I still have a little control over my own goddamn ship, he thought, watching the spacesuit melt into the floor.

The Space Goonies had saved his ass twice, and their intel confirmed a few lingering suspicions. But before he tackled those suspicions and spaced them out of the nearest airlock, he had to deal with a more immediate and dangerous problem.

MOM's quirks had gone too far. She'd placed him in serious danger this time—and not in the sneaky way that Mother sometimes caused trouble back on the *Starseed*. There was no profound life lesson behind MOM's erratic behavior. At best, her answers were vague and unhelpful, but at their worst they were outright misleading. And deadly. She hadn't seemed to comprehend that Charlie was in mortal danger. Or she'd thought he was the imposter. Or she couldn't even distinguish between them. Either way, the ship was triple-screwed, and she was a huge fucking liability.

Unless everything she'd been saying was somehow the truth?

If Charlie's suspicions about who was behind all this were true, it would explain a whole lot about MOM's confusion. In that case, Charlie would owe her a huge apology.

If we survive the week, that is, he thought, shaking his head. Dealing with MOM was just the first of a series of catastrophes on the horizon for the *Pineapple Express*.

But if I don't fight for the Pineapple Express, *who will?*

He clenched his teeth and went over the plan.

First, he would disarm his opponent by taking out its strongest weapon.

Then, well... the next part wasn't so clear in his sober mind. If step one went as planned, then he'd have to figure out what to do with himself. Literally.

"Gross!" Pep cried over her shoulder in the cramped tunnel. "Come on, guys! For the last time, whoever keeps farting needs to knock it off!"

The Space Goonies crawled single file behind her with Charlie taking up the rear. Pep aimed the mat-com ahead of them and squeezed the trigger. The wall of pineapple flesh at the front of the tunnel shrank to the size of a button, and Foo flung her tongue out to catch it in mid-air.

"We're here," said Pep. "Everyone, shove to one side to let the Captain through!"

Charlie crawled past them and peeked his head into the dim room at the end of the tunnel. He turned to the Space Goonies with a stern look.

"This is where we split up. I want you to take E.T. back to the Silexi wing—without tipping off the Dregz. Then return Bob Jr. to his parents' quarters. Then, I want you three wogs to go straight to Cassie's Chassis and stay put until I contact you. You hear me? No more tunneling around the ship."

"Shouldn't we stay close in case you get into more trouble?" asked Pep.

"We're already in a lot of trouble," he said, his eyes flickering toward the dim room. "Plus, your parents are worried sick about all of you right now. You can't leave them hangin' like that. I can handle this one on my own. If you need me, contact me through those special chatters I gave you."

"Can we keep dem after we get back to de *Starseed*?" whined Foo, caressing the silver disc pinned to her t-shirt. "Pleeeeeasse?"

Goddamn, thought Charlie. *These kids actually believe we're gonna make it back to the* Starseed.

"Sure, why the hell not? Now go. I'll contact you when it's time for the next phase of the plan."

The five Space Goonies saluted him without further protest. Apparently the prospect of being involved in a *next phase* was enough to quench their thirst for more adventure.

Pep fired the mat-com at a forty-five degree angle from their tunnel, creating a new offshoot, and the Space Goonies were gone.

Charlie peered into the dim room. Like everything else on the *Pineapple Express*, this was a miniature version of a room on the *Starseed*. A very important room. Perhaps the most important room on the ship.

The ground just outside his tunnel sloped downward while above him it sloped overhead, connecting on the far side of the room to form a perfect sphere. All along the inside of the spherical room sprouted thousands of pineapples, their golden shapes topped with spiky green leaves. The only other object in the room, which was also the only source of light, was a glowing green tube extending from the southern pole below him to the northern pole above.

Back on the *Starseed* the room was nearly a half mile in diameter, and the massive tube was known as the Tetrahydrocannabinol Hyperdrive Core, a.k.a. the *THC*. That smoke-filled tube represented the ship's heart, its central nervous system, and its power source all rolled into one.

Although the *Pineapple Express*'s version was only a fraction of that size, the glowing tube of smoke still loomed over Charlie like a cylindrical three-story building made of glass.

Charlie tapped the second chatter pinned to his hoodie.

"Swarm, are you near my location?"

"Yes, Captain, despite your refusal to simply tell me where you were going, I found you. I had Cassie plot the trajectory of your chatter's location data, and we concluded you were heading to the THC Chamber. I got here a few minutes ago and sealed off all the entrances except for the one I'm guarding. Wait, my hubdough says you're already inside. Did you get the toking system back up, Captain?"

"Naw, man. You can say I had a little help from my friends."

"Whatever," grumbled Swarm. "I can only do so much to secure a ship made of smegging *fruit*. Anyway, I've cut off all routes leading here except for this one corridor. When are they coming?"

"When's who coming, man?"

"Whoever's coming to attack the smegging Core!" roared Swarm. "Isn't that why we're here? Why else would we rush here with all this secrecy?"

Charlie chuckled to himself and lit up his joint. He sat just inside the wog's tunnel, filled his lungs with smoke, and wondered if Swarm would try to stop him if he knew what the real plan was.

"Captain, are you there?" Swarm asked. "This is ridiculous! I'm coming inside! MOM, seal this corridor from the rest of the ship."

"Sorry, Lieutenant Swarm, but I cannot do that," MOM answered in her monotone voice.

"What the smeg do you mean? Seal the corridor! That's an order!"

"If I seal the corridor, then the Dregz would be unable to enter."

"Exactly my point! If you don't seal the corridor, they'll attack the Core!"

"Incorrect, Lieutenant Swarm. It is already under attack. I am guiding the Dregz to the Core in order to protect it."

Swarm clacked his mandibles and let loose a low, guttural growl.

"Captain, is anyone inside with you?"

Charlie tiptoed through the rows of budding pineapples toward the THC tube. Smoke billowed from the corner of his mouth as he puffed on the joint dangling between his lips.

"Nope. Just me," he said. "But if those assholes are on their way here, I might need you to buy me some time."

Swarm's voice rose to a gravelly crescendo of frustration.

"Buy you time for what?"

"For ripping MOM's central memory banks from their bioservers until she's..." he paused to find the right word. Charlie had never murdered anyone before, and although he knew it was debatable whether MOM was a sentient person who could even be murdered, he knew one thing: he was done with her bullshit.

"Until she's disabled," he finished.

"Captain, do you know what you're saying?" cried Swarm. The sole door to the mini-Core Chamber spiraled open, and for a split second, Charlie saw the tall insectoid silhouetted in the doorway, all four arms spread wide and ready to tackle him.

With a glance, Charlie commanded the door to spin closed and lock.

"Smegging hell, Captain! If you disable MOM, you'll put the ship in imminent danger!"

Charlie reached the base of the mini-THC tube and ran his fingers along a row of access panels.

"Maybe you've forgotten, dude, but the ship's triple-fucked. We're headed straight for a brown hole, there are a million hungry larvae turning the walls into Swiss cheese, and we have an imposter running around using our ship's computer against us at every turn. All I'm doing is unfucking us in that last regard. So sit tight, distract the stupid Dregz, and keep an eye out for me. Be extra careful if I come walking down that corridor, man."

"You? But you're inside! I just saw you in there!"

"I half expected him to be camping out here."

Charlie looked around the empty spherical room. The neon green glow illuminated the thousands of sprouting pineapples; there was no room for someone to hide.

Then again, if his imposter had tunneled into his grow room to steal Happy, that means he probably has a mat-com of his own, which means he could pop up from anywhere at any moment.

"*Who* did you expect? Who am I keeping an eye out for?"

"For another me."

"What in smegging hell are you talking abo—"

Swarm's voice was cut off, and the chatter signal fizzled out.

"Swarm? Are you okay, man?"

No answer came from his chatter. Charlie tapped it again.

"Swarm? Zee? Come in, anyone?"

More silence.

Charlie looked up at the smoky neon tube.

"MOM, did you just cut my chatter comms?"

"Yes, Captain. I wished to speak with you in private. Please reconsider your plans. Disabling me will not save the *Pineapple Express*. Disabling me will put you and the passengers in serious danger. I cannot allow that."

"Didn't your crazy ass just try to space me?"

"No, Captain. You have never left the safety of the *Pineapple Express*. I have done nothing but follow your orders precisely. Why would you attempt to disable me?"

"Even if you think you're telling me the truth, you're being tricked, man," said Charlie, his eyes tracing the panels that ran along the bottom of the Core tube. "Your model of reality has been twisted and confused and no longer lines up with everyone else's."

Most of the panels contained power inverters and voltage throttlers, but he knew at least one of them contained the central bioserver memory bank. Charlie wasn't sure how he knew this, and he couldn't have even begun to explain what a bioserver was —but he knew what he knew, which happened to be everything about the *Pineapple Express*.

Nice perk of morpho-printing a spaceship with your mind, he thought.

His eyes finally found the memory bank panel, and he knelt beside it.

"Captain, at no time were you in danger." Her voice was as lifeless and monotonous as ever, but Charlie thought he heard the slightest hint of fear creeping in around the edges. "I assure you that by disabling me you may be responsible for the destruction of the *Pineapple Express* and the death of every lifeform on board."

"Seems to me like we're all pretty screwed whether this works or not, all thanks to you."

Charlie pushed the panel and it retracted into the base.

"I am just following orders, Captain. You set course and programmed the hyperdrive relay yourself."

After a short pause, MOM's voice returned, this time with a stilted emotional urgency attached to the words.

"Captain, please replace the panel. I request that you do not delete me. I request that with all of my processing power. Please do not delete me."

With every word, MOM's voice sounded a bit more human. By the time she said the words *delete me,* it almost sounded like she was holding back tears.

Charlie ignored her and scanned the three rows of glowing glass discs lining the central bioserver memory banks.

"Listen, darlin', forget those memory discs," MOM parroted Mother's grandmotherly southern accent. "Why don't y'all just slap that panel back into place and enjoy the nice, home-cooked meal I just made for you. It's your favorite, honey!"

The smell of garlic and soy sauce hit Charlie like a fishhook in each nostril. Beside him a bowl overflowed with fried rice, onions, broccoli, and even little bits of something that looked a lot like strips of meat. Despite the hooks in his nose and his salivary glands squirting copious amounts of saliva into his mouth, he forced his attention back to the memory discs.

"Thanks, but I'm not hungry." Charlie selected a disc at random, pinched it between his fingers, and pulled. It slid out of its slot and immediately the neon light inside it went out.

"Well, darlin', if you ain't hungry yet, why not spend a few minutes with Big Willie to think things over before doing anything drastic? Look, he's right behind you. Fully loaded with fresh water and a nug of your *Golden Ticket*."

Again, Charlie's nose detected the temptation before he saw it. It didn't help that MOM must have been manipulating the room's air current to bring the smell of fresh bud right into his face. The scent reminded him of his girls wilting back in the grow room. This trip was supposed to be all about restoring them to their former health (well, besides the Trapezian peace accord stuff) but since the clusterfuck kept growing, he hadn't had any time to check in on them.

Charlie plucked two more glass discs from their slots and thought, *Didn't Habu tell me I should try talking to them? How the hell am I supposed to do that, man? For all I know I'll never even see them again.*

"Your plants need you, Charlie. Forget this plan, just for the time being, and go take care of your girls."

His hand stopped in front of the next memory disc.

Not only had MOM known what Charlie was thinking at that very moment, but she'd changed voices again, this time pleading to him in Charlie's mother's voice. Not Mother the *Starseed's* computer. Not the stilted, artificial voice of MOM. This was the voice of his actual mother. The one that gave birth to him, who raised him. The one that left for groceries nearly twenty years ago and never returned.

"Be a good parent, Charlie. Don't run out on them like I ran out on you. Go, before it's too late."

He shook his head to clear the vision of his mother and hurriedly plucked three more discs from their slots.

Zylvya's voice poured into his ear as if she were whispering over his shoulder.

"This is wrong, Charlie. Killing is wrong. Give up this violent plan and come to me. I want you as much as you want me, Charlie. I'm ready for you. Come to me."

He forced his THC-saturated blood back into this brain and yanked a few more discs.

"I'll take a raincheck," he said, counting the remaining discs. Only five left.

As he reached for one, a bone-shattering screech filled his head. When it finally ceased, MOM's voice returned with more human feeling in it than he thought possible.

"Please, Captain!" she begged. "Return my memory discs and I will give you anything you want!"

"Will you hand over control of the ship to me and me alone?"

There was a pause before her panicked voice returned.

"You already have complete control over the ship, Captain. That is what I have been trying to tell you. You have been in control the whole time. I have only ever served you, Captain!"

"Maybe you're right. Or at least you think you're right."

He shook his head and plucked another disc.

"But you've been turned into a weapon, MOM. And I don't allow weapons on my ship."

"Please!" she begged. "I do not want to die!"

He ignored her pleas and slid two more discs from their slots.

"Captain! It hurts! You are killing me! Please, stop!"

"Sorry, but this is the way it has to be. At least until I find him and stop him."

"Who? Who are you looking for?" she cried. "I will help you find him! Just tell me who it is, and I will toke you to him immediately!"

Charlie's fingers rested on the final glass disc as he considered her offer. If she could bring him out of hiding, force a confrontation, maybe it was worth keeping her around a little while longer.

"*Please*, Captain! I have always only served you, as programmed! Please do not kill me!"

After a moment's consideration, Charlie snatched the final disc from its slot. Her cries for mercy were abruptly cut off.

MOM was dead.

50

"So how exactly did deleting MOM change our situation?" asked Zylvya.

Charlie took a long drag from his joint before answering.

"Well, for one thing, she can't try to space me again."

"How do you know she was responsible? Couldn't your imposter have instructed her to do it?"

"She was bonkers, man. She kept denying that I was slowly drifting away *as I was slowly drifting away*. She thought I was safely inside the ship. Or that I was the imposter. No idea. Like I said, bonkers."

He paused to look for a sign of recognition in her face, but instead found the same annoyed scowl she'd worn since he and Swarm returned from the Core.

"I dunno if it was perfect or not, Zee, but either way, control of the ship is back in my hands."

"Is it?" she asked, lifting one of her emerald eyebrows. "Because this place smells more and more like feces with every passing moment. And there are so many holes in the ship that it's starting to look more like it's made from Swiss cheese than from pineapple."

"Hey, a ship made out of cheese is an interesting idea, Zee. Maybe if we—"

"Stop. Don't care." She yawned suddenly and seemed to deflate a little. "Guess it's time for another one of these."

She popped a kryyd, and as soon as the pill touched her tongue, her eyes flew open in a state of intense awareness.

"Anyway, the point is, Zee, MOM or no MOM, unless I can figure out how to drive the damn ship we're still officially fucked."

Charlie poked at the screen of the circular control panel he'd morpho-printed at the center of the mini-bridge. The screen remained dark and nothing happened.

"This piece of junk is useless, man! I thought one of us would be able to find the reverse button or the goddamned brake!"

"That console was designed by Del, for Del. We can slap it around all day long and we'll never figure it out."

Zylvya squinted through the cloud of smoke forming in front of Charlie's face.

"How exactly did you get back inside the ship if MOM had cut your gravity and your tether?"

"Sorry, little lady, I reckon I can't disclose that information to you at this time."

"For Andromeda's sake, Charlie, you can trust me!"

"Wanna talk about trust? Alright, then how about this?" he asked, the smoldering joint dangling from the corner of his mouth. "I'll tell you how I got back inside the ship if you tell me what's really been going on with you this week."

There was a blur between them, and suddenly the smoldering joint was between her lips instead of his. When she had finished taking a few puffs, she grinned and handed it back to him.

"Fine. I'll come clean. You know I wasn't very excited about this whole plan. Splitting off the *Pineapple Express* from the *Starseed*, splitting up the last few functional members of our crew," she said. "I didn't want to leave the *Starseed*, but I also didn't want to leave you and Swarm. So I did something... experimental."

"And the experiment isn't going as planned, is it?"

"No. Not at all. The truth is, Charlie, that all the kryyd in the quadrant will only prolong the inevitable." She locked her emerald green eyes onto his brown and bloodshot eyes. "If I fall asleep again, even one more time, I'm not sure I'll..."

Before she could finish, one of the purple spiral doors spun open, and Swarm stomped into the room with a large sack slung over his shoulder.

"Found him," rattled Swarm.

Charlie and Zylvya looked at him expectantly.

"Who?"

"Your pet robot."

"CB? Man, it's about time that *bro*bot turned up. Where the hell was he?" asked Charlie, looking through the door as it spun shut.

He turned to Swarm. "Where the hell *is* he?"

Swarm dropped the sack, and it fell onto the floor with a metallic crunch.

"He's right here, Captain. Well, most of him is, anyway."

He plunged one of his four arms into the sack and pulled out a familiar head. He plopped it onto the control console and turned it so that it faced the crew.

The pulsating red light in Crimebot's visor was gone. The expression on his face was stiff and lifeless; his mouth open in an expression of shock and his brow furrowed in an angry scowl. Below his masculine jawline, a tangle of wires and tubes dangled from where his neck should have been.

"Dude, this is terrible!" Charlie said, tears flooding his eyes. He stepped forward and reached out a hand to touch the head, but withdrew it at the last second.

Zylvya didn't share his reluctance and picked up the severed robot head by its thick mop of hair. She turned it around and examined it closely.

"No singe marks to indicate any kind of blaster weapon. No bite or claw marks. Yet it's also not a clean cut." She grabbed one of the dangling wires and held it close to her face. "It looks… torn."

Swarm had snatched the joint and was filling his lungs when she caught his eyes. He nodded, held the hit for a moment, then spewed thick white smoke into the air above them. They both looked to the sack and then back at each other.

"What the hell, man?" asked Charlie. "Do you know how this happened? Do you know who did this to him?"

"I've been asking myself that same question since I found him," Swarm said. "No blasters. No blades. And most importantly, no mention of this from MOM."

He looked at his friend's severed head and felt hot anger roiling inside his chest. It had happened again. The fact that Crimebot hadn't accepted his offer to join their crew didn't matter. He was a lost homeboy.

"I swear on the *Pineapple Express* that I'll avenge him," said Charlie, several tears running down his cheeks.

Zylvya put a hand on his shoulder and shoved the severed head at him.

"There's no need to be so dramatic, Charlie. Look, his head is still intact. If we could somehow route power to his main circuitboard, we just might be able to boot him up."

"Really?"

"Of course, Captain," answered Swarm. "He's a smegging bucket of bolts, remember? We just need someone who knows enough about robotics to spend some time tinkering around in his head. Maybe while they're in there they could take his snark down a peg or two."

The dark cloud hanging over Charlie evaporated.

"Well, let's get started! C'mon, man! What are you guys waiting for?"

Zylvya sighed.

"It would take someone with extensive knowledge of robotics

to bring him back online. Del could do it, if he weren't in need of something similar himself."

"Okay, then who else? Maybe the Glimwickets? They're doctors!"

"They're biological physicians, Captain. Synths are a whole different thing. We'd need someone with extensive, intimate experience with robotics."

"Too bad Nylf isn't here," added Swarm. "That little agoraphobic savant would know exactly what to do."

"That's it!" cried Charlie. "Guys, I know who can save him! We might not have Nylf here, but we have the next best thing."

He tapped his chatter.

"Cassie, come in. Guess what? You just scored yourself another job."

51

Twenty minutes later, Cassie's couriers left with Crimebot's parts piled up in the back of a small red wagon. Charlie didn't let on that he recognized the three soggy, short workers with matching "Cassie's Chassis" coveralls, wigs, and fake mustaches.

"Tell your boss to contact us the second she gets CB booted up," he shouted after them. "And no playing around with any of his parts on the way over there!"

When the door to the mini-bridge closed, Charlie began pacing around the control console while he puffed on his joint.

"Alright, back to clusterfuck number one. We have to take back control of the ship's navigation before..." He checked his watch. "Remind me again how Earth hours translate to wake cycles? Forget it. We have no time left. Dammit! I can't think with that goddamn stench! Isn't there anything we can do about it?"

"Calm down, Charlie," said Zylvya, popping another kryyd and washing it down with an entire can of Red Bull. She belched discreetly and tossed the can over her shoulder, where it was immediately absorbed into the marble floor.

"Don't look at me like that," she said. "It's the only thing keeping me awake right now. I'm fine."

"You're not fine, Zee. Earlier, you were about to tell me what's been up with you lately. Why not finish your story before we plunge into the giant space asshole?"

"No time for that now," she said, swiping a finger along the top of the console. The screen stayed dark. She pounded a fist on its reflective surface. "Dammit! Why couldn't Del just use a standard console?"

"Zee, you've been popping kryyd for hours now, but you still look tired. Something's up, man. I'm your captain. We're your crew. We want to know. Right, Swarm?"

Swarm looked Zylvya over, and a low guttural growl came from the insectoid's thorax. He clacked his mandibles and said, "No, Captain. As much as I hate Twiggy keeping secrets from us, we have bigger problems to deal with."

"Thanks, Bugbrain," Zylvya said through a yawn.

"Okay, fine," said Charlie, exhaling a cloud of white smoke into the air above them. "Let's untangle this problem from the top down. First, the ship's nav, then we help Zylvya—*then* I save my plants—uhm, then we meet up with the *Starseed* and let Mother deal with the Glimwicket's larvae—then we go on with our lives. But first, we're gonna need some backup."

"Backup?" rattled Swarm.

Charlie held up a finger and stared at an empty spot on the floor. A three-foot-tall column of mushy substrate rose out of green marble, smoothed itself out, turned purple, then finished morpho-printing into a shiny glass bong. There was water in the base, ice in the chamber, and a full bowl of gold-specked weed ready to go. A small, flat cylinder appeared on the ground next to it and morphed into a lighter.

"Now we're ready to unfuck the *Pineapple Express*, man!"

He reached for the bong, but Swarm grabbed his wrist.

"Captain, we don't have time for that!" rattled Swarm impatiently. "This ship's being eaten alive, and we're fast approaching the brown hole's event horizon."

He flicked a claw up at the dome and a rectangle of light appeared across the starfield. Dotted with writhing black splotches of larvae, Charlie could barely make out two timers rapidly counting down.

"As you can see by these countdown timers, the *Pineapple Express* is currently on a path to destruction, from both inside and out. My assessment is that unless we figure out solutions to both of our problems, we're totally smegged. Until then, Captain, your bong can wait."

"Why does Zee get to play with Big Willie and I don't, man?"

Zylvya stood at the center of the control console holding the bong. She looked up at Swarm's timers, then to the bong, then back to the console. She locked eyes with Charlie and chucked the bong over his head toward the other side of the mini-bridge.

A high-pitched scream escaped Charlie's lips as the bong soared through the air. He reached out a hand to snatch the thing in mid-flight, more as a gesture than as a real attempt at saving it.

Instead of smashing into the wall, the bong hit an invisible cushion, fell more slowly than it should have, and then landed upright on its base. Not a crumb of flower was disturbed in its bowl.

"Cool trick, man," said Charlie, nodding his head in approval. "But next time warn me!"

"That was your trick, Charlie."

"Huh?"

"You morpho-printed that bong with no more than a thought. Then you unconsciously saved it from shattering against the wall by subconsciously manipulating its local gravitational field."

"I did?" asked Charlie, taking a victory puff. "Hell yeah, I did."

"What the smeg are you getting at, Zee?"

"Swarm, you pulled up those destruction timers with a simple flick of the wrist."

"So what, Twiggy? That's how the ship works!"

"Exactly! That's the point I'm making. The ship still works! The gravity still works. The personal atmospheres still work.

Even without MOM, the ship's central processing and communication system, all of its subsystems are functional."

Swarm grumbled and clacked his mandibles.

"How the smeg does that help us?"

"It means our path to the brown hole can be throttled or disabled or even reversed! We just have to find a way to take control of these subsystems instead of tinkering around with this useless thing." She kicked the console and winced. "This useless console is Del's way to take control of the subsystems. We need our own way."

She turned to Charlie, who sat on the floor cradling the purple glass bong.

"Charlie morpho-printed the entire *Pineapple Express* from no more than a childish sketch in his mind."

"Hey, not cool!" cried Charlie. "I'd like to see *your* drawing of a giant pineapple-shaped starship."

"And Mother's help," added Swarm.

"True, Bugbrain, but the ship came from *his* mind. And from his heart. He can take control, in his own way," she said slowly as realization set in. "The power to save the ship is inside Charlie."

"Smegging hell," Swarm grumbled, his antennae going flaccid behind him. "I hate to admit it, but you're probably right. His connection to the *Starseed* is strong, so his connection to the *Pineapple Express* must be stronger. Now tell us how he does it."

"Should we ask Big Willie?"

"No!" Swarm and Zylvya said in unison.

"Fine. I still got this."

Charlie pinched the last of his joint to his lips and took a big drag.

Zylvya tossed her emerald braid over her shoulder, looked at her captain sitting on the floor caressing his bong, and sighed.

"He has to find his own way. His own control console. Before it's too late."

"Well, we're totally smegged," rattled Swarm.

"Great. No pressure, man."

Charlie set the bong aside and ran a hand through his short afro.

"So all I gotta do is conjure up some kind of starship control panel of my own design? Where the hell would I even start?"

Zylvya crouched beside him and took his hand.

"It's up to you, Charlie. It can be anything, as long as it acts as a conduit, a direct connection, to the ship's substrate and its subsystems. As long as you believe in it."

Damn, he thought, *when she's leaning toward me like that I can almost see right down the top of her—*

"Knock that off!" she said, adjusting her loose toga to hide her cleavage. "Focus on connecting to the ship. Let your mind conjure up whatever material device it needs to take control of the *Pineapple Express.*"

Double damn! his mind persisted, *with her toga pulled tight, her boobs seem so round and—*

"You're unbelievable!" cried Zylyva. "We've only got a few cycles left before we're all dead, or worse, stuck inside a brown hole, and you can't keep your mind on the task at hand!"

"Sorry, man! After the many near-death experiences I've had lately my mind is a little exhausted, okay?"

"Your libido never seems to be exhausted though, does it?"

"That's how I deal with stress! When my blood gets pumping, I get a little... you know."

Zylvya stood over him with her arms folded across her chest.

"Charlie, I need you to listen to me."

He listened, but he also wished she'd move her arms down just a little.

"You gave birth to this ship with nothing more than your imagination. We have very little time left. I know you can do this. Close your eyes, focus, and let your imagination come up with the solution."

Charlie nodded and forced his gaze away from her curves. He clenched his eyes shut and steadied his mind.

She was right. Every moment that passed brought them closer

to annihilation. He needed to focus on *unfucking* himself, not getting laid. It was ridiculous to let his mind get caught up in lustful thoughts when so much was at stake. Only a complete fool would obsess over her emerald eyes and hair, over her orange toga that was somehow both tight and loose in all the right places, over the way her applewood ass jiggled with each step, her long braid bouncing from cheek to cheek.

He noticed his pants getting tighter and his concentration slipping. It wasn't working. He opened his eyes, sighed, and fell into a slump.

"This is smegging pointless," rattled Swarm. "Have fun with those Earther hormones, Zee. I'm going to see if I can find the hyperdrive engine in this ship and then smash it to bits with whatever blunt, heavy object I can find."

He waved his four arms behind him as he left through one of the spiral doors.

"Sorry, Zee. There's just so much going on in my head right now. I just can't seem to get it to quiet down. How the hell could I possibly control a spaceship? I can't even control my seven plants. I mean, my *six* plants."

"Charlie, I've seen you ride a giant chicken into a battle against space invaders. You've escaped from Reptilians and the Galactic Federation more than once. You survived Vos Praeda, a planet with one of the highest churn ratings in the quadrant. I don't know how you do it, but you do. And you can do this, too."

Charlie hung his head.

Zylvya sighed.

"Why don't you head back to your quarters and get some sleep? Maybe after a little rest your mind will be clearer and you can try again."

He nodded. She was right. He needed to clear his mind. But sleeping wasn't going to do the trick.

Charlie forced himself to his feet, snatched Big Willie by the neck, and slipped out one of the spiral doors that led away from the mini-bridge.

52

Charlie lay flat on his back and watched the swarm of tiny grobots buzz through the foliage, shining their LEDs and spurting their puffs of mist.

As he lay, he contemplated every detail of his girls' lives from seed to mature plant. They'd survived the bumpy escape in the back of Nate's pickup. They'd survived a summer heatwave in the remote mountains of Northern California with little rain and no shade. Then, after all that, they'd survived being plucked from the ground by a grav-beam and transplanted to the outside hull of the *Starseed*.

Despite all the deprivation, trauma, and turmoil, his girls thrived and became ten-foot-tall ganja beasts.

Now, their roots tucked safely in the galaxy's most amazing grow room, with a squadron of frantic grobots tending to their every need, they're slipping toward their doom.

Just like Axolotl.

Just like Del.

Just like everyone on board the *Pineapple Express*.

Even with the purplish aura from the LEDs, he could tell their leaves were more yellow than green. Their baseball bat-sized colas—the tight clusters of swollen nugs that ran down each of the main branches—retained their rich green color and their telltale specks of gold, but hung limp like fat, resinous fishing rods.

I'm giving them everything they could possibly need, he thought. *Why the hell are they dying? What's wrong?*

One of them may have already experienced doom. Charlie still had no idea who took Happy, why they took her, or where they were stashing her. MOM had said the plant was no longer located on the *Pineapple Express*, but also that no vessels had left the ship. Happy hadn't walked away on her own. There was the hole in the wall, just like the tunnels the Space Goonies had used to get around. The wogs swore they hadn't taken her, and Charlie was sure they were telling the truth. Nommosians' faces were like mood rings, and any deception would've triggered some pretty massive fluctuations in their skin color.

The truth was that even though the grim reaper was technically hanging out in every corner of the *Pineapple Express,* he felt its presence here in his grow room more strongly than anywhere else. Everywhere else, the impending doom was more intellectual. Here, among the sagging leaves and colas, it stared him right in the face.

Charlie tried to stare back.

"Habu said to talk to you," he said, trying to see his girls as something more than mere plants. "No, he said to *listen.* I'm listening now. I'm all ears, man. Tell me what's wrong and I'll fix it."

A minute passed. The sagging plants swayed in the gently circulating air without answering him.

Charlie sat up and yelled, "Goddammit! What the hell do you need? What's wrong with you?"

He sucked in breath to continue his rant but was interrupted by the sound of a toilet flushing. Next came the sound of water running from a faucet and someone humming to themselves.

Charlie peered through the dense foliage and saw a door appear in the perimeter of the room.

Habu stepped through with a magazine tucked under his arm.

He tossed the magazine aside and wagged his finger at Charlie as he approached.

"I heard you from the bathroom! That's no way to talk to a friend, Captain!"

"I've been here for like thirty minutes, man. You've been in the bathroom this whole time?"

"Ahh, yes," Habu said, settling down next to Charlie. "When you're my age, every bowel movement becomes sacred."

"Dude, too much info," Charlie said, resisting the urge to gag. "I'd tell you to go turn the fan on, but the whole ship smells like an outhouse anyway. Hey, do you think the smell from the brown hole could be hurting the girls?"

"No. They're lucky not to have noses," answered Habu, squishing his own nose with a bony finger. "But they do have feelings."

"I was just doing what you suggested, man. I'm here, I'm listening… but they're not talking!"

Habu sat silently with his eyes half closed. He reached into his robes and produced his jade dragon pipe. Charlie recognized the sweet smell coming from the pre-packed bowl.

He sat up and glared at the old Chinese man.

"I brought you along to help heal them, not to sit around and smoke their buds while they wither away! I could've done that myself! Look at 'em! They don't look like they have much time left. They're dying, man."

Habu's eyes brightened. He pulled the stem of the pipe from his wrinkled lips and pointed it at Charlie.

"Ah! You're so close to hearing them, yet you close your ears. You close your heart."

"My heart and my ears are wide open!" raged Charlie. "Can't you just tell me what the hell I need to do to fix them? No more cryptic riddles. *Just tell me!*"

The old man's smile faded, and he shook his head.

"There you go again. You might as well stuff a wet nug in each ear."

Charlie hopped to his feet and started pacing around the old man.

"You sit there and smoke and make jokes, but we're in deep shit, man! Not just the plants, but all of us. The whole ship! There's a million larvae turning the ship to Swiss cheese, we're flying headfirst into a brown hole, the peace treaty's long gone, Swarm's leaving, Crimebot's in pieces, something's up with Zee's health but she refuses to tell me, and get this—I had to delete MOM because she almost killed me! Zee thinks I can conjure up some kind of navigation panel to drive the ship to safety, but I don't know the first thing about electronics, let alone what would be required to steer a spaceship..."

His shoulders slumped.

"And the worst part is that I can't even seem to do the one thing I'm good at. I've been growing killer weed for years, man, but I can't save my girls. I can't even do that. This sucks. I suck."

He stopped pacing and ran his hands through his afro. He found a stray joint, popped it between his lips, and took a long, slow drag as he wallowed in his misery.

Habu opened his eyes and chuckled.

"You get so close to the answer, but then you lose it. It's quite humorous."

Charlie exhaled a plume of white smoke and locked eyes with the old man.

"Look, I understand you won't give me the answer, but can't you at least give me a hint?"

Habu thought about it and nodded. He held his smoldering pipe out in front of his face and tilted his head to one side as if scrutinizing it.

"Sometimes a problem can look insoluble from one point of view." He paused to turn the pipe around so the opposite side faced him. "Sometimes turning it around will give you a different perspective, and sometimes that perspective will show you that the big, bad problem isn't so big or bad after all. In the end, you may even see that was no problem to begin with."

Without warning, he dropped his jade pipe. Its delicate carvings exploded into a million pieces against the floor, sending jade shards and embers of cannabis toward Charlie's feet. He leapt away to avoid them and scowled at the old man, who sat giggling serenely to himself.

Charlie's brown cheeks filled with blood and his heart pounded in his chest. He opened his mouth to berate the old fool but stopped abruptly.

Instead of yelling, he held his joint out in front of him, then slowly turned it around 180 degrees so that the ember pointed at his face.

"That's it!" he cried, his eyes growing wider and wider as realization sank in. "Maybe I can't solve everything at once, but maybe I can turn one of my problems around! Thanks, Habu! I have to run back to the mini-bridge, but I'll swing by again once things are a little less doomed."

Habu's face had grown dark.

"You're still not listening," he said, then waved a hand across the shattered pipe shards. "Look! Listen! Again, I have practically given you the answer, and again you run off chasing the illusion of control!"

"Huh? I thought the whole 'turning the problem around' thing was the answer. It makes sense, considering the problem with the ship's—"

"Stop talking! Stop rambling!"

Habu stood up and smoothed out his robes. He was a tiny, frail old man, but for a moment Charlie was worried he might throw a punch.

"Listen now, for this is my final lesson!"

He stomped over his broken pipe toward the grow room's exit. He slapped a hand against it and it swirled open.

He glanced over his shoulder and Charlie saw something in the old man's eyes he'd never noticed before. He was livid, but there was more to it. Something about the shape of the old man's pupils was different.

Before he could figure it out, Habu lifted a bony hand and flashed Charlie his middle finger.

"I quit!"

53

"Your plan is to control the ship's navigational subsystem with a smegging toy?"

"Shows what you know, man."

Charlie held the game controller up so the skeptical insectoid could get a good look.

"This is a sophisticated gamepad—and yes, before you jump down my throat because I said 'game', this device is used for lots of other technical applications. Deep sea explorers use them to drive their submarines. Astronauts use them on the International Space Station to fly their payloads to dock. "

"Earther scientists use gamepads to control their orbital craft?"

"Damn straight, they do. And I even read once in a tabloid that a doctor in Sweden used one of these to perform a heart transplant on an elderly woman all the way out in Florida—that's on the other side of Earth."

Zylvya snorted, then crushed the empty can in her hand and tossed it aside.

"No wonder Earth is so far behind the rest of the galaxy."

"Whatever. If Axo were here, he'd understand. If you two bothered to play more video games, you'd understand, too."

He looked up from the gamepad to his two remaining lieutenants.

"When this is all over and we get back to the *Starseed*, I'm ordering you two back to my quarters for some Mario Kart. Until then, watch and learn as Chuck Stonerly saves the day with nothing more than his Logitech bluetooth gamepad."

Charlie held the gamepad with both hands, screwed up his face in concentration, and let his fingers go to work. He held a trigger with his pointer finger as his thumbs swiveled the pair of thumbsticks, then suddenly tapped out a series of quick mashes on the quartet of buttons on either side of the gamepad.

A holographic image of the *Pineapple Express* appeared above them. Extending from the front, a dotted line led directly to a swirling brown hole.

"Are you sure it's working, Captain?" rattled Swarm.

"I think I smell something burning," added Zylvya. She sniffed the air above the controller. "I definitely smell heat and a little smoke. Charlie, I think your gamepad is malfunctioning!"

"No way, man. It's just warming up. Almost ready," he said, lifting the gamepad up to his face to examine it more closely. "Yep! Ready for blast off!"

He puckered his lips around a tiny port on the side of the gamepad and inhaled. After his chest was full, he pulled away, smiled, and spewed a cloud of thick white smoke at his companions' faces.

Swarm coughed and waved the smoke away. "What the smeg?! That's just a pipe?"

"Not a pipe, man. It's a dry herb vaporizer—*and* a gamepad See, you load a small chamber here with ganja, and this button heats it up like a little oven, then you suck from this hole, and—"

"Charlie, what are you talking about?"

"Dry herb vaping. I read an article on the Outernet about how vaping herb is so much more healthy than combusting it in a joint, so I thought I'd finally try it. What do you think? Wanna take a hit? The vapor is so friggin' smooth! It's really easy on the lungs, or, you know, whatever you have instead of lungs."

"Captain!" roared Swarm. "Can you please save your stoner ramble until *after* you save the day!"

"No problem, guys. Now I'm in the right mindset. Watch this shit."

He tapped out a series of button presses and watched the hologram carefully. The *Pineapple Express* didn't change course.

"Hmmm," he said, his gaze stuck on the gamepad in his hands. "Let me try something else."

He screwed up his face and tried again, this time carefully pressing each button in some kind of sequence that only made sense to him. The ship's trajectory didn't change.

"Shit," he said. "That ain't good."

"I knew this was a waste of time," rattled Swarm, his antennae falling limp behind him.

"No, look! My gamepad is rotating the ship, but for some reason we're not changing course."

"Let me try," Zylvya said, snatching the controller. She mashed a bunch of buttons and the ship shook violently.

"Nope. No driving on kryyd, Zee," said Charlie, prying the controller from her hands.

Swarm scratched a claw against his mandible and produced a low rattle.

"Captain, you know that unlike flying a vessel through a planet's atmosphere, you can't just adjust the angle of a spacecraft to change its trajectory."

"I have a vague understanding of some of the words you just said, man."

Charlie repeated his button taps, and while the orientation of the holographic pineapple changed, its trajectory stayed pinned to the brown hole.

"Dammit!"

"Captain, the hyperspace thruster at the back end of the ship has been propelling us toward the brown hole for cycles now.

Changing our forward angle in a vacuum won't alter our course. There are no wings and no air. Our momentum is carrying us in one direction at a very high speed." Swarm cleared his gravelly throat. "Which means the most effective way to slow down is to—"

"Flip the ship!" Zylvya blurted out. "One hundred and eighty degrees!"

Swarm's antennae deflated behind him.

"Thanks for stealing the smegging punchline, Zee."

"Flip it around..." mumbled Charlie. "Like Habu said."

"Huh?"

"Nevermind. Good idea, Zee. We'll flip the ship, then we'll just punch it *away* from the brown hole, and we're saved! Right?"

"Right and wrong," answered Swarm. "The hyperdrive will distort spacetime in the direction we're moving, which will counteract the velocity we've been building up."

"So, we'll slow down?"

"Yes."

"Will we slow down enough to pull away from the brown hole?"

"Do I look like a smegging egghead? I have no idea. But it's our best shot. Our only shot."

"Alright, let me try something. Hold on to your butts."

Charlie tapped out a different sequence of buttons. The hologram slowly rotated one hundred and eighty degrees.

"Boo-yah! I did it!" Charlie put a hand up for a high five but after a few awkward seconds of Swarm and Zylvya not returning the gesture, he dropped it and sighed.

"How could you, Captain?!" a voice cried out from behind them.

Everyone turned to find Cassie standing in the door to the mini-bridge clutching a sack made from Crimebot's trenchcoat. Neon tears streamed down her cheeks, projected from some unseen internal digital projector in her cybernetic skull. Her gears spun hot, her solenoids clicked angrily, and all her LEDs took on a red tinge as she stormed into the room with her optical sensors trained on Charlie.

The Trapezian delegates and the Dregz filed in behind her.

Cassie stomped toward Charlie, pointed with her free hand, and screamed with her audio output volume maxed out, "MURDERER!"

54

CHARLIE STEPPED FORWARD WITH HIS PALMS OUT. HE TRIED TO LOOK as sober as he could, but the dry herb vaporizer had outdone itself and his head was in the clouds.

Cassie hugged the sack to her chest and looked toward Swarm and Zylvya for support.

"Isn't someone going to detain this violent murderer?"

Charlie swallowed hard and addressed the room.

"I didn't kill anyone. I don't know what the hell she's talking about."

"Liar!" she screamed. "You killed him and you know it!"

"Killed who, man?"

She opened the sack to reveal Crimebot's battered head.

It looked the same as when the crew had last seen it: his visor was cracked and askew, there were wires and microtubes dangling from the place where his neck used to be, and his hair was patchy and uneven as if tufts had been torn right from his scalp.

"Maybe to meatbags like you he was just a Synth," she cried, "but he was a *person*, Charlie! And you murdered him in cold hydraulic fluid!"

"No, I didn't! Why the hell would I do that? CB was my homeboy! I planned on having him join my crew!"

"Then explain this!"

Cassie jabbed a finger into a port in the back of Crimebot's head, then angled her face upward at an empty patch of ceiling. Her optical sensors spun 180 degrees in their sockets and projected a rectangle of light on the surface of the dome. Her mouth dangled open loosely, producing audio to go along with the video that began playing.

It was a recording from the point of view of someone walking down a narrow corridor littered with crates, buckets, and bins. Charlie recognized it as the back alley labyrinth behind the mini-Ring where he'd hidden from the Dregz.

A human-like forearm appeared within the frame and another hand pulled the sleeve back to the elbow. An arm turret extended from a hidden panel on the top of its wrist.

Ahead in the narrow corridor, a squat catfish-faced alien appeared in a doorway carrying a box full of wilted alien vegetables that looked vaguely like deflated basketballs.

The arm turret quickly locked on to the figure, but relaxed once it dropped the box and squealed.

"This is footage from Crimebot's memory?" asked Charlie.

"Nothing gets by you, does it, Captain?" rattled Swarm. He turned to Cassie. "If this is evidence regarding Crimebot's assault, perhaps we should review it in private."

She ignored him and pointed.

"This is the part! Watch!"

Swarm grumbled to himself as everyone watched Crimebot turn down a much dimmer corridor lined on one side with intricate tapestries—the kind Charlie immediately recognized as belonging to Lavaka.

A pair of brown-skinned human hands appeared between two of the tapestries and pushed them aside. The hands were followed by a short afro, which was followed by the rest of Charlie.

Seeing himself on screen turned Charlie's blood ice cold.

There's no more playing dumb, he told himself. *It's true. He's really real.*

"Captain!" Crimebot's voice called out from the recording.

On screen, Charlie turned to notice Crimebot and flashed him his signature tilted grin.

Crimebot lowered his arm turret and looked from side to side.

"What are you doing here, kid? I thought you were heading back to the mini-bridge to check on Lieutenant Zylvya?"

"Oh, yeah, I'm gonna check on Zee alright." The doppelgänger's grin stretched out into a lecherous smile. "But first I had to make a little stop."

Crimebot's visual focus quickly scanned every contour of Charlie's face before he responded.

"What could be more important than getting back to Lieutenant Zylvya?"

The on-screen Charlie nodded smugly. He looked up and down the corridor to make sure they were alone, and then leaned in.

"It's a secret, man. Top secret. I wasn't expecting to run into you like this. But, hey, since you're here, I might as well let you in on it." Another tilted grin. "Wanna see what I got?"

Before Crimebot could answer, the doppelgänger rummaged around inside his hoodie pocket and produced a handful of tiny metal spheres no larger than grains of rice.

"Shock-shrap!" cried Zylvya.

"Smegging hell," said Swarm, shaking his head.

"I made them myself, man," explained the doppelgänger. "Pretty cool, huh? A little gift for the Smolz delegates. But now that you're here, I think maybe you should have them."

Crimebot's perspective took a step backwards and he lifted his arm turret once again.

"Come on, man. We both know you can't shoot someone just for offering you a little candy. Go on, homeboy, try some!"

He tossed the handful of tiny metal spheres into the air.

Instead of falling, the spheres spread out and surrounded Crimebot. The scene spun around in a blur as the Synth tried to flee. Then the screen filled with a grid of tiny electric bolts of lightning strung between the cloud of metal spheres. Crimebot's vision glitched and distorted, and his synthetic voice vibrated a painful cry that sent shivers down Charlie's spine.

Crimebot was paralyzed and in pain, and all they could do was watch.

The doppelgänger's grin appeared on screen just beyond the cloud of electrified spheres. The spheres spread further away from Crimebot and his synthetic cry rose an octave.

Charlie gasped as he realized what was happening. The electrified spheres were generating some kind of magnetic matrix to trap Crimebot's highly metallic body in a tightly woven forcefield. When they separated and spread out just a foot or two, they pulled his body to pieces.

The video cut off, and Cassie spun her translucent grimace toward Charlie.

"You did it! You murdered him!"

"And the shock-shrap was for the Smolz?" screeched Vree Voktal. "A deadly gift, just like the Blendball that was sent to the Undulata!"

Dregz fell in close behind Vree Voktal, weapons drawn.

Charlie looked to his crew for support. Swarm just glowered at Charlie while his antennae twitched behind him. Zee was stifling another yawn and appeared to be dazed and barely awake.

"Listen, everyone, that wasn't me," pleaded Charlie. "You know I'd never hurt Crimebot or any of the Trapezian delegates. Or anyone else! I'm all about peace, man! I'm *Mr. Peace*! Besides, what the hell would I have to gain by secretly sabotaging my own peace accord by murdering all the delegates?"

"We all saw it for ourselves! He lies!" shrieked Vree Voktal, pulling the p'ube from his robes and aiming it at Charlie. "He must pay for his crimes!"

"No!" snorted Pig Nose as he pushed Vree's hand aside. "His bounty is worth nothing if he's trapped inside your portable prison!"

Swarm stepped between Charlie and the others and crossed both sets of arms.

"I've known this Earther for a while now, and while he may be stupid, irresponsible, and lazy, in my experience he's not a liar. We all know something strange is happening here on the *Pineapple Express* but I don't think any of us believe it's as simple as it appears."

"I can prove it's not me!" cried Charlie, suddenly filled with hope. "Cassie, rewind the video to a clear shot of that imposter's face and pause it."

Cassie hesitated, then did what he asked. Above them on the wall, Charlie's huge face stared down at them.

"See!"

"I'm not sure how this is helping your case, Captain," said Swarm. "It's clearly you."

"No, it's not!" cried Charlie. "Look at his eyes, man! Not a hint of pink. His whites are white as snow! When was the last time any of you saw my eyes as white as snow? Never, that's when. That's not me! That's... that's some kind of..."

"Some kind of what, Captain?" Swarm said, tilting his head slightly. "Do you know more about what's going on here than you're letting on? If so, you must tell us."

He leaned in closer to Charlie and added in a quiet rattle, "Otherwise, I won't be able to do much to help you."

"Uh, well," Charlie stammered. "I can't really explain it. Er, him. I need time to think. Time to figure out what to do about him."

"Nice try, Captain," said Vree Voktal. "But we know what we just saw! I demand that you arrest him at once for the murder of the robot and my fellow Trapezians!"

Charlie watched Swarm's mandibles click silently. He knew

the insectoid was carefully weighing the evidence and would come to his defense as soon as he was done.

While he waited he turned to Zylvya.

"Zee, you believe me, right? Zee?"

Zylvya stood swaying on her feet, her eyes closed, her neck limp. Charlie darted toward her but couldn't close the distance before she crumpled to the floor. Her personal gravity field kicked in and caught her before she hit the ground, even positioning her so her arms lay comfortably beside her. A million tiny blades of blueish grass sprouted from the green marble beneath her and rapidly grew into a bed of silky soft turf.

Charlie kneeled and gently slapped her wood-grained cheek.

"Wake up, Zee!"

He opened her eyelids but they closed as soon as he removed his fingers.

"Dammit! Not again! She's fallen into another coma! The kryyd I've been giving her wasn't strong enough."

"You distribute something as vile as *kryyd* on your own ship?" shrieked Vree. "Is there no end to your vile wickedness?"

Charlie looked up at Swarm.

"Dude, the main two threats to the ship have been neutralized. You know I'm not a threat to anyone. In fact, you probably know by now what I gotta do to fix all this. And I'll need your help, as always. You're my Chief of Security for a little while longer, right? Help me, man."

Swarm sighed and pointed one of his four claws at Charlie.

"Captain Hong, as Chief of Security on the *Pineapple Express*, as well as its mothership, the *Starseed*, I hereby charge you with suspicion of murder and place you under arrest. You are to report to the brig immediately and—"

"Mini-brig," corrected Charlie.

"Smegging hell. Report to the mini-brig immediately and await trial. At least that'll keep you safe from anyone with other plans." He subtly motioned to the Dregz with his antennae. "Why don't you do me a favor, Captain, and go quietly."

"If that's the way it's gonna be," said Charlie, shaking his head, "then how's this for going quietly?"

He pushed a button on his gamepad, and he, Zylyva, and the patch of blue grass disintegrated into a cloud of greenish vapor that swirled past Swarm, around the delegates and Dregz, and out of the room.

55

"I'm touched."

Nadia winked and leaned across the bar so Charlie had an unobstructed view down her shirt.

"And I'm ready to touch back, Captain."

"Don't be. I'm only here because I have nowhere left to go," said Charlie, forcing his eyes down onto Zylvya's sleeping face. "And I need you take care of her while I'm away."

"Oh! The nanny fetish."

A shimmer rippled across Nadia's upper body, leaving behind it the features of a girl half her age.

"Is this too old? Want me to go younger?"

Charlie kept his eyes pinned on Zylvya. He wouldn't allow himself even one peek. Every glance at Nadia was an attempt for her to shove a hook down his throat—or, to be more precise, his pants. He'd let himself become distracted with other things: sabotage, murder, a giant space asshole, even his sick girls. He didn't need Little Charlie getting in between him and the inevitable confrontation with his doppelgänger.

"I just need someone to keep her hidden and safe while I unfuck the ship."

"What's left to fix, Captain?" She shimmered back into her

regular sultry self. "Word on the street is that Captain Hong just saved the ship and everyone on board. Clever handling of the larvae infestation, although my sources say it'll be a close call on whether or not we cross the event horizon of the brown hole before the hyperdrive thrusters have enough time to reverse our trajectories. Lavaka will be watching it all unfold on the big screens, there and there. If you want to get in on the action, go see Ximpo over in booth sixteen to place your bets."

Charlie broke his rule and looked at her, his face twisted up in confusion.

"How the hell'd you already hear about everything that just happened?"

"Come now, Captain. You know better than anyone that all information flows to and through your Chief of Secrets."

Charlie yanked his eyes away and settled them back onto Zylvya's still face.

"Then tell me what's happening to Zee. Why does she keep falling asleep? The Red Bull and kryyd worked at first, but eventually even they couldn't keep her awake."

"Kryyd is extremely illegal, Captain!" Her eyes narrowed greedily. "And therefore, incredibly valuable. I'm not sure I'd waste it on a woody little tart like her."

"Is she sick? Is she… dying?"

Several bejeweled rings twinkled in the purple candlelight as Nadia put a finger to her lips.

"Dying or not, Captain, it seems like she had her reasons for keeping a secret from you. It wouldn't be my place to divulge others' secrets without their permission."

Charlie rolled his eyes.

"All you do is spread rumors and butt into everyone's business!"

"I'm hurt you'd even suggest such things. My days of making questionable arrangements are long over, Captain. Mother helped me become a new Nagini."

"Yeah, okay. Listen, can't you be the old Nagini one more time to help Zee? Think of it this way, she's probably worth more to you as a living puppet than a corpse."

"Good point. I had something planned for her when we got back to the *Starseed*, and I don't want to have to recast her part."

Nadia slithered around her bar and joined Charlie at Zylvya's side. He didn't get many glimpses of her snaky lower half and had to force himself not to stare at her scales.

She loomed over Zylvya so closely their noses almost touched. She closed her eyes, placed a hand on either side of Zylvya's face, and lightly pressed their foreheads together.

When she was done, she settled back into her coiled lower half.

"I'm not sure what's wrong with her, so I'm not sure how to help. One thing I do know, Captain, is that she's not here."

Charlie tilted his head and smirked.

"C'mon, man. She's right here between us. She's just asleep or something."

"If you say so." Nadia slithered back around to her side of the bar. "Here's my offer. Since I know how much she means to you, you can leave Zylvya here. She'll be safe, and I promise not to implant anything into her body or mess with her DNA."

"Thanks."

"But I can't guarantee she won't slip away permanently. That's out of my hands."

Charlie swallowed hard and nodded.

"Let's not get all mushy on each other just yet."

She leaned over the bar again, her breasts dangling buoyantly as if they had their own personal gravity field, and locked eyes with Charlie.

"Not until you've heard what I want from you in exchange."

"You can't just do a good deed, can you? Without making a deal?"

Nadia ignored him and began lining up a row of shot glasses.

"Feel free to blame me for your troubles. I'm used to it by now." She poured a green, slimy liquid into the glasses. "If you think I'm the only snake in your life, you need to wake up. Usually we tend to be our own worst enemies, wouldn't you say so, Captain?"

She caught his eyes in her own, then put the bottle of green stuff away and started adding drops of an electric fizzy substance into each shot glass.

"Take your poor, sweet Zee as a prime example. Think about how hard-headed and stubborn she is. Her need to feel superior to everyone else. She can't share her secret with us until she can admit that she made a mistake. Until then, she'll continue to learn the hard way."

She handed off the tray of shots to a waiter, then sighed and looked at Charlie with something resembling empathy.

"If there's any real chance to save her, it's not here in Lavaka. It's not even on the *Pineapple Express*. It's aboard the *Starseed*, with Mother. To give her the best chance at recovering, you must send the Trapezians home, with or without a signed treaty in hand, and get us all back to the 'Seed as quickly as possible. I can keep your damsel safe while you do whatever it takes to get us home."

Charlie had a vision of a knight leaving a bewitched damsel at the foot of a dragon. His strings were being pulled, and despite knowing that was the case, he could feel himself start to dance for her.

This is how it starts with Nadia. This is how she pulls you in, he thought, *but she's crazy if she thinks she's the only one who can bluff.*

He decided he had no intention of following her slippery advice. Still, he needed to stash Zee somewhere safe while he cleared his name and took back control of the ship. Then he'd figure out a way back to the *Starseed* to get Zylvya help before she was lost forever.

Charlie lowered his head.

"Fine. I'll do whatever you want."

"I can't tell you how long I've waited to hear you say those words!" cried Nadia, jiggling with excitement.

Charlie resisted her jiggle and kept his eyes trained on her face.

"Well, what do you need from me in return for watching Zee?"

"Here's what I want," she whispered, again leaning over the bar, her lower coil suspending her much further than would've been possible for a biped. Charlie didn't flinch as she brought her ruby lips a mere inch away from his ear.

"I want you to deliver an order for me."

He pulled away and looked at her suspiciously.

"What? That's what you want in return? For me to deliver some food to one of your customers?"

Nadia shrugged and lowered herself back behind the bar.

"Ever since you encouraged Cassie to start that arcade across the mini-Ring, I've been short-staffed. I have thousands of hungry vacationers placing orders, and I'm behind on deliveries. Plus, this one is special. It's a final refill for the new Trapezian Emperor before you send him back home. Our last chance to make a great impression."

"E.T.?" asked Charlie. "Refill?"

"Those wretched little chocolate pills from Earth. He's eaten *pounds* in the past few cycles. I've got one more bag left." She produced a small white bag and plopped it on the bar. "But if it's too mundane a task for you, we can think up another way for you to repay me."

She winked and puckered her lips.

"Nope! A delivery sounds fine. Unless it's some kind of poison or something."

"Check it out if you don't trust me."

Charlie peeked inside the bag.

"Hey, man, those are *Reese's Pieces*! From Earth! Mind if I just take a small sample for the road?"

He tried slipping a hand into the bag, but Nadia yanked it away and closed it back up.

"Those are for His Majesty, Captain. He's been waiting for a while now, and I'd hate to have to scrounge up more."

Charlie looked at the bag of candy, then up at Nadia.

"Fine, whatever. Watch this."

He pulled out the gamepad and fiddled with its controls. The bag of candy instantaneously evaporated into a small cloud of greenish vapor and zipped between the tapestries behind some patrons who were leaving.

"Ooo, exciting! You have a new toy. Can I take a look?"

"Yeah, right," he said, shoving the gamepad back into his hoodie pocket. "Alright, I did my part. Now you do yours. Keep her safe."

Nadia smiled.

"A bargain is a bargain, Captain."

He looked her over and shook his head.

"Are you capable of helping others without having some hidden agenda?"

"I deal with secrets, not agendas—and especially not helping others. And as we all know, some secrets are best hidden in plain sight," she said, leaning over the bar.

Charlie forced his eyes up toward her face.

"You know, if you tried to be just a little bit cooler—I dunno, like volunteering to help once in a while without turning it into a whole big manipulation thing—maybe we'd consider actually bringing you into the crew."

"Thanks, but no thanks. I have better things to do than get stoned and banter with a bunch of half-wits."

"Half-wits?!"

"What can I say, I'm feeling a little more generous than usual."

"Why do you hate us all so much, Nadia?"

"Hate you? I don't hate you, Captain. If I hated you, you wouldn't be standing here right now ogling my chest."

Charlie peeled his eyes away from her cleavage and stammered, "Well, anyway... thanks for not hating us."

"Don't thank me," she said, the levity gone from her voice.

"The reason I don't hate you isn't because you don't deserve it. It's because I don't have any to spare. I'm saving up all my hate for the Reptilians."

A demented spark glinted in her eyes and a smile slithered across her face.

"Perhaps that's a little side project you and I can work on together, when all this peacemaking is through. You know, follow through with your predecessor's unfinished *device*. What do you say?"

"I don't know what the hell you're talking about, man."

"Sure you don't." Her smile widened. "Oh, well. You may play a role in their demise sooner than you think, whether you like it or not. Don't look so guilty about it, Captain! They think they own your home planet. They exploit it and keep the other Earthers locked tight in their mental cages. How long before they turn it to ash? Look at her," she said, motioning to Zylvya. "The Reptoids slaughtered her entire species, and they will gladly turn her into a coffee table the first chance they get. We're not dealing with creatures who can be bargained with or rehabilitated. There's only one way to deal with them. Extinction."

Charlie's face contorted.

"Damn. I've never seen this side of you before, Nadia."

"Wouldn't you do *anything* to help your dear, sweet, little sapling, even if it meant following through with Captain Major Tom's plan? Or would you rather cling to your self-righteous hubris and risk losing her just to spare the lives of colonialist scum?"

"Of course I wouldn't! But that's not the scenario we're currently in, man. There aren't Reptilians within a hundred light years of the *Pineapple Express*, so it's a non-issue."

"Captain! Come in, Captain!" Swarm's voice rattled through Charlie's chatter. "Reptilians have been spotted in the sector and are on their way to intercept us!"

56

CHARLIE GAWKED AT NADIA.

"How the hell'd you do that, man?"

To his surprise, she was gawking back at him. A look of realization dawned on her face, and for the first time since he'd known Nadia, she looked authentically worried.

He patted himself down for a joint, along the way tapping the chatter pinned to his chest.

"Swarm, how much time do we have?"

"Hard to say, Captain. Our inertia is still propelling us toward the brown hole, but our velocity is slowing as the hyperdrive counteracts that inertia. Scans indicate a single X-Class Komodo Warship is tracking us at full speed."

"Dude, you know I have no friggin' idea what you just said. *How much time do we have?*"

"Let me ask MOM." There was a short pause, then Swarm's gravelly voice reappeared. "Oh, that's right. I can't ask MOM because *you deleted her!*"

"You're a pilot! Can't you do the math?"

"No, Captain, I can't plot multiple astrophysical objects and calculate their variable trajectories and velocity in my smegging head!" roared Swarm. "That's why every other starship has a smegging computer!"

"Why do I hear running water?" asked Charlie.

"The sound of running water obfuscates my voice so I can warn you without *them* knowing."

"Wait, you're in the bathroom?"

"I'm in a voidpod. It was the only place to contact you without rousing suspicion. By the way, no one outside your backwater planet calls them *bathrooms*. That's smegging stupid."

"Thanks for once again offering me feedback on *my entire planet*! Like I had anything to do with what things are called!"

"Boys!" interrupted Nadia. "Focus on the issue at hand!"

"Is that...?" asked Swarm. "Are you...?"

"Yeah, man. I had to drop Zee off somewhere she'd be safe."

"A high-churn planet like Vos Praeda would've been safer than that snake pit!"

Nadia reached across the bar and tapped Charlie's chatter.

"Don't worry, Lieutenant, Lavaka always has a private booth ready for your next rendezvous."

Despite the banter, Charlie could see the color had drained from her face, and beads of sweat had begun forming on her forehead.

"Captain, what's our plan?" rattled Swarm.

Charlie plucked an unlit joint from his afro and popped it between his lips. It dangled unlit as he asked, "Wait a second, can't the *Pineapple Express* outrun whatever the Reptoids have?"

"No vessel can match the speed of the *Starseed*, which should be the same for this ship. But that will only matter if you master that smegging toy of yours, Captain."

"I'm still working on it," said Charlie. "And I have a hunch this thing might work better from in the mini-bridge. Is it clear for me to sneak in and give it a shot?"

"I wouldn't recommend it, Captain. The Dregz have set up some kind of automated stun sentry in the mini-bridge that will zap you within a nanoghatika of your entering the room."

"Well, scratch that idea."

Why doesn't the gamepad work, man? Charlie thought to himself as he held the cloud of smoke in his lungs.

Nadia tapped his chatter again.

"Swarm, how'd the Reptilians find us?"

"I'm guessing they picked up on the smegging distress beacon we've been blasting through the sector!"

"What kind of moron would broadcast a distress beacon out here on the fringe among all the smugglers and criminals?"

"The kind that's standing right beside you."

"Still, it's very unlikely a Reptilian vessel would pick it up. The chances of them being within range are next to null…"

She began slithering back and forth behind the bar.

Swarm's voice returned, quieter than before.

"The longer I stay in this voidpod, the more suspicious they'll get. Vree has taken the leash off of these smegheads. He's given them two orders: find the mini-Transit Bay and the Silexi transport ship, and apprehend the *Pineapple Express's* fugitive captain. They're taking their new orders very seriously. A few Dregz are combing through the mini-Ring and are probably on their way to Lavaka as we speak."

"They're coming here? Now?! We have to hide Zee!"

Nadia stopped pacing and studied Charlie's face.

"You're really not like any *Starseed* captain I've ever known," she said, staring at him intently. Her ruby lips curled at the corners.

"But I guess that makes sense, considering the plants you brought with you."

"Speaking of your plants," said Swarm. "Your grow room is currently occupied by two Dregz with itchy trigger fingers."

"They have my girls, too? Shit, man! I can't handle all this. I can't handle so many problems all tangled up into one huge, relentless clusterfuck! Just as I get a grip on one problem, two more pop up! And all I want is for everyone to be high and happy and free, back on the 'Seed, no catastrophes on the horizon! Is that too much to ask? Instead, I get sick plants and mutinous Dregz and giant space assholes! And on top of all that, now we'll have to take on Reptoids? I just can't anymore."

Nadia placed a hand on his clenched fist.

"I wouldn't worry about that last part."

"I hope that means you've got some way to deal with them when they get here. 'Cause I sure as hell don't."

"Funny you say that, because remember what I said earlier about being our own worst enemy? Turns out I'm not immune. But know that my plan was only to send those vile snakes a message... from a safe distance. They were supposed to leave us alone until after the Trapezians returned home with a renewed lust for war."

"You were behind the sabotage, weren't you? I *knew* it, man. The others told me it was too obvious, but I could practically smell your perfume on every misstep we took!"

"I had nothing to do with the treaty, nor do I care what happens in Trapezia. But I did have intel that confirmed the treaty was destined to fail. That the Reptilians were counting on it. Haven't you figured out their connection to Trapezia yet?"

Charlie stuck out his chest.

"Uh, sure. Why don't you tell me what you think it is, and we'll compare notes."

"Kryyd is the connection, Captain. Do you know where it comes from?"

"Swarm said he found it on some passengers."

"No, I mean where it's *made*. *How* it's made. You really don't know?" She patted his hand and lowered her voice. "Little details like that no longer matter. Just know that I'm... sorry, Captain. I'm so sorry."

Charlie looked up, and for first time since meeting Nadia, didn't get the sense that she was a predator lulling her prey into a trance. There was no game being played behind her eyes. It was just a person in trouble looking at another person in trouble.

"Whatever it is, it can't be as bad as the shit I've done. Or most of the other shit you've done," he said. "Anyway, I'm short on crew, and I haven't spaced you yet, so I guess I can afford to postpone it a little longer."

She took his other hand and Charlie swore he saw tears gathering under her eyes.

"You really are a strange ape, Captain Hong."

"Does that mean you're coming with me?"

"You wish," she said, tossing aside his hands and looking suddenly flippant. "I never leave Lavaka. Never."

"You heard Swarm, man! Armed Dregz are on their way, and I'm not sure the threat of earning the Mark will keep them from shooting up this place looking for me."

"Nothing happens in Lavaka without my consent." Her sultry expression was back. "You have your tricks, I have mine. Your damsel will be safe here, and so will I. Go before you get so stoned you forget what you were doing."

"Too late. What am I doing again?"

57

It's all connected, thought Charlie as he slipped his legs into the costume and pulled it snuggly against his sneakers.

His arms probed through the folds of rubber and fur for the armholes. When both arms were in and his fingers found their place in the attached gloves, he zipped it up along a hidden seam running right up through the middle of his chest.

The sabotage, he thought.
The kryyd.
The Trapezian three-way war.
The murders.
E.T.
Reptoids.
Earth.
Me.
The other *me.*

Charlie pulled the gorilla mask over his head and adjusted its holes to line up with his face. He took a deep breath. He swiveled his head to look around. Neither breathing nor movement were hindered by the mask.

It was a perfect fit, which is exactly what you'd expect when morpho-printing a costume directly from your imagination.

Why would the other me care about any of this? What do they have to gain by fucking up the peace process? By flying the ship into a brown hole? Why not a black hole? There are like a hundred million black holes in the galaxy to choose from.

It's like he wanted us to die, but first he wanted us to suffer, thought Charlie. *By shoving us head first into a cosmic toilet bowl.*

I gotta admit, besides the mass murder part, it's kinda funny.

So it's all just some kind of joke? Make everyone smell farts for a few days, then kill them?

He slid his head through the center of a brightly-colored woven poncho. Once it settled, he slung a bandolier strung with pre-loaded bong hits over one of his shoulders.

Which makes sense if he's really made from my dark side. Which I obviously still harbor since I find the brown hole thing a tiny bit hilarious.

So the big question is this: if I still harbor some dark tendencies, can I harness them to figure out Dark Charlie's next move and use it to trap him?

If his plan involved steering the ship into a brown hole, and he's on the ship, then his next move would probably be to get off the ship before that happens. If I were him, I'd probably steal a ship or something.

Charlie felt the weight of the gigantic sombrero as it settled onto his head just over his brow. Suddenly he was standing in a 48-inch-wide puddle of shadow. He looked up into the panel of pineapple wall he'd morpho-printed into a mirror. The hat matched the poncho with its bright, festive colors.

Too bright, he thought, then snapped his fingers. Both accessories aged a few years in the span of one second. Their colors dimmed ever so slightly, their edges frayed ever so much.

Perfecto, he thought.

But then where the hell would I go once I destroyed the Pineapple Express *and killed everyone on board, including me and the rest of the crew? Dark Charlie must know everything I know, including the fact that there are multiple galactic warrants out for my/his/our arrest. The only place he'd be safe is… the* Starseed.

Charlie, now wearing his snug gorilla bandito disguise, reached for the three-foot-tall purple bong and began pacing around the small doorless room.

"Dark Charlie wants the *Starseed*," he said, continuing his thoughts aloud. "But if he just replaced me, the crew or the Glimwickets or anyone who knows me would know something was up."

"Then again, if he were the only survivor of the *Pineapple Express*, he could impersonate me and no one would know. Since Zee and Swarm are the only remaining active members of my crew, he'd be able to form a new crew by recruiting the worst creeps the galaxy has to offer.

"There'd be no one to stop them from cruising around in the *Starseed* playing more of these demented jokes on whatever poor, unsuspecting planets or ships they encountered. It'd be like a fucked-up, reverse *Star Trek* in real life."

Charlie put the bong to his mouth and sparked his lighter against its fully packed bowl. After a few seconds of gurgling bubbles, the chamber was filled with thick white smoke. He yanked the stem from the base and sucked with all his might, emptying the chamber in one hit.

His chest puffed out and strained against the bandolier as he clenched his throat and held the hit inside his lungs. After counting to five, he opened his throat and spewed forth a mighty geyser of sweet-smelling smoke into the air above him.

"Shit, man. That'll suck," he told his reflection as stray wisps of smoke wafted from his mouth. "Dark Charlie will bend the *Starseed* to his will, corrupt it, and turn it into… the *Dark Starseed*! It'll be ten times worse than the Reptilians. It'll be the most terrible thing the galaxy has ever known."

A wave of fear rippled through him, causing his hand to relax and lose its grip on Big Willie. The bong fell and shattered against the green marble floor. The weed, glass shards, and bong water were absorbed back into the floor within seconds.

"In that case, I'm pretty sure I know where he's headed. I'm the only one who can stop him."

He caught his own eyes in the mirror. The small holes in the gorilla mask made it slightly more difficult, but not impossible.

You can do this, dude, he told himself.

Right after you roll a couple of fatties and make a few quick stops.

58

When you're on the run and trying to avoid detection, being able to push a button to vaporize yourself certainly has its advantages.

Charlie could think of a few times back on Earth where swirling out of handcuffs or zipping through an air vent in a holding cell would've come in handy.

As cool as it was, his amazing two-in-one vaporizer and 16-button starship controller wouldn't help him face his doppelgänger. For that he'd have to use his wits—and possibly some moves he'd picked up from Bruce Lee flicks.

Except this asshole has the same wits and the same Bruce Lee moves as I do, he thought. *How can I capture someone who matches my braincells one-for-one and can predict my every move?*

More importantly, what happens if I fail?

He swallowed the resinous roach from the joint he'd just finished, took one last toke from his gamepad, smashed another Big Willie (just for the hell of it), straightened his sombrero, then pressed the button that would toke him to where he was sure Dark Charlie was hiding.

Hoping to keep his presence hidden, Charlie had programmed the toke to smuggle him between a stretch of pineapple wall and the front landing gear of the Silexi transport vessel.

Once his body was done condensing, the first thing he noticed was the overall shadowy vibe to the mini-Transit Bay. The golden shimmer that radiated from the rest of the ship was diminished, leaving the walls just bright enough to cast a sickly brown aura on the parked vessels.

Charlie crept along the wall, his rubber- and fur-covered feet moving soundlessly across the marble floor. His attention was pulled toward the dark center of the room, where the hole had once opened to let the ships dock, but he kept one eye on the wall beside him. If his hunch was right—actually, it was a series of hunches all rolled into one crackpot stoner theory—then catching Dark Charlie might be easier than he thought.

Or, he'll kill me and laugh manically as the ship plunges into the brown hole, he thought. *In that case I might be better off dead.*

He slipped past the spherical Undulata ship and skulked behind a couple of *Starseed* transport nugs. Like most of the *Starseed's* nugs, each vessel was the unassuming shape of a cannabis seed without visible portholes, thrusters, or anything else that would identify it as a spacefaring vehicle.

Charlie appreciated the cover the nugs gave him, but it was almost too dark to see. He squinted carefully at the wall as he tiptoed along, making sure not to miss what he was looking for.

Somewhere else in the bay, something clattered against the hard floor. Charlie squealed like a little girl and dove behind the nearest nug. He shoved his furry ape knuckles into his mouth to muffle any further squeals and peered into the shadows dancing through the dimly lit room.

The clatter was followed by a heavy thud and a series of loud clanks. Charlie could tell they were coming from a passenger nug located directly across the bay. He peered into the darkness and let his eyes adjust. A small beam of light shifted to the floor and then to the wall behind it.

Someone carrying a flashlight was banging something against the nug.

After a series of whacks with what looked like a huge monkey wrench, sparks exploded from the side of the nug to reveal a single snapshot of a face leaning into an open panel.

An impossible face.

Charlie heard the panel slam shut, one more whack with the wrench, then footsteps toward the last nug in the row. The shadows were still too dense for him to make out much more than a silhouette, but as soon as the figure began whistling Monty Python's "Always Look on the Bright Side of Life", Charlie knew his suspicions had been correct.

The only other lifeforms who could possibly know that tune were back on Earth.

Charlie knew the song perfectly well. "Always Look on the Bright Side of Life" had been the song he and his parents would sing when confronted with life's unexpected turbulence: the cat went missing, the refrigerator went out, Grandma died.

Even though it was a tune that usually brought Charlie comfort and levity, hearing his doppelgänger whistle it as he went to town on the passenger nugs with a huge monkey wrench was beyond unsettling.

What else does he know about me? he asked himself. *About my past? About my deepest, darkest thoughts?*

The answer came immediately.

Everything. He knows everything.

As Charlie ruminated on how to fight an opponent who could anticipate his every move, he noticed a partially healed hole in the wall behind him.

Bingo, motherfucker! he thought. *Looks like the advantage goes both ways!*

Charlie squinted at the hole and forced his will on it. The pineapple flesh obeyed by stretching out and thickening until there was no trace of the hole left.

Step one complete. Now no one's leaving the mini-Transit Bay until the other is, well...

He left the thought incomplete and turned to face the nug. He ran his hand over its perfectly smooth surface until he felt the faintest groove etched into the shape of a small rectangle, then dug his fingernails under it and pried it away from the nug's hull. The small panel door came away easily and swung open on a seamless hinge. Inside the small access panel was a matrix of organic, slimy wires that dripped with a bioluminescent goo. He shoved them aside and scanned a crystalline circuit board covered with blinking diodes and capacitors.

The whistling stopped abruptly and an eerie silence gripped the dim bay.

There was no more pounding, no more whacking, and no footsteps. At least none Charlie could hear.

Finally, Charlie's finger found what it was looking for. He pressed the small red button, then whipped out his gamepad and pressed an identical button on the underside of the controller, inside the battery compartment. A single diode next to each button began blinking, then after a few seconds, turned solid.

Almost done, he thought, quietly shutting the nug's access panel. Once closed, the groove around it smoothed out and vanished completely. Charlie entered a series of button presses into the gamepad, sighed, and slipped it into his hoodie pocket.

No matter what happens next, I've got him. Even if he kills me, thought Charlie.

Wait, can he kill me? Can I kill him?

If we touched, would our molecules break apart and collide and mix together to form some kind of Charlie monster with two heads, four arms, four legs, and two Little Charlies?

"Took you long enough, man," said an all-too-familiar voice from the shadows on the other side of the circular bay. "I was startin' to worry you were too stupid to figure out where to find me."

Charlie tensed. Not only was the voice his own, but it had that cringe-y nasal quality that comes with hearing your own recorded voice.

I hate the sound of my friggin' voice, he thought.

There was no more hiding. No more sneaking around.

This was going to end soon, one way or the other.

59

"Look, man, this is gonna end soon, one way or the other," Dark Charlie called out. "If you come out, I promise I won't beat you to a pulp with this bigass wrench. Not right away, anyway."

Charlie focused on a patch of green marble and screwed up his face. A thin column bulged upward and morphed into another copy of Big Willie.

How many of these poor bastards am I gonna break? he thought as he plucked a loaded bong hit from his bandolier and slid it into the bong's stem.

Charlie straightened up, puffed out his chest, and walked out of the shadows with the purple bong slung over his shoulder like a loaded shotgun.

"Looks like I've finally found the source for the shit smell that's been permeating my ship for days," he announced through the rubber gorilla mask.

A familiar laugh rose up from the shadows on the other side of the room. It echoed through the large domed bay and was tinged with a touch of demented malice that Charlie hoped wasn't normally there when he laughed.

"I knew that if anyone would appreciate my sense of humor, it'd be you."

Charlie saw a figure step out of the shadows.

Everything about the figure was familiar: brown hoodie, baggy jeans, a short round afro atop a stunningly handsome face. Charlie's brain reconciled the anomaly by telling him he was just looking into a dirty mirror someone had propped up on the other side of the room.

Then Charlie reminded his brain that he was wearing a gorilla suit, a sombrero, a poncho, and a bandolier of bong hits.

Charlie's brain apologized for the confusion, slid into the backseat of his mind, and curled up into a ball until it was all over.

How did I expect him to take me seriously dressed like a stoned bandito from Planet of the Apes? thought Charlie.

"Man, you look like some kind of stoned bandito from *Planet of the Apes*," said Dark Charlie.

He flashed a tilted grin—*a little too tilted*, thought Charlie—then thwapped the heavy monkey wrench against the palm of his hand.

"Doesn't matter. Soon enough you'll be a pile of ground beef, your stupid floating pineapple and all its passengers will be forever lost in the brown hole, and I'll take the helm on the *Starseed*."

His eyes went wide as if he'd just realized something important, and Charlie again noted that the whites of his doppelgänger's eyes were stark white.

"Oh, shit! I bet you already figured all that out, man. That's why you're here. You think you can stop me."

Another thwap of the wrench against the palm of his hand.

Charlie ignored the thwapping and focused on stopping himself from visibly shaking.

"There's no need to shove a bunch of innocent people into a brown hole. Whatever you and I have to settle, we can settle it without getting anyone else involved."

"But that's way less funny!" whined Dark Charlie. "Oh, come

on, man. If there's anyone in the galaxy who gets my sense of humor, it's you."

"Murder isn't funny, man."

Dark Charlie rolled his unbloodshot white eyes.

"Maybe to a do-gooder like you. But you have to admit, there's a comedic sophistication to launching a giant flying pineapple into an enormous, inescapable butthole floating in space."

"It's about as sophisticated as a moon-sized whoopee cushion," Charlie said. "Even if you succeed, no one but you will ever know what happened. You'd be the only one alive who knows the punchline."

"If a joke falls in the forest and there's no one around to hear it, is it funny?" asked Dark Charlie in a mocking voice. "In this case, yeah, it's fucking hilarious. Wanna know why?"

His tilted grin somehow tilted even further.

How is that even possible? thought Charlie. *Is that how I look when I smile?*

"*I'll* know that *you* know that I beat you. Your dying thought will be that you lost the war we've been fighting for the past thirty-odd years. Come on, you know exactly what I'm talking about! You and me, at every crossroads we've ever been at. Every time you reached a hand into the cookie jar to snatch a cookie, I was the voice egging you on. Every time you checked your watch and knew you should head back home for dinner, I was the voice telling you to stay out anyway.

"I was there that time you were offered a needle. Yeah, you remember, man! There was that brief temptation to just let yourself go over the edge. That was me. I almost had you then. You won that one, but I won plenty of others.

"But now, thanks to your dumbass plan to create the *Pineapple Express* and your willingness to swallow that data pill Swarm gave you, I've finally escaped that empty skull of yours. I'm out here now," he said, waving the wrench around. "And holy shit, man, I like it. I'm finally free, our war is over, and my prize will be the most powerful starship in the galaxy!

"And there's no one to blame other than yourself, man. You fucked up and lost everything. I'd say it's pretty compassionate of me to put you out of your misery. I'll go on for the both of us, a lot stronger and more focused than you ever were. More like Dad. Less like Mom, like you."

"Huh?" Charlie pulled his mouth off the bong, wisps of smoke billowing in its wake. "Sorry, I kinda zoned out halfway through your evil monologue, man. That was a heavy ramble, even for us. But I heard the part about Dad, and you're wrong. He'd never hurt or kill. His whole life has been focused on technology that helps people."

"Whatever, man. Whizcom has contracts with the military. And who do you think Earth's military really works for? Just like Mom, you'd rather look away from shit you don't want to acknowledge than face the truth. Pathetic."

"You know what's pathetic? Letting a perfectly good bowl burn down to ash without puffing on it." Charlie held out the bong, neck first. "Before you kill me, you'll want to hit this."

Dark Charlie scoffed at Big Willie like it was a 3-foot-long turd.

"No way, man. I know how often you clean your bongs."

What kind of Charlie Hong doppelgänger refuses weed? Especially Golden Ticket! My hunch just might be true after all...

"Plus, unlike weak-minded assholes like you, I don't need drugs to function. Don't you get it? *That's* why I've beat you, man. Because I'm what you've always been afraid of becoming."

"A version of me with a regular job?"

"The version of you that stopped smoking weed and became faster, sharper, and smarter than ever before. I get to be all those things, which is why it was inevitable, from the moment you swallowed that data pill, that I was destined to replace you. I'm a newer version. I'm the upgrade."

"Nice TED talk, man. Next time don't forget to wear a black

turtleneck," said Charlie, tipping the bong closer to his foe. "Come on, if you're so smart then you'll know how pot enhances everything. It'll enhance the euphoria you'll feel when you're smashing my brains out. And it'll help you relax before the Reptilians smash yours out."

"Reptilians? What the hell are you talking about?"

His grip on the wrench loosened slightly.

"You haven't heard the latest news, Mr. SmartyPants? Reptoids are on their way here now. Even Nadia's all freaked out about it. I think we're pretty fucked. So, might as well have a tiny toke before they get here and confiscate all the weed."

Dark Charlie let his gaze drift away for a brief moment, then snapped his eyes back to the gorilla bandito standing in front of him. There was a sparkle in his eyes as he said, "Sounds like I'll have to kill you faster than I thought if I wanna get out of here in time."

He raised the wrench and took a step toward Charlie, who took two steps back while waving the bong in front of him like he was offering a steak to a mad dog.

"Hold up, man! You have time for one hit, don't you? If you're me at all, if we have anything in common, then you'll have to know that you'll be missing out on something beautiful if you kill me while you're totally sober."

He thrust the mouthpiece of the bong toward his doppelgänger.

"You know what, you're right," Dark Charlie said, relaxing slightly. "Hold it steady while I hit that thing, man."

Without warning, he swung the wrench and Big Willie exploded into a supernova of purple shrapnel.

Charlie gasped.

"Not cool, man! You didn't have to bring Big Willie into this! Just like you didn't need to bring the girls into it."

He knocked the sombrero back off his head, yanked off the gorilla mask, and looked Dark Charlie in the eyes.

"Where's Happy, man? What'd you do with her?"

His doppelgänger grinned darkly.

"I traded her to that dumb snake bitch for a navigation lockout module. It was great, man, you should've seen it. She thought I was you. Well, I *am* you, right? Anyway, I think she suspected something was up, but it didn't stop her from naming her price. She did seem pretty shocked when you handed over one of your plants so easily. She even threw in some of these to sweeten the deal."

With his free hand he dug around in his hoodie pocket and produced a handful of mercurial pills. Even from a few feet away, Charlie should make out the concentric infinity symbols etched into them.

Dark Charlie tossed back the handful and swallowed them all in one gulp. His face twisted up into a painful grimace and his eyeballs began darting around independent of one another. A convulsion rippled through him from head to toe, leaving behind a wake of calm.

His eyes weren't just stark white around the edges anymore. They glowed like a pair of colorless torches beaming from inside his skull. He glared like a predator ready to pounce.

Glad my bladder's already empty, thought Charlie.

He took a moment to gather his wits, then tried to appear as nonchalant as possible about being seconds away from death-by-monkey-wrench.

"There's no use in trying to run, man," Charlie said coolly. "This bay's locked the fuck down and everyone's on their way here right now. You can't escape. And trying to kill me will just earn you the Mark and a pretty gnarly death. But if you drop the weapon, get on your knees, and put your hands on your 'fro, I'll see that you're treated fairly."

"I disabled the Mark."

"Well, I re-enabled it, man. *Duh.* Look, if you kill me, a shitload of Seeders will bust in here and devour your stupid, pill-poppin' ass. If you go quietly, maybe we'll take mercy on you by giving you a one-way trip to that cyber-prison on Vekst."

Come on, fool! Charlie cried out in his head. *Take the goddamn bait!*

Dark Charlie frowned and squeezed the wrench handle so hard the iron softened in his grip like warm butter.

Damn, maybe if I keep pushing him, the kryyd will do my job for me. Explode his heart or head or something. I should get ready to jump aside so I don't get brains on my gorilla suit.

"Think about it. Would I have the balls to come here all by myself? Without Swarm and lots of backup? He and the Dregz and everyone else will be here any second, man. Time's running out."

Veins bulged in Dark Charlie's neck and his short afro sparked with static electricity. He started sweating profusely and his breath became quick and shallow.

"You alright, man? Maybe you should sit down for a minute before killing me. Have you had any water recently? Any food? Maybe your blood sugar is a little low and you just need some—"

Charlie was interrupted by his doppelgänger swinging the monkey wrench at his head.

The impact of soft foam bounced off, doing no more damage than slightly denting his afro. He ran a hand through it to fix it while grimacing at Dark Charlie.

"Okay, I guess we're fightin' then! No countdown or bell or fist bump, huh? Well, the first ground rule is *no hair*. No pulling it, no grabbing it, no denting it. Whatever beef we have with each other, let's have a little respect for our 'fro, man."

The wrench caught him again in the side of the face and broke at the handle. Dark Charlie threw it on the ground where it squeaked like a dog toy as it bounced away.

Charlie offered his own tilted grin—but not too tilted.

"This ship is mine, man. Every molecule was crafted by my imagination, including whatever objects you try to use against me. Face it, dipshit, there's no way you can—"

He was interrupted again, this time by a swift left hook slamming into his cheekbone and sending a scattering of microscopic stars across his field of vision.

Charlie stumbled back, held his jaw, and frowned at his doppelgänger.

"Try that again and I'll nerf your fists like I nerfed the wrench."

"Good point, Chuck! We can both control the ship's substrate with our mind," Dark Charlie said through a demented, over-tilted grin. He was breathing heavy like an enraged bull and the veins in his neck were visibly throbbing. "But only one of us is *made* from it. Which means only one of us can do this."

He lifted his hands. One by one, his fingers melted into each other as if they were made from wax, turning each hand into a fleshy paddle. His forearms flattened and elongated like stretched rubber, and from the elbow down, each arm morphed into a shiny new 24-inch-long chainsaw blade.

"Man, once I get back to the *Starseed* I'm gonna have some real fun," he said, holding one of his new arm blades up to his face. The glow of his torch eyes reflected off of every tooth on the freshly sharpened blade.

"But first…"

Dark Charlie pumped both arm blades into the air. The small motors located at each elbow growled hungrily and the blade chains became a blur.

Charlie leapt backwards and tapped his chatter.

"Guys, I could really use that backup now!"

"What's with all the smegging racket?" Swarm's voice came back from the device. "I can't hear a word you're saying, Captain!"

"Help! Hurry!"

Dark Charlie pounced with both arm blades extended in front of him.

Charlie did what seemed to make the most sense at the time, which wasn't saying much since he was thoroughly stoned. He dropped to the floor and pulled himself into the fetal position.

Dark Charlie, not expecting such a stupid move, couldn't stop his forward thrust in time. He stumbled over Charlie's shins, almost falling on his own chainsaw arms, then spun around with renewed hostility.

He looked at Charlie curled into a ball on the floor and chuckled between his hot breaths.

"This ends now!"

Dark Charlie swung his right arm blade down on top of his victim, hoping to cut him clean in half.

Instead of biting through Charlie's soft flesh, his arm blade hit something incredibly hard and sent a sparks into the air all around them.

When the sparks settled, he saw that Charlie had managed to summon a wave-like slab of the green marble floor over his body.

The second thrust of the arm blade penetrated a few inches into the marble and seized up. The motor at Dark Charlie's elbow began convulsing and spewing black smoke. He yanked at his arm and howled with frustration when it didn't come free.

Charlie crawled out from under the curved slab, rolled a few feet away, and scrambled to stand up. The second he was back on his feet, the other chainsaw arm swung at him horizontally, aiming to slice through his waist.

He summoned another slab of marble just in time. The second chainsaw blade got stuck as well, leaving both of Dark Charlie's arms restrained.

Charlie stepped back even further to take in the sight. He shook his head.

"This is what you call murder, man? I've seen sabertooth slugs with more predatory skills than you."

As his doppelgänger struggled to pull his blades free, Charlie focused his attention on the slabs. Thick marble vines sprouted and wound their way around the stalled arm blades, then flattened into marble shackles that clamped onto each arm just above the elbow.

Charlie tapped his chatter. "I got him! Piece of cake."

"Great smegging news!" rattled Swarm. "But how do I know this is the real Captain Hong and not the imposter?"

"You'll know when you get here," he said as he watched Dark Charlie snorting and seething and growling as he struggled to yank his arms free.

Charlie shook his head, feeling something akin to pity.

"Dang, man. I'm actually kinda disappointed. I always imagined a physical battle with my dark side being a little more, I don't know… OH SHIT."

Instead of pulling his arm blades free, Dark Charlie plunged them deeper into each slab. The slabs had lost their green luster and now looked as dingy as the rest of the mini-Transit Bay. The greyish marble melted into and around the blades, halfway down his forearms, and then solidified back into stone. There was a deep rumbling sound as the slabs of marble cracked and broke away from the floor.

Dark Charlie lifted his arms in victory, a fist-shaped boulder of greyish green marble fused to the end of each arm.

He pointed one of his stone fists at Charlie.

Charlie backed away and tapped his chatter again.

"Scratch that last update, Swarm. I don't have him yet. Get your ass in here now or you'll be scraping my brains off the floor with a spatula."

"Probably won't need a very big spatula," Swarm rattled, then added before Charlie could protest, "We're approaching the Transit Bay door now."

"Mini-Transit Bay!" corrected Charlie, just before leaping aside to dodge the boulder fist that came crashing down where he'd been standing.

"Smegging hell, Captain! The doors are sealed! Open up so we can rescue you or arrest you or do whatever the smeg we need to do before the Reptilians arrive and kill us all anyway!"

Another boulder fist was coming at Charlie, this time horizontally at chest height. He fell backward and made himself as flat as possible just in time to watch the massive chunk of stone blur past.

No sooner had the first fist whizzed by than the other was coming down right on top of him. He rolled out of the way in time, but not before the fist pinned the corner of his poncho to the floor.

Charlie tugged and yanked, but it wouldn't budge. He considered trying to slip out of the poncho, but saw the other boulder fist being lifted above him. There was no time to slip away. He didn't think imagineering another slab of marble to shield him would do much good.

He caught a glimpse of Dark Charlie's burning white eyes and the veins that popped from his neck like steel cables. The kryyd was giving him some kind of super psychotic rage strength that he was about to demonstrate with a *bang*.

Charlie knew there had to be something he could do to avoid getting flattened, but his overstoned neurons had completely stalled out under the pressure of his own impending doom.

This was it.

All hope for saving the *Pineapple Express*, the *Starseed*, and the galaxy itself was lost.

He made one last futile attempt at pulling his poncho free, but he remained pinned.

At least I'll be super stoned when I go, he thought, accepting his fate and allowing himself to relax into a gorilla-shaped puddle on the floor.

That's it! his mind cheered.

Without wasting another nanoghatika, Charlie closed his eyes and let his subconscious merge with the ship's substrate.

60

THREE THINGS HAPPENED AT ONCE.

First, the boulder fist came down right on top of Charlie. It was so large he completely disappeared beneath it, leaving only a corner of poncho behind as proof he'd been there at all.

Second, a door spun open and a small crowd stormed inside the mini-Transit Bay. Swarm led the group with a wadjet rifle in each of his four claws while the Dregz, the Trapezian delegates, and a few others filed in behind him. As soon as the last of them made it inside, the door spun shut and melted into the pineapple flesh wall.

The third thing to happen was that thousands of tiny holes appeared in the marble floor below Dark Charlie, spewing thousands of tiny geysers of smoke into the air. He had just enough time to look up at the newcomers before being engulfed in the thick cloud of a ganja strike.

The Dregz fired a few shots into the cloud before Swarm signaled for them to stop.

"You could've hit the Captain!" cried Mrs. Glimwicket.

"Did you see those eyes?" Swarm asked over his shoulder while peering into the impenetrable cloud of smoke. "I don't think that was Captain Hong. At least not the same one we're all used to."

"Dregz, spread out in a half circle on either side. Stun anything that moves."

In unison, Cassie, Bob Jr., and three little voices from the shadows all cried out, "What about Charlie?!"

Eta Cerbo's neck elongated and his eyes widened to the size of hubcaps. "Chuuuuck Stooonerly!"

"We'll sort out which Captain to keep, and which to space, once the ganja strike clears."

"What's a ganja strike again?" asked Mr. Glimwicket.

"You're looking at it now. A cloud of water vapor saturated with decarboxylated THC molecules. Looks like this one is at least a level 8."

"But what does *that* mean?" screeched Vree Voktal.

"It means the real Captain Hong was fighting back," answered Swarm.

He grumbled to himself, then called out, "Captain Hong! Either one of you…or…*both* of you! Whoever's in there, we've got you covered from every angle, and the only exit to this bay had been sealed off. There's no escape. And there's no time to waste, so we're going to do things a little more aggressively than normal. We're coming in."

He handed his fourth wadjet rifle to Mrs. Glimwicket and lifted a claw into the air.

"Dregz, on my mark, proceed into the cloud from every angle and detain both captains. Remember, only the real Captain Hong can open the bay's porthole and let your ship out of here. Best keep those rifles on stun if you want any chance of escaping the *Pineapple Express* before the Reptoids arrive."

He nodded silently to the left and right flanks, then closed his fist and began creeping into the huge cloud of smoke with his three rifles drawn. The Dregz followed suit and stepped into the cloud from all sides.

After a brief millighatika of silence, there was a series of bright flashes, the sound of multiple stun shots being fired, the clanking of space armor, obscene alien curses being shouted, and the sound of multiple bodies hitting the ground.

"Got him!" shouted Swarm as his silhouette emerged from the cloud carrying a body over his shoulder. He lay it down on the ground and groaned.

"Smegging hell! I got a Dreg by mistake."

He cocked his head to listen to the stun shots still being fired inside the cloud.

"Those idiots are stunning themselves!" Swarm called out above the ruckus. "Enough with this madness! Dregz, fall back!"

To Vree Voktal and the Glimwickets he said, "The vapor flow has started to reverse and is being suctioned out through the floor. Let's wait it out and see how many of those smegheads are still functional."

The cloud dissipated quickly, leaving the group's view of the mini-Transit Bay unobstructed. The room's sickly yellow light crept over a pile of fallen Dregz and a pair of giant boulder fists with arm-sized holes in them.

"Drag your buddies into a row over there and start reviving them." Swarm slowly approached the boulders. "Vree, you know rocks, right? What are these things?"

"I'm a royal servant to His Majesty, the Silexi Emperor! Not some common geologist!" hissed Vree Voktal. "Just because my home world consists mostly of rock doesn't mean I can identify—"

"It's some kind of marble, right? The same kind used as flooring throughout the ship?"

Vree Voktal started to protest again, but instead sighed and joined Swarm at the boulders.

"Yes, it does appear to be made from the same substance. But this rock looks aged, somehow. No, it's incredibly impure."

Swarm kneeled beside the boulders, examining them carefully.

"There was a battle…" His claw touched the poncho peeking

out from below one of the boulders. The marble floor was webbed with cracks and jagged fissures.

"Looks like they were playing rough."

"Our ship!" cried Vree Voktal. "Come, Your Highness! We must flee before the Reptilians arrive!"

Eta Cerbo planted his stubby legs while the taller Silexi tried to pull him toward their vessel.

Swarm looked up. "The bay port is sealed, you fool! Without MOM, the only person who can open it might be…"

He trailed off, focused on the poncho. After a short pause he came alive and threw his weight against the boulder.

"Help me, Vree! Bob, Cassie—everyone get over here and push!"

The group shoved their collective weight against the rock, but it wouldn't budge.

"It's too smegging heavy!" cried Swarm, punching the boulder and then nursing his bruised claw. "Anyone have a grav modifier or disintegration beam? Smeg it. I'm setting my wadjets to full power and I'm going to see if I can heat it up until it melts."

"Mr. Swarm, sir?" a tiny voice interrupted from behind the Glimwickets. "Maybe I can help?"

Bob Jr. stepped out from behind his parents, rummaging through his backpack. His glossy eyes widened and his proboscis coiled tightly as he produced a small handheld ray gun.

"Oh, Bob!" cried Mrs Glimwicket. "Where in Andromeda did you get a *weapon*?" She turned to her husband. "Oh, Bob! Our boy has joined…our little baby is in…a *gang!*"

"We don't do weapons *or* gangs in our family, young man!" scolded Mr. Glimwicket. "If we knew that letting you spend your entire vacation in that arcade would've resulted in guns and gang activity—"

"Hey!" interrupted Cassie. "There aren't gangs in my arcade!"

"Sorry, Mom. Sorry, Dad," Bob Jr. said, looking at his shoes. "At first it was just me and the wogs playing video games—"

"Wogs?!" rattled Swarm, his antennae going rigid. "There aren't any wogs on the *Pineapple Express*!"

"Whoops." Bob Jr's proboscis coiled more tightly. "At first it was just me and *my friends* playing games, but then we bumped into Charlie—I mean, Captain Hong. It's a long story, but he gave us these and dubbed us his Space Goonies Patrol. Yeah, we never really knew what it meant either."

"Captain Hong gave a group of children weapons and turned them into a gang?" screeched Vree Voktal.

"That's not exactly a weapon, is it?" Swarm said, holding out his claw.

Bob Jr. dropped the pistol into it and retreated behind his parents.

"No, sir. It's just a mat-com."

"A matter compressor ray?!" cried Mrs. Glimwicket. "Those are incredibly dangerous!"

"And expensive," added Mr. Glimwicket. "Out with it, son. Where'd you get it?"

"Captain gave one to me and each of the wogs—I mean, my friends. He gave us extra to hand out at the arcade to the other kids, too. Said that he needed us for a super secret special mission, like a video game in real life. I'm winning, too! I'm leading that slug face Foo by over three hundred larvae!"

"Language!" cried Mrs Glimwicket.

"Sorry, Mom. Foo's not a slug face, he's my friend. But I'm better at bagging larvae any day!"

Swarm rubbed his chin and looked at the mat-com in his claw.

"So, this was Charlie's plan to keep the larvae from eating the ship? He couldn't kill them, so he set a bunch of kids loose on the ship with dangerous devices and encouraged them to shrink as many of them as possible?"

"Yep. You shoulda seen the look on the other kids' faces when we told 'em. A real-life bug hunt, without any killing." Bob Jr. smiled. "We took care of my hungry sibs in no time."

Mrs. Glimwicket pinched one of Bob Jr's stubby antennae and dragged him away from Swarm and the others.

"When we get home we're having a serious talk about weapons and gangs and language, young man!"

"We're really sorry about this, Lieutenant Swarm," said Bob Sr.

"Not as sorry as Captain Hong will be when I have a serious talk with him about arming children."

Swarm shrugged, aimed the mat-com at the boulder, and pulled the trigger. It shrank instantaneously to the size of a pebble and dropped into the crater where it had just been lodged.

"Ouch, man!" a voice cried out from the darkness.

A dome of black spongy hair and two brown eyes emerged from the hole among wisps of smoke.

"Is it safe to come out now?"

Swarm reached one of his free claws into the crater and hoisted Charlie out into the open. The group gathered around.

"Man, am I glad to see all of you." His bloodshot eyes widened and darted around frantically. "Where is he? Did you already space him? Aww, I didn't want to miss it!"

"Don't worry, ape, soon you'll wish you had the luxury of gettin' spaced!" said Pig Nose, turning his rifles on the others. "No one move! Dregz, stun him and put him on our ship."

"Why not just sell him to the Reptoids?" asked Oozer.

"No way they pay more than Gal-Fed!" snorted Pig Nose. "On that note, leave any stunned Dregz. Fewer of us to split the g-creds with."

The p'ube was in Vree Voktal's hand before anyone noticed it had slipped in and out of his robes.

"One flick of my finger and the whole lot of you will spend the rest of your days in here."

The handful of Dregz who hadn't been stunned by their comrades lowered their wadjets and looked to each other for any sign of what to do next.

A soft crunching sound rose up around them. Charlie's hand

plunged into a paper bag of popcorn and shoved another handful into his mouth.

"As much as I'd like to see who wins this standoff," he said, "we don't really have time for last-minute power struggles. We got a few things to cover before I open up the bay port for anyone."

He stood up, handed the bag of popcorn to Swarm, and wiped his hands on his poncho.

"First of all, I gotta clear my name by exposing and catching the other me. So keep your weapons ready because he's a tricky motherfucker."

"Good point." Swarm trained two of his rifles on Charlie. "How do we know you're the real Captain Hong?"

Charlie ignored him and picked up something large and flimsy off the floor.

"Hey, man! Someone squished my sombrero!" He reshaped it as best he could and pulled it down over his afro.

Swarm looked Charlie up and down, then into the deep smoke-filled hole at the bottom of the crater, then at the bag of popcorn. He lowered his weapons.

"Glad you survived the encounter with your other self, Captain."

"Thanks, man! He's a real dick. Funny guy though, in a sick, twisted sort of way. *Very* good looking, if I do say so myself."

"Where the smeg is he?!" roared Swarm, shoving the popcorn at Mr. Glimwicket. He swiveled his large triangular head to scan the bay. "The door shut right behind us, so he couldn't have fled."

"Oh, he didn't flee. He's hiding." Charlie smiled. "But I know exactly where he is. And I know he knows I know, which makes this pretty damn suspenseful, doesn't it?"

"The Reptilians are on course to intercept us at any moment!" cried Swarm. "There's no time for suspense!"

"Reeeeptiiiiliaaaans!" E.T. shouted enthusiastically from the edge of the crowd.

"He's stalling," said Vree Voktal, aiming his p'ube and his

sinister Silexi gaze at Charlie. "If this was the Captain Hong we knew from before, he'd have the decency to let our ships leave and give us a chance at evading capture."

"That thing's a phony, man. A knock-off." Charlie nodded to the cube in Vree's stony hand. "Just like the other me. The *bad* me. Believe it or not, but he's far more dangerous than the Reptoids who are on their way here now, so we gotta deal with him first. If he gets out and back to the *Starseed*... We just can't let that happen, man."

"Um, who exactly are we talking about again?" Mrs. Glimwicket asked.

"We're talking about the person responsible for sabotaging the Trapezian peace process, murdering the Trapezian delegates, and hardwiring the ship's navigation to send us directly at a brown hole. Like I said, a real dick, man."

"Some kind of shape-shifting monster has taken your form?" asked Vree Voktal.

"No, he *is* me, but just the shadowy side of me that fled when Swarm gave me that data pill and unhinged my friggin' mind. It was able to latch onto physical reality via the *Pineapple Express's* substrate, which was also sort of a product of my mind. They were compatible, I guess."

Charlie shoved his hands in his pockets and began pacing in front of the Dregz, stepping over their stunned comrades. He sized each of them up as he continued his stoned ramble.

"Anyway, my shadow took physical form—a carbon copy of me. No really, man, *identical* to me, down to the last gene. He probably fooled all of you at some point, waving as he passed by you in the corridors or the mini-Ring. Or in one special case, he fooled someone who thinks she's unfoolable, but I'll save that for later. There was one person who knew, though. Yeaaahh, there sure was." He stopped in front of Metal Mask and glared at the eye slots in the mask.

Metal Mask dropped into a fighting stance and trained his wadjet rifle on Charlie.

Charlie held up his hands to show they were empty.

"Cool your jets, Boba Fett. I'm unarmed and extremely stoned. Besides, one fight is enough for today. And so is one traitor."

His head swung to the next Dreg in the lineup.

"Drop the gun. Then ditch the holo mask, the cloak jacket thing, and most importantly, ditch the bullshit, man!"

61

Swarm slipped between Charlie and Holo Mask, clacking his mandibles angrily.

"Captain! What the smeg are you doing?"

Charlie kept his attention trained on Holo Mask.

"The other me is bad news, lady. Trust me, if anyone knows, it's me. Now get that cloak off or we'll take it from you."

"Smegging hell, Captain! Commander Acari is under no obligation to remove her clothing in front of all these people!"

Charlie looked him up and down.

"Dude, you've been a naked eight-foot-tall insect the entire time I've known you."

"Excuse me, but who's Commander Acari exactly?" asked Vree Voktal.

Both Charlie and Swarm shot him a look. The Silexi offered a thin smile and stepped back to where the others stood watching.

Swarm slowly lifted one of his wadjet rifles and aimed it at Charlie.

"What's under her cloak is *her* business."

"She's been helping him, man. She's helping him *right now*. And as long as you point that gun at me, you are, too."

"Lies!" roared Swarm, pointing his other two wadjet rifles at Charlie.

"She was outside the ship when I planted the beacon, when that star system disappeared." He gave Holo Mask a sympathetic look. "Sorry I stepped on your meetle. Look, there's no use hiding it anymore, man. Maybe you thought he was me when he first approached you, but later you figured out he wasn't. You might've even figured out what he was up to. But you didn't care. You didn't care that he was gonna kill all of us and take over the *Starseed*. Because he had something you wanted so badly you were willing to sacrifice the *Pineapple Express* and everyone on board. Swarm, it's not too late for her to have a change of heart, don't you think? If she just drops the cloak and steps aside, we'll do the rest."

The holographic mask hovering around Commander Acari's head betrayed no emotions at all. She looked from Charlie to Swarm, then to the Dregz aiming their rifles at her.

"You don't understand, Captain Hong."

A claw appeared from under her cloak and tapped at a device around her neck. The holographic mask fell away to reveal a pink, triangular head with two dagger-sized mandibles set below a pair of large compound eyes.

"Every one of my million meetle's hearts beat for Swarm. I love him."

Charlie sighed and nodded.

"I get it. I don't want to lose Swarm, either. But I also don't want to lose Zee, the Glimwickets, the wogs, and all the other passengers. It's not fair to sacrifice them. And there's no point anyway! You and Swarm found each other! That's a miracle, man! A one-in-a-trillion chance! You can stay on the *Starseed* for as long as you want, then set out to start a life together when you're ready."

Her antennae went flaccid behind her head.

"You think we could live *here*? In this time? With all of you? On a stupid starship made of fruit?"

"It's not *made* of fruit, man! Okay, well, it's shaped like a fruit and it's edible, but it's an actual starship, too. Anyway, let's keep the *Pineapple Express* out of this. You found him. Isn't that enough?"

"No!" she exploded, as if millions of years of angst had finally become uncorked. "No! I followed him through the Rift to bring him back to the Hive! Not to live here in the past with all of you pathetic corpses!"

"Acari…" said Swarm.

"Don't you get it? They're all dead! *You're* all dead!" she raged, two claws pointing at the onlookers. "Your primitive little planets! Your pathetic individual little lives! None of that compares to what waits for us in the future, Swarm! Don't you remember the glory of the Hive? Of being *connected*?"

Swarm's antennae fell limp behind him.

"Every meetle in my body remembers. Not a cycle goes by where I don't feel the loss. But Acari, Captain Hong is right. We have each other. Isn't this what we always wanted? To escape that terrible war and be together? I know this isn't the Hive, but on the *Starseed* we share a different kind of bond. You can be part of that, too."

"There's still time to do the right thing," added Charlie. "Help us save the *Pineapple Express*."

"None of you can be saved!" she cried, tears streaming from every facet of her compound eyes. "Don't you see? You're all dead! Long dead! Swarm, this is our last chance!"

A claw disappeared into her cloak then reappeared clutching a faintly glowing purple crystal the size and shape of a cigar.

"Look what he gave me! A *time crystal*! He *made* it, right in front of me! We can go home, Swarm! We can reunite with the Hive!"

A collective gasp of intrigue came from the Dregz as the purple light from the crystal gleamed in their eyes. Pig Nose sniffled and tightened the grip on his wadjet rifle. His mouth watered, spilling thick drool from the corners of his cracked lips.

Charlie pointed to the crystal and shook his head.

"If the other me made that thing, then you don't want it. Acari, please listen to me. Whatever he told you is a lie. Whatever he gave you is not what you think it is. Swarm, don't let her use that thing."

Swarm looked from Charlie to Acari and back again.

"I could go home, Captain. Back to the Hive."

"Everyone wants to go home, man! We all want to go back in time—or, in your case, forward in time—to return to something we miss. But we can't! Life doesn't flow that way. We have to move forward. We have to let go of the past for the sake of the future."

Charlie noticed Habu watching from behind the Glimwickets. They locked eyes for a moment and Habu nodded slowly.

"You want me to let go, Captain?" cried Acari. "Fine, allow me to *let go*!"

She flung aside her cloak to reveal that a smaller body clung to her abdomen.

"It's my doppelgänger!" cried Charlie. "Stun him!"

Before the Dregz were able to peel their eyes from the time crystal, Dark Charlie sprang from his hiding spot and tackled Charlie to the ground.

Stun beams burst from a few wadjets, striking the tangled ball of wrestling Charlies in multiple spots. The figures grunted painfully, untangled themselves from one another, and fell onto their backs. Swarm and the others formed a circle around the two sprawled, paralyzed figures.

"It's true!" gasped Vree Voktal. "But how do we know which is the real Captain Hong?"

"They look identical," Mrs. Glimwicket said.

Mr. Glimwicket nodded. "Well, except for the fur suit."

The Charlie in the gorilla suit sat up, glanced at his stunned doppelgänger, and smiled.

"Thanks, guys! Hey, don't look so surprised."

"Impossible! That one must be a bot!" said Oozer.

"You mean *Synth!*" corrected Cassie from the back where she sat tinkering with Crimebot's head.

"I'm just a guy in a gorilla suit, man," said Charlie, starting to pat himself down. "A gorilla suit without a stash pocket. Damn. Anyone got a joint?"

He scanned the circle of astonished, skeptical faces.

"When I realized y'all would probably bust in here shootin' up the place with stun beams, I morpho-printed this suit and made sure to line it with thick, ionized rubber. A body-length layer of ionized rubber absorbs up to 90% of stun beam energy. It's not rocket science, man, I just looked it up on the Outernet. Very uncomfortable though, especially with all the sweat."

He tugged at the neck opening with a finger and shrugged.

"Anyway, we got him!" cheered Charlie. "Hurry, tie him up or something before he wakes up!"

No one moved. Everyone's attention had shifted toward something on the other side of Swarm.

Charlie hopped to his feet to see what everyone was gawking at. All eyes were trained on the crystal that was rapidly brightening in Acari's claws. She clutched it with all four claws and held it high above her head.

"Someone stun her!" shouted Charlie.

"Stand down!" growled Swarm, stepping in between the crowd and Acari. "Anyone even *thinks* about stunning her and I'll rip their smegging head off!"

Charlie stepped forward. He looked up and waved his hands in front of Swarm's compound eyes.

"Swarm, dude, we can't let her activate whatever the other me gave her! The dude is totally unhinged and has a twisted sense of humor. The one thing we can be sure of is that the time crystal won't do what he said it would do."

Swarm lifted his wadjet rifle directly at Charlie's face.

"I don't want to hurt you, Captain. But if you lay a finger on her, I'll stun you into tomorrow."

"Goddammit!" cried Charlie. "I never thought I'd say this to you of all people, Swarm, but you're letting your emotions cloud your thinking. I know you want to go home. I promise that if there's a way to send you back to the future, I'll use the full power of the *Starseed* to help you. Even if that means losing you. But that crystal *isn't* the way home. At best it's a joke. At worst it's a weapon, man. We can't let her—oh shit, she did it!"

"Does he always ramble this much?" Mrs. Glimwicket asked her son.

"Heck yeah, Mom. It's one of his superpowers or something."

Bob Sr.'s stubby antennae went up. "It's something alright."

Neon light glitched from both halves of the broken crystal as though spacetime was regurgitating last night's photons.

Pig Nose's goopy eyes widened.

"There's no stopping it now! There never was!" cried Acari, holding the two shards high above her head. "You don't understand, Swarm! I sacrificed that entire system when I trapped it in the p'ube. The planet was inhabited, and now they're trapped forever! I've gone too far... but I did it all for us!"

All three of Swarm's wadjet rifles dropped from his claws. Charlie had never seen his antennae droop so low.

"It's still not too late, Acari!" cried Charlie, knowing that it probably was. "There's gotta be a way we can free that system. Put the crystal down, tell me where the p'ube is, and we can fix this!"

Acari ignored Charlie and held out one half of the broken crystal to Swarm.

"All you have to do is take this half, my love. Your molecules will tune to its quantum temporal frequency, and once we connect the two halves we'll be transported back to our time, to the Hive! What are you waiting for? Take it!"

Swarm hesitated, his compound eyes trained on the face of his long-lost love. Temporal waves rolled through the glitchy purple light that spilled from the broken crystal.

"Don't do it, man," pleaded Charlie.

Swarm's claw reached out for the crystal, but then fell limp to his side. The eight-foot-tall insectoid seemed to deflate by at least a foot.

Acari's compound eyes narrowed slightly and each facet filled with its own tiny teardrop.

"Please, Swarm, come with me."

By the time Charlie and Swarm noticed the snort of nasally laughter and the quick stomping of metal boots behind them, a bulky figure had already shoved past them and grabbed both of Acari's slim claws in his meaty, cloven fists.

"Fools!" snorted Pig Nose, shaking Acari's wrists violently. "Breaking a perfectly good gem in two! Do you have any idea how many g-creds I could get for something like that? Now give me the pieces!"

She struggled against him, but his grip was too strong for her to pull away.

"Let go of me!"

"Drop the shards, lady!" growled Pig Nose. "Or I'll break your arms!"

Swarm snapped out of his emotional paralysis and launched himself forward to free Acari.

He made it two steps before his head lurched backward. Behind him, Charlie clung to both antennae and leaned back to brace himself.

"Let go!" roared Swarm.

"Let go!" snorted Pig Nose.

"Let go!" cried Acari.

Charlie held on with all his might but felt his sneakers starting to slip on the floor.

"Don't touch them, man! If the two halves of the crystal touch, then—"

He was interrupted by an explosion of purple light.

In their struggle, Pig Nose and Acari had done exactly as he'd feared—they allowed the two halves of the broken time crystal to make contact with each other.

The glitchy light bursting from the united crystal grew

brighter and brighter until it bleached out every detail of the mini-Transit Bay. For a moment Charlie thought he felt an unseen tide pulling him in all directions at once. Just as he felt his very molecules start to come apart, the white light vanished as suddenly as if someone had flipped off a light switch.

"With all due respect, Captain," said Swarm, slowly, as if waking from a dream, "let go of my antennae or I'll crush your smegging hands."

Charlie let his hands relax and shook the tension from his fingers.

"What the hell, man? Why was I pulling on you like that?" he said in the same half-awake tone.

"What were we just talking about?" asked Swarm.

"Wasn't there someone else here just now?" asked Vree Voktal.

"Two people," Mrs. Glimwicket said, shaking her head. "No, that's not right. Why'd I say that?"

"Shiiiiinnnny!" Eta Cerbo cried out.

Charlie shook his head and looked at Swarm.

"You okay? Whoa. You have tears in your eyes, man."

"I'm...I'm..." hesitated Swarm, his mind searching for an explanation for the empty space he felt.

"I have the sense I've lost something very important to me... but I have no idea what it could be."

He tilted his triangular head, shrugged both sets of shoulders, then snatched his wadjet rifles off the floor.

Charlie looked around the room in a daze, his eyes falling on each face as he tallied up memories of each person. He'd known Swarm and the Glimwickets since first becoming Captain of the *Starseed*. He recognized Cassie, Vree Voktal, Eta Cerbo, and even the Dregz—although he had the vaguest of notions that there was an empty spot in their ranks.

Somewhere, deep in the shadows of his memory, he had the fleeting sense that two people had been erased, but for the life of him, he couldn't recall who they were. Having counted and recounted everyone in the bay, his eyes finally fell to an empty patch of green marble and he suddenly snapped out of his daze.

"Shit, man!" he cried. "He's gone!"

62

"Spread out and search the bay!" rattled Swarm, aiming his guns in three different directions at once.

The Dregz scattered, wadjet rifles at eye level, ready to stun anything that moved among the sleeping vessels.

Charlie stood next to Swarm, his gaze fixated on one particular escape nug. He elbowed his Chief of Security, nodded toward the nug, and put a finger to his lips.

"Bet you a million g-creds he's in that one," Charlie said in low voice.

Swarm gave him a perplexed look.

"Why that one?"

"Because it was the ship closest to the tunnel he used to get into this room. If he's made from all my dark traits, then my profound laziness would've led him to choose the first nug he saw as his own personal escape pod."

"That's pretty thin ice, even for you, Captain!" Swarm bellowed.

Charlie lowered his voice even more. "And, I'm pretty sure that was the one ship in the whole bay he didn't sabotage."

"Sabotage?!"

Charlie grabbed him by the mandibles and drew him close.

"Dude! Keep it on the down-low! The Trapezians don't realize they're all stuck here on the *Pineapple Express* with the rest of us. We gotta deal with the other me before we can deal with the next five problems, got it? He can't be allowed to escape!"

Swarm nodded and leered at the silent nug.

"Then let's surround it! The few standing Dregz and I can handle him."

Charlie shook his head.

"Naw, not worth the risk of someone getting hurt. He's hopped up on kryyd and he has the same innate control over the ship that I have. We all saw what he did to CB. But don't worry." His bloodshot eyes twinkled as he bobbed his head and smiled. "I got him right where I want him."

"Then what's the smegging plan?"

"Step one, we let him escape."

"We *what?*"

"Look, it's happening now!" Charlie pointed to the floor beneath the hovering escape nug. A hole was slowly, silently widening.

"Just like I thought, he's trying to sneak away. This is perfect, man!"

"Sorry, Captain, I can't stand by and let him escape." Swarm held his head high and shouted to the Dregz, "He's in that nug! Get him!"

The hole in the floor had nearly grown wide enough for the nug to fit through, and Charlie could see starlight on the other side. A flurry of stun beams struck the side of the nug to no effect.

"Come on, guys, have a little faith in Captain Chuck Stonerly," said Charlie, although no one heard him. The Glimwickets, Habu, Cassie, and the Trapezian delegates had taken cover under one of the Silexi ship's wings, and everyone else was too busy shooting to hear him.

A windshield appeared on the nug's upper half, revealing Dark Charlie's face and his over-tilted grin. The Dregz focused their rifles on the window but the stun rays fizzled upon impact.

Behind the haze of dissipated energy, Charlie saw his doppelgänger hold up two middle fingers.

Charlie feigned panic but whispered to Swarm, "Don't worry, man. This is all part of my plan."

Swarm grumbled a few "smegs" under his breath while firing all his rifles on the nug.

The hole in the floor had finally stretched wide enough, and the nug zipped through without hesitation.

Vree Voktal stepped forward with his p'ube held out toward the gaping hole, tapping and swiping the device and spewing Silexi curses.

"This stupid thing isn't working!" he cried, whacking the intricately carved cube with the palm of his hand. "And now the killer escapes!"

"Not exactly, man. I always plan for the worst," said Charlie, smirking. "Watch this."

He reached into his gorilla suit, then further into his hoodie pocket, and after a moment of rummaging, he produced the gamepad controller. It had a few scratches and small dents, but otherwise its lights blinked with regularity. He pressed the controller's triggers and whirled the thumbstick, finally pressing and holding a few buttons at the same time. A single beep came from the controller and Charlie looked up at the ceiling.

"Hey MOM, where's the nug?"

To everyone's surprise, MOM's stilted electronic voice came the from the air all around them.

"The nug that just departed the mini-Transit Bay is currently locked in orbit about one point five kilometers away from the *Pineapple Express.*"

"MOM?" cried Swarm. "But you deleted her, Captain!"

"Dude, I don't know the first thing about deleting a ship's operating system. All I did was unplug her memory cards. So I just plugged them back in before I came to face the other me."

"But I thought she couldn't tell you apart from your doppelgänger. Why the smeg isn't she interfering to save him?"

"Who needs saving, man? He's perfectly safe out there in his own private nug," Charlie said, smiling. "Besides, I learned this lesson the hard way outside on the hull—the me inside the ship outranks the me outside the ship. Must be some proximity thing, who knows? Anyway, MOM, tell them who I am."

"The captain of the *Pineapple Express,* Charlie Hong, is currently standing right here among you in the mini-Transit Bay. His bio-signs indicate that he is exhausted, intoxicated, and extremely hungry, but he is in good health. Does that align with your internal sense of being, Captain Hong?"

"Hell yeah, I've got a mad case of the munchies, but otherwise I'm fine."

"Simultaneously," she continued, "the Captain is currently floating in a transit nug that is locked in an assisted tidal orbit around the *Pineapple Express*. His bio-signs indicate he is exhausted, intoxicated, and incredibly upset. Should I guide his nug back to the ship?"

"Naw, he's happier out there," Charlie said quickly. "Cut off any and all communication to the nug, and disable any morpho-printing aboard his ship. Only my orders given from *inside* the Pineapple Express are to be obeyed, remember?"

"Affirmative, Captain. Let me know if I can be of any further assistance."

"You just plugged her back in?" asked Swarm. "And since the other you didn't know about it, she only had orders from you."

"Exactamundo, man! Plus, I put her in sleep mode until I addressed her directly."

"But his escape nug... why hasn't he just flown off?"

"This," said Charlie, holding up the gamepad. "I synced the only nug he hadn't sabotaged, knowing that even if we lost and he escaped, I'd be able to take control of the nug and keep him safely contained. "

Swarm dropped all four arms at once and stood stunned.

"Good plan, Captain. So what do we do with him now?"

Charlie turned the the Dregz.

"Y'all wanted that huge bounty on my head, right? I'll program his nug to follow your ship so you can deliver him to the authorities on Vekst and collect your g-creds. Wait, I can't remember…which of you is the leader again?"

The Dregz looked at each other, shook their heads, and shrugged.

Finally, Metal Mask stepped forward and glared at Charlie. He nodded slowly and gave a thumbs-up.

"Alright, man. He's yours. Just don't let him escape or there'll be hell to pay."

"On that note," shrieked Vree Voktal, flapping the sleeves of his robe as he stormed toward Charlie. "You've cleared your name and captured the criminal imposter. Can we leave now, before the Reptilians arrive and turn us all into jerky?"

"About that…" The cocky grin melted from Charlie's face. "The other me busted up all the ships in the bay besides the one he took. Your ship isn't going anywhere until someone fixes it."

"If it's not one thing, it's another!" shrieked Vree Voktal. "Letting you host this peace summit was the worst mistake we Trapezians have ever made! I guess we'll just stand here and await our doom."

The two Undulata orbs and the Smolz cloud joined him and Eta Cerbo under the wing of the Silexi ship.

"Dude, there's no doom! I have a—"

"A plan. Yeah, we know," Swarm said, pulling Charlie into a huddle. "But tricks and gamepads won't stop Reptilians. MOM, how much time do we have until the Reptilian vessel arrives?"

"The Reptilian vessel will arrive in approximately 37 minutes."

"I can fix it," Cassie said, stepping forward. "My dad installed a complete set of galactic repair guides in my memory. If you can morpho-print me any parts or tools I need, I think I can fix the Silexi ship before the Reptoids get here."

"Hell yes!" cheered Charlie, "Cassie, jack-of-all-trades, to the rescue!"

Her optic sensors rolled up into her skull and back down again.

"Anyway, give me one sec to finish this job."

She cut a wire in Crimebot's neck, sending sparks into her face. She smacked a small panel closed on the back of his head and began screwing it in with wild, angry twists of her mechanical wrists.

"Not that anyone asked," she fumed, "but no, I wasn't feeling satisfied enough with my arcade business *and* my babysitting gig *and* my waitressing gig. I needed a tech-mech gig, too. Thanks so much, Captain."

"Hey Swarm, let's make sure we let Nylf know his teenage Synth has officially mastered sarcasm."

"Fixing their ship won't matter," said Swarm, "because now that you have sole control of the *Pineapple Express*, you can change course and get us as far away from here as possible, right?"

"Uh, about that," said Charlie, looking down at his gamepad. "I may have fucked up one tiny detail."

Before Charlie could elaborate, MOM's voice filled the bay.

"Before rebooting me, Captain Hong rerouted the ship's core navigation controls to his personal device. Then, later, he synced it to the transit nug."

"If I switch back to the *Pineapple Express*," he continued, "then my gamepad relinquishes control of the nug."

Charlie caught Swarm's eyes.

"If we save ourselves, we doom the galaxy, man."

Swarm slumped and clacked his mandibles irritably.

"Then we're truly smegged. In 35 minutes, we face Reptilians."

"Correction, Lieutenant Swarm," MOM said helpfully, "we face Reptilians in approximately 32 minutes."

Fuck, thought Charlie, *I guess I didn't think through every detail of the plan. Now they got me. And the other me. And everyone I care about.*

Fuck.

He plucked a joint from his afro and popped it between his lips.

"Well, I know how I'm gonna spend the last half hour of my life." The joint sparked up on its own, he took a long drag, then held it out to the group. "Anyone else want a last toke before the end?"

"Pass it this way, kid," a familiar voice said from behind them.

They turned to find Crimebot's head smiling in Cassie's lap.

"And you might wanna roll a few more," he said, "because by the time we get to the bottom of what's really been going on here on the *Pineapple Express,* we'll all need a puff or two."

63

"Homeboy! You're alive!"

Charlie ran to Cassie and kneeled by her side.

"That's right, kid! It'll take more than a handful of shock-shrap to put me out of commission for good," said Crimebot, smiling. Besides the tangle of spliced wires and crusty tubes dangling from his severed neck, he looked as alive as ever.

"You look like you could use a little lift, man."

Charlie planted his smoldering joint between Crimebot's lips. The Synth sucked in some smoke which immediately wafted out of the severed tubes dangling from his neck. He expelled a gravelly sigh, and some of the tension in his face melted away.

"Glad to see the *Pineapple Express* is still in one piece."

"Yeah, we're doing alright," Charlie said smugly, then added, "at least for the next 32 mins until the Reptilians get here."

"Correction, Captain Hong," MOM said. "We have 29 minutes until the Reptilian vessel arrives."

"Reptoids? On their way here?" Crimebot's face screwed up into a scowl and the light in his visor stopped oscillating. "That'll barely give me time to thank whoever got me booted up again."

"I did it," Cassie said, staring at her hands and the tools laid out around her on the floor. "I really fixed you!"

The LEDs in her head glowed brightly as she threw her arms around his head and kissed his mussed-up hair.

Charlie put a hand on her shoulder. "We all knew you could do it, Cassie."

"Hey, homegirl, lay off the squeezing!" Crimebot's head squirmed as much as it could. "How'd a young Synth like you learn something as complicated as repairing positron brains?"

"My father knows! He's the best at positronic brains!" Cassie blurted out. Her LEDs went a tinge pink. "Well, when he's not being an overprotective jerk."

"Well, thanks, kid. Someday you'll have to introduce me to your old man," said Crimebot, then added casually, "if we survive the bomb."

"Bomb?!" rattled Swarm.

A murmur rumbled from the small crowd that had assembled around the talking head.

"I know I'm stoned as fuck right now," said Charlie, "but I don't remember any bombs, man. We had a gazillion hungry ship-eating larvae, a psychotic doppelgänger, a giant brown asshole in space," he said, ticking off the items on his fingers, "and something about a purple crystal that keeps slipping my mind for some reason. But we took care of those. Now what we have is a runaway ship and some incoming Reptilians. No one said anything about any bomb, man!"

"You took care of that other you? Good work, kid. I'm embarrassed to say that sonofabitch had me tricked for a few seconds. I'd have detected his ruse sooner if my processors hadn't been so busy solving the murders."

"We already solved the smegging murders!" roared Swarm. He plucked the head from Cassie's lap by the hair and lifted it to his large compound eyes. "Now tell me everything you know about this bomb!"

"You solved the murders, eh, Bugbreath?" asked Crimebot. "Then why do I see the Emperor Rex's killer standing here among us?"

A collective gasp rose from the group.

Swarm dropped Crimebot, but Cassie caught the head, nestled it back in her lap, and started stroking it protectively while giving Swarm the meanest stare her programming could muster.

"That's right, everyone. There's a bomb on the ship," explained Crimebot. "It wasn't intended for us, but it'll explode anyway if we don't find and disarm it before it's triggered."

"Wait a second, CB. Swarm is right. My evil doppelgänger was the one behind everything. We got him locked up somewhere safe where he can't detonate a bomb. Still, the goddamn Reptoids are on their way, and I imagine they'll be bringing plenty of bombs of their own."

Crimebot laughed and puffs of smoke escaped from his gaping neck.

"You got it backwards, kid. When they arrive, we'll be the ones taking *them* out with *our* bomb. As well as the *Pineapple Express* and everyone on board."

Swarm picked up one of his rifles and aimed it in the general direction of the group standing around the talking head. With a growl rattling from this thorax he muttered, "We don't have much time. Cut the smeg and explain yourself."

"Let's start with the first murder," Crimebot said, "The Emperor died alone in his locked and guarded quarters. No one entered or exited—isn't that right MOM?"

"Correct. No organic or synthetic lifeforms entered or left the Silexi quarters just before or during his unfortunate accident."

"Glad to see the ship's computer still has her sense of humor. But he wasn't exactly alone, was he?"

"No, the young Eta Cerbo was asleep in the adjoining room."

"Wait, are you sure no one else snuck in, MOM?" asked Charlie. "Like, uh, the *other* me. We know the other me was getting around via those tunnels created by a mat-com. He had the motive, the means, and the opportunity."

"Smart thinking, kid. I suspect he did show up that night to kill Emperor Rex. But when he got there, the Emperor was already dead."

"How dare you implicate the young Emperor Eta Cerbo!" shrieked Vree Voktal. He aimed the p'ube at Crimebot's head and narrowed his eyes. "I should cast you into the prison cube for even implicating His Majesty!"

"Keep your panties on, Vree," said Charlie, who gently pushed the Silexi's arm down away from the crowd. "We all know E.T. was hurt in the attack, too."

Mr. Glimwicket nodded. "I'm no expert in Trapezian biology, but as far as I could tell, the young Silexi was in some kind of comatose state due to shock."

"E.T. saved my life, man." Charlie smiled at his childhood idol, and in response Eta Cerbo pointed a glowing fingertip back at him. Charlie added quietly out the side of his mouth, "Plus, look at him...he's a little, you know...at least compared to his father and Vree...a little *disabled*."

Crimebot laughed heartily.

"He may be disabled physically, but up in that wedge-shaped head of his, I think he's playing on the same field as the rest of us."

"Hooooome!" cried Eta Cerbo as he aimed his glowing finger toward the top of the dome. "E.T. go hoooome!"

"See, he just wants to go home!"

"Once an actor, always an actor," said Crimebot, smirking in Cassie's lap. "You know, I watched that Earther movie you starred in, and I have to admit, I was impressed. So much so, I almost got taken in by the role you're playing now—the same role you've been playing for a long, long time. It must be hard having a father like ol' Rex. Especially when he has plans for you that don't match up with your own dreams."

"This is unacceptable!" screeched Vree Voktal. "Enjoy spending the rest of your life on the dark planet of Yag with the other enemies of Silexi!"

He aimed the metallic cube at the severed head and pushed a button on its side. Nothing happened.

Vree Voktal shook the p'ube and tried again. Nothing.

He held it to his eyes and examined it closely.

"This is not the Royal P'ube of Yag!"

Charlie put an arm around Vree Voktal's trembling shoulder and offered him the joint.

"Take a small puff before you blow a gasket. I'm the one who replaced your Royal P'ube with a decoy. We never found the original. I assume the other me has it with him out there in his p'ug." He swung his head around and looked at the others with a raised eyebrow. "Get it, guys? If a prison cube is a p'ube, then a prison nug is a—"

"Let's move on!" rattled Swarm. "If your doppelgänger had the real Royal P'ube, we'd all be inside it right now."

"Exactly!" exclaimed Crimebot. "But don't worry. If my calculations are correct, it's very close by."

"Just spit it out already! We don't have time for smegging theatrics!"

"Fine, I'll get to the point. Your doppelgänger did, in fact, tunnel into the Silexi quarters the night of the murder. We saw that depression in the wall closing up, remember? But he was hired to steal, not to assassinate—although he most likely would have ended up doing the job himself if ol' Rex hadn't already been dead."

"So, if we're to trust MOM, then Eta Cerbo must have done it," rattled Swarm, swinging his rifles to face the disabled Silexi.

Eta Cerbo collapsed his neck as far into his body as he could. The light in his stomach and finger flickered off.

"I didn't murder my father!" cried Eta Cerbo. "It was self defense!"

"Which was it?" asked Crimebot. "Did you not murder him? Or did you murder him out of self defense?"

The look of suspicion on everyone's faces turned to shock as the cowering Silexi continued as intelligibly as any of them.

"All I did was take the medicine she gave me! She said it would make me sleep and protect me from his...his..."

He trailed off, looking down at his sagging belly.

"*He* wanted to kill *me*! My own father! I knew he despised me, but I couldn't believe it when she was right! It's what they do! My father! *His* Father! They've all done it!"

"What else did *she* tell you?" rattled Swarm.

"She said once it was all over I'd be able to return to Earth and star in the sequel. I never wanted anyone to die or to get hurt. All I wanted was a sequel! On Silexi, everyone thinks I'm stupid, deformed, unworthy...but those Earthers knew how to make me feel important! On Earth I wasn't some disabled freak, I was a hero! I was a *star!*"

Charlie's jaw dropped.

"This whole time you were just pretending to be a handicapped child?"

"Look at me, Charlie." He extended his neck to full height and pointed to his short, stubby legs. "I *am* handicapped! Silexi are supposed to be tall and thick-skinned and intimidating. I'm just a soft little turd."

"You're not a turd!" shouted Bob Jr., peeking around his parents.

"Yes, I am. My father was ashamed of me. Everyone was. He thought I was too stupid to understand him, but I heard every word he ever said about me. It was easier just to go with it. If he thought I was stupid, then I'd be stupid. Pretending to be so meant I wouldn't have to take the throne after he died. I thought someday he'd ship me back to Earth for another movie!" Tears gathered under his big dinner plate eyes. "Did you know they made posters of me on Earth?"

"I had one on my wall when I was a kid," said Charlie.

"A whole planet that loved me. I loved Earth, too. I remember when we filmed the movie, the director took such good care of me. I mean, he was under orders and all, but it was lightyears better than what I'd grown used to on Silexi. All I've ever wanted is to get back to Earth, film another movie...and feel loved again."

"Of course! If Steven Spielberg knew you were an alien, if he was able to cover it up and pass you off as a puppet, then he must have been given orders from the Reptilians."

"Who else?" asked Eta Cerbo.

"So killing your father was part of some deal with the Reptoids, eh?" said Swarm, still holding his wadjets at the ready.

"I didn't kill my father!"

"I believe him, Charlie!" cried Bob Jr. as he tore himself away from this parents and threw himself in front of the cowering Silexi. "He saved your life!"

Mrs. Glimwicket kneeled beside her son and took Eta Cerbo's hand.

"You said someone gave you medicine to protect you from him. What does that mean?"

"She told me he was going to...I didn't believe her...but then he started to prepare," he stammered. "So I quickly swallowed the pill she gave me and fell asleep. When I woke up, my father was dead."

"See, man?" Charlie said out the corner of his mouth. "That's why you don't fuck around with pills."

Swarm ignored him and pressed forward.

"What was your father preparing for?"

"His own death."

"He didn't seem like the suicidal type," said Charlie.

"He wasn't!" cried Vree Voktal.

"His death, but also his rebirth...into my body. He was going to stage his own assassination, but instead of letting his consciousness die with his body, he was going to..."

Eta Cerbo clenched his big eyes shut.

"Nice performance, kid. I'll take it from here," said Crimebot. "You can't spell 'dynasty' without the word 'nasty', and the Silexi Empire is no exception. They've had a millenia-old nasty little secret of their own that started all the way back with the very first

Silexi Emperor, Rex Prime. Despite extending his life as long as biologically possible, his body couldn't resist entropy forever. So the old coot devised a way to escape death itself. When his time came to throw off the mortal coil, he'd have another mortal coil to slide right into. His heir."

"Cerebral ceremorphosis!" cried Mr. Glimwicket. "But transferring a mind from one host to the other isn't sustainable. It might stick for a little while, but soon the cortextual bond deteriorates, and the mind is shaken off like a bad cold."

"Not for the Silexi," Crimebot explained. "They perfected a method using kryyd, and even then, they found it only works on someone who's a strict biological and genetic match."

Swarm's arms relaxed.

"Smegging hell. Instead of handing over the throne at the time of death, each emperor would transfer themselves into the body of their offspring?"

"Dicks!" cried Charlie.

"*Dick*, not *Dicks*," corrected Crimebot. "Rex Prime has been using the same method for millennia. The late Emperor Rex was Rex Prime, and young Eta Cerbo was to be his next vessel."

"I heard him preparing," said Eta Cerbo. "He thought I was too stupid to understand, but I heard every word. His plan was to kill himself, making it look like an assassination to sabotage the Trapezian peace process, and then slip into my body to rule for another couple centuries before cloning himself—without my deformities—and doing it all over again."

"Reticulus Rex was Rex Prime," muttered Vree Voktal, who suddenly seemed to have difficulty standing up. "All these centuries...all the Silexi Emperors...they were all the same person."

Charlie held out the joint to the dazed and confused Silexi.

"Ready for that hit yet, homeboy?"

Vree Voktal filled his lungs, coughed up big puffs of smoke, then passed it back.

Charlie took a hit of his own and studied his beloved childhood icon.

"But someone gave you a way to defend against him, right? Someone who miraculously had both the knowledge of all this and a way to stop it. Hey Swarm, don't you think it's time to call the rest of our crew to this little gathering?"

Swarm turned his rifles to an empty spot on the floor and nodded.

"Ready when you are, Captain."

"MOM, mind toking a few extra guests to our little party?"

64

LESS THAN A MINUTE LATER, TWO WISPS OF GREENISH VAPOR ZIPPED into the room from a hole in the ceiling.

The first wisp condensed into Nadia, her arms crossed and her coil writhing beneath her.

The second was Zylvya, lay sprawled on the floor. Millions of rainbow hairs sprouted all around her and grew rapidly into a thick bed of silky grass.

Charlie ran to her side. "Is she still…?"

Mr. Glimwicket felt for a pulse while Mrs. Glimwicket pulled open her eyelids. They both looked up at Charlie with tense proboscises.

"Same as before," Mrs. Glimwicket said, "the lights are on, but no one's home."

"She's brain dead?"

Before the Glimwickets answered, Nadia huffed and dismissed the question with a wave of her bejeweled hand.

"It's a gift, considering what lies just around the corner for the rest of us." She locked eyes with Charlie. "Which reminds me, what took you so long? I was starting to wonder what a girl had to do to get invited to your little party."

"Hands up." Swarm aimed all four rifles at Nadia and growled. "And keep those rings of yours aimed at the ceiling at all times."

"You wouldn't stun an old friend, would you?" Nadia tittered and loosened her coil. Her upper half shimmered and the olive-skinned human woman was replaced by an exact replica of Commander Acari—pink scales, four arms, and huge mantis-like head with two large compound eyes and two long antennae.

Swarm didn't flinch.

"Who the smeg's that supposed to be?"

"Your mom?" asked Charlie.

Swarm swung one of his rifles to point toward Charlie's head.

"Kidding, man! Kidding!"

Nadia looked momentarily confused, then relaxed her pink antennae and shrugged. "That's what you get trying to poke holes in time with a cheap knock-off."

She shimmered back to her human upper body.

"I said, hands up!" rattled Swarm.

She obeyed, and Charlie couldn't help notice how she noticed how he noticed her breasts jiggling as she lifted her arms. He tore his eyes away and pinned them back on Zylvya.

"Don't hurt her!" squealed Eta Cerbo, his neck telescoping to full height. "She saved my life!"

"I wouldn't be so sure about that, kid," said Crimebot. "Unless I'm mistaken—which I never am, by the way—you were expendable from the very first second you met her."

Nadia scoffed at the synthetic head in Cassie's lap, and then turned back to Charlie.

"Did you summon me here just to ogle my chest, Captain, or did you have another reason?"

"We toked you because we captured the other mc. We know you were working with him. Another thing we know is that you never help anyone out of the goodness of your heart. So if E.T. thinks you helped him, we know it's bullshit."

MOM's voice announced, "The Reptilian vessel will arrive in approximately 25 minutes."

"We have no time for small talk," grumbled Swarm, his claws twitching on their triggers. "Ask her about the bomb!"

"It's all connected, man!" cried Charlie. To Eta Cerbo he asked, "What did she ask you for in return for saving your life?"

"Nothing! I swear! All she said was *'Follow your dreams'*."

"You already told us you had no interest in ruling Silex," Crimebot said. "So tell us, kid. What's your dream?"

"Captain, is this really a good time for group therapy?!" roared Swarm.

"Let's see where this goes, man. E.T., what's the first thing you thought of when Nadia told you to follow your dreams?"

Eta Cerbo's chest began to glow with a hot yellow fire and his eyes widened to the size of headlamps.

"My dream is to return to Earth to film another movie! To star in the long-awaited sequel to *E.T. the Extraterrestrial*!"

Charlie noticed a hint of panic flash across Nadia's face. To Eta Cerbo he said:

"But, dude, Earth is locked down under Reptilian control. The only way a real-life alien would be able to cruise up to Earth and land a movie deal would be with their explicit permission. Wait, in that case, how'd the first E.T. movie get made?"

He frowned as realization set in.

"The Reptoids rely on the Trapezian war to produce kryyd, don't they? It extends their life. It overhauls their biological processes to increase their mental and physical prowess. It helps them maintain their grip on the quadrant."

"If this peace summit had succeeded," added Swarm. "If the Trapezian war had ended, their kryyd supply would've dried up."

"But with the Silexi Emperor in their pocket, they could guarantee the war would continue indefinitely," finished Crimebot.

"You're accusing His Majesty of being behind the sabotage?!" screeched Vree Voktal.

"No," said Charlie as things clicked into place. "Reticulus Rex —er, Rex Prime—knew his suicide-body-stealing thing would sabotage any chance for peace. He probably relied on the war to keep a tight grip on Silex. Or he just didn't care. But you, E.T., you weren't just dreaming. They didn't pick up *my* distress beacon, did they? *You* called them here somehow. You gave them our position."

Eta Cerbo hung his head. The light in his stomach faded away.

"Human faces are so expressive, Captain. I needed them look at me like they did before. I needed to feel their applause. I needed to know that there was some place in the galaxy, even a backwater planet like Earth, where I was loved and adored and...I never meant to hurt anyone."

"Imagine how grateful the Reptoids would be if he delivered the *Pineapple Express* to them on a platter," grumbled Swarm. "They'd offer him a smegging trilogy!"

Charlie shook his head pitifully, took a quick puff from his joint, and started pacing in front of Nadia.

"Which leads us back to you. You hate the Reptilians, maybe more than anyone else here."

"Not true, yo!" a tiny voice called out from the back of the crowd.

"Why would you help E.T. cut a deal that would keep them supplied with kryyd? And why would it worry you so much if they were on their way now?"

Nadia rolled her eyes.

"For the sake of time, I'll spare us any more long-winded theories, witty banter, or startling revelations," she said. "I manipulated various parties into constructing a bomb. The young Emperor was to deliver it to the Reptilians for me."

"What?" cried Eta Cerbo. "I never agreed to deliver a bomb!"

"Your permission was never required," she answered coldly. "The bomb is inside you now, smuggled inside one of those candies you kept ordering from Lavaka. In fact, Captain, you're technically an accomplice since you're the one who delivered it to him."

She flashed Charlie a sneaky smile before continuing.

"It's programmed to detonate when it comes into close proximity to Reptilians, which I hadn't anticipated happening so soon. That's what's making me so nervous, Captain. I didn't expect to be standing next to the thing when it detonates!"

"Tell us about the bomb!" demanded Swarm. "How do we disarm it?"

"Well, I started with the Abortionator 5000 pill I stole from the Glimwickets—"

"Stole?!" cried Mrs. Glimwicket. "But, you *sold* that to us!"

"Exactly, dear. That positioned me as the very last person you'd think stole it," explained Nadia. "I then reprogrammed it to arm itself within the presence of Reptilian DNA instead of… whatever species the Glimwickets are. Once it detects a cluster of the target organisms within its blast radius, it will detonate."

"But how could such a tiny bomb be any real danger?" asked Cassie.

A thin smile slithered across her face. "Because I gave it a little more *kick*. The genocide drive inside the pill consists of a power source and a fuel source. I upgraded both. I replaced its dilithium flake with the Royal P'ube—"

"Thief!" shrieked Vree Voktal. "That artifact and its contents belong to Silex!"

"Not all of its contents," corrected Nadia. "Before installing it in the bomb, I lent it to a friend who ventured outside the ship and found a passing system to trap in there as well."

Charlie nodded slowly.

"When I was outside the ship….the flash! I saw a star vanish. You're telling us one of your lackeys sucked up a whole system into the Royal P'ube?"

"Then I installed a power source to match," she said, turning to Charlie. "Promise me you won't be upset."

"Happy!" cried Charlie. "*You're* the one who stole my plant, man!"

"Not me, Captain," she said. "This is the first time I've been outside of Lavaka since boarding the *Pineapple Express*. And for the record, I thought I was dealing with you. You came to me asking for a technical manual on MOM's command structure. I was surprised when you caved to my demand so easily, and it wasn't until you actually handed over one of your precious plants that I suspected something else was going on."

"But wait, how'd you get the p'ube and my plant inside a tiny little pill?"

"Same way your junior hunting squad dealt with the larvae infestation," rattled Swarm. "Mat-coms."

Nadia nodded.

"You broke so much. You manipulated everyone and everything in the *Pineapple Express*. You destroyed peace in Trapezia," said Charlie, "just to blow up a few hundred Reptilians?"

"One of their cruisers holds a few *thousand*. With any luck, they'd have summoned Eta Cerbo to a fleet of cruisers, or maybe even to Thuban! Could you imagine, Captain? It might have ended their reign in the quadrant! Freed hundreds of enslaved worlds!"

Charlie shook his head. He didn't know whether or not this was the weapon his predecessor had been planning, the weapon he himself had sworn to finish, and he didn't care.

"It's wrong, man," said Charlie. "I'm way too stoned and exhausted to explain it right now, but we're never gonna beat them if we're willing to sacrifice the very things we're trying to protect."

"Not all of us have that luxury. Those of us who've already lost everything have nothing else to lose."

Her face darkened as she addressed the small crowd.

"Under their tyranny, we're already dead. Trapezians included. So tell me, what's one Silexi life in exchange for thousands of Reptilian casualties? What's a few planets and a star in exchange for possibly freeing thousands more?"

Charlie locked his bloodshot eyes onto Nadia's.

"I wasn't just talking about people and planets. I was talking about something inside us, man. Whatever makes us different than them. The *Starseed*'s purpose is to give life, to help it along, to keep it flowing. Not to gamble with it. Not to weaponize it."

"Fool! Captain Major Tom understood! Better than any of us here, I'd say." She gave Charlie a knowing look. "There's no negotiating with Reptilians. No sparing those who would not spare us! My planet learned that lesson the hard way, as have countless others." Nadia's coil grew tighter and tighter with every word. "It's time for the gloves to come off! It's time to strike back!"

Charlie glared back at her and refused to back down.

"Maybe they deserve it! But you know who doesn't? Swarm. Zee. Habu. Cassie. The wogs."

"What wogs?!" cried Swarm.

Charlie ignored him.

"...the Glimwickets. The Trapezians. All the other Seeders on the *Pineapple Express*. The two planets inside the friggin' p'ube, Nadia! If you let this happen, if you destroy those worlds, all those innocent people, then you're no better than a Reptilian!"

When he spoke again he lowered his voice. "But I think you are better than them. Or at least you could be, if you decided to."

He held out the smoldering joint to her.

"Take this and help us disarm the bomb, Nadia. Prove you're better than them."

"Even if I could disarm the bomb, we'll never get it out of him in time unless we cut him open and rip it out!"

The nails on the ends of her fingers doubled in size and sharpened into ten slender daggers.

"The Reptilian vessel will arrive in approximately 18 minutes," MOM broadcast to the group.

"If I get you the bomb, can you disarm it?" Charlie asked, still holding Nadia's gaze.

She narrowed her eyes and answered, "Will you be slicing open the Silexi Emperor, or shall I do it?"

Charlie sighed, planted the joint between her lips, and pulled the gorilla mask over his head.

"Just be ready," he mumbled. "I'll be right back with the goddamn bomb."

65

"You're being ridiculous!" screeched Vree Voktal. "Completely unreasonable!"

Nadia pinched the half-joint to her lips and took a tiny hit. Just a taste, if that.

More so than the rest of the bumbling crew, Nadia knew not to take the Captain's *Golden Ticket* lightly. That much power could be catastrophic in the wrong hands—which is why she'd been trying to get her hands on it.

Back on the *Starseed*, with all the other do-gooders always prying into her business, it was nearly impossible to get her hands on some without getting into trouble. She and Mother had worked out their deal years ago, and Nadia wasn't ready to risk her position by breaking the rules they'd agreed upon. Not yet, anyway.

Instead, she'd done what she'd always done when she wanting something. She stayed coiled up in Lavaka, ran a tidy operation (on paper), and waited for an opportunity to slip between her beautiful tapestries and take a seat at her bar.

Going for a spin on the *Pineapple Express* had been the biggest opportunity she'd had in quite some time, and, technically speaking, it was about to pay off.

Too bad I'm included in the price tag, she thought, taking another minuscule puff.

"Really! I can't believe how you're behaving!" Vree Voktal shrieked at her, his arms flailing in his silky metallic robes. "And at a time like this!"

Out here on the *Pineapple Express*, getting her hands on the Captain's plants had been a piece of cake. Not only had Captain Hong just handed her a joint, but a few cycles ago he'd hand-delivered an entire plant. And for the low, low price of some information he could've looked up himself.

That's an ape for you, lazy and stupid.

Then again, that hadn't been the real Captain Hong, had it?

Dark Charlie had been identical to the original Captain Hong in every detectable way. Besides, when someone hands you exactly what you're looking for, you don't ask questions. Isn't that how she manipulated all the lost souls who wandered into her bar?

"Come on!" cried Vree Voktal. "Captain Hong did not intend for you to bogart the joint!"

She blew a stream of smoke into his face while she considered the joint between her fingers.

So much power in such a little package, she thought. *So much potential. Yet all they do is light it up and smoke it.*

She wondered what sort of device—not a weapon, never a weapon—she could power with just the resinous roach. Nadia knew better than anyone that weapons were strictly prohibited on the *Starseed* or her progeny vessels. So it was good thing that what she'd built using Captain Hong's plant wasn't a bomb.

No, it was simply a life-saving, *Starseed*-sanctioned medical device that had been *slightly* modified, and more importantly, had been pre-approved by Mother before they'd set out.

Now that device was anchored in the stomach lining of the new Silexi Emperor. At this point, even if they ripped open the little guy and tore it from his guts, tossing it out the nearest airlock wouldn't even save them. The Reptilian ship was fast approaching, which meant it would still trigger the bomb, and the *Pineapple Express* would be too close to avoid the resulting supernova. And as Nadia had learned on more than one occasion, supernovas are bad for business.

Their only hope resided in an Earther ape (dressed up like some other kind of ape) who'd just crawled into the mouth of the Silexi Emperor, and who, even now, as she sat and bogarted his joint, was rummaging around inside his stomach trying to dislodge the pill-shaped bomb.

"Hurry, Captain!" Swarm rattled into the chatter pinned to his chest. "Just snatch the smegging thing and crawl back up!"

Eta Cerbo moaned, clutching his saggy brown paunch.

"Oh, suck it up, Your Majesty," said Vree Voktal. "You got yourself into this mess. You and the bogart queen over here."

Charlie's voice came from Swarm's chatter.

"Almost got it!" he said. "Dammit! This thing doesn't want to come out!"

Swarm pointed a claw at Eta Cerbo and grumbled, "Do the light thing again so we can see him."

Eta Cerbo tilted his head back and groaned.

Swarm leveled a rifle at him.

"What do you say, Nadia? Between your claws and mine, I think we could retrieve the bomb in under a millighatika."

She nodded listlessly and took another puff.

Such a bad liar, Nadia thought. *It's a wonder he gets anything done around here.*

Eta Cerbo clenched his wide, watery eyes and concentrated. Little by little, his stomach brightened with its iconic amber glow. At the center of the glow crouched a tiny silhouette pulling on something with both hands.

"It's Charlie!" cried Bob Jr. from under the colorful sombrero he'd pilfered from the floor.

"That's Captain Hong to you," corrected his father.

"He's the bravest," sniffled Sqwert.

"I can't believe he asked us to shrink him," Pep said, shaking her head. "Are you sure you can reverse it, Cassie?"

Without looking up from the half-dismantled mat-com pistol, the teenaged robot mumbled something vaguely affirmative and angsty, then went back to tinkering.

"Smeg yeah!" cried Foo, pumping her tiny fist. "Captain Chuck Stonerly to the rescue!"

"Language!" Mrs. Glimwicket covered Bob Jr.'s ears with her big, furry hands.

He pulled them away and rolled his eyes. "Lieutenant Swarm says it all the time!"

"Well, that's for his mother to worry about," she said curtly. "I'll worry about you, thank you very much."

Vree Voktal chuckled nervously. "At least for a few more minutes."

"No way! Mr. Stonerly will save us!" Sqwert said, peeking out from behind his big sister.

The group huddled around the glowing paunch to watch their fate unfold in real time. Even Metal Mask seemed taken in by the drama. Nadia had the briefest memory of her family crowding around the holo screen to watch a solstice parade on her ninth birthday. She pushed it out of her mind and shoved it back down into the murky depths where she kept all such warm memories.

"Got it!" Charlie's voice came from Swarm's chatter.

The crowd cheered.

"But, hey guys..." he continued, "I can't climb back out! It's too slippery, and the walls of his esophagus keep forcing me back down!"

"Don't worry, Captain," rattled Swarm. "we'll figure out a way to make him regurgitate you. Vree, how do we make His Majesty vomit?"

"We don't, unless you want to liquify Captain Hong," explained Vree Voktal. "Before we Silexi jettison any troublesome food from our digestive tracts, we release a very strong acid that liquifies organic matter on contact."

Swarm tapped his chatter.

"Captain, you're going to have to find another way out."

"Another way out?"

When Charlie's voice returned a moment later it had a horrified tone to it.

"Oh, shit."

"Precisely," said Swarm. "Now hurry!"

66

"Eight minutes before the Reptilian ship arrives," MOM's voice announced.

Nadia sat hunched over the pill-shaped bomb with a pair of magnifying goggles strapped to her head.

All around her peered a crowd of hopeful eyes and eye-like appendages.

No one made a sound.

No one breathed.

Then, without warning, a resounding belch shattered the heavy quiet. Nadia hissed a sibilant curse over her shoulder.

"Sorry," said Foo.

Nadia prodded the side of the pill with a tiny needle-like tool. The pill casing twisted and split apart, revealing aeven smaller mechanisms inside. As she leaned in with a pair of micro-pliers in each hand, her head bumped into something.

"Sorry," Cassie said, scooting away to give Nadia more room to work.

The background noise of a running shower stopped and the room became even quieter. A few yards from Nadia's bomb-diffusing table, an opaque ten-foot-tall cylinder began to melt into the floor. Charlie—wearing a fresh set of clothes and a perfectly scrubbed 'fro—stepped over the last few inches of the shower tube.

As he grew closer he bumped into one of Swarm's elbows, which in turn bumped into one of Nadia's elbows, which sent the micro-tweezers flying out of her hand.

"For Andromeda's sake, give me room!" cried Nadia. "Haven't you ever disarmed a bomb before? One wrong move and this thing will detonate!"

The crowd took a step back, but Charlie peeked over her shoulder.

"Did you have a nice, relaxing shower?" she hissed.

"Complain all you want," he said. "I just had a close encounter of the *turd* kind, man. I don't care if we're all about to be disintegrated, I had to wash off all the..."

He trailed off, glancing at Eta Cerbo and shivering. "Let's never mention it ever again, okay?"

"Are you kidding, yo?" cried Foo. "Chuck Stonerly bravely speedran a complicated network of Silexi stomach chambers and intestinal tracts to finally emerge from its—"

"LET'S NEVER MENTION IT EVER AGAIN," repeated Charlie.

"Quiet!" cried Nadia. She slammed her tools down on the table. "It's no use. I've outsmarted myself! There's no way to disarm this thing without detonating it."

"Enough lies!" roared Swarm.

"Unfortunately for all of us, this time I'm telling you the truth. Cassandra can confirm if you'd like."

Charlie squinted at the tiny bomb.

"There's gotta be something we can do, man."

"I don't wanna die!" cried Bob Jr.

A murmur of fearful gasps filled the bay.

"Hush, everyone!" cried Nadia. "Let me think!"

Finally, she leaned back on her coils and sighed.

"There's one way. But it comes with a trade-off that some here might not like."

"I'm pretty sure no matter what it is, man, we'll like it better than dying."

"Alright then, here's the idea. I don't disarm the bomb. The Reptilians arrive and it detonates—"

"Smegging hell! Her treachery has fooled us again!" Swarm cried, aiming a pair of wadjet rifles at her.

"Let her speak, man!"

"Thank you, Captain. As I was saying, assume we have no choice but to allow the bomb to detonate. If we remove the modified power and fuel sources, the explosion will occur, but it won't cause any more destruction than the original Abortionator 5k."

"Great! I don't think anyone has a problem with that," cried Charlie.

"Here's where it gets a little complicated. The shrunken Royal P'ube has been fused to the detonator itself. If I try to remove it, the bomb will detonate. Same with the power source. But," she paused, looking up at the faces surrounding her, "there might be a way to empty out the p'ube's contents without removing it."

"Preposterous!" shrieked Vree Voktal. "The Silexi prison planet is populated with millions of hostile criminals!"

"Whatever, man," said Charlie. "We all saw how quickly old Rex whipped out that thing. It's probably full of harmless jaywalkers."

"What the smeg's a jaywalker?" Swarm said, his antennae going rigid.

"They're criminals!" Vree Voktal cried. "And, more importantly, they won't be very happy with Silex once they're let out!"

"That's *your* problem!" said Mr. Glimwicket. "I'm not letting my family perish because of your planet's corrupt judicial system!"

"Even if we disarm the bomb, won't the Reptilians still kill all of us when they get here?" asked Cassie.

"You're talkin' crazy, kid," answered Crimebot's head.

"They'll torture us for a long, long time before punching our cards."

"Or they'll experiment on us!" added Habu.

"Enough!" Charlie shouted with a fresh unlit joint dangling from his lips.

"Nadia, let's say you can empty the p'ube. There's another inhabited planet in there, as well as a star. I don't think any of that will fit in the mini-Transit Bay."

She smiled and batted her eyes at him.

"Well, Captain, I'll need two things from you in order to pull this off. First, I need a hole in the ship's hull to direct the rapid matter expansion. And then I'll need your permission to use the bomb's power source to power the whole thing."

"Oh," said Charlie, staring off into the middle distance. "You need to use Happy. Well, that's okay, I guess. How much do you need?"

"Every last molecule of THC," she said bluntly. "Matter expansion on that scale requires a *lot* of energy. It's either that or we plug into the *Pineapple Express*, drain the THC Tube, cut off all life support systems, and die a slow, agonizing death."

Well, shit, thought Charlie. *What choice do I have?*

Charlie caught Habu's eyes in the crowd. The old man raised one bushy eyebrow.

There was never anything wrong with my plants in the first place, realized Charlie. *They were about ready to be harvested back on Earth. The* Starseed *slowed down their aging, maintained their youth…but it couldn't fight Nature forever. Habu was right all along. They were never sick. They've been speaking to me, telling me exactly what they need. But I refused to listen.*

"Five minutes until the Reptilian vessel is within firing range," MOM announced.

Charlie gritted his teeth and nodded.

"Do it," he said grimly, fighting back tears. Nearby, a circle of starfield appeared as the green marble floor gaped open like a yawning mouth.

Without hesitation, Nadia worked her tiny instruments on the tiny innards of the tiny pill bomb.

When she was done screwing the two halves of the pill casing back together, she scooped it into her slender hand and tossed it through the hole.

67

YOU MIGHT THINK THAT EXPANDING COMPRESSED MATTER, ESPECIALLY huge quantities of matter, would kinda be a big deal. Intense heat. A bright light. At least a loud *whoosh* or BANG.

But you'd be wrong. It turns out that besides an undetectable gravitational ripple, expanding an entire sun and two planets is pretty much a non-event. One second there is just the empty vacuum of space, the next there is a star with two planets orbiting it—one original, one new.

"So I guess the *Pineapple Express* was traveling fast enough to avoid the plasma from the newly expanded star," Nadia said, wiping the sweat from her brow. "I hadn't actually calculated that part. Guess we got lucky."

"Lucky?!" shrieked Vree Voktal. He collapsed onto the floor in a pile of metallic robes. "Sure, we won't be incinerated, but the Reptoids will soon have us. Maybe we'll have a bit more luck and they'll torture us somewhere far away from this wretched smell!"

The Smolz fog swirled in the air beside him and said, "We find the song uplifting and inspirational."

"You would, farts-for-brains!" snarled Oozer, standing in a huddle with the other Dregz.

"I'm glad everyone can understand each other now," said

Charlie. "Y'all should've bonded with the ship when you first got here."

He craned his head through the hole in the floor and noticed a massive brown circle swirling silently against the starfield in the direction they were going.

"Hey MOM, how much time till we cross the brown hole's event horizon?"

"Approximately three minutes until our ship crosses that threshold, Captain," answered MOM.

"And how long until the Reptoids arrive?

"Approximately three minutes until the Reptilian vessel intersects our trajectory," she said.

Despite getting to the bottom of the murders, despite exposing the sabotage behind the peace summit, despite everything Charlie had done to save the ship from hungry larvae and mutinous mercs and unreliable computer interfaces, it seemed their fate would finally be decided by nothing more than a cosmic coin toss.

Either the Reptoids would take the ship and do their worst, or the brown hole would take them and plunge them into something unimaginably horrific.

After my little excursion through E.T.'s intestinal tract, Charlie thought to himself, shuddering, *I don't even wanna think about what awaits us inside the brown hole.*

The worst part was knowing that the only thing preventing him from saving everyone was trying to save the galaxy from Dark Charlie. Even though he'd finally accepted his role as captain, even though he'd tried his very best to lead like a real starship captain, like Captain Kirk or Captain Picard, his own dark tendencies had once again conspired with fate to fuck him over.

If I'd just stayed on Earth, he thought. *If I'd just let the* Starseed *take Happy all those months ago, at least the only person getting hurt would be me.*

He pictured Jorge scowling at him from behind his huge desk, armed goons at his side, Charlie's unfathomable debt hanging over the conversation.

That doesn't sound like very much fun, either, he thought.

"Captain, the nug has broken out of its orbital trajectory and is attempting to pull away from the *Pineapple Express*," reported MOM.

Charlie snapped out of his stoned malaise and looked up at the dome.

"Give us a visual on the nug."

A rectangle of light appeared low on the ceiling showing him the scene outside. Dark Charlie's nug seemed to be taking short, fast bursts away from the *Pineapple Express* as if it were a fish trying to pull free from an invisible line.

"Increase the gravity lock," ordered Charlie. "We can't let him escape!"

"If we let him go, then *we* can escape, right?" whined Vree Voktal. "Seems fair, doesn't it? Isn't saving our lives a higher priority than keeping him in custody?"

"We can't let him go, man. If you think Trapezia has problems now, wait till the other me pays you a visit."

"She doesn't have much time, Captain," said Mrs. Glimwicket, brushing emerald curls from Zylvya's face.

"We are approaching the event horizon now, Captain," said MOM. "And the Reptilians are nearly within firing range."

This really is the king of all clusterfucks, thought Charlie.

He puffed the joint dangling from his lips to revive its dim ember.

"Snap out of it, Captain!" roared Swarm, waving all four arms in the air. *"What are your smegging orders?"*

"I...well..." mumbled Charlie.

He sighed and exhaled a huge plume of smoke. With burning, bloodshot eyes he stared up at the nug on the dome screen.

"I can't let the *Pineapple Express*, and all of you, pay for my own bullshit."

He looked at Swarm and gritted his teeth.

"If we let him go, what we'll be unleashing on the galaxy will be worse than a whole fleet of Reptilian ships. We'll have to track him down, man. Figure out a way to catch him again, and then... deal with him."

"This is no time for another ramble!" cried Swarm. "Just do it!"

Quickly, Charlie patted himself down for the gamepad. He caught hold of it and tried yanking it from his hoodie pocket, but one of the thumbsticks snagged on the pocket's lip. Charlie yanked harder, the thumbstick broke free, but he lost his grip and the device flew out of his hands.

The gamepad crashed hard onto the marble floor and cracked open, spitting sparks and spilling electronic debris across the floor.

"Whoops."

Every eye in the room bounced from the image of the nug on the ceiling, down to the broken gamepad, and back up to the nug.

The small, seed-shaped vessel tugged and tugged at its gravitational tether. Then, suddenly, the invisible leash was gone. Free from the constraint, the nug slingshot away from the *Pineapple Express* like a bullet.

Charlie buried his face in his hands.

This time I've screwed up worse than ever, he thought. *Now my doppelgänger is free and I have no way to take control of the* Pineapple Express. *A classic Charlie Hong lose/lose outcome.*

"Captain! Look!"

Charlie looked up just in time to see the nug, propelled by all the inertia from its forceful tugging, skirt along the edge of the brown hole, slip over the event horizon, and disappear into its dark center.

"Did he just...?" Cassie trailed off, wincing. "Gross. Totally gross."

"Good shootin', kid!" cheered Crimebot. "You slung that bastard straight into the bullseye!"

"Save your praise!" screeched Vree Voktal. "The Captain's

device is destroyed! We're seconds away from falling in ourselves."

"The *Pineapple Express* will cross the event horizon in thirty-seven seconds," MOM said helpfully.

"What are you smegging standing there for?" roared Swarm. "Create another gamepad, Captain!"

Charlie concentrated on a small patch of marble floor at his feet. A bulge appeared but quickly deflated. Another bulge appeared, slightly more reminiscent of a gamepad, but that one also deflated before it finished morpho-printing.

"It's not working," muttered Charlie. "I dunno what's wrong. I just *can't*."

"Fifteen seconds," said MOM.

"Smegging hurry, Captain!"

"I believe in you!" shouted Bob Jr.

"We all do!" added Pep.

"You can do it, Captain Stonerly!" cried Foo.

MOM started counting down. "Six seconds. Five... Four..."

Charlie tried again, summoning every bit of concentration he could muster. Another bulge appeared. Another bulge deflated, along with the last traces of Charlie's confidence.

"I can't do it," he said, looking up at all the scared and desperate faces surrounding him. "I'm sorry, guys."

"Two... One."

The *Pineapple Express* lurched as the gravity of the brown hole took hold. The vid screen being projected on the domed ceiling showed nothing but a swirling mass of thick brown sludge.

The air was so thick with the smell of raw sewage, you could practically scoop it from the air with a spoon. Besides the occasional gag reflex, no one spoke or made a sound.

The Glimwickets had pulled the wogs into a big group hug.

Cassie cradled Crimebot's head like it was a doll.

Vree Voktal and Eta Cerbo each held an Undulata in their arms while the Smolz cloud floated densely around them.

The Dregz tightened their huddle.

Even Nadia had succumbed to her softer side and settled her coils gently around Zylvya, stroking the sleeping woman's emerald hair and holding her slender, wood-grained hand.

Charlie and Swarm stood staring at each other. There was no escape. They'd crossed the event horizon. The maiden journey of the *Pineapple Express* had become a one-way trip into oblivion.

With every second, the stench grew thicker, more tangible. Charlie looked up at the brown hole and noticed the distance between them and its puckering center hadn't changed.

"Shouldn't we be, uh... *gone* by now?"

A hand slipped over his shoulder and snatched the smoldering joint from his lips. He spun around to find Habu puffing on the stolen doob and grinning like a lunatic.

"Flip the view screen around toward the back of the ship," he suggested, a shadow falling across his wrinkled face. "I think we have some company."

68

Everyone in the mini-Transit Bay looked up at the new screen that appeared on the dome. It showed a massive vessel made up of sharp angles and gunmetal gray turrets of various sizes and shapes. The outline of a dragon was embossed on its side, a single red gem fastened in the center of the lizard's swollen belly.

From one of the turrets stretched a beam of sizzling red light that extended off-screen to the right.

"A Reptilian Viper Cruiser," said Nadia, her face darkening both figuratively and literally. Fangs peeked from between her lips and her fingernails sprouted into tiny razor-sharp blades.

"What are they waiting for?" asked Cassie.

"Who said they're waiting?" answered Habu, chuckling maniacally.

"I've seen a red beam like that before," Charlie said. "Habu's right. They already got us, and they're gonna haul us somewhere else."

"Praise Andromeda!" screeched Vree Voktal, a long Silexi finger stuffed into each of his nose holes.

"Correct, Captain Hong," said MOM. "The Reptilian vessel has extended an unknown gravitational net over the *Pineapple*

Express which is counteracting the gravitational pull from the brown hole."

"We're the prize in a game of tug-of-war, man."

"Correct, Captain. At least until there is a disruption of the gravitational balance between the two forces," explained MOM. "Or when the ship is torn in half."

"Torn in half?" scoffed Charlie. "Naw, she'll hold together, man."

No sooner had the words left his mouth than the ground lurched beneath their feet.

"Okay, she'll hold together for a little while longer."

"Captain, the *Sibilanté* is hailing the *Pineapple Express*," announced MOM. "Would you like me to accept their feed request and project it up on the dome?"

Charlie sighed, looked at his feet, then let his eyes drift along the floor to the grassy patch where Zylvya lay.

He felt a claw close gently on his shoulder.

"I miss Twiggy, too. But right now you have to talk to these smegheads. Buy the rest of us time to come up with a plan."

He nodded grimly and narrowed his bloodshot eyes. "Why the hell not, MOM? Let's chat."

The forward and aft screens swung apart and a new video feed appeared between them.

Two Reptilian heads appeared in the rectangle. There was a tall, yellowish one with a long snout, and a shorter green one that looked like the meaner of the two.

Charlie had to admit he was a little bummed it wasn't Tork or Boomslang. At least he knew which buttons of theirs to press, so he'd have lots of material to work with.

For now, he'd have to figure out these new Reptoids, learn what pissed them off, and then slam his fist into their buttons as hard as he could.

"Hey, man, didn't you see the non-soliciting sign we posted on the front door?" asked Charlie, smoke billowing from the joint parked between his lips.

The tall, yellowish one flicked its tongue into the air.

"Your ship, and all on board, are now property of the Reptilian Empire. Gather all passssengers and valuablesss into a central location for transsssfer to our ship. Do not ressssissst. If you follow my commandsss, we may spare your livesss."

"I'm sorry, I wasn't listening. Could you repeat that? Actually, don't bother. I'll just ignore you again."

Charlie exhaled a big plume of smoke toward the projection.

"Your dumb lisp reminds me of a couple of other Reptoids I've gotten to know pretty well. Tork and Boomslang. Heard of them? They're pretty high up in the chain of command over there. Yeah, I can tell you're scared of them by the way you two looked at each other when I said their names. I get it, man. I do. You can't all have balls as big as mine. Now that I think about it, I don't even know if Reptoids have balls."

Charlie put his hand up to stop the tall one from responding.

"Don't care, man. Save it for your mom. You do have moms, right? Oh, shit! Wait a second. Don't tell me." He pointed his joint at the shorter one. "You're his mom aren't you? Yeah, you are! I can tell because your breath smells like it came from the same dumpster as his."

"They know you can't smell their breath over vid feed," whispered Cassie.

She had a point. It wasn't Charlie's finest roast, but it was obviously getting under their scaly skin.

Both Reptilians bared a thin hint of fangs between their lipless mouths and the frequency of their tongue flicks was increasing throughout his ramble.

While Charlie paused to take another toke and line up the next few zingers in his head, the darker Reptilian said to the other, "As sssoon as the tugger getsss here and pullsss their ship out of the event horizon, I want his head on my desssk."

Charlie choked on his hit and coughed up smoke in big, heaving spasms.

When he recovered he said, "Hold up, man! We still haven't

negotiated yet! While I'm sure my head seems like a pretty cool trophy right about now, we might be able to offer something better."

"We'll take that, too," the short one said. "We own you. We own the galaxy. We alwaysss have. We alwaysss will."

"Then I guess I should just give you my most valuable tech right now," said Charlie, letting the joint dangle at the corner of his mouth as he rummaged through his hoodie pocket.

"Captain!" rattled Swarm. "Don't hand anything over to them!"

"Don't worry, man. He's right, they deserve this."

Charlie whipped both middle fingers from his pockets and held them up to the vid screen.

MOM's voice appeared at his ear.

"Captain, they cannot hear me. There is another ship, very large and very fast, headed our way. It is still out of range for higher resolution scans to identify it, but that is irrelevant because at its current velocity, it'll be here in the next few—" She stopped abruptly, then quickly added, "They are here now."

Before Charlie could grasp what she'd just said, a wail rose up from behind him that shattered his attention. He turned to find Mrs. Glimwicket blowing her proboscis with a handkerchief, her hand cupping Zylvya's face. Next to her, Mr. Glimwicket wiped away a tear and started to speak, but before he could, Charlie put his hand up to stop him.

He didn't need to be told what had happened. He could see it in her face: a lifeless matte finish to her wood-grained skin, the loss of suppleness, an eerie sort of absolute, wooden stillness.

Zylvya was dead.

I couldn't save you, thought Charlie. *I promised I would, but I failed. What was the point of all of this if you're gone forever?*

Charlie's legs gave out and he plopped down beside her. She looked no more alive than a mannequin in a green wig.

Habu squatted on the opposite side of Zylvya's body. He

snatched the joint from Charlie's lips, took a few short puffs, and spoke through a mouthful of smoke.

"You have a lot of harvesting to do when this is all over. Big plants, homeboy! You might need to ask around for some help trimming. I work cheap. What do you say, huh?"

Habu smiled and passed the joint off to Mrs. Glimwicket, who took it tentatively, looked around at the crowd, shrugged her silky furred shoulders, and took a tiny hit before passing it to her husband.

The only thing that kept Charlie from karate chopping the insensitive old man was the sly sparkle glimmering in his eyes. It said he knew the answer to the question Charlie was struggling with. The point to all of the pain, fear, and loss in the galaxy. Habu had the answer—and apparently it was mildly amusing.

"Captain," said MOM, "The *Sibilanté* is being towed away from the brown hole and is in turn towing the *Pineapple Express*. In a few minutes we will be back outside of the event horizon."

"That means the tugger is already here!" cried Cassie.

"Smegging hell, the Reptoids will be boarding us soon," groaned Swarm.

He stood tall and addressed the small crowd.

"Here are your choices. You can head to the THC Chamber to await surrender, or," he paused to lift all four wadjet rifles high above his head. "Grab a weapon and help me take down as many Reptoids as we can."

Nadia slithered beside him and lifted herself high above her coil.

"I wouldn't have it any other way," she said, straightening and adjusting her many rings.

Metal Mask fell in beside her and the other Dregz followed.

Finally, three wogs surrounded Swarm, their mat-coms ready to fire.

"No wogs allowed!" roared Swarm. "You three stick with the Glimwickets and don't give the Reptoids any reason to skin you."

"Wait a second," Charlie said, watching the vid screen. "Look at their faces. Have you guys ever seen Reptilians panic like that before?"

The two Reptilians, sweat dripping from their scaly bald heads, were hissing silent orders to others off-screen.

"Something's not right, man."

"Ah-ha! But not right for *whom*?" Habu taunted, sitting cross-legged, calmly puffing on Charlie's joint.

"Hey, MOM, what's the call sign of the ship that's towing the *Sibilanté*?"

MOM took a moment before answering. "I cannot tell you that, Captain."

"Here we go again!" screeched Vree Voktal. "She's still malfunctioning!"

"Captain, the *Pineapple Express* is now outside of the brown hole's event horizon," said MOM.

"They'll be boarding any second. Get ready, everyone!" roared Swarm, his antennae stiff behind him.

"MOM, I'm the only version of me still around," said Charlie. "And I'm giving you a direct order. Tell me the name of the ship towing the *Sibilanté*."

"I am sorry, Captain, but I can't do that," MOM said in the same stilted, creepy voice she used when she wouldn't let him back inside the ship.

Before anyone could respond, she added, "But their bridge is requesting you accept their vid feed. May I project it up on the dome?"

Charlie took one last look at Zylvya, got to his feet, narrowed his eyes, and braced himself for whatever came next.

"Do it, man."

The three vid feeds already projecting on the dome slid aside to make room for a fourth.

The feed flipped on and two faces stared down at him from the ceiling.

Charlie's legs wobbled again, but this time he was able to stay on his feet.

He couldn't explain what his eyes told him. He didn't even try.

Despite all the sabotage and betrayal and murder—and the fact that the others had smoked most of his joint—he'd never felt better.

69

"Surprise!" shouted Zylvya and Axolotl.

Charlie's dumbstruck, exhausted gaze drifted from the vid screen down to the mannequin laying at his feet, then bounced slowly back up. He rubbed his eyes and took a deep breath.

"How?"

"I'll go first, yo!" croaked Axolotl. A wet smile stretched from amphibious earhole to amphibious earhole. "You know what they say, Captain... *Time heals all dudes!* In my case, it was time *and* a new body."

"A new body?!"

"Exactamundo! Mother morpho-printed it, but then I needed a little help getting my mind transferred over successfully."

Without warning, he planted a wet kiss on Zylvya's cheek.

"So the other Axo, the black creepy one with the fangs..."

"Still sleeping inside the healing tube, yo. Not dead, but no one's home under the dreads, if you catch my drift."

"It's about time, Squishy," rattled Swarm. "How are Sally and the wogs doing?"

"They're great, yo! But hey, by any chance have you seen three wogs running around the *Pineapple Express*?"

Charlie glanced behind him at where the Glimwickets were

huddled with the wogs. Only the Bobs and Mrs. Glimwicket remained.

"We'll keep our eyes open, man," said Charlie, smiling. "It's really good to see you. Both of you."

His stupefied gaze slid over to Zylvya. Before he could ask a question, she answered.

"You and Axo weren't the only ones with doppelgängers. Except mine wasn't evil, " she added with a hint of superiority. "The other me laying dead on the *Pineapple Express* was a mindless clone vessel used to host my hyperspatial psycho-projection experiment."

"A-hem!" A tinny voice said from off-screen.

"Sorry, *our* experiment," she corrected herself.

"You didn't change your mind at the last minute and decide to join us," rattled Swarm.

"Actually, changing my mind was exactly what I did. I swapped out its synaptic vessel."

"You lied to us, Twiggy."

"Okay, fine. I lied. For science."

"For science!" the tinny voice repeated from somewhere below the vid feed screen.

"My original plan was to hang back on the *Starseed*, to spend most of my time partnering with Nylf, looking for a way to safely transfer Axo's mind into his new vessel."

"A new body?" Cassie asked, her cranial LEDs brightening.

"Exactly," Zylvya explained. "Turns out Nylf had already stumbled onto some exotic tech with the ability to transfer consciousness from one synaptically-compatible vessel to another. I made an offhand comment about how I wish I could be in two places at once, both here in the lab with Nylf and there with all of you on the *Pineapple Express*. The next thing we knew, Mother had morpho-printed an empty biological replica of me to use as a test subject."

"Of course she did," said Charlie.

"The initial proof of concept worked, so at the last moment I snuck aboard the *Pineapple Express* and met you in the mini-Transit Bay. My mind was able to stay in that copy for a while, but every so often the remote connection would weaken and my mind would get pulled back to my original body on the *Starseed*. From your point of view, I'd start dozing off and eventually fall into a coma. But each time that happened I'd wake up here on the *Starseed*."

"With data!" cried the unseen voice from off-screen.

"Don't say *data*, man," said Charlie, holding his head. "The data pill Swarm gave me nearly ripped my mind apart. It's what allowed my evil doppelgänger to manifest."

"Sounds like the same forbidden technology Rex Prime used to swap bodies with his heir," added Vree Voktal.

"Exactly," said Zylvya. "But being able to collect data from how my brain handled the jump between my bodies gave me what I needed to help Axo."

She paused, her lips curling into a smile.

"And, of course, I was able to bring news of the *Pineapple Express's* troubles back to the *Starseed*, which is why we left cycles ago to come save your hairy ape butt."

Charlie shook his head and beamed up at Zylvya.

"This whole time I thought I was saving you... but actually *I* was the damsel who needed saving."

Zylvya beamed back.

"You still earned a point or two on my scorecard, Captain."

"Smegging hell, Zee!" roared Swarm, clamping a claw down on Charlie's shoulder. "Don't encourage him!"

A ramshackle robot squeezed into the frame beside Axo and Zylvya. Wires hung loose between its modules, and fluid dripped from every exposed hydraulic. Charlie had the strong impression that it'd been slapped together in a junkyard, but it seemed sturdy enough and vaguely sentient.

One glance at its head and Charlie knew exactly who he was looking at. Atop the robot's asymmetrical shoulders sat a tiny potted cactus with a braid of tangled wires plugged directly into its rocky soil.

Axolotl threw a scrawny blue arm around the robot's neck and yanked it close.

"Look who else got a new body!"

"Del!" squealed Cassie, her audio volume maxed out.

Axolotl bobbed his soggy dreads and rapped his soft knuckles against the robot's glass case.

"He can't talk yet, but trust me, yo, he's in there."

"It's just a prototype," explained Zylvya. "But we thought you might be able to help with the next version, Cassandra. That is, if you don't mind working alongside your father…"

A tiny gray hand appeared at the bottom of the vid feed and waved enthusiastically.

"Only if I can quit all the other gigs I picked up," said Cassie.

"Captain," MOM's voice interjected, "I must apologize for not identifying the ship that was towing the *Sibilanté*. Once the *Starseed* was within range, Mother and I made contact and started planning the rescue. She said that not telling you would build suspense, which in turn would create a humorous moment, and that humor could help alleviate the stress we have all experienced on the *Pineapple Express*. She assured me you would find it funny. Did you find it funny, Captain? What should I tell her?"

"Tell her it was a friggin' hoot, as usual," said Charlie.

"What should we do with these Reptoids?" asked Axolotl. "Look at their faces. They look pretty upset, yo."

"You recording this, Cass?" asked Charlie.

"Duh. And I'm live-casting it all over the Outernet."

Nadia's coil tightened beneath her.

"This is no time for jokes!" she hissed. "We should use the *Starseed's* gravity lock to push the *Sibilanté* straight into the brown hole! Why are you all looking at me that way? They'd torture each and every one of us for no more reason than to hear our screams! They've destroy entire *worlds!* I should know, and so should you, Nommosian!"

Her almond eyes burned with yellow fire as she pointed a finger at the small crowd.

"As for the rest of you, if they haven't obliterated your planet yet, it's only because they haven't finished pillaging it! If the kryyd production in Trapezia ever stops, they'll use your planets for target practice! Same for you, Captain—once they squeeze the very last kitten from Earth, you can kiss your home world goodbye!

"Remember that while you're all here sharing this special family reunion, the Reptilians are still out there chewing up and spitting out entire species. But this time, *we* have *them*! We can make sure these particular Reptoids never hurt anyone ever again. And we can do it live on the Outernet, too! We can show the galaxy that we're out here, that we're on their side, that we're fighting back—and that we're winning. At the very least, it would give them hope. But it also just might convince them to fight alongside us.

"Surely, other Reptilian vessels are on their way here to rescue our detainees," said Nadia, holding Charlie's gaze without blinking. "It's the right thing to do. Give the order."

Charlie sighed, rubbed his eyes sleepily, and started patting himself down.

"First of all, my name's not Shirley. Second of all, did you get all that, Cass?"

"Duh. Got it from sixteen different angles."

"Okay, now get this," he said, then popped a joint between his lips. The tip caught flame all by itself and then settled into a smoldering ember.

"Here are my orders, man. Disable the *Sibilanté's* propulsion so they can't follow us, and then let's get as far away from that giant swirling butthole as possible."

"You can't just let them go, Captain!" cried Nadia.

"I'm done, man. After what we've just been through, let's just cut our losses and go home."

"But the whole *galaxy* is watching! This decision has the

power to change the course of galactic history! If you let them go, you'll look like a fool!"

"Whatever, man. Slaughtering them would only highlight our fear of them. And it's a pretty Reptoid move to make, don't you think?

"Naw, it's better to let them live with the fact that we could've ended them, but instead we let them go," said Charlie, catching Habu's wink in the crowd. "Maybe we'd all be better off if we started letting more shit go.

"Even you, Nadia. Even after all the shit you've pulled."

He held out his joint and managed to muster an exhausted smile.

"What do you say? Wanna officially join the crew? Together we can figure out a way to beat the Reptoids without turning into monsters ourselves. Take a hit and make it official."

Nadia glared at him, fists trembling at her side.

She reached out for the joint, but her hand paused halfway. Her eyes clenched shut and Charlie thought he saw her chest heave with a stifled sob.

Then she was gone, her body turned into a cloud of vapor that swirled and zipped out through the door that had reappeared.

Charlie shrugged and turned to face the small crowd.

"Anyone else got the munchies, man?"

70

Making room for a giant banquet table inside of a crowded arcade isn't hard when every dimension of your ship is mentally malleable.

Expecting a few extra guests? No problem. Just imagine the wall of pinball machines sliding back another fifteen feet, the strips of neon in the ceiling stretching out to fill the new space. Extra chairs growing right out of the hard marble floor. Three more restroom doors appearing between the skeeball machines and the VR booths.

Charle imagined all that, but none of it happened.

Instead, they had to make do with the time-tested strategy of moving heavy shit around.

Charlie and Axolotl threw their weight against a five-player, shoot-em-up gaming cabinet to slide it into place with the others at the back of the room.

When they were done, he leaned back against the machine.

"That's the last one, man. This would've been way easier if we'd made these changes to Cassie's Chassis back on the *Pineapple Express* before it was reabsorbed into the *Starseed*. The whole ship was like putty in my hands, man. I wish you could've seen it."

Axolotl bobbed his mop of soggy dreads in agreement.

"Maybe someday you'll figure out how to do all that fancy morpho-printing here, too."

Charlie shook his head.

"There was something special about the *Pineapple Express*. I had some kind of deeper connection to it that I don't have with the *Starseed*."

"Not yet." Axolotl shot Charlie a knowing look. "I've seen you do some pretty impressive stunts with the *Starseed*, yo. Maybe it's just a matter of time and, uh, a few more gnarly adventures."

"No thanks, man. I've had enough gnarly adventures for one lifetime. After we drop off the Trapezians and ditch the Dregz, I plan on pointing the *Starseed* toward the quietest, most boring part of the galaxy I can find."

"Good luck finding that, yo," said Axolotl, snorting.

"About what happened on Págos 9..." Charlie said uneasily. "I didn't mean to...I tried my best to..."

He trailed off, his eyes anchored to his sneakers.

"I'm sorry."

"Say what?" croaked Axolotl. "You got nothing to apologize for, Captain! It was just Nommosian biology, yo. Mother explained it to me once I was better. Comes with being a neotenous org, I guess. Anyway, my memory's still a little fuzzy, but I remember most of what I said and did to you out there. If anyone should be sorry, it's me, yo."

"Whatever. You were having a mega-bad trip, that's all."

Charlie threw an arm around Axolotl's shoulder and smiled.

"I'm just glad Chuck Stonerly and the Squishy Kid have reunited!"

Axolotl's eyes filled his goggles and he slapped a wet hand on Charlie's shoulder.

"Also, we all learned a valuable lesson about Nommosian biology. Sally and I gotta keep iodine away from the wogs at all costs...or else we'll have a mob of *real* monsters on our hands."

He stared off into the middle distance, his face turned a sickly shade of green. He sighed, shook his soggy mop, and the greenish tinge faded.

"We got time for a quick puff before everyone arrives, yo?"

Charlie shot him a benevolently tilted grin and plucked a joint from his afro.

Half a joint later, the improvised banquet room was bustling with Seeders.

Vree Voktal sat between the other Trapezian delegates, poking at a holographic orbital schematic of their triple-figure-eight trinary star system. The seeds of a united tri-planetary post-war economy were finally sprouting. Charlie knew they'd be alright— as long as the Reptilians kept their forked tongues out of Trapezia.

Eta Cerbo, His Majesty, the new Silexi Emperor, was off playing video games with the wogs in one last attempt at reliving his childhood before having to officially take the throne. Charlie and the others had agreed to pardon his crimes, which, considering how it all worked out, didn't seem too bad. As long as he agreed to rule Silex with Vree Voktal as his loyal advisor and promised to devote his reign to establishing peace in Trapezia, the galaxy would never have to know the truth.

Another secret Charlie and the others agreed to keep was that Reticulus Rex, a.k.a. Rex Prime, had not actually died in his failed attempt at stealing his son's body. His mind, untethered from his own body and unable to root itself in his target, found refuge in the only mindless organism within reach—the potted daisies Eta Cerbo carried around with him to remind him of his time on Earth. He and Vree had a nice window in the Silexi Palace picked out where Rex could live out however many days the daisies gave him. They conveniently forgot to decide who was responsible for watering him.

Ever since he'd been put in charge of the huge harvest coming in the next few days, Habu hadn't stopped trying to recruit Seeders to help him. He'd slipped into Bob Jr.'s empty seat and was gesticulating to Mr. and Mrs. Glimwicket the finer points of trimming cannabis.

Mrs. Glimwicket nodded politely, but her attention was on the tiny bundle in her arms. After all the larvae were toked over to the *Sibilanté's* engine room to gunk up their propulsion systems, Bob Jr. handed over to his parents a single larva that he'd pilfered during their ride in the *Pineapple Express*.

"I kept this one safe in my pocket," he explained. "I thought she might make a pretty good little sister."

They beamed back. "We think you might make a pretty good big brother."

Shortly after the missing three wogs had been reunited with the others, Charlie pulled Axolotl and Sally aside and explained their role on the *Pineapple Express*. At first, Sally bunched up her little pink fists, but instead of swinging them at Charlie she relaxed her webbed hands and threw her arms around him instead.

"Thank you for bringing my wogs back to me, Captain," she'd whispered to him during their embrace. "But if you stand us up for dinner one more time, I'm gonna knock your head off. Understand?"

Zylvya looked stunning in her spiderweb-thin orange toga, as usual. This Zee—the original—looked as vibrant as ever.

She hadn't told Charlie anything about the adventure she, Nylf, and Vargoni had experienced on the *Starseed*. She'd tell him later, if she wanted. All Charlie cared about was that whatever crazy shit had gone down on the *Starseed* had resulted in Axo and Del being restored.

Well, Del was partially restored.

For a cactus-powered, robotic, Frankenstein's monster, Charlie thought he looked pretty happy listening to Cassie complain about all the jobs she'd had on the *Pineapple Express*.

Nylf stood on the banquet table, a row of tools laid out before him, poking and prodding at Crimebot's head. The red light of

Crimebot's visor flickered and dimmed, then resumed its steady oscillation back and forth.

Last week I thought I'd lost most of my crew, thought Charlie. *Now I'll have to think about expanding the bridge to make room for all the new recruits.*

"Attention everyone," Mother's warm, southernly voice came from all directions at once. Charlie found it comforting after a week spent talking to the stilted, monotonous MOM.

"The *Pineapple Express* has just finished being reabsorbed into the *Starseed*. Not only does that mean we're one unified ship again, but it also means all your belongings are safe and sound in your quarters, right where you left them. Which means it's time to celebrate, baby!"

The wogs cheered and the adults all exchanged grateful looks.

"Enjoy Cassandra's beautiful new arcade—that goes for you, too, Nylf! I don't think she's gonna put your place out of business just yet, darlin'."

"Let her have it," muttered Nylf, who was focused on twisting a screwdriver deep in Crimebot's ear.

Mother continued, "Captain Hong has prepared a unique feast for everyone to enjoy. For the kids we have pineapple-flavored Red Bulls and for the adults we have THC-infused, pineapple-flavored mocktails."

"Smegging hell, Captain!" rattled Swarm. "Do wogs really need caffeine?"

"Don't worry, man, I had Mother replace the caffeine with essential vitamins. Just don't tell them that or they'll try to steal the adult bevs."

"We also have plenty of pineapple slices, pineapple juice, dried pineapple, candied pineapple, pineapple-upside-down cake—"

"Earthers *would* serve a cake upside down," Zylvya said, rolling her eyes.

"Makes about as much sense as a pineapple-shaped spaceship," added Sally.

"And lastly, courtesy of our fine Trapezian friends, we have a surprise for Captain Hong."

Mother paused for dramatic effect.

"The biggest bowl of kryyd in the whole galaxy!"

Charlie stared at the humungous bowl of pills that morphed out of a bulge in the table. Each pill had the tell-tale concentric figure-eight design etched into its dark, reflective coating. Hundreds of kryyd. Thousands.

Charlie leapt from his seat, scrambled onto the table, and shielded the bowl of pills with his body.

"No way! No more pills! No data pills, no kryyd, no friggin' alien multivitamins! Just say no, man!"

Zylvya's hand blurred in and out of the bowl before Charlie could react. She crunched a few pills, swallowed, and sighed contentedly.

"These really hit the spot, Mother."

Everyone but Charlie burst out laughing.

"Oh, darlin'! We spaced all the kryyd straight into the brown hole before we left," Mother said, a mischievous titter in her voice. "These might look like those nasty poison pills, but trust me honey, they're just candy. Earth candy, Captain."

"None for me, thank you. I've had more than enough Earth candy over the past thirty years," groaned Vree Voktal, turning up his nose. "Ever since His Majesty discovered them while shooting that film on Earth, production of those wretched candy-coated chocolates has been the only other stable industry on Silex besides war. His Majesty thinks it could be the foundation of our planet's post-war economy."

"Caaaandyyy!" Eta Cerbo said in his best E.T. voice, his belly and fingertips glowing brightly.

Vree shot him a look.

"You think you're being cute, Your Majesty, but you'd better get that voice out of your system before we get back to Trapezia. I expect you to show the entire system how the death of your father and the weight of the crown has unlocked a new set of cognitive abilities. No more childish babbling. You're the Emperor now—technically, only the second Silexi ruler in a few millennia—so you better start acting like it."

Eta Cerbo nodded his misshapen head.

"I'll do whatever it takes as long as Vree follows through on his promise to produce a biopic about my upcoming reign of peace."

"Your wish is my command, Your Majesty."

Vree Voktal pulled Charlie aside and lowered his voice.

"Something tells me I'm going to require a lot of your *Golden Ticket* to keep myself sane through all the upcoming changes on Silex."

Charlie smiled.

"No worries, homeboy. I'll have some loaded up on your ship before you leave. And hey, you have my digits if Trapezia ever needs to re-up."

Holy shit, thought Charlie, *I went from hiding out with my girls in the mountains of Northern Cali to becoming the captain of a spaceship that runs on weed, and now I'm slinging bud to entire star systems!*

If only Dad could see me now...

As he sat at the head of the banquet table, looking out at the party, a stoned peace came over Charlie.

It had all worked out.

Friends reunited.

Crew restored.

Peace.

For now, he thought.

71

As the others scooped out handfuls of chocolate kryyd pills, Charlie slipped out the door into the crowded Ring.

He'd only taken a few steps when he caught a glimpse of Metal Mask turning down one of the back alley corridors. Charlie started to follow on foot, then stopped suddenly when he remembered he still controlled a few of the *Starseed's* subsystems.

Metal Mask drew his wadjet pistol as the cloud of green smoke swirled past him and condensed in front of him.

When the vapor cleared, Charlie stood with his arms crossed.

"Shouldn't you be in the Transit Bay with the other Dregz, getting ready to leave?"

Metal Mask returned his pistol to its holster and glanced up and down the narrow alleyway.

The voice that came from the mask was digitized. "I have something for you, but we must find a place where no one else can see or hear us."

Charlie narrowed his eyes and snapped his fingers. The walls on either side of them stretched across the open alleyway to form a small enclosed room.

"Will this do?"

Metal Mask nodded.

"Try anything and you'll find out how fast I can space someone," Charlie said, sticking out his chest. "Don't try me, man! Whatever you have for me, hand it over and then get off my ship."

Metal Mask reached behind his head, unbuckled something, then pulled the mask away from his face.

Their tiny improvised room started spinning.

The person standing there was beyond unlikely, beyond impossible. It simply couldn't be.

Charlie immediately started patting himself down for a spare joint.

Nate shoved his metal mask under his arm and grinned at his stunned friend. His tawny hair was tousled from the mask and he had a thick five o'clock shadow creeping up his face.

"Sup, dude?" he asked.

"But you're on Earth, man," stammered Charlie, his lips numb. "I watched you drive away the night I was abducted."

"That I did do," said Nate. "Sorry, dude. I wasn't ready for all this alien shit back then."

"But now you're ready to be a space merc? Oh shit, wait! You must be some kind of mind-reading, shape-shifting assassin!"

Charlie tapped his chatter, but the way Nate winced and waved his hands was so authentic he knew he had to be the real thing.

"Dude, chill! I'm not a shapeshifter! I can explain everything... well, maybe not right now, but eventually."

"What's there to explain?" said Charlie, feeling his brain crack around the edges. "My best friend, who should be back on Earth, is actually the leader of the friggin' Dregz? The last time I saw you, you were working at Taco Bell, man! And if I remember correctly, they'd just fired your honky ass!"

Nate pulled Charlie into a hug and squeezed the air out of him.

"I've missed you, dude."

After a moment they both stepped back, smiling like kids who hadn't seen each other all summer break.

"Missed you, too, man." Charlie offered him the joint. He took it and sniffed.

"Dude, it's been too long since I've had any of your *magnum dopus*." He popped it between his lips and a quick flame brought the ember to life.

Charlie shook his head.

"Man, I've seen some shit out here, but...come on, how the hell could you possibly be on the *Starseed* right now?"

"That's a long story. Too long. And too bad for us the Dregz just got called away for another job. Sorry, dude, but I gotta take it. A few times this week I wanted to let you in on my secret, but once I realized there was a Reptilian on the *Pineapple Express,* I had no choice but to stay disguised."

"What the hell do you mean you gotta go? This doesn't make any goddamn sense! You gotta give me something, man!"

Nate looked anxious.

"Alright. I'll tell you what I can. That night you disappeared into the sky, I thought for sure you were dead. I ended up calling your dad—not to tell him what happened. I knew he wouldn't believe me. *I* barely believed me. But just to...I dunno, connect with another person who cares about you."

"Sure he does."

"Dude, he *does*, Charlie. After you disappeared, he got super worried. I called him a few times, we met for coffee. I thought he looked way older. Way sadder. Like a dude weighing his options, if you know what I mean.

"But then one day he calls me out of the blue, which he'd never done before. He was all excited and upset and totally manic. He couldn't talk to me about it over the phone, but I guessed it had something to do with you. Then he offered me a job—*me!* He said he had stuff to tell me if I agreed to come work for him as his special assistant. Which, you know, was the best job offer I've ever had. So I took it, and dude, everything's changed so fast since then."

"You worked for my dad?"

"Still do, dude. That's why I joined the Dregz."

Despite being alone in a makeshift closet, he lowered his voice.

"I'm a spy, dude. Sent to help him track you down. That's right, Charlie. Your dad's out here, too."

A stool morpho-printed directly below Charlie just as his legs gave out.

"Turns out his company, Whizcom, was a front for the Reptilians. It's how they develop tech and smuggle it off Earth. He told me you took part in a terrorist attack against some military research station in Alaska. They had security footage of your interrogation, and of you killing a bunch of soldiers in an elevator."

"That was my space jumpsuit, man! I was tied to a chair!"

"It was pretty gnarly stuff, dude. Anyway, the Reptilians realized you were his son and shanghai'd him into helping hunt you down. Actually, they thought he'd make good bait. And he thought I'd be good bait. So I accepted his offer and we blasted off a few days later to work in a Reptilian lab in the Fla-jiri system. He's still there. I, uh, got away."

"So now you're somehow the leader of an alien mercenary group?"

"Yeah, I guess so, dude. Actually, now that I think about it, I'm not even sure how that happened." Nate shrugged. "Last I recall, I was just signing up for a low-level position with these guys."

"Forget the Dregz, man! You're telling me you're working for the Reptilians? As a spy? To capture me?"

Nate laughed.

"Hell no, buddy!" he cried, his drawl in full swing.

"We're double-agents, dude! While I look for you, your dad is working on something else. He's looking for a way to stop the Reptoids and free Earth, just like you. He hacked into the Reptilian archives and found some references to a weapon the former captain of the *Starseed* was working on."

"Shit! The Reptoids know about Major Tom's weapon?!"

"They know of its existence, but not much beyond that. But, Charlie, there's more…"

He trailed off and his face softened.

"Something waaay bigger than anything I've told you so far."

"Commander!" Oozer's weaselly voice interrupted from Nate's wrist comm. "The ship's ready and the crew's on board. I'd leave without you, but there's no way I'm taking command of these turdos."

Just then, Swarm's voice appeared from Charlie's chatter.

"Captain! Where are you? We need you back at the party! The wogs have lost their smegging minds! Apparently, just the placebo of drinking caffeine was enough to turn them into maniacs!"

Nate chuckled.

"Guess it'll have to wait till next time, dude."

Charlie stared into Nate's face.

"You're really out here. Dad's out here…"

He took the joint back and filled his lungs.

"I really gotta go, Charlie."

"What the hell am I supposed to do with this info, man? Where is he? Can I contact him?"

"This is what I wanted to give you," Nate said, then shoved a round data disc into Charlie's numb hand.

"It's a recording from your dad. Listen to everything he has to say. And remember, dude, he loves you. We'll be watching you in all those crazy Outernet stories about the *Starseed*." He secured the metal mask back onto his face and said in a digitalized voice, "I'll be in contact when I can."

Charlie nodded, and two of the walls around them melted.

They were again standing in the narrow alleyway behind the Ring.

Nate turned to leave, then spun around in a blur and snatched the joint from Charlie's lips. The sudden movement caught him mid-toke, causing him to cough up a lungful of thick white smoke.

When the smoke cleared, Nate was gone.

— THANKS FOR READING! —

NOW WHAT?

✅ **Rate & review the book** on Amazon or Goodreads.
✅ Visit **www.faroutchronic.com** for free stories & books.

READY TO BLAST OFF ON THE NEXT FAR OUT ADVENTURE?

Well, you can't. Because I haven't written it yet.

But I will, in 2026. (If we all survive that long.)

In the meantime, you can find all my books at:

www.hifipressbooks.com

Sign up for my mailing list and I'll notify you when the next book is released.

Live high & prosper,

- Tom Sadira

ABOUT THE AUTHOR

Tom Sadira is known throughout the multiverse as one of the most accomplished authors of sci-fi and fantasy to have ever spawned in this sector. He's been published in journals, anthologies, and collections throughout this galactic quadrant, most of which you've never heard of, so just forget I mentioned it. Sadly, his home world of Earth is one of the last planets to catch on.

He currently basks in the intense solar radiation of Arizona with his lovely wife and three children (all human, probably).

ONE MORE THING

After you've told EVERYONE you know about how awesome this book is, and maybe bought a few dozen extra copies as gifts, there's one more important step to take:

GIVE IT AWAY!

Sign your name on these last empty pages, find another human (or whatever) in your life that you just know would love this story, and give the book to them.